What Happens on Vacation

ALSO BY JO WATSON

What Happens on Vacation

JO WATSON

by wattpad books

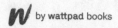

An imprint of Wattpad WEBTOON Book Group

Published in Canada by Wattpad WEBTOON Book Group, a division of Wattpad Corp.

36 Wellington Street E., Suite 200, Toronto, ON M5E 1C7 Canada

www.wattpad.com

First W by Wattpad Books edition: October 2023

ISBN 978-1-99077-891-9 (Trade Paper original)
ISBN 978-1-99077-892-6 (eBook edition)

Library and Archives Canada Cataloguing in Publication information is available upon request.

Printed and bound in Canada

1 3 5 7 9 10 8 6 4 2

Cover design by Sophie Melissa
Title design by Elliot Caroll
Interior image © Alina Tsimanovich, © poganka06 via Adobe Stock
Author photo by Gareth Paul
Typesetting by Delaney Anderson

For my dad, who will never get to read this book.

(Not that romance was his thing and not that he would ever have read it anyway, because reading sex scenes written by your daughter is just . . . No!)

But it's for him anyway, romance and all.

Chapter **One**

Everyone has a defining characteristic. That one thing that makes them who they are. For example, perhaps you're a particularly upbeat person who always finds fullness in the glass. Or maybe you only ever see a small dribble of droplets at the very bottom, not nearly enough to quench your thirst. Or perhaps you don't give a crap about the glass! Perhaps you push it off the edge of the table like an obstinate cat might do, watch it shatter on the floor, liquid gushing out in all directions; you're a rebel like that.

Me? If I look at the glass, I will take out a ruler and measure the liquid before I pass any judgment on where it may or may not be. I'll double-check the glass, too, make sure it's not one that's wider on the top and narrower on the bottom. *Is the glass even on a flat surface?*

I like details. I'm a perfectionist—nothing wrong with that! And as far as I can see, it's stood me in good stead through the decades, especially in my work as a journalist. I think it gives me a certain edge, an ability to hone in on all the details, bringing them into crisp, microscopic focus; to ask every conceivable question in the quest for a well-balanced article. *But lately I've discovered I have a new defining characteristic . . .*

"What's this?" I pointed at the suspicious mauve smudge on *my* side of the desk. Under normal circumstances, I might not have noticed the smudge so quickly if it hadn't been for all the other irregularities in the office.

The first irregularity was the loose partition in the middle of the desk, dividing *his* side from *my* side, so I didn't have to stare directly at him all day. There was a definite slope to it this morning, which had not been there yesterday when I'd left work. The other irregularity was that my pink highlighter was lying on the carpet and my trash can was also in the wrong place.

My office nemesis didn't look up. Had he even heard me?

"JAGGER!" I shouted, and his head snapped up.

"What?" He rubbed his temples with his fingers, a sign that he was, as I like to politely call it—*although I have no idea why the hell I even bother with politeness when it comes to him*—"under the weather."

"This!" I pointed and snapped my fingers. He visibly winced at the sound. Clearly he was a lot more under the weather than I'd initially thought.

"Whaaat?" Jagger groaned and finally released his temples.

I sighed. Well, it was more of a very pointed and purposeful loud inhalation followed by an equally purposeful loud exhalation. I followed it up with a tap of my foot, which was not nearly as effective as I'd hoped, given that the floor was carpeted.

"This! The mauve smudge on *my* side of the desk. And don't think I haven't noticed that the middle partition has also been moved and my pink highlighter is on the floor. And as for my trash can"—I bent down and picked it up—"it belongs on the right side of my desk."

Jagger raised his red-rimmed eyes to meet mine. "Nothing escapes you, Detective Maggie May."

"Margaret! Stop calling me that. How many times do we have to—" I stopped talking and inhaled slowly, drawing an imaginary infinity symbol in my mind with my breath—something my therapist had taught me. Jagger was riling me up, again. As if that was his sole purpose for existence. And he'd been doing it from day one, from the second we'd been made to share this way-too-small cubicle.

I'd been forced to hand construct—with very little experience in such things, I might add—a partition to divide our desk in half. *Did you know that using a nail gun is not as easy as they make it look in those DIY YouTube tutorials?* That had been precisely six months, three weeks, and two days ago, *yes*, I was counting. Because that was the day when my entire work life changed. When it went from normal and pleasant to downright hell on earth, all thanks to him—Jagger Villain! I'm also not entirely sure that's his real surname, by the way. Although there is definite poetic sense to it!

"So," I said, "what is it, and why did you move the partition?"

Jagger gave me one of his signature shrugs, a move that totally ticked me off. Everything about him did, but it was these shrugs that really grated on me. They were always accompanied with this casual, bordering on utterly uninterested in everything around him attitude that he seemed to ooze around the office. I say *ooze* because Jagger Villain never walks—*oh no*—he slips and slides through the office like shiny liquid mercury. Glinting and gliding under desks and doors, flowing through small spaces and somehow always managing to be everywhere at once. *And we all know how poisonous mercury is!*

"God, it's *waaaay* too early in the morning for this interrogation." He gave me that stupid lopsided smile of his, which I've noticed has quite an effect on all the females in the office. It seems to make them positively lopsided themselves. In fact, some seem so lopsided that they look as if they might fall over onto their backs. Not me, though. I remain upright.

"It is after nine, Jagger. I'm supposed to be working but, thanks to you, I'm officially"—I glanced down at my watch—"two minutes late!"

He chuckled. God, I hated that chuckle of his.

"Has anyone told you how funny you are, Maggie May?"

"Stop calling me that!"

"But it's such a classic song . . . *Doo, do doo, du, waaah!*"

"Uh, what are you doing?" I watched in horror as he made some strange noises and did something with his fingers in the air that I couldn't interpret.

"Catchiest guitar riff ever."

"Stop!" I held my hand up.

He smiled, leaned back in his chair, crossed his legs, and put his hands behind his head, another one of his signature moves. I glared right into those silver-gray eyes of his, which only seemed to make his smile grow.

"The mark!" I pointed down at the desk. "What. Is. It?"

Jagger rose from his seat with a dramatic *swoosh*. He was tall. Taller than most men. This was the other thing I'd noticed women got lopsided about. They always seemed to gaze up at him with a ridiculous look in their eyes, as if they'd been living in a nunnery for years and were encountering the last male on earth.

Jagger straightened his T-shirt, although I have no idea why. His T-shirts were always old and crumpled and looked as if they'd been lying around on some floor in a twisted pile all night. Whose floor they'd been lying on, though, was anyone's guess.

"Heeey, Jag." I heard a voice and turned. It was Denise from Accounts. "Hey," she said again, her voice sounding like the slow, high-pitched drag of a bow across a violin. The sound made my skin crawl, and I wasn't sure how to interpret her tone, but it did give me pause. It seemed to imply something. *Something*. And then her lips twitched into the slightest smile and . . .

"Oh. My. God!" I turned back to Jagger and scowled at him. *Surely, he wouldn't.*

I reached down and wiped the stain with a piece of paper and then raised it to my eyes; my suspicions about its origins were instantly confirmed. I glared at Denise's mauve lips and then turned my attention back to Jagger.

"You did not! On my side of the desk? *My side!* I can't believe you—*well, I can*—but I can't and . . . oh my god, it was Mark's birthday last night, everyone stayed late for drinks, so of course you did!" Denise was looking decidedly sheepish now, and that pink flush in her cheeks really did not complement her lip color. Not that the brown melamine surface of my desk did either. She lowered her head and dashed off.

I analyzed the situation. Lipstick smudge, partition that had clearly been taken down, highlighter on floor, moved trash can. It all pointed to one undeniable thing.

"You had *s-e-x* on my desk!" I whisper-screamed at Jagger. "We have rules about being on my side of the partition and this is a clear violation of those rules. Not to mention that having s.e.x. at work, with a co-worker, has to be a clear violation of about a million other HR rules!"

"Maggie May, please—"

"Stop calling me that!"

"Fine, Maggie, then—"

"My name is Margaret, which you know but choose to ignore!"

"It's not what you think, Margaret."

"Not what I . . . *ha*!" I threw my hands in the air. "How can it be, 'not what I think'"—I wiggled my fingers dramatically—"when someone else's cosmetics are smudged on my desk. I mean, how did she even get her lipstick *there*?" I looked back down at the smudge and tilted my head from side to side, trying to imagine what position a person needed to be in to produce this kind of . . .

My hands flew over my mouth when I figured it out. She would have had to have been on all fours—*no*! I couldn't think about it. It was terrible enough imagining it happening in the first place, but like that! Doggy style! On *my* side of the desk.

But what did I expect from a man like Jagger Villain? A man whose entire job revolved around dating and hooking up with women, and then writing a weekly column about his single-man sexcapades. A man whose job it was to go to concerts and parties, get drunk with celebrities, and pen trashy, scandalous gossipy articles about who screwed whom, or who came back from the bathroom with a white-tipped nose, for what was once a very respected newspaper. Whose job it was to consume strange foods—like the time he'd eaten that one hundred-year-old egg—and film himself doing it.

But now due to—what had my boss called it?—the need for clickbaity content, whatever the hell that meant, he'd been hired and placed next to me. And now he was having co-worker coitus in my once calm cubicle. No, this time Jagger had crossed a line, and I wasn't just referring to that line that clearly divided our cubicle in half.

"Margaret, it's not what you think. I know you think you hate me—"

"I *do* hate you," I snapped.

"Well, thanks," he said sarcastically, "but I'm not so bad that I would have sex on our desk!"

"Stop talking," I managed to say, even though my throat felt tight. "In fact, please don't say another word to me for the rest of the day. The rest of the year, if possible." I looked down at the stain again. "I'm going to get some coffee, and when I come back, I expect you to have disinfected the desk!"

"Don't leave like this," he called as I walked away. "I swear, it's not what you think."

I brushed him off with a flick of my wrist and didn't look back.

"'Maggie May' is one of my all-time favorite songs by the way."

I swung around. "Well, I think it's time you got a new one!" I said, and then stormed out.

Yes, my new defining characteristic was that I definitely *hated Jagger Villain.*

Chapter **Two**

"He is the most selfish, egotistical, womanizing, unnecessarily tall—*why is he so tall?*—uh, uh . . ." I grappled for a word that would sum him up sufficiently. "Asshole!" I jabbed my fork into my cheesecake several times and then violently pushed it around the plate. "Why does he have to sit next to me? Can't they put him somewhere else, preferably a cold, dark, moist, spider-infested pit with black mold!"

"That's specific," Lesego said with a mouth full of cake. Lesego was my work bestie, and, as such, was all too familiar with my Jagger issues.

"It doesn't even have to be dark, or moist, or even spider infested." I downgraded my fantasy. "I would settle for mites and dim overhead lights. But put him somewhere else. Out. Of. My. Sight."

"You know,"—Lesego raised another piece of cake to her lips—"you've been talking about Jagger for the last five minutes. And yesterday you spent ten minutes telling me why he wasn't a real writer. You talk about him so much one might think you fancy him."

"WHAT? . . . *no!*" I spluttered. "Trust me, talking about him is not an indication that he is preoccupying my thoughts in *that* way. On the contrary, he is preoccupying my thoughts in a very different way."

"But he is preoccupying them."

"Preoccupied thoughts are not an indication that I fancy him. And besides, he isn't a real writer!" I pushed the plate away from me now. Usually, I could inhale cheesecake like air, absorb it through my pores, but today I couldn't even look at it. The mulberry topping was just too damn mauve. "I have a degree in political science as well as journalism. And he did what? His LinkedIn profile says he studied at the 'School of Hard Knocks'!"

Lesego laughed, and I shot her my best unamused look.

"You have to admit, it is kind of funny."

"It's not funny. It's cocky and purposefully facetious in that way that he thinks is so damn cute but isn't."

"Most of the women around here do find it cute, actually."

"Do you?"

"I mean . . ." she started, and looked down.

"You *do*. You think he's hot!" I eyeballed Lesego in a way that I hoped conveyed the sense I was certainly judging her. But not too harshly—after all, I did love her.

"I don't know what you see in him," I said.

"I see a lot, I mean . . . *look at him*." And with that her perfectly cat-lined eyes moved over my shoulder and fixed themselves on a spot behind me. I didn't need to look around to have it confirmed. I knew it was him. I could see it in the way heads were turning and feel it in the way the air in the room was becoming sticky and musky with female pheromones. I straightened in my seat. I was not going to acknowledge him.

"Come on, haven't you ever wanted to be with a bad boy?" Lesego asked.

"No!"

"Tattooed, probably has a ring through his dick, or nipple!"

"Stop!" I cringed; Lesego was never shy about saying exactly what she was thinking.

"I'm sure he's filthy in bed, too, if those articles he writes are any indication of what he gets up to. That one about threesomes being the new nightcaps, or how to have sex on a stripper pole, or that one he wrote about that furry fetish when people dress up as woodland creatures and screw each other in the bushes or . . ." Her voice softened and she giggled. "Hey, Jag."

I rolled my eyes. I hated this shortening of his name that everyone did.

"Hey, Lesego," he said in that smooth voice that I was sure was completely put-on.

"Margaret," he said very pointedly, as if he now wanted congratulations for getting my name right.

"Mmmmm," I mumbled, still not looking in his direction.

"You can come back to the desk now."

"Can I? Have you disinfected it after the s-e-x you had on it? Not that I trust your disinfecting, and will do it again myself anyway."

He laughed, and this time I did turn to give him a glare.

"Why are you laughing?" I asked.

"Firstly, I didn't have s-e-x on our desk, and secondly, why are you spelling it? Can't you say that word?"

Lesego also laughed, and I aimed my gaze at her now.

"He has a point, you know. You haven't actually said the word once to me either."

"I can say that word. I just choose not to be hideously inappropriate by walking around the office talking about s . . . that, at work!"

"Ha! You almost said it." Lesego pointed at me, looking way too pleased with herself.

"Just two more letters and you're there," Jagger added.

"Come on, you can do it!" Lesego teased me. *Whose side was she on?*

"That's it!" I stood up and pushed my chair toward the table. Its legs squeaked against the floor, which I thought added something to the moment. "I don't have time for this puerile, immature, egregious behavior. Unlike some people, I have *real* work to do!"

9

"I have real work," Jagger said.

"What?" I put my hands on my hips and felt them wobble beneath my palms. "Dressing up as a panda to have a furry threesome while sliding down a bamboo shoot?"

He burst out laughing. Real, loud, big laughter that made everyone in the cafeteria turn. I physically shuddered; I didn't want anyone to think Jagger and I were on friendly terms. When the laugher ended, he also put his hands on his hips, mirroring my pose. If he thought this would somehow build rapport between us—as behavioral psychologists claimed—he was sadly mistaken.

"No pandas, threesomes, or bamboo today, but I do have to shoot a video. I'm going to the worst-rated barber in Joburg to see how it goes. Then I'm going speed dating tonight and writing about it for my column, and then I have to review the latest trends in male sex toys and—"

"That is *not* real work."

"Well, what are you doing today?" he asked, smiling from ear to bloody ear like a clown.

"I am going to be writing an article about the new proposed wealth tax in South Africa and the impact that will have on ultra-high-net-worth individuals. In fact, I have a phone call with someone from the South African Revenue Service in an hour, not to mention the CEO of Falcon Wealth Management and the head of private banking at First National Bank!"

Jagger whistled. "Wow. Very important and impressive sounding. But not very fun, is it?"

I folded my arms across my chest, as best as I could anyway—my big boobs usually interfere with this activity somewhat. "Well, it is quite obvious that our definitions of fun are wildly different."

"Or maybe you just don't know what fun is," he said quickly.

"I know what fun is," I insisted.

Not that I'd had any in a while. My life hadn't exactly been fun these past few years.

"You know what, Jagger?" I stepped closer to him. "This used to be a very well-respected newspaper, reporting on serious, relevant global and South African topics. It's bad enough that we had to go online because print is dying, but now we are online and you—you—are making a mockery of everything we're supposed to be, with your Swipe Write column—which, by the way, is such a poor and cheap stab at a pun—and your belligerent *Jagger Tries . . .* videos. Why would anyone want to watch you try to beat a lie detector test?"

"That video got five hundred thousand views," he chirped with a smile.

"But who, pray tell, is viewing it?"

"Now you're insulting my audience," he shot back, his smile faltering, which I took as a sign that I was finally getting through to him, breaking through that clownish exterior that seemed to see everything as a damn joke.

"Well, *you* are insulting *me*!" We silently glared at each other for a while before Jagger sighed.

"Okay. Come on, I need to show you something. I wasn't going to, but I can see it's the only way to settle this." He started moving away.

"I have to work."

"This will only take a minute." He was exiting the cafeteria.

I looked at Lesego, who was smiling from ear to ear. I raised my brows in a question.

"Maybe he's finally getting a room for you two. God knows you both need it!"

"What do you mean?"

"Well, it's kind of obvious, isn't it?"

"What is?" I pressed her.

"You two."

"Us two, what?"

"Oh please. Don't act like you don't know what I mean."

I stared at her for a moment and then shook my head. *No, I had no idea what she meant!*

"You secretly want"—she mouthed the next two words—*dick ring*! She winked at me, and I think I threw up a little in my mouth.

Chapter **Three**

To say I followed Jagger down the brightly lit passage reluctantly would be an understatement. I had no idea where he was taking me, and I didn't like that. I'd asked him multiple times and been dismissed with halfhearted hand gestures. He led me down the main passage that divided the huge building in half. Media 365 was an institution, and I'd always wanted to work here. It published more magazines and newspapers than any other media company in the country—from political to financial, trade publications for the banking and insurance industry, property magazines, travel magazines, and even a magazine called *Submerge* for submarine enthusiasts (there are more than you would think!).

I'd always wanted to work for one publication and one publication only: *The Daily Tribune*. I'd made this decision at the tender age of seven after seeing an article about *Pathfinder* landing on Mars. The red-tinged pictures were splashed across the front page, with a headline that read THE ROBOT MAKING PATHS 248 MILLION KILOMETERS AWAY. I'd read that line over and over again, sounding out all the letter and words to get them right. *How could something be so far away?* It was almost impossible to imagine, and yet here was the photographic evidence.

That's when I realized how powerful newspapers could be, bringing the seemingly impossible to life in the first high-definition pictures of a planet that no one had ever been to before. I felt as if my world had opened up and expanded to encompass not only the planet I lived on but the solar system too. *That's what news does.* From that day onward, I'd known I wanted to be a journalist and I'd planned my life accordingly. Every step I'd taken after that was to ensure that one day I, too, would open people's worlds. And I had. *I did.* Those journalism awards sitting on *my* side of the desk told me so. But now that desk was being shared with someone who laughed in the face of all the things I stood for, and somehow that took away from the importance of the awards that had once meant so much to me. Not to mention the fact that *someone* had probably been bent over doggy style across my Nat Nakasa Award for Media Integrity, *all thanks to him.*

I mean . . . *sex toys?* How was that going to open your mind to a bigger world view? *And male sex toys?* What the hell were those, anyway? I was glad I'd reached the three-decade plus mark and had never found out.

I'd encountered sex toys before, of course, but only the female versions. My ex-husband and I'd had a brief period where—on our marriage counselor's suggestion—we had tried spicing up our sex life. The whole experience had been more cringe producing than climax producing, though. I wasn't a sexual prude but there was something about a bow tie–wearing penguin sex toy that really didn't turn me on.

"Here we go." Jagger's hip swaggering finally ceased. He stopped by a door I'd never seen before in a passage I never knew existed.

"Where are we?" I tried to hide my growing anxiety.

"Don't you trust me?" He smirked and leaned against the door, which was another thing he did a lot. *He leaned.* On everything! As if he couldn't be bothered to hold himself upright in the world. It was very disrespectful. While all of us were going about keeping ourselves straight in the face of challenges and adversity, he didn't give a crap. Screw social norms and expectations—that's what his kind of lean said, anyway. In fact, everything he did reeked of someone who stuck up their middle finger to just about everything that I found sacred: order, routine, self-discipline, real journalism, and having the decency to stand up straight in an ironed shirt.

"I don't trust you, actually." I scanned the walls for some kind of sign that told me where I was.

"Well, now I'm just heartbroken," he quipped.

"Get used to it."

"We've been working together for six months already, and you still don't—"

"Six months, three weeks, and two days! And calling it working together would be a stretch."

"See, this is what I love about you."

"What?"

"Your attention to detail. You're the only person I've ever met who would know, right down to the day, how long I've been working at the office. Not to mention notice a slight tilt in an office partition or a tiny mauve smudge."

"The tilt was at least forty degrees."

Jagger leaned even more now, and a big smile slipped across his stupid lips.

He rapped his knuckles against the door, which only piqued my anxiety further. And then a man I'd never seen before peered around the door with one eye, looking suspicious as hell.

"Hey, Tebogo," Jagger said in a low, equally suspicious voice.

"Jag," Tebogo said with a sense of familiarity, and then he looked at me.

"Margaret." I pointed at myself.

He nodded, didn't say another word, and then swung the door open with a flourish. My stomach dropped as I tried to imagine what could possibly be behind this door. Jagger and Tebogo stepped inside what I could now see was a dark room, apart from a strange blue glow emanating from the very back of it.

"What is this place?"

"The place that shall surely vindicate me," Jagger said, and disappeared inside.

"Mmmm . . . vindicate?" That seemed like a rather large word for the likes of Jagger Villain. I took a deep infinity symbol–shaped breath and walked into the room and . . . not what I was expecting. Firstly, I could see Tebogo now—he was more than just a suspicious left eyeball—and I could see that he was wearing a security uniform. The room was full of rows and rows of small TV screens. I glanced from screen to screen, recognizing the images in front of me.

The parking lot. The building entrance. The cafeteria. And then there it was: our open-plan section of the office.

"I didn't know the building had so many cameras."

"Ever since the riot," Tebogo said.

"Yes. That," I said, a slight sense of guilt creeping up in me, since I'd played a role in it. One of the political youth parties stormed the building after I'd published an exposé about their corrupt leader. But apparently, they would rather take up arms and stand up for him than believe he'd stolen money to buy two Porsches, a seaside mansion with a helipad, and a Birkin bag for his wife that cost millions because it was made from the albino skin of a Floridian alligator.

"Security here is top-notch," Tebogo said.

"I'm sure it is." I smiled at him, validating the obvious pride he had in his job. "So, why am I here?"

"For this." Jagger pressed Play on one of the TVs. "It's from last night." I leaned in to look as our desks sprang to static life.

"You brought me here so you could show me you're—"

"*Not* having sex on our desk." Jagger stepped closer to me, and a deep, rich sandalwood smell wafted in the air for a second, then was gone.

"I'm not watching that." I made a move for the door.

"I didn't do what you think I did, and I want to prove it to you!" I stopped dead when I heard his tone. There was an air of desperation to it. A plea. Why on earth would Jagger be pleading with me? He didn't seem like the kind of guy who would ever plead for anything. *Why did he care what I thought?* Surely, having me think he'd used our desk for some late-night fuck would have suited him and further cemented his reputation as the country's number one dirty playboy bachelor.

"Please," he said, his voice sounding even softer now.

Despite myself, I felt something inside me slacken.

Shit, I was going to give in. I could feel it.

"Two minutes!" I said fast, and then pushed past him and back into the room.

Chapter **Four**

I folded my arms tightly across my chest as I watched the figures of Jagger and Denise stumble into the office on the small screen. I could see they were both inebriated. There was a looseness to their limbs that you only got from alcohol. Screen Jagger pointed at something on his desk, and then walked over to it. He picked up his bag and slung it over his shoulder.

"I was leaving the party and realized I'd left my bag at my desk," he piped up, as if narrating the event. "Denise followed me. I never asked her to come."

I rolled my eyes. "Come" she indeed did. She probably came a few times if that smudge was anything to go by. I kept watching and then it started.

Denise slid onto Jagger's desk seductively, put her hand on his bag strap, and pulled him toward her.

"Uh . . . I thought you were going to show me you *not* having sex!"

"I am. Watch!" Jagger turned, his steel-colored eyes momentarily connecting with mine. I threw mine skyward, just to make sure that he still knew that this was the last thing I wanted to be doing. But then something strange happened.

I turned my attention back to the screen: Jagger took a step back, placed his hand on Denise's shoulder, and said something to her. She reached up, put her hand over his, and nodded. They looked at each other for a while, saying nothing, but I could see some kind of communication had passed between them. And then she pushed off his desk, straightened her skirt, and walked away. Jagger pressed Pause and turned to me.

"See."

"What did you say to her?" There had been something in their interaction that had fascinated me, and the reporter in me wanted to know.

"I told her I was flattered. But that she'd had too many drinks to be in any kind of position to give consent and I would not be a gentleman if I took her up on the offer. And if she wanted to, we could share an Uber so I could see she got home safely."

"Oh!" I couldn't imagine words like that coming out of Jagger's mouth. Of course, he could be lying to me, pausing it at a convenient spot, two seconds before the desktop screw, because this still didn't explain the partition and the smudge. I pointed at the screen.

"Press Play again."

Something like a grimace moved across Jagger's face. "I don't want to."

"I knew it! You're conveniently pausing it at just the right moment. Just before it all goes down."

"I'm not. But I don't want to embarrass Denise by letting you see what happens next. But it's not sex, I promise."

"It's not," Tebogo piped up.

"How come Tebogo gets to see it and I don't? That doesn't seem fair."

Jagger sighed. "I get it. You're a woman of facts. Some people collect stamps—you collect facts. You want to be able to see it with your own eyes before you believe it. Touch it to know it exists. You want nothing to be left to chance."

His surprisingly accurate insight into me made me freeze for a moment. "Just press Play!"

"Fine, but please don't tell anyone about this." His eyes collided with mine.

I nodded. "Agreed."

"Off the record," he teased me.

I nodded again and turned my attention back to the screen. The image started moving and, as it did, Denise stumbled back into frame. Her shoulders began to heave up and down and then she grabbed the desk as if she couldn't hold herself up. Jagger placed a hand on her back and rubbed it in a small, almost comforting circle. Something in me softened for a second; this care seemed contradictory to the man I knew. These were the actions of someone with genuine concern—or maybe of someone who knew how to feign genuine concern. That was the thing with Jagger. I found it hard to read him. I could never tell what was a joke and what was not. If he was being serious or sarcastic. Understanding him was like trying to critically examine a piece of modern art—an entire canvas painted red with one yellow stripe in the middle. Everyone extrapolates something different: some see meaning in the colors; some read into the significance of the stripe; others, like me, just think it looks like crap.

The back circles abruptly stopped when Denise launched herself across the desk, knocking the partition aside to grab my trash can.

"She threw up in my trash can!" I pulled my hands away from my body. "Unbelievable!" Exasperated, I slammed out of the room and back down the corridor. I heard Jagger call out behind me.

"Maggie! Come back!"

I ignored him totally.

"You seem angrier about the trash can than about the imagined sex." I heard a chuckle and stopped rushing. I turned to face him. He was smiling his mocking smile at me, and this time, *this time*, I really hated him. Gone were any softer thoughts I might have had about him earlier, or the fact that when Denise had been throwing up he'd pulled her hair back like a best friend might do at a party. I gave Jagger one last scowl before turning away.

Chapter **Five**

Jagger was absent from his side of the desk when I got back from the bathroom. When I'd seen the empty seat and his missing notebook, which I was sure he never actually wrote in, and his absent laptop bag—this old, worn leather thing that reeked of pretentiousness—a warm happy feeling descended. When the laptop bag was gone, that usually meant he would be out of the office for a large part of the day. It was an opportunity to get work done in silent, uninterrupted bliss.

Jagger hindered my productivity. It was his incessant chatting, as each person that walked past stopped at his desk to have a quick chin-wag. That music he played on his AirPods that was just audible over the general white noise of the office, which made my toes curl while making his feet tap. On several occasions when the foot tap got so bad that the desk wobbled, I was forced to kick his shoe under the table. I know, so childish. But this is what he'd reduced me to, especially when the foot kick was always met by a low-toned laugh and smile, as if he was actually enjoying it. There have even been many days when I've wondered what would happen if I simply took the pencil I was holding and jabbed it into his kneecap.

I'd made it through my article and almost through the day when Jagger slipped back into the office. I knew he was there before I saw him because the energy in the room seemed to increase, like a beehive coming to life in the morning. A plume of laughter filled the room like a cloud of cheap perfume that catches in the back of your throat. A few wolf whistles sounded and calls of "looking good there."

I refused to look up. Instead, with a laser-like focus, I leaned closer to my screen and scrutinized the words in front of me. But after reading the sentence ". . . the deceased's estate is regulated by the Estate Duty Act and is levied at 20 percent on the first R30 million . . ." ten times, I gave up.

Jagger was surrounded by a small crowd. They were all smiles and joviality and outstretched hands touching his head. I still had no idea what was going on, so I forced my eyes back to the screen. I managed to make it through that sentence and then the rest of the article before I pressed Send and closed my laptop. The crowd had dispersed somewhat, and I was finally able to see him.

"What do you think?" he asked, sounding so smugly self-satisfied.

"What is it?"

"A checkerboard, it's their specialty." He chuckled as he ran a hand over the side of his head, where, indeed, a rather poor and disproportionate attempt at a checkerboard had been made with a razor blade.

I shook my head in disapproval.

"What?"

"Nothing," I mumbled, and started packing up for the day. Why everyone in the office found this kind of thing so funny was beyond me. To me it reeked of a sort of narcissistic exhibitionism that was highly distasteful.

"No, seriously. I want to know."

I slapped my book down and stopped what I was doing, and then made very deliberate eye contact with him. "I think it looks ridiculous."

"That's the point." He shot me one of those cheeky Jagger grins that lit up his eyes.

"I don't get it, then," I said. "Clearly I'm the only one missing the point."

His smile grew. "You get the point. You just don't want to admit that you do, because god forbid that anything I do would ever be even vaguely amusing to you. God forbid I actually make Maggie May . . . sorry, Margaret, smile."

Our staring intensified and I tried to pull my eyes away from his, but for some reason, couldn't. I was ever so grateful when Lesego walked up to my desk. But as soon as she saw Jagger, she burst out laughing.

"Oh my god." She snorted. "That's the worst thing I've ever seen. Where did you get it done?"

"Dye Hard," Jagger said, which caused more mirth.

"Even the name!" she squealed in hysterical delight.

"They have seventy reviews on Yelp with an average of two stars!"

"Isn't it funny?" Lesego asked, turning to me when she knew I would *not* find it funny at all.

I *humph*ed my disapproval and continued packing up.

"So, quiz night on Friday," Lesego said, changing the subject.

"Yes." I slipped my notebook into my bag. I actually *did* write in my notebook.

"No guesses as to who's going to win." She pointed at me with a smile.

"What's quiz night?" Jagger asked.

"It's this company tradition—we do it every year. One or more of the advertisers usually sponsors the prize and Margaret always wins. And this year the prize is the best one yet." She swooshed her hands around in the air. "All expenses paid long weekend in Zanzibar, business-class flights, and luxury accommodation. That prize is so good that even I'm tempted to enter, although my general knowledge only extends to who wore what on the red carpet and what bangs are in this season. Although last year Margaret did take me with her on that spa weekend . . ." She eyed me hopefully.

I smiled apologetically at her. "No. This year I'm taking my mom. We need the break."

Lesego's smile faltered. "That's a good idea. You guys really deserve it."

"A general-knowledge quiz?" Jagger piped up. I'd almost forgotten he was there or maybe I'd just blocked him out. "My general knowledge is pretty good."

I was just about to scoff at this when someone else ran up to him and suggested that they attempt to play a game of actual checkers on his head. This sent the office into more hysterics, and a call to find checker pieces sent people running in all directions. This was clearly my cue to leave. A man who would allow people to play a board game on his head could not be good at general knowledge—of that I was sure.

I arrived home that evening at the usual time, after stopping to grab Wednesday-night takeout for my mom and me. I'd been living back in my childhood home for just over a year now, in my teenage bedroom, staring at the posters of Linkin Park and Nickelback, which had never been taken down. During my teen years I'd gone through a somewhat emo, rebellious phase and probably, percentage wise, had spent the majority of my monthly pocket money on the purchase of copious amounts of black eyeliner. The black clothes and raccoon eyes had really been the extent of the rebellion, though; while other teens had been out partying and falling down drunk in their parents' flower beds, I'd been indoors diligently studying—while wearing said black clothes and dark eyeliner. I'd once fallen asleep with my head on a history essay and woken up to find an eye-shaped black smudge on the paper. Unable to get rid of it, and utterly embarrassed to explain it to the teacher, I'd painted the cat's paw with eyeliner and pressed it over the smudge.

"Cats!" I'd said when handing it in.

Mrs. Drake had looked up at me and smiled. "Don't I know it." Clearly a cat lady. I'd still gotten a solid 95 percent for the essay, though.

I felt a mixed bag of emotions living here. I'd moved back home to help my parents toward the end of my dad's illness. When he'd gotten sick, there'd been a lot of driving to medical appointments, and since my mom didn't drive, it just became convenient for me to be there instead of running back and forth—besides, I was also going through a divorce at that stage, and the fact that my husband had decided he wanted to live in our house with his new girlfriend made my living in the garden cottage rather awkward.

My dad had gotten sick one year and eleven months ago. It had been a Wednesday. An unremarkable, midweek day. I suppose I had a notion in my head that when a day came around that changed your life forever there should be some kind of a sign warning you about it. Like those on the highway, counting down the distance until the offramp, giving you adequate time to check your blind spot, put the indicator on, and change lanes. But I wasn't given any time at all. Neither was my mom.

One minute the doorbell rang and my dad was going to fetch his delivery—one of those DIY diamond-art kits. He'd recently retired after thirty years spent working in insurance and now he was "ready to embrace his creative side." He'd opened the box, taken the picture out, and placed it on the kitchen counter. Then he turned to my mom to complain that they'd sent him the wrong design. He'd ordered an underwater scene, complete with dolphins, not this. And the next minute he was on the floor, shaking.

"Glioblastoma," the doctor had said.

I'd never heard the word before. Isn't that strange—that a word I never knew existed had the power to alter everything. As it turns out, as brain tumors go, a glioblastoma is the worst type you can have. Not that you would want any kind of tumor, but if you were forced to pick one under duress, this would be at the bottom of the list. At my dad's age, he had a 5 percent, five-year survival rate—not the greatest odds. But as my dad had said, the odds of dying someday were 100 percent, so he had a better chance with the brain tumor than with death itself. He'd cracked these stupid jokes right up until the very end. I know he only did it for Mom's and my benefit, so I would always force a smile, even though they broke my heart.

My dad survived for another 364 days, one day short of a full year. I'd planned a party for him, invited all his friends and family, to mark "kicking cancer's butt for an entire year." I'd been so careful about organizing it, and only weeks before the date, when I was sure he was going to make it, went into full party-planning mode. Turns out, his party became his funeral, except I couldn't use the same decorations. My dad would have probably found that funny.

He deteriorated so quickly after his diagnosis, with all the chemo and radiation and fistfuls of pills, he never did get to finish his diamond-art thing. Looking back on it now, the diamond art might have actually been the sign I'd been looking for. Instead of an underwater scene they'd delivered an image of an angel sitting astride a cloud, the sun setting in the background and a white dove hovering in front, backlit by the last ray of sun. I'm reminded of that Alanis Morissette song, crooning about irony after irony in her husky voice. Well, if that wasn't the ultimate irony, I don't know what is.

I don't necessarily know what I believe in, but when I'm alone and that feeling of loss creeps up on me and fills my chest, I like to think of him like that: very, very shiny, existing in a sparkly diamond world of fluffy clouds and doves and angels blowing trumpets.

To mark the one-year anniversary of his passing, I'd opened the diamond-art angel kit and started doing it. I'd only managed one tiny corner. There was something so final about the act. Each colored crystal placed was just another pointed reminder that he wasn't here anymore.

There's something about losing a parent when you're an adult that no one tells you about. It reduces you to feeling like a small child all over again. You think of that person as the man who carried you on his shoulders when your little legs were too tired to walk, who held the seat of your bike as you tried to pedal for the first time, who threw you up in the air and caught you in the pool, who drove you to school in the mornings on his way to work. And you crave those moments more than anything and wish you could go back and relive them all one more time, taking note of every single detail: the sights, the smells, the way the air felt against your skin. Because when they were happening you didn't know how precious they would be one day.

"Hey, Mom," I called as I arrived. I walked into the lounge and looked at the garden cottage: the light was on inside and the door pulled closed. That usually meant she was busy with a client doing one of the many things she does. Quite honestly, I've lost track of them all. Angel healing cards? Reiki? Transcendental meditation? Crystal aura cleansing? Who knows.

My parents' house definitely pays homage to all the things that go on in the little purple-painted cottage outside. The interior is absolutely festooned with chimes and feathery mobiles, crystals and little cross-legged Buddhas on windowsills peeping out from behind small mountains of rose quartz that only ever gather dust. The smell of incense has seeped into the walls and carpet, so that even if it's not burning, it's always there. The only rooms that had escaped my mother's exuberant decorating were my bedroom and my dad's home office. His office used to be my refuge when I was younger and wanted to escape the purple *everything*. A big, dark mahogany desk and a big leather chair. Brown bookshelves and a dark-blue Persian carpet. I would spend hours in there reading from his set of *Encyclopaedia Britannica*, and he would sit in the chair behind his desk and read the newspaper cover to cover. Those were the quiet moments that I missed most. We were two kindred spirits; I'd never felt more like I belonged than when I was lying on that Persian rug that always tickled my bare skin, a thick encyclopedia open in front of me, and the soft sounds of newspaper pages turning from time to time.

"Margaret-Skye," my mom called as she walked inside. Lucy bounded up behind her and greeted me with a million wet Labrador kisses. My mom is the only one in the world who calls me by my full name. My hippie mother had wanted to name me one of those earthy ethereal names, Moon-Catcher or Forest-Fern, the kind that bare-breasted women dancing in the mud at Woodstock might have, and my dad had wanted to name me after his late mother. Margaret-Skye was their compromise. Even though I didn't use it, I quite liked it. I liked it I suppose because in some ways it was the perfect representation of my parents' marriage. Even though they were complete opposites, they always made it work.

"Hey, Mom," I replied, grabbing two wineglasses after putting some kibble in a bowl for Lucy.

Mom waltzed into the kitchen, her purple flowing dress flapping behind her. She had this ghostly way of walking, where clothes always seemed to float on her, as if a mysterious breeze was perpetually following her around. Her long gray hair was in its usual side braid, falling down over her shoulder, tied at the end with a purple hair band. She sat at the kitchen counter, stretching her hands out across the top of it; her various crystal-encrusted rings always made a drumming sound when she placed them on any surface. Her rings were bulbous affairs, made from aged pewter and amethysts and opals. The only traditional ring she wore was her wedding ring, a plain gold band with a single diamond on it. She always said it was her favorite, even though all the others completely dwarfed it.

My mom and I have the same type of body. She likes to call hers abundant; I'm more a fan of plus-sized. I'd watched my father love my mother passionately over the years, and growing up in that environment had instilled in me this notion that our size was not an issue. It was certainly not a hinderance to love; in fact, my mother's favorite saying was that there was just more of us to love.

"How was your day?" she asked.

"Good," I lied. I've learned that lying about these kinds of things is usually better, because if I tell her anything other than this, she will want to know every single detail of the day, and I mean *every. single. detail.* I once made the mistake of raging to her about Jagger, only for her to pull out her pack of well-worn tarot cards to "get a better understanding of him and what he is trying to bring into your life." My mom firmly believes that nothing happens by accident—that every event, every moment, holds some kind of grand cosmic relevance, and contains within it a valuable life lesson. She'd even tried to find this kind of meaning in my father's death, something I just couldn't wrap my head around.

As far as I was concerned, from what I'd observed in my own life, and as a journalist often having to report on the bad rather than the good, it seemed to me that life was very random in how it doled out misery and sadness. In my opinion, most tragedies seemed utterly pointless and held no intrinsic hidden meaning other than just being downright shitty. But apparently Jagger had been put into my life for some grand reason. I'd cut her off before she could tell me anything. I didn't need to be told. I knew what that reason was. He'd been put in my life to upend it—to bring chaos to my peaceful work environment and to irritate me constantly.

"How was your day?" I returned the question.

"Wonderful. Your father's favorite roses started flowering today even though it's too early. It was such a beautiful message from him."

I smiled at her. I didn't really believe in these messages my mom was always getting from my dad, but they made her happy. Sometimes I think it's easier for people who believe in this sort of thing to come to terms with death, because then it's not finite. A constant line of open communication remains between you and your loved one: white feathers falling from the sky, roses that flower ahead of schedule, and even that rainbow that comes out when there's been no rain.

"And look at these gorgeous flowers that arrived today." She gestured at the enormous, opulent vase on the dining-room table, and I knew who it was from immediately.

"What did he say this time?" I walked over to the table and opened the card.

This is not a gift—this is a bribe! I expect you to send back a batch of those little lavender lemon meringue tarts that you make! L.

I smiled. My best friend Leighton never liked to be sentimental; he found sentimentality to be utterly disdainful, even though deep down inside he was one of the most sentimental people I'd ever met. He was a closet sentimentalist. This was a gift—everyone knew you could not post lemon meringue tarts.

My phone suddenly beeped at the same time as my mom's, and we looked at each other and sighed. This could only mean one thing.

The neighborhood WhatsApp group. Possibly as irritating as Jagger. *Possibly.* If you want a front-row seat to people behaving badly, join a WhatsApp group. There's something about WhatsApp groups that bring out the worst in people.

"The neighborhood vandals are back," my mom said, somewhat amused. "Apparently, they wrote *Fuck Off* on Jean and Basil's mailbox."

We both burst out laughing and then watched the stream of horrified messages cause our phones to flicker like Christmas lights. Jean and Basil were probably the most uptight neighbors on the street, the kind of people who spent their weekends manicuring their promenade of lollipop-shaped trees with nail clippers and taking photos of the neighbor's cats using their flower box as a toilet. I'd often wondered why they'd moved into this area. My mom lived in an old, arty neighborhood. It was mainly inhabited by creative people, but the addition of a university made for an interesting melting pot of drunken vandal students, old hippies, and theater doyens. It probably had more esoteric shops per square meter than anywhere else in the city, those and vaping cafés (as they liked to call them), as well as shops that sold handmade trinkets and, with the word *artisanal* attached to the product, felt that they could charge a lot more than market value.

But this also meant that many a drunken student incident occurred, which were always reported and then discussed ad nauseam on the group. In fact, recently one of the neighbors' gardens had been broken into by a group of partying students late at night who all skinny-dipped in the pool and then made a half naked run down the street when the police were called. But as my mom always says, a real university experience is not complete without at least one run-in with the law. Hers had happened when she and her friends had been caught ripping up National Party posters at an anti-apartheid rally. I'd not had a run-in with the law, despite my mother always encouraging me to "at least try and get into some kind of trouble."

"In all the years she was at school, I was never called to the principal's office! Not even once," she told people—but not how other parents would, with a sense of pride, but rather as if she'd missed out on something. In kindergarten my mother had encouraged me to color outside the lines. At university she'd offered to put me in touch with her weed dealer, who sold quality stuff, in case I was thinking of "smoking that crap you buy from the campus dealers that has god knows what in it." She'd looked so disappointed when I'd informed her that I had absolutely no desire to partake in illegal substances.

We ate our takeout the same way we always did, in front of the TV, Lucy sprawled out on the carpet between us, watching one of the very few things my mom and I have in common—our love for reality TV shows about finding "love." This week we were catching up on last season's *The Bachelor*. We hadn't seen it while my dad was sick, and were currently binge-watching it together.

"He's not going to find his true love on this show!" my mom said suddenly, sipping the glass of wine she'd been nursing for so long that the ice cubes had melted. "She's not here."

"Here?"

"His soul mate is not on this show. I can tell. None of these girls are right for him."

I laughed. My mom did this every season with the most uncanny accuracy. She was good at reading people and would often call the winner way before I even had my suspicions. When the bachelor was still kissing them all and telling the camera how shocked and confused he was because he'd developed such strong feelings for so many women in such a short amount of time, my mom just knew. Personally, I think anyone can fall in love with anyone on that show. A coldhearted psychopath could probably fall in love on *The Bachelor*—that's how romantic it all is. If my ex-husband and I were put on it together and wined and dined and helicoptered and yachted around like those contestants, we might also fall in love again. Although that would be very unfortunate.

"I like this bachelor," I said thoughtfully. "He seems . . . solid."

"Solid. That's how you would describe the foundations of a house. He's hot!"

"Mmmm . . . he's not really my type."

My mom turned in her seat and looked at me. "You know, maybe I should enter you in *The Bachelorette* so you can get out there again."

"Mommm!" I moaned. "Not this again. I'm not ready to be out there. Whatever 'out there' means these days. You know, when I last dated, people actually met each other the old-fashioned way, face-to-face. Now it's all on Tinder. I'm too fucking old to be on Tinder."

Of course, I didn't tell her that, somewhat against my will, Lesego had created a profile for me and was currently screening all my likes until someone worthwhile came along. Apparently, I'd received a few dick pics, which I declined to look at, even though Lesego regularly pulled them out to show me and others. There was one of them in particular that she'd shared with several other women in the office, who'd even held a conference over it. The question asked was, is it really as thick as the can of beer he is holding next to it, or is this forced perspective or some kind of Photoshop trickery? Although opinion on the girth had been divided, the takeaway had been unanimous: I was not to go on a date with a man who took a photo of his dick while clutching a can of milk stout in the other hand.

And if they were not sending one-eyed selfies, they were saying something about my size. How they liked a woman who had some meat to grab hold of, or my particular favorite: "thick thighs to wear as earmuffs." I didn't want someone who fetishized my size sixteen body. I didn't want that to be the reason men wanted to date me, so they could "spank my big juicy booty" as one man had charmingly put it.

"You're thirty-three! You're a spring chicken! Of course you should be on Tinder," my mom said, ripping me from my thoughts.

"Well, then I feel too old! Besides, I can think of nothing worse than going on a million dates in the hope that I might actually meet someone who isn't a weirdo, a pervert, or who lives in his mom's basement, or worse, is a social media influencer who ditched his home to downsize and live in his converted panel van only to make his own kombucha and use a composting toilet."

"I drink kombucha," my mother answered.

"But at least your primary residence doesn't have wheels and has a toilet that uses water."

"You've become so cynical, Margaret-Skye."

"Do you blame me? When the guy I'd been with since I was twenty suddenly decided that I wasn't really his thing anymore and left me for someone else?" I will admit that my divorce had left me more suspicious and cynical in general. I think prior to my divorce I was a pretty trusting person, not with the people I interviewed of course—Journalism 101, assume some degree of lying—but when it came to people I met in real life. I had trusted Matthew implicitly, even when he'd been away on those book tours. It had never crossed my mind for a second that he could be cheating on me. And when Matthew had started going through his "crisis of self-identity," as our therapist had called it, it had never occurred to me that the nature of the identity crisis was really about no longer wanting to identify as my husband. Matthew had taken the trust I'd put in him and our relationship, and he'd chewed it up and spat it out at my feet like an old piece of gum that had long lost its flavor. And because of this, I had no idea how I was ever going to trust anyone else again.

My mom rolled her eyes. "They won't last."

I rolled mine back. "Well, so far so good. In fact, in many ways, they're far more suited than Matthew and I ever were."

"You know what you need?" My mom raised her brows at me, and I had a feeling I knew what was coming.

"Enlighten me."

"Sex!"

"Mom! I don't want to talk about my sex life."

"Sex *life*, darling. When last did you even have sex?"

"I have sex. I do. I just don't want to talk about it."

"Obviously it wasn't very good then."

I sighed. "No. Not particularly."

"Sex is not worth having if it's not good. Your father and I—"

"Okay, stop! Not you and Dad again, *please*." My mom had never been shy when it came to talking about sex. My "talk" had been her coming into my room when I was sixteen with a pack of condoms, telling me she wasn't ready to be a grandmother and asking if I knew how to put them on?

"I think I need sleep," I said, rising from my seat, trying to avoid this conversation.

"It's vital that one's root chakra is stimulated, you know. Nothing wrong with doing it yourself either. It's—"

"Mom! Absolutely not! I'm officially parking that conversation in the cul-de-sac of *NO*."

She smiled at me. I don't know when and where the saying had come about, but over the years when there were things I really didn't want to talk about, we parked them in this made-up "cul-de-sac of no." Strangely enough, she actually respected the boundaries of this imagined place.

"Stimulating my own root chakra, and yours and Dad's sex life! Both are in the cul-de-sac."

"So, basically, all the fun things in life to talk about."

"I have no doubt you will find many other fun things to talk about, Mom." I squeezed her shoulder good night and then traipsed down the passage I'd walked more times than any passage in the world. I pushed the door to my bedroom open and looked at my small single bed as Lucy bounded into the room and ran in circles around her basket before settling down. Matthew and I'd had sex in that bed so many times in the beginning of our relationship. Those times when we couldn't get enough of each other, when every touch felt like fire, every kiss was lava, and every time we had sex it was the best sex I'd ever had.

But now my ex-husband was having sex with someone else. It wasn't that I was pining for him and wanted him back—on the contrary. I suppose my only complaint was that the relationship had to end under such dramatic circumstances. Me barging in on them together on our newly acquired leather couch while my dad was having brain surgery was the kind of gasping season-ending cliffhanger that only a scriptwriter could conjure up. It was all so embarrassingly soap opera–ish. All the moment needed was bad lighting, big hair, and for me to look directly into a camera and narrow my eyes as if I was constipated.

Want to know what his first words to me were?

But you said you would be at the hospital all night!

As if this was my fault. As if coming home at eleven o'clock because I felt utterly desperate for a shower so I could wash off the sterile smell of the hospital that had embedded itself in my skin, was *my* fault.

And you know what I did?

I took my fucking shower and went straight back to the hospital. I did three things the next day: one, I called the home decor shop and exercised my seven-day, no-questions-asked refund rights (although I did tell them why I was getting rid of it and the lovely woman on the other end of the phone was only too happy to refund me and give me a complimentary R100 voucher for my next purchase); two, I moved out and into the cottage in the garden; and three, I called up my lawyer friend Laura and began divorce proceedings. I knew from the moment I saw *her* shiny red heels in the air—one had come off her foot a little and was bobbing up and down as he pounded away, exposing a tattooed snake that coiled down her foot—that the marriage was totally over. We'd been in therapy for well over a year by then; Nadezhda, that was her name, was not really the problem. She was simply the red-soled tip of the iceberg. Besides, I also knew that if Matthew was screwing a gorgeous Russian contemporary artist—someone who wore such high heels, had lime-green hair, snakes tattooed on her body, and a tongue ring—then he and I really stood no chance, because the change that he'd undergone of late was far more drastic than I'd initially suspected.

I sat on my small single bed as I did every night and pulled my phone out while Lucy started snoring from the corner. I messaged Leighton every night before I went to bed. It was our little daily ritual—one I looked forward to. I could have had the worst day imaginable, and these five minutes messaging my best friend somehow made it all right again.

Leighton and I met thirteen years ago, when I was just starting out as a journalist for my college newspaper, the *Rattle Tattle*. It was 2010, and I was doing one of those New Year retrospective articles, looking back on the decades and writing about all the trends, the news happenings, the music and movies that had defined them. And Leighton George— the lead singer of the wildly successful New Romantic band Le Mode Yeaux—had definitely defined the 1980s.

After a quick Google search, I discovered that he'd moved to South Africa in the '90s to pursue "a gorgeous man who'd stolen his heart over the rim of his martini at a nightclub in London." The relationship hadn't worked—Leighton's the first to admit it had been a toxic, drug-fueled, sex-fueled relationship doomed to fail, especially when he stopped taking drugs. But he'd stayed in South Africa, and I'd reached out via an email address I'd found on his website, not expecting him to get back to me.

As it turned out, Leighton George was only too happy to regale me with stories from his debauched glory days. We just clicked during that interview, even though we were complete opposites: me with my penchant for order and control, and him all wild and spontaneous. Because even though he's no longer high on a cocktail of cocaine and Dom Pérignon, or sporting a spiky, bleached blond mullet, wearing fingerless lace gloves and a Napoleon Bonaparte jacket with gold shoulder tassels, or partying with Bananarama, he's still the craziest person I know, in the best way possible. He'd been amazing through my divorce and my dad's death. In fact, I don't know how I could have survived without him. As he's so fond of saying, we're each other's ride-or-dies. "Or in my case more die than ride," he says.

Leighton is always talking about what little time he has left. He's only sixty-two. But when he was in his twenties he died twice, of two different drug overdoses, and is convinced that ever since then he's been living on borrowed time. He's even given me a spare key to his house so that when he does "kick the fucking bucket," I can go in and delete his browser history and empty out the top left drawer of his cupboard.

> **Margaret**: Totally exhausted, climbing into bed. Crappy day. Jagger was his usually crappy self. How you?
>
> **Leighton**: Grand. I'm out having coffee with this gorgeous boy I met at an NA meeting

I chuckled.

> **Margaret**: Don't they call that thirteenth stepping?
>
> **Leighton**: I would never. I'm simply offering a sympathetic ear . . . and if the ear turns into a head, neck, torso and the rest of my body, well . . .

Margaret: You're incorrigible

Leighton: No seriously, I'm honestly just lending an ear. He's just relapsed and needed someone to talk to

Margaret: Remember your rule!

Leighton: If I find them hot, don't sponsor them!

Margaret: Yup!

Leighton: Listen, I hung up my slut heels in the '80s. They're at the back of the closet gathering dust. Speaking of slut heels…

Leighton: How is our favorite ex and his paint thrower?

Leighton had called Nadezhda the paint thrower ever since he'd seen her "art." He liked to use dramatic air gestures whenever he said that. *She threw pink fucking paint on a canvas and actually sold it to someone. Someone parted with their hard-earned cash for pink paint on a canvas tossed by a green-haired woman with an unpronounceable name!*

Margaret: They seem fine. Apparently, he's started writing his new book

Leighton: Good! And I hope it tanks and reviewers call it pedestrian, with weak, vapid characterization, stilted dialogue, and an asinine plot. A book that quickly descends into the bowels of literary hellfire

Margaret: Have you been practicing that?

Leighton: Of course, for when I need to review it on Goodreads.

Margaret: Well, it's better than your last review. "I hate this book and I especially hate the person who wrote it." A bit of a giveaway

Leighton: Not my finest work, I admit. But it is a best friend's duty to hate the ex! And I hope when I get into a relationship that ends dramatically with me throwing his clothes over the balcony, that you will also exercise your duty!

Margaret: I promise to hate your future ex-boyfriend!

Leighton: I shall count on it. Got to go. XX

Margaret: XX

I was about to slip my phone away when I looked at the clock. It was time for the publication to go live.

I opened the web address and tomorrow's paper lit up the screen. I sighed when I saw what was dominating the page, not that I was surprised anymore. My articles used to lead the page before Jagger came along. His latest *Jagger Tries . . .* video took up the bulk of the screen. I scrolled down. My article, a really insightful and interesting piece on Busisiwe Mkhwebane, South Africa's public protector, was there too. Sitting next to Lesego's new piece on the mental-health impact of beauty filters. Then another one of mine, "Green Is the New Black," a look at alternative energy sources and their effect on the economy, as well as another one of mine, a detailed probe into government corruption. And then, *then*, bigger than all of those articles combined, Jagger's Swipe Write column.

There he was, his face plastered across the top of it. Smiling while holding his phone in his hand, his other hand poised millimeters from the screen, ready to swipe "write." I sneered and tossed my phone down; it bumped my knee, and I heard Jagger's voice. I picked it up and Jagger's latest *Tries . . .* video filled the screen. I was about to press Pause, but for some reason, I didn't.

Chapter **Six**

"*Today I tried the worst-rated barber in Johannesburg. I went there with low expectations. After all, the reviews I'd read called the place 'hell on earth' with 'chairs that feel like torture devices' and 'a butcher as a barber.' While it's true that the interior of Dye Hard is not that of a trendy vintage barbershop—black-and-white checkerboard floor tiles, a big, brown, purposefully aged leather couch—it certainly was not hell on earth. But Dye Hard is not trying to be a trendy barbershop. With cuts that cost R70 and beard trims that cost a mere R30, you know you're not going to get warm lavender-scented face towels. So if that's what you're expecting, I suggest you don't go to Dye Hard. And did I find a butcher there? I certainly did not.*

"*In fact, Naseem, a third-generation barber from Iran who came to South Africa with his family in the 1980s to flee the war, is one of the nicest people I've ever met. He couldn't have been kinder, more attentive, or prouder of his daughters and grandchildren—all the photos of them on the walls of the shop and the endless stories he told me about their many achievements were testament to this. The chair, I will admit, though, was not comfortable. Would I compare it to a medieval rack designed to pop your bones out of their sockets? No, I would not.*

"*Naseem will be the first to tell you that he had a barbershop decades before it became trendy to have a barbershop. And with limited income, he is* not able to keep up with the latest trends, like serving patrons artisanal coffee while they wait. But that doesn't mean that Naseem has been left behind when it comes to all trends. In fact, to keep up with 'changing men's fashions' he offers an array of men's hair art, his checkerboard being his specialty. So, naturally, I asked for it.

"Is it perfect? Is it vaguely proportionate? Does it even remotely fade into my hair? Well, the answer is a loud and resounding no. But have I ever seen a man try so hard, put so much effort into something, or seen a man in his seventies stepping out of his comfort zone, trying something new and attempting to be 'on trend'? Well, that is also a loud and resounding no. And you can't fault a man for doing his best. And that's what Dye Hard is all about. It's about one man's fighting spirit—a man who fled a war-torn country to give his family a better life, who worked seven days a week to put them all through school and college. Who tried to innovate and keep up, not be left behind in the fast-changing world of men's grooming. The fact that Dye Hard has been standing on that same street corner for thirty-seven years is proof of all that. And he does it all with a smile and one of the most genuinely positive attitudes of anyone I've ever met. Naseem definitely put a smile on my face, and I must say, his checkerboard design put a smile on the face of everyone in the office too.

"Was it worth it? Absolutely! And bearing all this in mind, I give Dye Hard 4.5 stars and recommend that everyone go there and meet Naseem and order his checkerboard specialty. A haircut doesn't last forever, but meeting Naseem and hearing his stories, sitting in the aura of his positive attitude, is something that will remain with me. The reason I'm not giving him five out of five stars is that that chair really was uncomfortable, but it won't be for long because, thanks to one of our sponsors, Naseem can expect a delivery of a brand-new barbershop chair. So that's this week's Jagger Tries . . . and I hope you'll all give Dye Hard a try too."

And then Jagger paused. He leaned closer to the camera and a smile crept across his face.

"I definitely got it, and I'm sure you'll get it too if you just try."

The video ended and his words prickled at the back of my neck.

I don't get it. That's what I'd said to him today. *Was that . . . did he . . . ?*

No! I was imagining things. That was surely not directed at me. A strange feeling washed over me. I couldn't quite put a name to it. All I knew was that it was an uncomfortable one. I put my phone down on the bedside table and climbed into bed. With quiz night only a few nights away, I was keen to get my requisite seven hours. I wanted to be as fresh as possible. My mom and I really needed this holiday. I was emotionally and physically drained from the last few years. I felt sick and tired of talking about it to my therapist every Tuesday as well. I'd been at it for four years already. My general anxiety was what had originally made me seek her out. I'd noticed it increasing over the years, like a soft hum that gets progressively louder until it can no longer be ignored.

At first the anxiety just seemed to be one of those things that made me who I was. The fact that I was an anxious flyer, the fact that I was overly concerned about deadlines, and rules, and driving at night, and making sure I took my vitamins, and googling what the appropriate resting heart rate was for someone my age. That I didn't like germs or dirty kitchen sponges—and that sometimes I couldn't fall asleep until I'd disinfected the kitchen sponge. I'd once read that kitchen sponges were the dirtiest part of any household.

In the early stages of our relationship Matthew had found these traits endearing. He used to tease me about them, in that way that couples in love tease each other about things like always losing their car keys or always forgetting to buy butter every time they go shopping. But as the years passed, the teasing had started to feel a little less like loving and a little more like loathing. My anxiety reached a sort of fever pitch in the year that Matthew took off to write his book. If I look back on it now, it all makes perfect sense, but at the time it didn't. Hindsight is always so much clearer.

Four years ago, Matthew's deep dissatisfaction with his life in general became apparent to me. I remember the night as if it were yesterday. It hadn't come out all at once—it came in drips, like a tap you haven't quite closed. What followed was a slow revelation of things. I often wonder what would have happened if that tap had burst open all at once, spewing out all the dissatisfaction like old, smelly dishwater. But perhaps he hadn't grasped the full breadth and depth of his dissatisfaction yet. He'd only just started to feel it, and it had begun with his job.

We were seated at the kitchen counter eating dinner. Matthew had been particularly quiet that night. This wasn't unusual. He hadn't been enjoying work lately (he was the in-house writer for a medical magazine, a job he hated but that paid quite a lot more than mine). He'd been working there for two years, getting more and more frustrated with articles like "How to Vanish Your Verruca" and "Understand Your Uterus." I could understand his frustration, but we'd just bought our first house together, so needed his income.

"One more year of working there," he'd said. Until my salary increased and we could cover the mortgage more comfortably. That was the agreement we'd made together. But of course, it didn't work out like that.

"I've quit my job," he'd said suddenly.

"What?" I thought I'd heard incorrectly at first.

"Quit my job. Today." I remember him putting another bite of food in his mouth and then chewing it slower than I'd ever seen anyone chew before.

"Okay, okay," I said, trying not to panic. "You can look for a new job while you work out your notice period. It's three months, right? And I suppose you'll be able to keep your medical aid for that time too. Perhaps we should line another one up, just in case there's a gap in cover and . . ." I stopped talking and looked at him when I saw the strange look that had moved over his features.

He took another mouthful of food and chewed again. His chewing seemed very deliberate and purposeful. "No!" he said when he finally swallowed.

"No, what?"

"I'm not going back . . . *I can't.*"

"Why?" I asked, and he told me. The story goes something like this.

On being asked to write a piece called "Let's Get Candid about Candida" he'd cracked. He'd gotten up out of his seat, slammed his computer shut, and said "Screw this" to the entire office and walked out.

He hadn't looked for another job. Instead, he'd lain on the couch in a kind of black and gloomy haze as we dipped into our mutual savings month after month to pay the bills. It was the kind of black, gloomy haze that caused half-drunk coffee cups to gather green bits of mold on the surface and empty potato chip bags to *not* find their way to the trash can. I gave up on emailing him jobs I spotted online after month three, and also gave up on picking up the cups and trying to clean the crumbs that had accumulated on the carpet. My anxiety skyrocketed. And then one day when I came home from work, the coffee cups were in the sink, the packets in the trash can, and he was furiously typing on his laptop. The gloomy cloud was gone—in fact, he seemed to be beaming. I imagined a new and wonderful job that he'd landed. Maybe a copywriting job at an ad agency—he'd always wanted to branch out into that kind of writing.

"I've decided to take the year off to write a book!"

A year! I got instant eczema trying to figure out how we were going to stay afloat, and how I was going to support us both while he stayed at home to fulfill this dream I never knew he had. My anxiety deepened over the next few months when sleep and stress-free waking minutes became a distant memory. Matthew typed away during the day and slept like a happy baby at night, while I burned the candle at both ends teaching English online to Japanese students for extra money.

Anxiety, the need to clean and keep as much control over my environment as possible—even though it was utterly out of control—overwhelmed me, until Leighton suggested I go to therapy. As he said, "You need someone to bitch to other than me about your husband's early-life crisis."

That's what he called it. The early-life crisis. And, honestly, I thought that's what it was. At the time I thought the crisis was linked only to his work life, but I'd been mistaken.

Chapter **Seven**

Friday mornings were always my day to drop Lucy off at Matthew's house, the house that we used to cohabit together. Lucy had been the only contentious item in the divorce, because like all childless (by choice) millennial couples, our four-legged pet had become our baby. It had been so contentious that a pet psychologist had been summoned to weigh in on what would be in Lucy's best interests. It was concluded that that was a continuous, ongoing relationship with both human caregivers, and so a doggy joint custody agreement was entered into.

I was feeling rather exhausted that morning. The previous day at work had been hectic, and then to top that off, I'd gone to dinner with friends that night. They were more Matthew's and my mutual friends. We'd been a couple for so long that we'd accumulated a group of friends like a planet might attract passing rocks and debris. These friends had been orbiting our relationship for years. When we announced the divorce to the larger group, the general consensus had been that this was going to be a very complicated thing to navigate socially.

But the longer I'd been divorced, the more I'd begun questioning my friendships with these people. We'd all met at university—that time when you're the most exaggerated version of yourself. You're yourself but a high-definition version of it. Infused with all that exuberant, defiant energy that only a university student can have, before the realities of adulthood dull its shimmer. Each annual tax return and car insurance payment strip it away more and more, until you wake up ten years later and look back on that time with a combination of sentimentality and cringe in equal measure.

I was also starting to question my friendships because it seemed that none of them could handle my newfound singledom. It was as if it upset the balance of things in the group to such an extent that they were constantly trying to set me up. Last night was no exception. And each time they attempted to set me up, I became more and more convinced that they hardly knew me at all; What could I and a "cutthroat personal injury lawyer who likes Porsches" (their latest attempt at matchmaking) possibly have in common?

I rang the doorbell and waited. This ringing of the doorbell like a visitor might do had been the first in a series of events that had made me feel like this house, and the life I'd once lived in it, were no longer mine.

"Hello." Nadezhda answered the door, as she always did on these Fridays since Matthew had his early-morning jujitsu class. He'd taken up strange sports and extramurals after our marriage had ended. He was always so fond of telling me how Nadezhda really encouraged him to do things "like that"—the subtext being that I hadn't.

"Morning, Nadezhda," I replied, and as usual, Lucy bounded up to her happily and wove between her shapely legs. Lucy was the ultimate traitor when she needed to be!

"I have something for you," she said, and I raised my eyebrows in surprise.

"Oh?"

"Well, it's for Lucy, but for you too. Let me get it." She smiled at me and walked off.

Nadezhda had always been overly nice to me since stealing my husband and, to be honest, despite trying really hard to absolutely despise her and direct all my rage at her, I just couldn't. Instead, I pitied her. During the last few years with Matthew and the countless Imago marriage-counseling sessions we'd had—

What I heard you say was that when I asked you how much you had written today, you felt that I was undermining you and your creative process, which must have made you feel judged. Did I hear you correctly?

Mirroring, validating, empathizing.

—I had learned that Matthew was actually a selfish, narcissistic man-baby. There was a part of me that was utterly relieved when she'd taken him off my hands. She had given me a concrete reason to leave him. If that hadn't happened, I might still be sitting around unhappily, trying to figure out whether Matthew and I would work or not, a thought that had taken up so much of my time and energy.

I leaned against my old front door frame and looked inside. The house looked totally different now. It had gone from clean and minimalistic to bohemian and artsy. There were Moroccan rugs tossed haphazardly on the floor, crocheted wall hangings, and everything wicca.

"How's the office irritant?" she called from inside.

"Irritating," I called back. Yes, one morning when I was feeling particularly weak, I had also vented to her. Ever since then, Nadezhda had taken a keen interest in Jagger, reading all of his columns and often messaging me about his latest *Tries . . .* video. She would message me a string of emojis that I often found hard to interpret. Nadezhda mostly communicated with emojis; if I was running late on Friday, she might text me a dog emoji, followed by a clock emoji, question mark emoji, smiling-face emoji. Communicating solely in emojis was just one of the many things that made us very, very different. There were other things that made us different too.

When Matthew had jumped up in horror that night, his appendage still pointing north, my eyes had drifted down to the couch, which in retrospect I really wished they hadn't. What had struck me most about Nadezhda was that hers had not been hairless. In fact, despite my going for a Brazilian because Matthew had purported to fancy smoothness (again, when attempting to spice up our sex life), she was sporting a full bush. Her armpits, too, were unshaved. I was later informed by Lesego that *not* shaving has become somewhat of a trendy, feminist statement. Pubic hair was apparently back in fashion after it had been MIA since the early 2000s. I'd tried to tell Leighton about my run-in with Nadezhda's feminist bush, but he'd refused to listen. There was only one thing you couldn't speak to Leighton about, and that was it.

Nadezhda finally emerged from the house and held out her hand. "Here." She passed me some tick and flea treatment. "I put it on her last weekend. The vet said to apply it again in three months, so I thought you should keep some too."

"Thank you," I said, and took it graciously. Nadezhda was intent on winning me over with kindness. She'd always claimed that Matthew had told her we were already separated when they'd started sleeping together—something I wouldn't put past him—and had never wanted any "hard feelings" between us. So I'd tried, quite successfully, to push those hard feelings down. Labradors can live up to twelve years; Lucy was only four, and as far as I could see, Nadezhda was going nowhere.

When I arrived at work, Nadezhda sent me a message that read: dog emoji, ball emoji, water emoji, duck emoji, exploding-head emoji, exclamation mark emoji. I took this to mean that when she took Lucy for her walk in the park, Lucy had jumped into the dam again and tried to catch a duck. Perhaps this time she had succeeded, given the exploding head and red exclamation mark. I replied with a screaming ghost-face emoji (I wasn't sure if that was the right one) and Nadezhda replied with a laughing-face emoji followed by tombstone emoji. I assumed that either the duck hadn't made it or she was laughing so hard she was dead. It was difficult to tell.

"Margaret." Jagger said my name very pointedly and then sat down at our desk. I didn't look up. Instead, I glanced down at my new garbage can, the one I'd bought yesterday on the way to work to replace the one Denise had vomited in.

I pulled my laptop out of my case and flipped it open. The screen saver of Leighton, Lucy, and I holidaying on the beach together sprang to life. Out of the corner of my eye, I saw Jagger reach out his arm. He gave the middle partition on our desk a little shake. It didn't even wobble.

"Hot-glue gun," I mumbled, not looking up. Also something I'd bought yesterday to fix the issue of our leaning partition.

"Impressive." I could hear a smile in his voice. I was happy when Lesego came up to the desk and stopped Jagger from trying to make conversation with me, as he usually did for at least the first ten minutes of every morning, despite the fact I never responded to him.

"How was last night? Do you have a boyfriend yet?" Lesego teased me.

"Thankfully, no."

"Who was it this time?" she asked, all too aware of what happened when I went to dinner with those friends.

"Brian. Personal injury lawyer who likes talking about himself in the third person, taking his new Porsche out on long drives, and suing people."

Jagger snickered, even though he hadn't actually been invited to join in the conversation. "He sounds utterly charming."

I looked up at Jagger. "That's perhaps the first thing you and I have ever agreed on," I said sarcastically. "He works for Smith and Simmons," I added, and Jagger and Lesego both gave the appropriate "oooh"s. Anyone who had a television had seen their tasteless, testimonial TV ads which always ended in a . . .

So, if you think you've been wronged, call 0800 letssuethem!

"I gather you won't be going on a date with him anytime soon?" she asked.

"I won't be going on a date with anyone anytime soon." I looked down at my laptop and pressed Refresh on my emails.

"Not even—" She pulled her phone out and swiped at the screen a few times. "Andy, thirty-two, chemical engineer looking for someone to create an exothermic reaction with. Fire emoji. Beaker emoji. Winky-face emoji. He swiped right on you and sent you two DMs."

"DM him back and tell him that exothermic reactions also cause rust."

Lesego burst out laughing as she typed back to him.

"Why is Lesego impersonating you on Tinder?" Jagger asked.

"I'm not impersonating her—I'm her official dating PA. I separate the wheat from the chaff on her behalf."

"No, that's not the reason. It's because she was the one who insisted I put myself up on the app, and when I said no, she did it anyway, without my permission."

"Well, that too," Lesego said, with that same wicked smile she'd had when she'd shown me my new dating profile. Apparently, I'm "looking for real connections, fun, and adventure" (she said to keep it broad) and my likes are tennis, reading, skydiving, and chess (again, to keep it broad). I'm also a writer, not a journalist, because journalist might make me seem pushy, and we all know that men don't like pushy. And apparently, as a dater, the most important thing to remember is to obviously pander to whatever the man wants from you—god forbid you were an outspoken university-educated women.

"And why would she do that?" Jagger was still trying to insert himself into this conversation.

"Because, like everyone else in my life, Lesego believes I should be dating."

"Well, that's only half true. As a married woman, I'm also selfishly looking to date vicariously through you."

"And you don't want to date?" he asked, looking at me with those steely eyes.

"No. I don't want to date. And if I did, I would *not* want to do it through an app."

"You wouldn't?"

"If I wanted to find someone, which I don't, but if I did, the last place on earth I'm going to look is on Tinder, if the three Tinder dates I got talked into going on are anything to go by." I clocked Lesego, the one who'd talked me into those dates.

"Sorry, Barry was a bad idea," she said quickly.

"Barry was on parole! For smuggling exotic lizards! In his trousers! Literally, he had a bearded dragon in his pants on a plane!"

"I admit maybe I didn't screen Barry as well as I should have, but Martin wasn't *that* bad. He was a vet."

"Martin was fine, if you enjoy hearing in great detail, while eating spaghetti, how he managed to pull a metal slinky out of a dog's intestines."

"Mandla was utterly gorgeous, though."

"He was," I admitted. "But he was meeting up with another date straight after our date. She pitched up early and joined us at the bar for a drink. I think he might have started hinting at a threesome."

"Interesting," Jagger said, and then leaned back in his chair slowly. He brought his pencil up to his mouth and bit the back of it, looking very thoughtful.

"What?" I asked.

"It's just very interesting—that's all."

"What's interesting?"

"That someone like you won't go on a dating app."

"What is that supposed to mean?"

Lesego smiled and took a step closer. "I also want to know." I could see she was hoping for some grand dramatic moment to transpire.

"Well, believe it or not, not all men on dating apps just want casual hookups."

"*Pffft!*" I scoffed loudly and Lesego joined in. I was glad she appeared to be on my side this time.

"It's true! Not all men are looking for one-night stands. Many are also looking for real connections. It's not as if women are the only gender who want that, otherwise no man would have ever gotten married."

"And your point is?" I tried to fold my arms again but my boobs prevented me from carrying that activity out in the way I imagined it would look in my head. A stern, detached-looking arm-cross. One that gave off the vibe that I was casually unimpressed by this conversation and wanted it to be over as soon as possible.

"My point is, if you're a guy looking for a real connection, or a real relationship on that app, you're the type of woman he's looking for. But if you're not on the dating app, if women like you aren't on the dating app, then what chance does he have of meeting anyone he can make a real connection with? I mean look at Lesego—she's on it only to have fun. So the people who really should be on it, aren't on it."

"Huh?" I blinked at him. "What do you mean, I'm the type of woman he's looking for?" I looked at Lesego, who was smiling from ear to ear, as if she was about to bloody explode.

"Well, you're . . . you know . . . relationship material."

"What does that mean?" It sounded vaguely like an insult.

"You're the kind of woman that men marry."

"Ooooh! Damn!" Lesego exploded next to me. "If that's not the best pickup line ever then I don't know what is."

"It's not a pickup line—it's the truth," Jagger countered.

"Double damn. The guy has skills." Lesego winked at me and then mouthed something, again, that looked like *dick ring*, and for the first time in my life, I think my cheeks went Jagger pink. I looked over at Jagger quickly and . . .

Wait! Had his cheeks just changed color, too, or was I imagining it? That usual cool façade, all cement gray and impenetrable, seemed a little pink now too. Jagger met my eyes but then looked away so quickly that I started to doubt we'd made eye contact at all.

"I have to work." I flipped my laptop open again.

Lesego gave an audible disappointed sigh. "Well, I suppose I do need to go and write an article about how early 2000s fashion trends are coming back. God help us all trying to squeeze our thirty-plus fupa's into those low-cut jeans, but I swear I will throw myself out that door and down the stairs if pink velour tracksuits with rhinestone bedazzling and frosted lip gloss return." Lesego nudged me. "I'll let you know when to dig out your old emo eyeliner from the back of your makeup drawer."

I blushed.

"Wait . . . you . . . emo?" Jagger asked.

"Oh, you should have seen her, full-on goth girl over here!" Lesego went on to embarrass me further.

"Now, that I would pay to see."

"How do you know what I looked like as a teen?" I turned to Lesego.

"When I was looking for a profile picture for your Tinder I delved deep into your online photos. Deeeep. One of your old school friends had tagged you in a photo from your prom."

"Aaarrhhhgg," I groaned in embarrassment.

"Hey, don't feel bad." Lesego patted me on the back. "My two friends and I dressed in matching Destiny's Child animal print." She sang "Say My Name" with a smile before she strolled away. I could feel Jagger staring at me, and my indignation flared.

"What?" I challenged him.

"Nothing." But a smug smile was plastered across his face.

I went back to looking at my emails—I always started the day with emails—and after the third one, my inbox pinged.

From: Jagger Villain

Subject: Don't feel too bad . . .

The message had an attachment. I looked up quickly, but Jagger's head was down. I opened the attachment and tried to stifle a laugh but failed miserably. Because there was a photo of teenage Jagger. Braces, pimples, and pitch-black choppy hair with green streaks in it that swept across his face. One heavily black-lined eye peeped through the curtain of hair. He had a neon-purple lip ring through his bottom lip, which was smeared with black lipstick, and he was wearing a leather choker with silver spikes on it, pulling a defiant blue-painted middle finger to the camera. When I looked up again, Jagger was also smiling, even though his eyes were still glued to his computer screen.

"Looks like we have something else in common," he mumbled.

Chapter **Eight**

Of course I forwarded that email to Lesego, who forwarded it to someone else, who forwarded it to someone else, and by twelve that day, everyone in the office had seen it and Lesego came running up to the desk.

"I have the greatest idea ever!" She jumped up and down on the spot. "I want to do an article, complete with photo spread, of what everyone in the office wore to their respective proms. We'll all dress up like we did back then. It will be a feel-good, funny retrospective piece about looking back on awkward teenage fashions through the years."

Jagger burst out laughing and declared that he, too, thought it was the greatest idea ever and to count him in.

"I'm not going to do it," I quickly cut in. "My prom is *not* a memory I want to ever relive again, thanks very much."

"What happened?" Lesego asked.

"Just your usual teenage angst. The guy I thought I was madly in love with made out with my so-called best friend on the dance floor to *our* song. I was utterly heartbroken."

"Asshole," a voice said. I turned to see who it was. Shawn, our social media expert, had somehow inserted themselves into the conversation.

"What was your song?" Jagger asked.

"Why, do you want to mock me?"

"Not at all."

"Well, I'm not telling you."

"Is it awfully embarrassing?" he asked.

"Tell us." Lesego smacked me on the shoulder. "Now I have to know."

"Me too," Jennifer, our editor, piped up. I hadn't noticed but she, too, had joined the conversation.

I lowered my head and mumbled into my hands.

"What?" Jagger leaned in. "No one heard you."

I mumbled again.

"Still not." Jagger teased me.

"Nickelback! Okay! 'Photograph.' Happy now, everyone?" I looked around and everyone was smiling, except for Shawn.

"What's Nickelback?" Shawn was so totally Gen Z.

"Nickelback is like the pimple you cannot squeeze in the middle of your back," Jagger quickly said.

"Nickelback is like that cringy uncle who always gets too drunk at family gatherings and insists on making speeches," Lesego chimed in.

"They're like the chaff between your legs," Jagger said enthusiastically, as if this had become some sort of a game.

"That recurring chin hair that you have to pluck out every week now that you're over fifty," Jennifer added.

"Okay, okay, I think we got it. If you don't mind, I have work to do!" I raised my voice so everyone got the message.

"This is fun, though," Shawn said. "Let me try one, Nickelback is like the woman yelling at the cat meme."

Shawn's comparison was met with silence and blank looks.

"Did I not get it?" they asked.

"No, that was actually perfect," Jagger said, and everyone nodded.

"So, let's schedule the shoot for soon!" Lesego said.

"I'm not doing it," I reiterated.

"Party pooper," Lesego said. "Besides, you have to—just about everyone in the office has agreed!"

I rolled my eyes. The thought of dressing up like my awkward teenage self and posing for photos sounded about as fun as having an annual pap smear.

"Everyone is doing it," Jennifer reiterated.

"That's what all the lemmings said before they hurtled off the cliff and plunged into the icy waters below. Besides, this isn't a fashion magazine, this is a newspaper—we'll look ridiculous. No one is going to take a political piece I write seriously if I have raccoon eyes, black lipstick, and purple hair."

"You had purple hair?" Jagger was clearly amused.

"Only for, like, a week," I said, trying to wiggle out of the fact that I had once attempted to dye my hair purple with gentian violet and had stained the entire bathroom, which my mom just incorporated in the general aesthetic of the house.

"Hard-core," Jagger said.

For some reason, I reached up and touched my straight, shoulder-length blond hair. My hair was actually curly and naturally very unruly, and I had to spend a great deal of time in the morning to get it like this.

"It's just a little fun," Jennifer said. I couldn't believe she liked this idea. She was usually so composed, so serious, so *not* like this. "Besides, you shouldn't feel so bad. My prom was in '83 and Eurythmics were my fashion icon!"

"What's Eurythmics?" Shawn asked, looking genuinely confused through their overly thick-rimmed glasses.

Lesego blinked at them. "You've never heard of Eurythmics?"

They looked totally blank and then a spark of recognition flickered across their face. "Oh, is that like when you guys put things on your dating profiles like Gryfandor and Huffington Puff?"

"It's Hufflepuff and NO!" I corrected them quickly.

"Whatever," they replied, and then turned to Jennifer. "This idea is sending me, though. It'll gain a lot of traction on social."

I watched Shawn walk away. Gen Z really confused me, not to mention made my millennial self feel much older than I really was. The way none of them used Facebook anymore, said things like "bet" and "sending me" and couldn't name a single Harry Potter house.

"Great. So you'll do it too?" Jennifer asked Shawn.

"Big yikes, no," they replied. "That's not my vibe." They turned and swished off down the passage and it looked as if they were tweeting while taking a selfie of themselves sipping a matcha latte at the same time—it was impressive. Although I still couldn't wrap my head around the fact that so many seem to have rejected coffee in favor of vegetal-tasting green drinks.

"I didn't take you for a Potterhead," Jagger said when Lesego and Jennifer finally left.

"I'm not." I felt my cheeks go warm. "I am. Okay. Nothing wrong with it!"

"Let me guess . . ." He leaned back in his chair again and looked thoughtful. Why did Jagger always need to announce his thoughtfulness with a lean? Couldn't the two things remain separate? "Ravenclaw?"

He was right, but I wasn't going to tell him that. "Let me guess . . ." I met his steely eyes. The light bouncing off the blue carpet seemed to have given them a slightly oceanic quality. "Slytherin?"

"Nope. Gryffindor."

I scoffed loudly and then shook my head. "Doubtful."

There was a pause. I could sense Jagger wanted to say more. It wasn't a silence, but rather felt like a beat in conversation. If this was a play, the playwright would have written *Pinter Pause*, a hellishly long pause that actors make onstage for the audience to glean some kind of subtext from. But what was the subtext of this particular pause? I finally had to know.

"What?" I asked.

"You'd look good with purple hair." I blinked at him. Not in my wildest dreams had I expected him to say *that*.

That day I wrote my articles as quickly as I could. Not that I needed to, but I wanted to brush up on some extra general knowledge ahead of the quiz tonight. The annual office party always contained a quiz. It took place on the anniversary of the paper's inception over a hundred years ago. *The Daily Tribune* was one of South Africa's oldest and most respected publications, which was why it was so devastating to see it go the way it was—online, clickbaity—and now we were all going to dress up in our prom outfits and pose in an embarrassing photo shoot! This was the newspaper that had interviewed Nelson Mandela first on coming out of Robben Island, had opposed apartheid in the face of death threats, had broken so many stories over the years about government corruption, and had done incredible investigative pieces, like the one on Durban's heroin trade!

And now we were dressing up in old dresses, shaving checkerboards into our heads, and writing about Fleshlights (apparently this was the world's number one selling male sex toy—an artificial vagina in the shape of a flashlight!). As I said, I'm not a sexual prude. I once attempted airplane-toilet sex en route to our honeymoon (utterly disastrous and dirty), in a changing room at H&M (too many mirrors—very distracting), and even attempted the Reverse Pretzel (a chiropractor had to realign Matthew's back after that). I suppose it wasn't the sex toys per se that were bothering me, but the fact that the sex toys appeared alongside an article on the global climate crisis. Global warming and warming lube were two things I think should never be near each other. And yet Jagger had brought them together with total disregard.

The annual quiz was a tradition, rooted in the very story of the newspaper's inception. It was founded by two university friends who only intended it as a means of posting about the local social events in town and as a means of entertainment: printing crosswords, quizzes, and cartoons. The quizzes became so popular that they were the main reason people bought it. A local paper that had not being doing well then bought it out, and included its puzzle section in their paper, and theirs took off. The back-page quiz is the one thing that has remained part of this newspaper for over a hundred years, and so, each year, to celebrate its birthday, the quiz writer writes a special quiz. And tonight I was going to win that quiz and soon I would be lying on the beach and floating in the warm, crystal clear waters of Zanzibar.

I went online and did a few general-knowledge quizzes, acing them, and then packed up in time to go home, freshen up for tonight, and come back. The quiz and party were always held downstairs in the huge cafeteria. Not the small cafeteria that we now used, but the older, bigger one that had been closed when staff had been cut by almost half two years ago. I always thought it was sad how it stood so empty. It was the one thing in the building that reflected the change that print media as a whole had gone through. Magazine and newspaper sales had declined by 44 percent in the last few years, and soon, if we weren't careful, like video stores and CD shops, print editions would be gone. Soon it would all be online, and the feeling and sound of a crisp, new newspaper being turned and flipped would be a distant memory.

Leighton was always telling me to get with the times; if he, an aging '80s pop star could embrace Spotify and Apple Music, let go of the ego kick it used to give him to walk past a shop and see his face on album covers, then I, too, should move with the times. But I wasn't ready to lose another thing in my life. I didn't think I was strong enough for that. I had lost too much recently.

Chapter **Nine**

When I arrived, the cafeteria was full. Staff from other publications and other departments whom you only ever saw once a year were there. They all knew who I was since I won this quiz every single year. The tables had been set up as they usually were, and the same contestants who challenged me each year were sitting at them. They already had defeated looks on their faces, but I tried to hide my smile and instead wished them luck as if I was the most generous sportswoman around. *I was not.*

Our CEO told the same story every year. We'd all heard it before, but he did it anyway, for the benefit of new staff—although there had hardly been any new staff recently. Then he spoke a little about the prize and the sponsor and wished us all luck. He glanced at me with a look that seemed somewhat defeated, too, and I think just before he turned away I saw him roll his eyes. I looked around, and everyone seemed to be doing the same thing. They seemed totally uninterested in what was going on, and all seemed to be looking at me and each other with a kind of exasperated . . . *something*? What did that look mean? The only person who smiled at me was Lesego, and that's when it dawned on me: no one wanted to see me win again! Everyone in the room wanted someone else to win. I straightened up and pushed my shoulders back. *Well, screw them!* I was definitely going to win now.

Shawn was the official quizmaster this year, and they took their place behind the podium. I gazed at the crowd again; most had turned their backs on us. Champagne and snack platters wafted around, and everyone seemed to be more interested in little slivers of smoked salmon on dry crostini than in this quiz. Even Lesego was following a tray of pink cocktails around.

Shawn cleared their throat and whipped their phone out to take a selfie of themselves before starting.

"Welcome to our annual quiz night," they said. Only a few people clapped; only a few people turned. "The rules are simple. As you know, we will ask questions from a variety of general-knowledge topics and the first person to raise their hand gets to answer it. If you get it incorrect, the question is turned over to the next person who held up their hand. And if no one knows the answer, we move on to the next question . . . so shall we get on with it?" No one answered back—the enthusiasm from the crowd and other contestants was underwhelming, to say the least. "Fine. Okay. First question is from the history category. When did Jan van Riebeek come to South Africa?"

I was just about to fling my hand up when a voice cut through the room.

"WAIT!" it shouted. The atmosphere in the room changed—everyone turned; people craned their necks and almost spilled their champagne to see where the voice was coming from. A commotion began, a low hum of voices that got louder and louder. Frustrated that I couldn't see what was going on, I stood up, and that's when I saw *him*!

"Sorry I'm late, was busy shooting a video"—he rolled his sleeve up and waved his arm around in the air—"at the worst-rated tattoo parlor in Joburg."

The crowd laughed. I rolled my eyes.

"We've already started, though," I said, having to raise my voice over the laughter. "You can't just join in now." I looked at Shawn; they looked confused and then started googling something on their phone. I tapped my foot against the floor as Shawn's eyes flicked back and forth across the lit screen.

"I can't really find anything specific about this online, so I'm just going to make a call as quizmaster. Since no answers have been given yet, so no scores locked in, I think Jagger can join the quiz."

"No. I object!" I raised my hand in the air and waved it back and forth.

"Relax, Maggie May, this isn't a court hearing," Jagger teased me, and everyone chuckled.

"Oh, let him join," someone from the crowd yelled. I wanted to know who they were so I could scold them. And then someone else yelled, and then Lesego—whose loyalty I was seriously starting to doubt—whistled.

"It's my decision," Shawn said, eyeballing me.

I lowered my hand and sighed. "Fine." Jagger rushed up to the stage, looking pleased with himself. I caught sight of his tattoo—it looked like a crudely drawn face—and shook my head in disapproval. He sat down at one of the tables and Shawn was about to start again when . . .

"It's 1652, by the way. Jan van Riebeek came in 1652." My blood ran cold, and I turned slowly to look at him. He was leaning again. Leaning all smoothly and smugly like he was something superspecial. A diamond-encrusted Wagyu beef hors d'oeuvre was something special, not him. My stomach rumbled. I was hungry too. Hungry and angry and sick of men who leaned and got silly tattoos and bad haircuts.

"Someone clearly understood the assignment. One point to Jagger," Shawn shouted.

"Wait. *What?*" I protested. "But we hadn't started the game. You even said so, we hadn't started."

"I'm the quizmaster," Shawn said firmly.

"Well, then I object to you being the quizmaster. You're obviously bending the rules. It's clear you're biased. Don't you think?" I turned and asked the audience for support. No one gave it to me.

"Just give him the point," someone yelled. And then someone else, and soon more people had joined in this rallying cry to award Jagger a point that he did not deserve.

It was clear by now, if I hadn't already guessed it, everyone in that room wanted Jagger to beat me. I straightened in my chair and took a few deep breaths. That was not going to happen.

"Right, let's get started. Jagger is in the lead with one point. Next question is from the geography section."

Ha! I was good at geography.

"What is the driest place on Earth?"

I knew the answer and started to raise my hand, but before I could get it fully up, Jagger broke the rules and called out.

"Antarctica!"

"Hey, you have to raise your hand. You can't just shout it out."

"Correct!" Shawn said, and suddenly the crowd was applauding.

"Hang on, wait . . ."

"Two points to Jagger." Shawn pointed at him with a smile.

"No. Wait!" My objections went unheard, and I was objecting so much that I nearly missed the next question.

Which European country technically shares a border with Brazil?

World's largest ocean?

What is the painting La Gioconda *more usually known as?*

In what year was the first-ever Wimbledon championship held?

About how many taste buds does the average human tongue have?

Who discovered penicillin?

Which African country was formerly known as Abyssinia?

Which South African artist is better known as the people's painter?

France. Pacific. Mona Lisa. *1877. Ten thousand. Alexander Fleming. Ethiopia. Vladimir Tretchikoff.*

I was officially sweating. Jagger was answering one question after the other—correctly! He was beating me, and the more questions he got right, the more the crowd cheered and the more I sweated. I was sure if I stood up I would have a big wet mark under my boobs, because I was flinging my arm into the air so violently with each answer. Most of the time Jagger beat my arm, probably because mine were just naturally heavier than his and, as a male, he had more muscle. I tried to point this out, that I was at a disadvantage because of his male musculature, but everyone just laughed!

"Last question of the night," Shawn finally said, and I could feel a bead of sweat dislodge itself from my hairline and trickle down my face. "The score is twenty-four all!" Shawn squealed. "This is soooo exciting!"

Everyone was watching now; not even those little tempura prawns that were floating around were pulling people's attention away from me and Jagger. I could taste salt in my mouth as the bead of sweat ran into the corner of my lips. I tried to wipe my hairline discreetly. Shawn cleared their throat into the microphone and a hush fell upon the crowd.

I had to get this right! This was *my* holiday! I needed this more than Jagger needed it. I deserved this! And also, I still wasn't quite sure he wasn't cheating. How on earth did he know all the answers? I had stopped the game at one stage and demanded that Shawn search him for some secret earphone or a piece of paper, or something! Shawn had just laughed, and Jagger had made a joke of it by lifting his shirt up for the audience to see and asked if I wanted to pat him down for a wire!

I looked at Lesego. She was the only one in the crowd not smiling. In fact, she had a very worried-slash-sympathetic expression etched across her face. She mouthed something to me. I thought it looked like *Sorry*. She thought I was going to lose.

"And the final question, the one that decides the winner of the luxury trip to Zanzibar is . . ." They paused for added dramatic tension. "What . . .

is . . . the . . . world's . . . highest . . . lll . . ." Everyone leaned forward as they dragged the *L* sound out. "Lake?"

Finally!

For a second or two my brain felt dead, and then, it fired to life, just like I hoped it would. I scanned my internal memory files, I could feel the answer just out of my reach, I grabbed for it inside my mind and then . . .

"Ojos del Salado. Argentina." I jumped out of my seat and waved my hand in the air, not caring that I was probably flashing underarm sweat marks. I was ecstatic. I knew I was right. No one in the audience cheered, though, because I could hear my own whoops of excitement bounce back at me like an echo. I looked at Shawn, waiting for them to officially declare me the winner. They looked down at the sheet of paper they'd been reading off, and then looked up at me unenthusiastically.

"That is correct," they said flatly. I whooped again, and I swear this time I think I heard someone boo.

"Well, actually . . ." Jagger stood up.

"Well, actually, what?" I turned to face him.

"Well, actually, you are correct, but you're also incorrect."

"That doesn't make sense. How can I be both correct and incorrect?"

"Until very recently Ojos del Salado was considered the highest lake in the world, but recently, a few weeks ago, actually, explorers found a lake in Nepal that is higher. I believe they call it the Lake of the Gods. It's yet to be officially named, that's how new the discovery is."

"That is totally made-up." I glanced at Shawn. "He's clearly making it up."

"No, I'm not. Shawn, why don't you google it?"

I felt a little knot in my stomach, a tight pulling of panic beneath my rib cage as everyone in the audience, including Shawn, looked as if they'd just perked up with hope. Shawn googled so quickly that their fingers blurred.

"Oh my god. He's right—Jagger is right!" Shawn exclaimed, and the crowd cheered.

"Let me see that." I rushed over to Shawn and stared down at the phone in their hands. I felt my blood drain into my toes. My lips and fingers and face went cold and clammy. "Well, it doesn't matter if he's technically right. The answer that's written on that piece of paper should be considered the correct one, and since I got that correct, I should—"

"It's a tie!" Shawn shouted, almost straight into my face.

My jaw dropped open. "It can't be a tie. My answer was right."

"His answer was also right."

"B-b-but . . . we can't go together! To Zanzibar," I argued.

"But there're two tickets," Shawn pointed out.

"I know, let's do a tiebreaker question. Like in tennis. Whoever gets the next question right, or maybe best of three or . . ."

"Oh, come on, Maggie May. It will be fun," Jagger said.

"No, it won't."

"It will give us a chance to get to know each other better."

"I already know more than I want to know about you," I hissed at him. "Tiebreaker! What do you say, Shawn? Shawn?" But Shawn had turned their back on us. Shawn had moved off into the crowd and was starting to drink pink cocktails with everyone else.

I felt Jagger slip up next to me. I could feel his presence in the same way someone might feel the presence of evil in a haunted house. I turned slowly and glared at him.

"How did you do that?" I asked.

"What?"

"How did you know all the answers?"

"I told you, I'm good at general knowledge."

"You cheated. I know you did."

"Look, we don't have to hang out together when we're there," he offered.

"We kind of do, since we'll be sitting next to each other on the plane and sharing a room with a four-poster, king-sized bed."

"I could build a pillow wall in the middle of the bed if that would make you feel more comfortable?"

"I am not sharing a bed with you!"

"It will be fun." He grinned.

"Fun? We can barely stand each other at work. How are we meant to—"

"Hey, speak for yourself. I like you. You're the one who took an instant dislike to me for some reason and then refused to get to know me."

I scoffed. "Oh please! You don't like me!"

Jagger's smile faded and his features knitted together to form something that looked serious. "I like you." He put great emphasis on each word, meeting my eyes as he spoke. I didn't like it when he looked at me. For some reason, I always found it so hard to look away. But when I finally did, I'd made a decision. The real reason I wanted this trip was so that I could go on it with my mom. And if she wasn't going to come, it was pointless.

"You can have the tickets. Go with whomever you please." A pink drink wafted past me, and I grabbed it and downed it.

Chapter **Ten**

I walked to my car in the underground parking lot, my legs wobbling more than I thought they would. I'd only meant to have one pink cocktail, but in an attempt to drown out the horror of the night, I may have had four. It had not been a good idea, because now I felt less steady on my feet than I knew I needed to be in order to drive home.

I finally arrived at my car, my trusty white Toyota steed, which I'd been driving for almost ten years. But no matter how trusty my steed was, I could not be trusted behind the wheel. I pulled out my phone to call an Uber, but accidentally dropped my bag. It landed on the ground with a crash, followed by a whooshing sound as it burst open and its contents spilled onto the parking lot floor.

"Fuckity!" I dropped to my hands and knees and crawled around, locating all the bits and bobs from my bag. I was almost finished when I heard a voice above me.

"Now why would someone need two hand sanitizers?"

I knew exactly who the voice belonged to, and it was confirmed when an old, worn sneaker came into my field of vision.

"I do," I said flatly. "Especially when the person I work next to invites women to empty their stomachs in my garbage can."

He laughed. "I didn't exactly *invite* her to do that." And then he bent down, his knees now just centimeters from my face. "Can I help you?" It was clearly a rhetorical question, because before I had time to answer, he was already touching my things! I tried to grab them from him, but wobbled embarrassingly on my knees.

"Easy there," he said, as if he was trying to calm down a bucking horse.

I steadied myself and looked up at him, determined to shoot him the most devastatingly vicious glare. A glare to end all glares. The kind of glare that seared through flesh and bone and set things alight it was so powerful. What happened was not that. Instead, I steadied myself, looked up at him, and hiccupped.

He smiled, picked up a small jar, and raised it to his face. "'Calming oil, serenity blend, contains lavender, chamomile and neroli.'" He turned the glass bottle around in his hands, looking at it curiously before passing it back to me. "Huh!"

"Huh, what?" I took it and shoved it back into my bag.

"I just didn't think you would be the kind of person who'd be into essential oils."

"I'm not into essential oils." I stood up. "My mom is. She gave it to me."

"Do they work?" he asked, and then stopped himself. "Okay, sorry, silly question."

"Silly question?"

"Well, you know, you're not exactly . . . *calm*," he said, and then leaned, *bloody leaned*, against my car. I shot his arm a look, the arm that was touching my car, and he quickly pulled himself off it. He gave a low chuckle and raised his brows at me, as if to say that I'd just proved his point. I wasn't going to deny it—I wasn't calm. I'd never purported to be calm. I was not Zen and into meditation and ASMR apps and putting my fingers together in strange poses and breathing out on a sustained *om* sound.

Jagger looked back at my open car door, and then at me. "I hope you're not planning on driving home."

"It's not really any of your business, but I'm planning on taking an Uber."

"Where do you live?"

"Again, none of your business, but Melville."

"Really? I live in Parkhurst. Right around the corner from you."

I *hmph*ed and looked back down at my phone, trying to put an end to this conversation. The reason I needed to take an Uber in the first place was because of Jagger. I wouldn't have drunk those bloody pink things had it not been for all the big back pats and loud congratulations he'd gotten all evening from everyone. I wouldn't have drunk those pink things if I wasn't devastated, thinking about that holiday that I'd wanted to take so badly with my mom.

"Let me take you home," he said, and I burst out laughing. Because it was late and relatively empty, my laughter echoed around the empty parking lot, sounding manic and strange.

"I don't think so."

"I'm going in that direction anyway."

"Good for you." I cringed at that sarcastic response of mine. It was so embarrassingly petulant.

"I insist," he said.

"Really?"

"You like logic, right?" Jagger asked.

"I do."

"How much does an Uber cost to Parkhurst? Three-fifty, three hundred rand?"

I glanced down at my phone. "Three hundred and twenty-one rand."

"So by *not* taking an Uber, you save three hundred and twenty-one rand. Think about it this way—you like one tall flat white from the canteen every morning."

"Wh—how did you know?"

"We've been sharing a desk for six months, three weeks, and I believe it's now seven days, as you pointed out."

This still didn't answer my question, though; How did he know what I drank each morning? He would have had to have been paying attention.

"One of them costs thirty-seven fifty rand, so how many cups of coffee is that Uber ride?" He paused and looked like he was thinking. "Eight point five."

I opened my phone calculator and did the math quickly. "Eight point five six," I corrected, trying not to show my surprise at how accurate his math had been.

He smiled. "Give or take. It's also about eight slices of red velvet cake, which I know you enjoy."

I think I blushed like a red velvet cake. I wasn't sure I wanted him knowing how much I enjoyed my red velvet cake. In fact, I didn't know how I felt about him taking stock of what I ate and of course my absolute devoted love of . . .

"Cheesecake." He finished my thoughts.

"What about it?"

"Forty-four rand a slice! Don't you see how much coffee and cake you could eat and drink if you just let me take you home? Not to mention the fact I'm a hundred percent safe."

"Safe?"

"Well, you know me. I'm not a stranger who might be a secret serial killer or kidnapper or who may or may not have just smoked a giant joint before fetching you. He might also stink and have a dirty Uber. My car is clean, and I'll even let you run one of your sanitizing wipes over it if you want."

"Um . . ." I looked back at my car, then looked at my Uber app, and then at Jagger. He met my eyes, and again, I couldn't look away. I tried, I really did, but my eyes felt frozen to his. My eyes stung as the staring continued. And then my mouth opened, and before I knew what I was saying, I'd agreed to let him take me home.

Chapter **Eleven**

In my head Jagger Villain drove like a hooligan in a big black muscle car. In reality, he drove a small Kia like my ninety-year-old grandmother: at least twenty kilometers below the speed limit, checking and double-checking, nay, triple-checking his mirrors when he put his indicator on. As a result, the drive back to my place took a *lot* longer than anticipated.

Finally, we made it.

"Thanks," I said as we pulled up to the house.

"It's a pleasure," he said with a massive smile. I did a double take. Why was he smiling like that?

"What?" I asked when I could no longer take the not knowing.

He shrugged, smile still plastered on his face. "You've just never thanked me for anything. It's a first, that's all."

I was about to open my mouth and argue with him but stopped. He was right, I had never thanked him for anything before. But he'd never done anything that warranted a thank-you, except for now. I gave Jagger a small nod as I opened the car door and climbed out. He also opened his car door and climbed out.

"I can walk to the house alone. It's literally twenty steps away."

But Jagger wasn't deterred, and he walked the twenty steps behind me. But as I got closer to the wall, I stared. There, in black spray paint, for all the world to see, was a giant . . .

"It's a dick," Jagger said, standing next to me.

I bestowed him with my best sarcastic *Do ya think?* look.

"It's a giant dick!" he said again, as if I was still in any doubt about what that shape on my wall was. As if I hadn't fully recognized that big, upright form festooned with two large circles, and was that . . . ? *How creative.* The artist had even tried his hand with pubic hair. The neighborhood vandals had clearly been here.

"Dick! It's a dick."

"Can you bloody stop saying *dick*!"

Jagger burst out laughing and I swiveled. "You would find this funny, wouldn't you?"

"What does that mean?"

"You men are so all obsessed with your genitals. You don't see women running around making jokes about their vulvas, talking about them nonstop or spray-painting their labias on the sides of buildings."

"Well, I suppose that statement does hold some truth."

"*Some* truth? I think it holds more than *some*. You're all obsessed! It's clearly some throwback to your primitive days. It's ridiculous."

Jagger kept silent, but I continued.

"You want to know the other reason I don't want to be on Tinder? Dick pics! That's why. I don't know how you all have it in your head that it's okay to send unsolicited pictures of your genitals to absolute strangers. You know if you did that in public it would land you in jail. But it's okay on social media. Well, let me tell you something: I don't know of one woman who actually finds an unsolicited picture of your erect penis—especially one where you are holding something next to it to show us how big it bloody is—sexy! We don't find it attractive. It's gross, not to mention the height of entitled toxic masculinity." I looked back at the wall. Until recently, I'd found the vandals somewhat amusing, but now, not so much.

"I'm sorry," Jagger said.

"For what?"

"I apologize on behalf of all mankind for this di—" He cleared his throat. "Inappropriate phallic symbol on your wall."

I was about to say something when the neighbor's lights switched on and I heard someone calling.

"Who's there?"

"It's just Margaret, Daphne," I replied.

"What's wrong?" she called from behind the wall.

"Seems like the neighborhood vandals have struck again."

I heard a loud *click*, and the gate next door opened. A slippered and gowned Daphne walked into the street. She was one of those old eccentrics who wore bright-pink eyeshadow and pink flamingo earrings. She walked up to us, folded her arms, and stared.

"What's going on out there?" another voice called. It was her husband, Steve.

"Someone's painted a giant cock on the neighbor's wall," she shouted back.

I choked on my in-breath as the word came out of her mouth, and I heard Jagger laugh next to me.

"What kind of cock?" her husband asked.

"What do you mean what kind of cock? There's only one kind of cock!" she shouted back as his face appeared from behind the door.

"Nonsense, you got the Jersey Giant cock and the white-faced cock and the bearded cock and the naked-neck cock and the long crowing cock." He rattled the names off, each one sounding worse than the previous one.

Daphne turned to us. "He grew up on a farm. I'll have to explain to him that this is just your standard one-eyed trouser cock."

Jagger was almost in hysterics next to me as Daphne turned and walked back to the house, promising her husband that she would explain it all when she got inside.

"I love your neighbor. She's a total character."

"You have no idea," I said. "She's a retired special effects makeup art-ist. You must see the stuff she has in her house! Latex alien and monster heads from some of the films she did."

"I bet you have all sorts of interesting neighbors in this area."

I nodded. My mom was definitely one of them, but I didn't share this. "It's getting late." I looked up at the sky, though I'm not sure why I did. It's not as if I could predict the time using the movements of the moon through space.

Jagger peered at his watch—a far more appropriate gesture. "I'll go now, unless you need anything else?"

"Anything else?" There was something strange in the way he'd said that. "What else could I need?"

He shrugged. "Paint thinners?"

"Nope. All good. But thanks for the lift. I really appreciate it." Second thank-you for the night, and Jagger smiled at me.

"Anytime." He walked back to the car and stopped. "Do you want me to fetch you on Monday morning for work, since your car's still there?"

"I . . . uh . . ." I stumbled at the question. "I'll take an Uber."

Jagger shook his head. "I knew you'd say that." And with that, he climbed into the car and drove away.

As I climbed into bed an hour later, I got a message from a number I didn't recognize. But the second I opened it, I knew exactly who it was from.

Jagger: I have an idea about our trip. I'm going to run it by Jennifer, see if it's possible and will let you know the outcome

Margaret: What's your idea?

Jagger: A way for us to still both enjoy it

Margaret: There's only one way I will enjoy it, and I think you know what that is

Jagger: 😄

Margaret: That's not meant to be funny

Jagger: I know, and that's what makes it so funny

Jagger: Is it weird to say that I really enjoyed tonight?

Margaret: Yes!

Jagger: Well, I did. You were a very worthy quiz opponent, and you also gave me an idea for a column. So thank you for the eventful evening. X

I read and reread his message a few times and, because I had no idea what to say back to that, I sent the most random emoji I could. A pimento olive. He sent me back a martini glass, pimento olive in the bottom of it.

And then something strange happened.

I felt the tiniest smile flutter in the corner of my lips.

I quickly bit it back and tossed my phone onto my side table before turning my bedside light off and rolling over.

Chapter **Twelve**

The weekend went as most of my weekends go. You really notice that you're divorced on weekends. When work is not there to occupy your mind, your singledom really sinks in. Not that I'm lonely. God, you could never be lonely living with my mother, but . . . no, that's not entirely true. I am lonely in some ways. Not in the big ways, but the mundane ways. The ways where someone is there to help you reach for the glass that is too high because you have short arms. Or when someone is there to tell you that you have spinach in your teeth or call your cell phone when you've misplaced it. Those small things don't really mean anything when you have someone but mean a lot when you don't.

The neighborhood WhatsApp group lit up with the dick, so to speak. The neighbors all helped paint over it, and I must say, the experience did make me feel as if I was part of a community of people who cared. A strange sense of camaraderie was created as we painted over the shaft and balls together and then all went into my mom's house for homemade minty lemonade after we were done. Leighton had been on the phone all weekend amusing only himself with his barrage of messages:

> **Leighton**: It's riDICKulous
>
> **Leighton**: Well, if someone ever got lost on the way to your house, you could always give them DICKrections

Leighton: I wonder if the students were just trying to write their DICKertation

And so it went on like this. By Sunday night when I climbed into bed I was fully DICKed off, and for the first time in a while, I was vaguely okay with tomorrow being Monday. I was curious to read Jagger's column, which apparently I'd help inspire, and I was also curious about this idea for the holiday.

Swipe Write *by Jagger Villain*

Men, we need to stop sending dick pics! I would have thought that not sending unsolicited pictures of your perfectly lit genitalia, no doubt at a perspective-distorting angle chosen to make it look bigger than it really is IRL, to women would be a given, but obviously not. Because in this golden age of superspeedy 5G and wonderous Wi-Fi, it seems that millions of dicks are flying through cyberspace at any given second right into the inboxes of unsuspecting women. Women who have not asked for them.

According to a recent study, four in ten women have been sent a photograph of a penis without having asked for one. That's a lot of women who are just going about their days, sitting in meetings, picking their kids up from school, cooking dinner, working out at the gym, reading a book, living their lives not expecting to open their phones to find your hairy balls and shaft illuminated on their screens.

Never having sent a dick pic myself, I decided to investigate the world of dick pics to see what they are really about. What blew my mind was how much artistry and time clearly went into these pictures. Some were so beautifully taken, black-and-white filters, soft lighting, some silhouetted against brightly lit backgrounds, that I don't think Annie Leibovitz could have done better herself. I could almost appreciate these pictures as photographic works of art that might grace the walls of an avant-garde art gallery in Paris. And then there were the others, the ones where the sender is clearly trying to make a bold statement about the sheer magnificence of his bulging manhood. The ones where the sender has purposefully put his cock next to a can of beer, or a wine bottle (if you're really confident), some leaving no room for misinterpretation with a ruler propped up next to it. Then there were my least favorite kind, taken from below: the looking-up perspective. I'm not sure why any amateur cock photographer would use this angle, because it always has the hairy balls and crack firmly in focus.

One of my colleagues, a smart, successful, attractive woman who, as a result, is regularly bombarded with knob pics, has assured me that she does not find them sexy at all. In fact, she says that she's never met a woman who does. So, if turning a woman on is your desired effect, perhaps it's time to adopt a different strategy. A strategy that doesn't perpetuate the cycle of toxic masculinity that enables men to feel so arrogant and entitled that they would smack you across the face with a picture of their erect dick.

The same colleague also posed a very important question: Why are we men so obsessed with that organ that dangles between our legs? But this fascination we have is far too big (excuse the pun) and long-standing (another pun) to cover in this piece, so I'll look at it in the next Swipe Write.

Since reading Jagger's article, I'd felt awkward. Four words rang in my head over and over again.

Smart, successful, attractive woman.

Was that how he really saw me? It seemed unlikely, and yet when I'd read it, my cheeks had flushed a little. Jagger's article was all anyone talked about that day: the women in the office praised it and the men nodded in agreement, even though I'm sure one or two of them (maybe more) had sent dick pics themselves. The article was trending on socials, Shawn said, and women from all over the world were now weighing in and sharing their worst dick-pic stories. In a matter of hours, Jagger Villain was a mini celeb; everyone walking past patted him on the back, sang his praises, and vomited congratulations all over him. The barrage of adoration stirred something inside me that I didn't like—it reminded me of how it was with Matthew after he published his book. Any vaguely warm feelings I may have had for Jagger were gone as I watched him bask in the adulation. I rolled my eyes; his article was like a dick pic in disguise. It had gotten him the kind of attention that those men who send them craved. Leighton had sent me a message earlier that day stating that he wouldn't turn down an unsolicited dick pic from Jagger. I'd thought the only adequate response to that would be the kind that Nadezhda would send, so I returned an eggplant emoji, two tennis ball emojis, a vomit-face emoji, a knife emoji, a monkey "see no evil" emoji, and then threw in an exploding meteorite for good measure.

He responded with an avocado emoji. I had no idea how to interpret that but had a vague suspicion, given that he loved avos and put them on everything, and he wasn't even a millennial.

The incessant buzz around Jagger's desk, *my desk*, had been so distracting that I hadn't been able to ask him about his so-called genius plan for the holiday. Between all the people and his Twitter notifications, which were beeping like a car alarm, my nerves were shattered.

"Do you think you could take your phone somewhere else?" I finally said. "It's beeping. Nonstop."

"That's because his Twitter is blowing up," Shawn said from two desks down, as if they'd tuned their ears into anything that pertained to our social media today.

"Blowing up or not, it's kind of blowing my concentration," I said pointedly.

"I thought you'd be interested, since you are my esteemed colleague who contributed to the success of this piece."

Shawn rose from their seat and walked over. "Wait—*you* are the colleague?"

"Apparently," I said flatly.

"Interesting." Shawn drifted off to that place where Shawn goes when they're about to get an idea, usually one I don't understand. "This hits differently."

"Sorry, what?" I asked, unfamiliar with this lingo.

"It's a different vibe. A new angle. Jagger's columns are all about dating for single men, but he writes something about what it's like to date as a woman, and it blows up. Margaret, I think you should be the voice of the single-female dater! I think you should contribute again to Jagger's piece. Maybe do a follow-up column about your dating experiences, compare it to the male dating experience, something like that."

"Certainly not!" I responded quickly.

"Certainly not what?" Lesego walked up carrying a coffee and looking so fabulous in what she'd called "color blocking" in her latest piece.

"I said that Margaret should contribute her dating experiences to Jagger's column. Give a single woman's perspective on dating."

"That's brilliant!" Lesego slipped her purple-covered bum onto my desk, and I shot her a look. She smiled and removed it.

"'Dating after Divorce.'" Lesego swooshed her arm in the air, making an imagined headline.

"You're divorced?" Shawn asked.

"Who's divorced?" Jennifer piped up, also standing by the desk now.

What was with this desk? Did it radiate some magnetic pull? Some gravitational force that caused co-workers to orbit around it like particles of space dust?

"Margaret's divorced," Shawn filled her in, and I lowered my head. This was a nightmare for me, my personal life splattered across the office walls for all to see.

"What divorce are you on?" Jennifer asked.

"One."

"The starter marriage. Been there, done that, got the T-shirt, and now I have the bag and shoes to match too. Next, I'll be going for the hat and gloves. Divorced hubby number three last year."

"I am not dating!" I declared loudly. "I'm not dating after divorce and I'm not contributing to Jagger's Swipe Write column. I'm busy with an article on whether or not the ANC will lose its fifty percent majority in the 2024 elections and what that will mean for the social and political landscape of this country as well as investor confidence."

Everyone looked at me as if they were totally uninterested.

"Elections that are over a year away do not get you a one point seven percent engagement rate on Twitter. Dick pics do!"

"'The Single Girl's Guide to Dating after Divorce.'" Lesego swiped her arm through the air again.

"'Sex after Divorce.'" Jennifer joined the arm swipe now.

Shawn arm-swiped. "'Dating after Forty.'"

"I'm not forty!"

"You aren't?" Shawn looked me up and down. I could see they were scanning me top to bottom. Taking me all in, from my shoes to my head. "Oh, I just thought you were. My bad." They moved off as quickly as they'd appeared.

"God, how could they think I was forty!" I said, hoping everyone around me would laugh, but no one did. "What? Do I look forty?" I asked Lesego.

She shook her head. "No, but sometimes you can seem older than you really are, maybe."

"Bet! A lot older!" Shawn said from two desks down, clearly still tuned in to the conversation.

"How? How do I seem older?" I looked from Lesego to Jennifer and then back to Shawn, demanding answers.

"Well, you can be a bit serious sometimes. I mean, I love that about you, but maybe that's it," Lesego offered.

"Serious?"

"And you're also, like, really into politics." It was Shawn again.

I swung around in my office chair and looked at them. "Being into politics is my job."

"But it's also so booooorrring." They dragged out this last word.

"What are you even doing working at a newspaper, then?" I asked.

"Just making a living while I'm building my TikTok. I do gender-neutral beauty and makeup tutorials."

"Your TikTok. Of course."

I wasn't going to admit that I'd never been on TikTok. That would probably make me look over fifty.

"I'm serious. Okay!" I declared, swinging my chair back to my desk and flipping open my laptop again. "That's just me." I put my fingers on the keyboard and began typing, a little angrily. I was feeling somewhat picked on, to be honest.

"Jennifer, about the prize for the quiz, the holiday to Zanzibar that Margaret and I jointly won," Jagger said.

"What about it?" she replied, and I was glad the conversation had moved on.

"Well, the two tickets are business class, right? And the room is a deluxe suite? I had a look at the pricing of that all, and if we downgrade the flight from business to economy we'll get four tickets instead of two. And if we take a standard room we will also get two rooms, not one. In fact, if we downgrade rooms we could even stay there a few extra nights."

I looked at Jagger and a glimmer of hope rose in me.

"Is that what you two want to do?" Jennifer asked.

"YES!" The word came out very loudly.

"The prize is from Travel Away. Contact them and see if it can be done, but I don't see why not." She walked away, and Lesego followed.

I looked at Jagger over the partition. "That was a good idea," I said to him.

"You know what was a good idea? The idea of you contributing to my column. Giving a woman's perspective on dating, especially after a divorce. I think that would resonate with a lot of women, especially a story about . . . you know, what Jennifer suggested."

I slammed my computer shut again. "You want me to tell you what it was like having sex for the first time after my divorce?" I rose out of my seat.

"No, I don't want you to tell me—I want you to share your story with other women who are probably going through the same thing. It would also help men—they could use some insight into the female psyche too."

"That is the most ridiculous thing I have ever heard. Why, *why* would I share something so personal with you, not to mention all those readers who read your bloody columns and watch your videos."

"I didn't mean to offend you. I just think it's a great idea. Everything I write is from a guy's perspective; it might be nice to have something from a woman's perspective."

"Why would you want some serious forty-year-old's opinion on sex anyway?" I started walking out of the office.

"Hey, I like that you're serious," Jagger called after me, and I turned around.

"You just like it because it gives you one more thing to ridicule me about."

"Not true! And you don't look forty. At all."

"I've never been on TikTok! And I still use Facebook."

"You still use Facebook?" I heard Shawn say from behind me, and then they laughed. "I'm weak."

I rolled my eyes at them but made a mental note to google what *I'm weak* meant.

I turned again and started walking out of the office once more.

"I also use Facebook," Jagger shouted after me as I exited. "And I used to have a Myspace page!"

Chapter **Thirteen**

I sat on the toilet seat seething somewhat. Since when had my personal life become something that everyone could talk about openly and give their opinions on? And especially my sex life! Jagger had, once again, crossed a line.

Not to mention the fact that my sex life after divorce was nothing to write home, let alone a column, about.

The first time I'd had sex after my divorce had been eight months after Matthew and I were over. Leighton insisted that I couldn't let it get to one year: if I didn't have sex in the first year after my divorce, then apparently I would *never* have sex again. So I decided I might as well get it over with. I'd done all those things that a woman in my position needs to do in order to have sex: I'd gone for a wax, I'd shaved my legs, and pulled that stray hair that started recurring after I turned thirty out of my chin. I'd bought some decent underwear—in my case underwear that matched. I'd splashed out on a new perfume, Sensual Mist, by someone with a very French-sounding name; it took way too much out of my monthly salary but the woman behind the counter had insisted that it would drive any man wild.

I'd been on five dates with a man named Byron. I'd accidentally called him Simon for the first date, and he'd only corrected me on date two. On date four, I knew that the next time I saw him we would have sex. There had been that look in his eyes that men seem to get, and I knew that, despite the fact I only found him mildly attractive and even less interesting, he would be the perfect person to end my drought with. There was no way I would get emotionally attached to Byron. He was an orthodontist—not that I have anything against orthodontists—but he was also shorter than me, had thin wispy hairs at the top of his head that stood up straight and, because his hair was such a shocking blond color, every time he turned his head to talk, the wisps, like gossamer threads, caught the light and looked like they were dancing. It was so hard to concentrate on what he was saying when he looked like a baby that had just had its head rubbed with a balloon that made their hair static. He also stared at my teeth a lot when I was talking, and on date three he'd said, "I hope you don't mind me saying this, but you have the most stunning cuspids." That's one of those comments that perhaps only comes around once in a person's lifetime. The kind of comment you're not sure is a compliment or red flag.

We went to a hotel after the date and it soon became very obvious that Byron had a mouth like a vacuum cleaner, the kind that seemed to move and suck everywhere. He'd tried to go down on me but I'd pulled him straight back up by those thin blond threads (which I was now grateful for). The idea of that was just *too* intimate for what I was planning on making a strictly one-off affair. The sex had taken *way* too long for sex that I really just wanted to get over and done with. He paused between every thrust, as if savoring a Michelin-star meal or stopping after each sip of wine to catch the hint of raspberry on the back of his palate. He'd even tried to cuddle me afterward, which was just as awkward as trying to go down on me. In a bid to get the sex over with, I'd been forced to fake several loud orgasms in very quick succession. I think he rolled over and went to sleep that night with the false impression that he was some kind of sex god. He was not.

Leighton suggested I simply ghost him, a term I'd never heard until recently. I had no idea that *ghost* could also be used as a verb, not just a noun. Instead, I simply chased him away with the best excuse a woman like me can use.

I'm sorry. I'm not over my divorce yet. I thought I was, but I'm not. It sends them running straight for the hills every time, pleased that they have clearly dodged the bullet that is a baggage-laden divorcé.

My phone beeped, startling me back to reality. When I looked down at it, I realized that I'd been sitting in this cubicle for twenty minutes.

> **Jagger**: Pack your bags for seven nights in Zanzibar!

> **Jagger**: I contacted the sponsor and it's all sorted. 4 tickets, 2 rooms, and 7 days on the beach

I jumped off the seat as if the water in it had just exploded out of the bowl and forced me into the air.

I typed back quickly.

> **Margaret**: Seriously?

Jagger's message was just a thumbs-up, followed by a big red hundred. And in that moment, I almost forgot why I was pissed off with him . . . almost.

Chapter **Fourteen**

I had a real Monday-night text marathon with Leighton later. I quizzed him on whether or not he thought I was boring and too serious and whether or not I needed Botox because people in the office thought I was over forty! Apparently, my seriousness was what Leighton loved most about me— it was my most "endearing and entertaining quality." And so when I did throw caution to the wind, it made it even more enjoyable, and apparently everyone could do with Botox. I was about to go to bed when a thought hit me. I downloaded TikTok, typed in Shawn's full name, and found them immediately. Their first video, and most popular one, started playing.

"Hey fam, it's Shawn again, and today we're doing an everyday look that will make you look snatched. I'm going to give my skin a very light covering of foundation, because who wants to conform to these societal norms of always having perfect, dewy skin? Since when did having imperfect skin become some kind of flaw? Our faults and flaws are what make us all unique, so I'm not going to try and cover all my freckles. And see this scar, the one on my forehead? Well, I got that building a fort with my brother in the garden when we were kids, and that's a memory I'm more than happy to have on my face. And then, as you guys know, I like to thicken my eyebrows. I'm all for a dark brow, so I'm going to be more liberal with the eyebrow stuff. But I'm not going for a Johnny Rose Schitt's Creek look."

I chuckled at the reference. Shawn was funny.

"But I do want to give them a bit of a glow up. Eyebrows accentuate the eyes, and as they say, eyes are the windows to the soul—well, that's what my mom always used to say to me growing up. She used to say that everything you ever wanted to know about a person is right there in their eyes. But my mom also used to say things like if I didn't wait for twenty minutes after eating to swim, I'd drown, and that if I sat too close to my computer screen I would go blind. So we take what my mom says with a pinch of salt. Hey, Mom, if you're watching, I love you!"

Shawn stopped what they were doing and waved at the camera.

"Seriously, I love my parents. They were so great when I came out as nonbinary and I told them what my new pronouns were. My little brother was a bit confused. He was like, 'But there's only one of you, not two of you!'"

Shawn laughed at the memory and suddenly I felt a little overwhelmed with emotion.

"I know some of you probably haven't been as lucky as I've been with parental support, but just know that we are all here for you. If you're having a hard time, drop it in the comments section or DM me."

I watched right up until the end of the video, listening to Shawn dispense a mixture of beauty advice and life advice. In fact, that's when Shawn was most magical, when they looked into the camera and talked to you as if they were sitting next to you. When it was finished, I put my phone on the bedside table and closed my eyes with a greater sense of well being than I'd felt in a while, and wondered what I would look like with a thickened eyebrow.

In a week my mom and I would be on a beach in Zanzibar. I needed a break from this house and all the memories in it. Sometimes it felt as if my dad's ghost still walked the passages at night. His presence could not be taken out of the bricks and foundation if you tried. But I also hoped that the presence of Jagger and whomever he was bringing was not going to take away from the holiday either. I took a deep breath and resolved that I wouldn't let him ruin my holiday. This holiday was a gift, and I was going to enjoy it to the full. My father had always wanted to travel when he retired. He and my mom had spent so many evenings together planning the trips that they would take: Kenya, Iceland, New Zealand. But he wasn't going anywhere. In fact, right now he was still in a box at the back of my mom's cupboard. Neither of us knew what to do with his ashes. We hated the idea of him holed up in a wall somewhere in a depressing graveyard, and yet we didn't know where his final resting place should be. And neither of us was ready to talk about it either. My mom was certain that one day we'd just know what to do with them, and that it would be the right decision. It would be what my dad would have wanted. But we were both still waiting for that day to come.

The next week leading up to the holiday flew by. Jagger and I hardly saw each other, and before I knew it, it was time to start packing. I love packing—there's something so therapeutic about taking your clothes out, laying them on the bed, and then folding them all precisely. And then came the fun, challenging part: getting them all to fit in your bag like a jigsaw puzzle.

"Are you taking a suitcase?" my mom asked as we pulled our bags out to the Uber we'd ordered.

"Yes. Why?"

My mom looked at it curiously and then slung a small backpack over her shoulder. "The weather there is going to be in the midthirties every day. I'm going to be living in bikinis, sandals, and sarongs. No need for actual clothes, so I just threw everything into a bag."

I looked at my mom's bag and shook my head. "What if the weather changes? What if you want to go into town? What if you want to go to a restaurant? What if you don't feel like wearing a bikini?"

My mom laughed. "Well, then it will make things interesting."

"I don't want interesting. I want all bases covered."

My mom walked over to me and placed her hand on my cheek. "I know you do."

"What's that supposed to mean?"

"You're like your father. I once organized him a surprise birthday party."

"Oh god! You didn't," I moaned. I knew how much my predictable father would have hated that, because it was exactly the sort of thing I would hate too.

"It was the first and last time," my mom said, smiling as if she was remembering a happy time. "You should have seen his face. I thought he was going to have a heart attack! His cheeks went crimson and that vein in his forehead started to bulge—you know the one he got every time he mowed the lawn or climbed a ladder to fix the gutter or hung pictures on the wall?" She laughed that deep, throaty laugh of hers. My mom had a great laugh. It was like no one else's laugh. When she laughed, the world stopped and laughed with her, even if they had no idea what the joke was.

"What did he do?" I asked, greedy for another story about my father that I could hold on to like a tiny piece of paper I could tuck away somewhere safe and, when I needed to, bring out and read over and over again.

"That's the thing: he was trapped. I'd invited all the family and all his work colleagues! He had to stick it out."

"Dad would have hated that."

"Oh, he did. I realized the error of my ways pretty early on. But we'd only been together for a year at this stage, and I hadn't learned yet that your father hated surprises and anything spontaneous." She cleared her throat. *"If it's not in my diary, it doesn't exist,"* she said, imitating my dad's voice so perfectly that it gave me a shiver. She stopped and looked up at the sky. "We were like a seesaw, your dad and me. On opposite ends, different weights, but somehow we balanced each other out perfectly.

You should find someone that totally throws you off balance, and because of that, balances you perfectly."

"That makes no sense."

"Find someone who drives you crazy!" she added.

"Again, no sense, Mom."

"Crazy in a good way."

"Is there a good way?" I asked.

"Find someone who pushes you out of your comfort zone and challenges you."

"I like my comfort zone. It's very comfortable."

"Are you ladies getting in?" We both turned when the Uber driver spoke from the front seat.

"Sorry. Coming." We climbed into the car, and it started moving. I wondered if my mom was right, whether that was the secret to a long and happy relationship. It certainly had been with my parents. They'd been utter opposites in almost every single way possible and they had definitely challenged each other. I don't think either one of them had been in their comfort zones since they'd married each other, and they certainly drove each other crazy sometimes. Not many people drove me crazy, other than my ex and Jagger. And both of those options were off the table. Off the table! *Ha*, that was an understatement. They'd fallen off the table and rolled like marbles across the floor and into another room. Out the front door. Down the street. Into another suburb. That is how far-fetched both of those scenarios were.

We got into the ticket line at the airport as soon as we arrived. The line was long, people standing like upright sardines winding around the barrier ropes. I looked over at the business- and first-class check-in line. So short. So quick. It seemed so much calmer over there, too, instead of this hustle and bustle. If I'd not tied with Jagger, me and my mom would be in that relaxing-spa equivalent of a line. They even had a soft, plush-looking red carpet underfoot and a giant orchid at the desk. I wondered if they were giving out warm, scented hand towels and a glass of champagne on arrival. Perhaps even a scalp massage to relieve the stress of first-class travel. Well, at least there was one thing I could feel relieved about: we hadn't seen Jagger and whomever he was bringing.

I took a moment to imagine what this woman might look like—the kind of woman Jagger would date and bring on a vacation. I wondered if she would have tattoos of snakes around her ankles and be an edgy, pixie-cut gal with pink tips, or if she'd be more classic and supermodel looking, impossibly tall and wearing a baggy, worn shirt with a hole that looked as if it came from the local thrift store but was actually YSL couture.

I breathed in, inhaling the buzz and excitement that an airport always has, but also feeling my own anxiety. As much as I loved vacations, I didn't love the traveling part, especially being flung into the air at 250 kilometers an hour and suspended on wings that didn't seem substantial enough for the considerable load.

"How are you?" Mom asked.

My lips strained into a self-placating smile. "Fine. I'm okay. Fine."

My mom ran a hand over my back in comforting circles. "It's a short flight."

"Yes. Only three hours and thirty-five minutes." I'd obviously googled the flight time, as well as the plane we'd be flying in and the safety rating of the airline itself. We were flying Kenya Air, which boasted a fairly impressive aviation safety record, but a recent midair engine shutdown had given me pause. However, the pilot had managed to land the craft safely, which spoke to high pilot competency. This thought soothed my anxiety somewhat, that was until . . .

"Margaret." The voice I'd been dreading was here, weaseling its way into my space. I suppose it was best to get this over and done with, though. Say hello, meet his traveling companion, and then part ways. It wasn't as if we'd be dining together, sitting poolside and sipping cocktails, frolicking in the warm sea. I probably wouldn't see him again after this— it was a large resort. I'd checked. No doubt he'd be in his room having whatever kind of sex he was into having. I turned slowly.

"Jagger." I scanned the sides and back of him for the woman he was with but found no one. *Maybe she was meeting him here.*

"Hello. You must be Jagger." My mom placed her hands in a namaste position, one of her signature moves.

"Well, namaste to you too," Jagger said, also placing his hands together. Then he turned to his left and I noticed the man standing next to him. The man was tall and had the same color eyes as Jagger, but he was much older. Shoulder-length gray hair, a beard, an earring in his left ear, and wearing a black leather jacket, in weather like this! "And this is my dad, Eddy Villain." Jagger pointed at the man.

I scoffed. It was one thing him having a fake surname to write under to give him an edgy mystique, or whatever he was trying to achieve with it, but it was quite another thing to introduce his father to us with the fake surname. *And why was his father here anyway?*

"Villain, that's such an interesting surname. Do you know its origin story?" my mom asked.

"I would *love* to know that too." I looked straight at Jagger. The truth about this made-up surname was about to be a cat leaping from a bag, and I personally couldn't wait for that reveal, even if I was allergic to cats.

"Well, the story of the Villains is not what one might call very distinguished. But it is an interesting one," Eddy said.

"I love interesting stories," my mom chirped.

"Hundreds of years ago in England, the Villains were all servants and slaves, the lowest of the low. The word actually meant peasant. And over the years, as you know, the word became a derogatory term, which we all know today as villain."

"Wow, fascinating. I love learning about a family's lineage. I think it's so important to know where you come from, both physically and spiritually. Don't you agree?" My mom leaned forward.

"I couldn't agree more." And then Eddy leaned forward too. "And what is your surname?"

Why were they both leaning?

"Well, that's funny you should ask. My maiden name was actually Bierman—my ancestors were Dutch. It means beer man, a surname given to tavern owners or heavy beer drinkers." My mom and Eddy burst out laughing. Together. At the same time. As if they were the canned laughter played on the set of a '90s sitcom.

"And do you enjoy beer?" Eddy asked.

"Not at all," my mom replied, and their laughter escalated.

I stepped back. *What the hell was going on here?* My eyes drifted across to Jagger, and for the first time ever, I suspected we were both thinking the same thing. I didn't know if this was a comforting thought or whether I should be very concerned.

"So you're of Dutch heritage?" Eddy asked.

My mom nodded coyly.

"That explains the startling blue eyes."

"It's funny you should mention my eyes—"

"Mom. No!" I warned. Oh god, I knew what was coming now. It always came whenever her eyes were brought up. The story, nay, the *legendary* tale of my mom's missing eye that has been etched into our family's mythology and that over the years had taken on a life of its own. It was the reason my mom could no longer drive a car—her good eye wasn't as good as it used to be.

"This one is actually a prosthetic." My mom pointed at her eye and the utterly entranced Jagger and Eddy moved closer to her. My mom had this way of pulling people into her "aura" as she always said.

I rolled my eyes. My mom loved telling people about her missing eye. Her favorite time of year was Halloween, when she got to scare the trick-or-treaters by taking it out. Of course this mortified me when I was younger, but I'm used to it now. My mother is an acquired taste, like marzipan, or pineapple on pizza. She requires someone with an adventurous palate to appreciate her.

"I would never have guessed! It's perfect," Eddy said, before a very familiar mischievous smile parted his lips slightly. "You're a pirate!"

Wait! I stared at my mother in horror. Had her cheeks just flushed pink? I'd discovered a new color, and it was called Villain pink. What was with these Villain men and their ability to flush female cheeks wherever they went? And then Eddy held up his hand. It was my turn to move closer; something about his middle finger looked strange.

"You're missing an eye, and I'm missing the tip of my middle finger," Eddy said triumphantly.

My mom stared at his finger in wonder, as if he was holding a shiny gold thing.

"How did you lose it?" she asked.

"When I was four, I did what my parents always warned me not to do. Played with my father's woodworking tools."

"A rebel," my mom replied.

"And you?"

"A cobra."

"You're kidding!" Jagger piped up.

"No, it came out of the bush and almost bit my sister, so I stepped in front of her. It was a spitting cobra, though, and got me right here." She pointed at her eye. "We were far from the house and didn't have any water to wash it out, and the hospital was miles away too. So that was the end of this eye!" Eddy and Jagger stared at my mom with looks I'd seen many times before. My mom often inspired this expression of amazed disbelief.

"It's true," I said. Because it was, no matter how unbelievable it sounded. My mom had grown up on a small trading station in a very rural and remote part of the country.

"I'm in the presence of a true hero," Eddy said, and then he did something that floored me. He took my mother's hand and kissed it, as if she was the pope and he was kissing her ring in appreciation. I gasped, and because it had happened so quickly, I immediately started coughing.

"You okay, Margaret-Skye?" my mom asked while whacking me on the back.

"Skye?" Jagger asked, a mischievous tone in his voice.

"That's her full name."

"It's stunning," Eddy said, and my mom's hand left my back immediately as she moved closer to him. "What's your name? We weren't actually properly introduced."

I was utterly horrified when my mom let out a breathy giggle. "Anke, it was my great-grandmother's name. She was . . ." Her words tapered off.

"Dutch," Eddy filled in and then placed his hands together in the namaste position.

"You do that so well," my mom gushed.

"I've been doing yoga for over thirty years."

"Really?" My mom's face lit up like a supernova. "What kind of yoga do you practice?"

"Ashtanga."

"Meee toooo!" She dragged out the vowel sounds until she ran out of breath and then stared at Eddy as if receiving some revelation from God Himself.

I stepped back from the scene and surveyed it as if it was a nightmare tableau laid out in front of me. A chill ran over my skin, even though the airport was perfectly climate-controlled. I had a bad feeling about this.

Very bad.

Chapter **Fifteen**

"Uh, Mom," I called as she continued to walk up the airplane aisle. "Our seats are here." I pointed at them.

"I think I'm going to sit with Eddy," she called back.

"Oh. I see," I said flatly.

"You know, when he was younger, he did a road trip across South Africa and stopped at our trading station to buy a Coke. Can you believe that?"

"Really?"

"I know, unbelievable! I wonder what else we have in common?"

Common. That seemed like a really large reach there. I watched as they continued up the aisle, craning their necks like ostriches to keep talking as they went. I hadn't been able to get them to stop talking for the last two hours. All the way through the security checkpoints, and then in the airport lounge while waiting for our flight to board. I'd not been able to get a word in sideways, and now . . . *shit*! It dawned on me—if my mom sat with Eddy, that meant that I would be sitting with . . .

"Looks like we're neighbors again," Jagger said, putting his luggage in the overhead compartment. I was about to protest when he reached for my laptop bag and slid it in next to his bag.

"Window?" he asked.

"No. I don't like looking down."

"Fair enough." He sat, and I hesitated for a second. Maybe I didn't need to sit here. Maybe someone had missed the flight! Been hit by that baggage carrier on the walk across the tarmac (one could only wish). But the flight was filling up before my eyes and each new bum in a seat saw that little sliver of hope melt away.

"I could build a wall between the chairs, if that would make you more comfortable?" Jagger's voice pulled me from thoughts of deliberately stealing someone else's seat. I turned. He was grinning from ear to ear. Mocking me.

"Yes, actually, that would make me more comfortable." I lowered myself into the seat and Jagger went to work, propping his laptop on the arm of the chair and then balancing the in-flight magazine on top of that. His face appeared around the side.

"Better?"

"Much."

Moments later the flight attendant was next to us. "I'm sorry, but you're going to have to take that down for takeoff."

"Can I put it back up after takeoff?" Jagger asked, his eyes peering over the top. The flight attendant looked confused but smiled politely at us.

"Sure, if you like."

"Great. You see, my neighbor purports to hates me," Jagger explained. The flight attendant looked appalled. She shot me a look, and I forced a smile back at her.

"She built a wall between our desks at work!" he carried on.

"It's more of a partition than a wall," I qualified when the flight attendant narrowed her eyes at me.

"She made it out of a piece of drywall."

"It was actually plywood."

"She secured it in place with a glue gun and nails, so really very permanent."

"It can be taken down," I insisted.

"But she won't."

"It's complicated."

The flight attendant had pulled her lips together tightly in a duckish fashion. "You can put it back up after we take off." She eyed us one more time, puckering her lips even tighter, and then walked off, shaking her head.

"Why do you do that?" I spun around and glared at Jagger.

"Do what?"

"Oh, don't act all innocent! You constantly goad me. It's as if you want to get a reaction out of me."

"I do." He took the wall down and slipped the laptop bag under the seat in front of him.

"Why?"

"Well, you mostly ignore me and pretend I don't exist, so I'll take any reaction I can from you. Besides"—he smirked that sly smirk of his—"it's fun!"

"No, it's not!" I said so loudly that the couple in front of us turned. I lowered my voice and leaned closer to Jagger. "It is not funny. It is intrusive and irritating and distracting and—"

"And makes you smile sometimes." He cut me off.

"NO!"

"Admit it, sometimes I make the serious Margaret-Skye smile."

"Stop talking about me in the third person and calling me by my full name."

"Okay, Maggie May."

"Oh my god, you are infuriating, you know that? Why do you do that? You know what my name is, *my real name*, yet you deliberately refuse to use it. It's completely disrespectful."

Jagger's smile faded as he contemplated what I'd just said. "You're right. I'm sorry. The last thing I want you to think is that I don't respect you when I have a great respect for you."

"You do?"

"Yes. Even if it's not reciprocated." He paused. Something in his voice had changed, and it made me stiffen. But a second later his smile was back. "I know I said I liked your seriousness, but we are going on holiday—maybe you could try loosening up a bit."

"Loosening up like you? The man who sees life as just fun and games and has a checkerboard shaved into his—" I looked at his head; the checkerboard was barely visible.

He ran his hand over it. "I shaved it a little—I knew it would irritate you the entire holiday."

"Oh!" I was taken aback. "But you do still have a hideous tattoo on your arm. What's it meant to be, anyway?"

"Bart Simpson." He chuckled. "I actually don't just view life as fun and games, but I do think that we have to laugh at ourselves sometimes. We can't take it all so seriously."

I *hmph*ed and turned to watch the flight attendant as she began the safety demonstration.

"You're really watching that, aren't you?" Jagger commented.

"It's important."

"Haven't you seen it a million times before?" He cleared his throat and put on a voice. "The exits are located here, here, and there."

"Here, here, and there—that's wildly unspecific and not what they say."

"In the unlikely event of cabin decompression, pull the mask over your nose and mouth and breath normally."

I reached for the safety manual in the pocket on the back of the chair and opened it. "As if anyone will breathe normally when the plane decompresses midair."

"Are you concerned about a midair decompression?"

I shook my head, making sure I remembered how to get the safety jacket out from under my chair as we were flying over water.

"Wait, are you scared of flying?" Jagger asked.

I put the safety brochure back in the chair and looked at him. Our shoulders were touching, more than touching—they were pressed together, and when I turned my face I realized how close we were.

"I don't like flying, but I'll be better once the plane reaches cruising altitude. Even though Kenya Air does have a very good safety record."

"Did you google Kenya Air's safety record?" He sounded amused.

"You clearly know the answer to that question."

"I also googled it. Pretty good, apart from that midair engine shutdown, but the pilot did manage to land the plane so we should be fine!"

"Why did you google it?"

He shot me an even bigger Jagger grin. "Perhaps if you got to know me, you'd find that we have far more in common than a shared teenage love of eyeliner and a vast knowledge of the Potterverse. Plus, our general knowledge rocks!"

"What the—" I hadn't meant to, but I grabbed Jagger's arm as the plane moved without warning. "Sorry, it moved." I pulled my hand away.

"It sort of has to move to get into the air—well, if Isaac Newton's first law of motion means anything."

I glared at Jagger again. "Stop being such a . . . a . . ."

"A what?"

"Don't act dumb, you know what you do."

"What do I do?"

"You're all snarky and sarcastic because you think it's cute in some way. Well, let me assure you, it's not."

He laughed. "It usually works for me."

"Well, it doesn't work on me."

"Oh, I'm aware of that. You make that very clear, on a daily basis."

"I'm impervious to your charms," I said, and then immediately regretted it.

He turned dramatically in his seat. "You admit I have charms."

"I didn't say that!"

"Yes, you did. You said I have charms, but—"

Loud laughter cut Jagger off and we both turned to look at our parents.

"Looks like someone else has charms too," Jagger said in a hushed tone.

"What do you mean?"

"Well, your mother seems to have totally charmed my dad."

"She has not! Your dad is the one trying to charm my mom with his jokes and his 'you have such blue eyes, you brave pirate snake stopper'!"

Jagger burst out laughing.

"It's not funny. My mom is in a very delicate and vulnerable stage in her life."

"Your mom seems anything but delicate and vulnerable."

"Well, you don't know her like I do," I countered quickly. "And she doesn't need someone trying to charm her."

Jagger laughed again, and I didn't understand what he found so funny about this. All the world was a joke to him. Was he incapable of being serious for one bloody secon . . .

"Oh my god!" I gripped the seat as the plane picked up speed. I reached down for my seat belt and tightened it as far as it would go.

"This is an Airbus A320," Jagger said.

"And?" I closed my eyes.

"Well, the A320 is considered one of the safest planes in aviation history. Also one of the most technologically advanced, and it can fly perfectly well on one engine in an emergency situation. The chances of us having an issue in an A320 are very, very slim. Does that make you feel better?"

"Not entirely," I admitted.

"Do you want me to distract you?"

"How?"

"What's the capital of Bolivia?"

"La Paz," I said without thinking.

"Incorrect!"

"What? No, it's not." I turned in my seat.

"I'm afraid you have it wrong, Maggie May."

"No. La Paz is the capital of Bolivia."

"Nope!" He shook his head. "You only have it half right. La Paz is the executive and legislative capital, but Sucre is its other capital. It has two capitals."

"That's a deliberate trick question, then!"

"It's not. It's a pretty straightforward question, actually, if you were au fait with your South American geography."

"You're deliberately trying to trick me. Some might call that cheating."

"No, if I was deliberately trying to trick you, I might ask you something like this: What are the two things you can never eat at breakfast?"

"Huh?"

"Lunch and dinner." He smiled.

"Well, that's just . . ." I couldn't help it. I tried to stop it, but I smiled.

"Waaait . . . did I just see a smile?"

"No!" I quickly wiped it off my face.

"I saw it!" He pointed at my lips, and I pursed them together and shook my head.

"Okay, here's another one. What never asks a question but gets answered all the time?"

"I don't know," I confessed.

"Your phone!" He smiled at me stupidly, and the bright-white lights of the cabin interior seemed to transform his gray eyes to silver. I pursed my lips together even tighter.

"Trying hard not to smile, I see. All right, try this one on for size. If a train is traveling north at night at a speed of a hundred kilometers an hour on a track that is a thousand kilometers long and a wind is blowing east at four knots an hour, with heavy rains falling at a six-degree angle, what color shirt is the conductor wearing?"

"That's not a real question."

"Yes, it is!"

"Uh . . . it is absolutely in no way a real question, Jagger."

"You just called me Jagger," he said, the playful tone in his voice gone.

"Well, that is your name. Isn't it?"

"It is, but you've never actually said it in all the months we've been working together. You've never called me by my name."

"No, that's impossible, of course I've—" I stopped talking. My brain caught up to my mouth. "I haven't called you by your name," I acknowledged.

"And why is that?"

I shrugged. "I don't know."

Jagger's eyes clung to mine, and for a moment it looked as if he was about to say something, but he pointed out the window instead.

"There we go, cruising altitude."

"Really?" I leaned across Jagger, careful not to press any more of my body against his and looked out window. He was right. The plane had leveled out somewhat, the clouds were no longer flying by at perturbing angles, and my spine no longer felt as if it had been sewn into the seat.

"Feeling better?" he asked.

And, I had to admit, I was. "Thank you," I said softly.

"Wow, two thank-yous and calling me by my name. Better be careful, Margaret-Skye. Some people might think that you're actually starting to like me."

I shot him a look. "I wouldn't push it."

"Who knows? We might even come back from this holiday as friends."

I laughed. "That's really pushing it."

Jagger made a big show of stretching his long legs out and slipping them under the seat in front of them. "Mmm, I don't know. I have a good feeling about this holiday for us," he said, and then put his head back against the chair and closed his eyes.

Chapter **Sixteen**

The rest of the flight was relatively incident free. I'd slipped in my AirPods and listened to my latest book. I loved audiobooks, and this one was a particularly dark and twisty novel about a serial killer, the troubled female detective hunting them, and dead bodies in ice. But every now and then loud laughter penetrated the sounds of the Scandinavian-accented narration. I'd look up to find my mom and Eddy *still* laughing. I watched them for a while, a sense of unease growing.

It had never occurred to me that my mother might ever be interested in another man after my dad. That she might flirt and date and one day maybe even settle down again. But as the thought crossed my mind, I realized that it wasn't that insane. Because ultimately that's what I wanted too—*even if it was very hard and terrifying to admit.* Despite the letdowns and heartbreaks, the dividing of wedding cutlery sets and arguing about who gets the good coffee machine, I wanted that comfortable *"Hey, how was your day?"* as I walked through the front door at night. I wanted someone to sit on the couch with me and watch lame reality TV, to climb into bed with me and engage in a half-asleep game of tug the blanket on winter nights. I wanted the smell of hair gel and old cologne on the pillow next to me, and I wanted to be so comfortable with someone that when I'd run out of toilet paper in the washroom, I could shout for another roll and they would bring it to me.

A part of me was scared to admit this, and I had no idea how I was ever going to trust anyone enough to get close to them again. And the other part of me was just embarrassed for still wanting it. How could I, after everything I'd gone through with a spectacularly failed marriage, still want that?

I put my head back and closed my eyes, too, as images of Matthew and me in happier times played in my mind. We'd been happy, once upon a time. We'd been in love, once upon a time. But that was then, and this was now, and right now there was no way I was putting myself out there again. Putting my heart on my sleeve, putting my trust in someone else's hands, putting so much faith in someone else that I was almost blinded by it. Lesego and everyone else could fantasize about me dating as much as they liked, but that was just not something I was ready for . . . or wanted.

Sticky heat engulfed me as I climbed off the plane, and we made our way inside to stand at the luggage carousel for what seemed like the most inordinately long amount of time. I was also the only one who'd checked luggage. Both Jagger and Eddy had backpacks on their backs, those brown military-style ones in which I imagined all their clothes were crumpled, and then there was my mom with her bag of sarongs and swimwear.

I stood there watching as the last bag was picked up and the conveyor belt came to a halt. A sinking feeling grew in the pit of my stomach. The sinking feeling came with a thought, loud and clear and undeniable.

"Your bag's not there." Jagger put words to my thought, and for some reason that irritated me. I felt like saying something childish, like *No shit, Sherlock,* when . . .

"No shit, Sherlock!"

I swung around and stared at Eddy. "I'm going to the baggage claims desk," I said, and walked off in the direction of the desk.

"Hi, there," I said, and then introduced myself to the young lady wearing a bright-purple hijab that was very eye-catching. After I explained what had happened, she went into absolute overdrive trying to locate my bag. She called the airline, the airport, checked in the back, checked on the tarmac. But an hour later, we were still no closer to finding my bag.

"I'm so sorry!" she gushed, looking truly devastated. She took my details and promised to call as soon as she'd found it. I hoped she'd find it. I didn't like losing things. Didn't like not knowing where something was. It made me feel anxious and out of control. But I thanked her for her hard work and turned back to my travel companions, who'd long since found themselves seats and were sipping cool bottles of soft drinks. My mom held out a Fanta and I walked over and took a long, slow sip of it.

"So?" she asked. I shook my head as the bright, fizzy citrus flavor quenched my parched throat.

"Well, it's not the end of the world," my mom said. This was one of her favorite sayings. Nothing was ever the end of the world. The world could actually be coming to an apocalyptic end and my mom would still not think it was ending and would be able to see the silver lining. In fact, the silver lining was usually her next line.

"I'm sure there's a silver lining to this."

I waited for her to tell me it was meant to be, that nothing happened for no reason.

"And you know what they say, nothing happens by accident."

Eddy echoed my mother's sentiments. "I couldn't agree more." Of course he agreed.

"You can always borrow some of my clothes," my mom added.

"Mom, you didn't bring clothes—you bought bikinis and sarongs."

"Those *are* clothes—besides, we're about the same size. Except for your boobs, of course." And then she said the most mortifying thing ever, even for my mother: "Margaret-Skye has always been blessed with abundance in that area."

"Mom!" I folded my arms across my chest as everyone looked at me.

"What?" she asked innocently. "Breasts are a perfectly normal and natural thing to talk about. They give life." She turned to Eddy. "That's the problem with modern society—all this Instagram and tweeting. Everything's just become so unnatural, you know what I mean?"

And of course he agreed wholeheartedly. I couldn't help the involuntary eye roll.

"Well, I'm not wearing only your bikinis and sarongs for the next week," I said, and marched off defiantly to the curio shop in front of me. I walked out of there five minutes later with two shirts—one that said "I Love Zanzibar" and the other "Welcome to Paradise"—and two bright skirts made from beautiful traditional fabric. Eddy and my mother were deep in conversation, discussing one of their newfound commonalities, while Jagger sat near them, looking at his phone. I stopped and stared at the scene in front of me.

Why hadn't Jagger and Eddy gone to the hotel yet? Why were they still here? In fact, why had they stayed with me while I'd looked for my bag? This was *not* how I'd imagined the holiday. I'd planned to never see Jagger again after the airport, and here he bloody was, with his dad. It was as if you couldn't get rid of them. Like mosquitos in the height of summer, buzzing around, making you itch and spreading diseases. I walked over to the little group tentatively.

"Are you done?" Jagger stood up.

I nodded at him.

"Let's call the taxi, then," he stated. It was not a question. Apparently, while I'd been shopping, it had somehow become an irrefutable fact that we would all be sharing a taxi on the forty-minute drive from the airport to the resort.

"You don't have to come with us," I said, and everyone looked at me blankly. Apparently, this was no longer up for discussion—I just hadn't been privy to the discussion.

My mom and Eddy still seemed to have so much to talk about and, on the taxi ride, continued their never-ending conversation. I eventually zoned out as their words blurred into a kind of background static. I looked out the window and got lost in the sights and sounds of the place. Zanzibar was fascinating. Architecture with a Middle Eastern influence, next to buildings that came straight out of British colonial times, and yet it was still very much an African country. This was one of those places that seemed to be a true melting pot of colors and cultures that had come together to form its own unique identity.

There was such a sense of energy to the place. It hummed and buzzed with activity wherever you looked. Hundreds of people on motorcycles, scooters, and bicycles wove in and out of the cars. There was a sense of organized chaos to the roads and somehow it worked. Men with caps covering their heads and women wearing bright traditional dresses rushed across the street. There was a sense of movement and color to everything here; the kind that you only found in Africa. Rainbow-patterned umbrellas dotted the sides of the roads with street vendors under them selling pallets of fruits. Taxis jostled for space on the road, and pedestrians pushed past each other, rushing to get to work, or home, or school. Tall palm trees crammed the pavement, their green leaves breaking up the gray cement buildings behind them. A scooter drove past us and I marveled at the balancing act of an entire family—dad, mom, and two children—all sitting on the scooter as it darted between the cars. Food vendors pushed wheelbarrows in the road beside rows and rows of parked bikes whose handlebars glinted in the sun as you drove by them. And as for the noise, it was a cacophony of hooting cars, shouting street vendors, crows cawing from the tree branches, and the rumbling revving of motorcycles everywhere.

After a while, our journey took us out of the city and into the lush green countryside. Small potholed roads wiggled through thick, dense vegetation that came straight up to the sides of the road. The greens here were so bright and vivid, popping against the powder blue sky. The drive through this dense, never-ending greenery seemed to go on forever, and at times the trees on the side of the street were so big that they spread their green canopy over the roof of our car. And then the landscape changed again, as the tarred road gave way to soft white sand. The taxi flicked the sand into the air as the road became narrower and the greenery doubled in volume and size.

"Look!" I pointed as calm turquoise waters came into view.

My mom and Eddy actually stopped talking and leaned toward my window.

"Like blue tourmaline!" my mom said, and of course Eddy agreed immediately.

"It's beautiful," I said, and felt Jagger edge toward the window next to me.

"I can't wait to get in," my mom said, and Eddy agreed. An image of the two of them frolicking together in tourmaline waters sprang into my mind.

The sea was so flat it looked as if it was made of exquisite blue glass, rendered even more blue by the contrasting bright-white sand of the shoreline. After a few more minutes of driving, the resort came into view. We turned off the main road and made our way down a long, sandy driveway lined on both sides with enormous palm trees. But they were nothing compared to the tree I saw next. A giant baobab came into view. It looked as if it had been standing there for hundreds of years. It probably had, judging by the size of its trunk. Its branches shot out in an upward direction, like wooden arms, holding up large green clumps of leaves. Almost offering them up to the sky.

We climbed out of the air-conditioned car and back into the wet heat. The hotel reception was a thatched, open-sided structure built around the giant baobab, and as we walked inside, we were immediately lulled into a state of relaxation. Soft music, the smell of tropical flowers, and the calm trickle of water from a fountain soothed us into immediate holiday mode. The rush and stress of the airport, the hustle and bustle of the streets, had all melted away by the time we'd walked up to the front desk and the woman behind it. But a minute into checking in we realized that there'd been a booking error that brought the stress crashing back.

"Oh, I'm sorry. We thought it was for two couples—the rooms are doubles. We don't have any single rooms left." The receptionist looked worried.

"That's okay—we can share. Jagger over here still climbed into my bed when he was ten years old anyway! Deathly afraid of the dark, this one."

"Dad." Jagger moaned, and his cheeks went a little red with, wait, was that . . . *embarrassment*? Jagger Villain looked embarrassed for maybe the first time since I'd known him, and I was going to relish it.

"He still sleeps with a lamp on," Eddy said, rubbing salt in the wound.

"Oh, does he?" I said with unbridled glee, which was quickly crushed by my mother.

"You know, Margaret-Skye used to be terrified of lightning when she was young, even wet her bed once during a particularly bad storm."

"Mom!" I chided her.

"Jagger used to be scared of the pool cleaner vacuum!" Eddy added.

"So was Margaret-Skye. It once sucked on her leg and all hell broke loose."

"Jagger was so scared of it that he jumped out of the pool and hit his nose. He still has the scar." Eddy pointed at the scar on the bridge of Jagger's nose.

"I love this!" my mom declared loudly, waving her hands in a circular fashion.

"What?" I asked.

"That we're all such kindred spirits."

I burst out laughing, apparently the only one who found this funny. "Just because Jagger and I share one common childhood fear, we are not kindred spirits. If anything, we are the opposite of kindred spirits."

Everyone stared at me blankly. I ramped it up a bit. "The antithesis. Antipode. Inverse. Converse. Opposites sides of the coin." I paused and waited for acknowledgment. None came.

"Margaret-Skye has always been so good with words," my mom said, completely dismissing my point. I was about to open my mouth and argue when the receptionist cleared her throat in what I assumed was an attempt at regaining our lost attention.

A few minutes later we were led down a path that wove through the tropical undergrowth. The two members of staff accompanying us showed us the various resort facilities as we walked past them. We slowed down when we reached a fork in the road and the staff members began walking in opposite directions. My mom and Eddy came to immediate standstills—so quickly that I almost walked into the back of them.

"Mom." I put my hand out to stop myself from slamming into her back. "What's wrong?"

"Are our rooms in different areas?" Eddy asked, bringing the hotel staff to a stop. When one explained that the rooms were basically on opposites sides of the lodge, my mother and Eddy looked at each other with a kind of longing.

"I'm sure we'll manage," I said sarcastically, slipping my arm through my mom's and pulling her down our path. They were acting as if they were going off to war or a deep-space expedition. For heaven's sake, they were only going to different areas of a resort; this was not the end of the world, and yet they were both acting like it was. I, for one, was glad we were finally leaving the Villain men behind. I'd had my fair share of Villains—enough to last me for a very long time.

Moments later we arrived at our room and were escorted inside. It was a small thatched cottage set into the undergrowth, and I loved it. I cranked up the AC and walked into the bathroom, which had one of those bath/shower combos. It was small, but perfect for what we needed. I was sure I'd hardly be in here anyway. I could see myself spending all my time outside reading by the pool, floating in the warm ocean waters, and grabbing afternoon naps under the shade of the palm trees.

"I'm heading to the beach," my mom said, wasting no time in peeling her clothes off and slipping into one of her bikinis.

"Since we're sharing a room, can we have a few boundaries, please?" I asked.

"Like what?"

"Well, how about no nude sleeping and always closing the toilet door?"

My mom laughed. She knew exactly what I meant. Too many times when I was growing up I'd caught her on the toilet, reading one of her latest esoteric magazines, door wide open as if she didn't have a care in the world. Not to mention the times I walked in on her naked in the morning because she didn't sleep in clothes. Not since her time spent at that nudist camp, as she was always so fond of saying.

"I can't sleep in clothes, though, not since the time I spent—"

"Nudist camp. Yes, yes. I remember. Shaking off the confines of our Western something or other."

"You should try it, darling. It's very liberating. Makes you feel so . . ." She paused and looked into the air, as if plucking the word out of it. "Free!"

"I'm sure it does, Mom!" I said with obvious sarcasm. But I could think of nothing worse.

"I'll sleep on top of the covers, okay?" I said, knowing full well that no amount of begging would get my mother to relent. Instead, we'd find ourselves knee-deep in some philosophical debate about feminism or

Western standards or something with the word *heteronormative* thrown in, another one of her favorite nebulous terms that honestly you could use as an excuse for everything these days.

"So what should we do today?" I sat down on the only other piece of furniture in the room, a small rattan chair. I picked up the resort brochure and leafed through it, familiarizing myself with the location, the things to do at the resort, as well as the activities and sights close by.

I looked up at my mom as she released her hair from its braid, and her gray tresses settled over her shoulders and down her back. She had the most amazing thick hair. She put it down to never dying it. *No chemical has ever touched my hair*, she was fond of saying. She also made her own shampoos and conditioners; our household went through a lot of shea butter and coconut oil—this was even before those two things had become popular along with things like nonmeat meat and collagen smoothies.

My mom had grown old gracefully and resisted, nay, railed against things like injecting neurotoxic proteins into her face and inflating her lips. Every line, wrinkle, and scar told a story.

"Well, actually, darling, we're meeting Eddy and Jagger for cocktails at the beach bar."

"We are?" I rose from the chair in surprise.

"I said we'd be there as soon as we'd settled." She picked up her handbag, a gesture that confirmed she'd settled and was ready to go. "Shall I wait for you, or go in the meantime?"

"Uh . . ." I stumbled on my words. "Why don't you go ahead? I'll join you later."

She sashayed up to me and pulled me into an enthusiastic hug. "This holiday is going to be great," she said, and then exited.

I wished I shared her sentiments. *But I didn't.* Ten minutes later, and wearing one ridiculous tourist outfit, I stood by a palm tree and looked at the beach bar where my mom, Jagger, and Eddy all sat laughing together, tropical drinks in hand. I held back for many reasons—I just wasn't in the mood for this group activity; I'd never really been one for them under the best of circumstances. I always cringed and feigned illness whenever some kind of office team building was on the cards. It usually resulted in a group of adults playing adventure golf, or that one year when our managing director had thought it a good idea to have a fun day complete with three-legged and egg-and-spoon races. It had not been a good idea.

But this, *this* gathering here, was an even more bizarre sight to behold than that of grown men in suits running across the grass desperately trying to keep eggs from falling. I turned my back on the strange view and walked to a rock that protruded from the sand and sat down. Everything was so beautiful here; the weather was a perfect combination of sunny and warm, with a slight cool breeze that kept your skin from feeling too hot. The sand was soft and fine and white, and the sea was so pale near the shore that the water was completely translucent. My phone beeped in my bag. I pulled it out and smiled when I saw who the message was from.

Lesego had sent me a voice note. If I didn't like her as much as I did, I would have held this against her.

Lesego: Heeeey, so make me jealous. Where the hell are you?

I took a photo of the scene in front of me and sent it.

Lesego: Look where I am

She sent me a photo of the office, which looked extradrab.

Lesego: So, how's dick ring?

I typed back as fast as I could after quickly looking around to make sure no one was in earshot.

Margaret: Stop calling him that

Lesego: When he gets into a bathing suit, I want aaaaaaaaaaall the details

She unnecessarily stretched out her *a*'s and I quickly typed back.

Margaret: I am nooooooooot giving you details. Besides, I have no intention of seeing him in a bathing suit

Lesego: Who did dick ring bring?

Margaret: Stop calling him dick ring

Lesego: Ha-hah! *[She actually laughed—since it was a voice note, she didn't actually type* Ha-hah.*]* I only say dick ring because I love how it makes you blush

Margaret: I don't blush

Lesego: Dick ring! Quick, take a photo of your face and send it to me

"Who's dick ring?" A voice startled me, and I threw my phone in the air. It landed in the sand and I made a panicked scramble for it.

"Was that Lesego's voice?" Jagger asked.

"No!" I tried to wipe the sand off my phone but feared I'd just pushed it farther into the little speaker and charger holes. I blew on it, trying to delay having to speak to Jagger and also trying to figure out why I'd said it wasn't Lesego, even though it obviously was her. My blatant lie made me look as if I was hiding something. Which I was.

"Why aren't you at the bar enjoying cocktails?" I quickly changed the subject, giving him zero chance of asking again about the speculative ring that he might, or might not, have.

"I was starting to get the feeling I was the third wheel." Jagger looked at the rock next to me and raised his brows in an obvious question.

"You might feel like the second wheel here, but if that's what you want." I shuffled to the edge of the rock. I didn't want to sit too near to him—all I'd done since this morning was sit next to him. In fact, my last six months had been spent sitting next to him.

"Nice outfit." Jagger gave me the once-over. "Very touristy."

I looked down at my "Welcome to Paradise" T-shirt and my sarong, which was just a little too small for me and exposing a large chunk of my untanned thigh. I pulled it closed as much as I could and made a mental note to stick my legs in the sun as soon as possible, to shave the hairs on my toes that were now glinting in the light and collecting beach sand, and to inspect my bikini line for any strays that might have been missed by the razor.

"Here." Jagger passed me a glass full of bright-yellow slushy liquid. Beads of condensation trickled down the side of the glass, making it look very inviting.

"What is it?"

"Pineapple daiquiri. Apparently, Zanzibar is known to have the sweetest pineapples in the world."

I sipped the drink, and the icy pineapple flavor filled my mouth. It was cool and refreshing and sweet and tart all at the same time, and when you swallowed, that warm feeling of alcohol slid down your throat.

"Tasty." I raised the glass in a thank-you gesture, which made Jagger smile at me in a way I wasn't sure he'd smiled at me before. I leaned back and looked at him curiously.

"What?" he asked.

"Your smile. . . . it seems . . . I don't know. . . . there's something different about it." I couldn't find the words to explain it exactly.

"Maybe I'm just happy to be here, *with you*."

I burst out laughing at the crazy notion but stopped when I noticed zero amusement on Jagger's face. I eyed him curiously.

"You're a mystery, you know that?" I took another sip of my drink as I gathered my thoughts on the matter. "I never know when you're being serious. When you're joking. When you're teasing me and when you're just full of crap—which is often, by the way. I never know anything with you."

"Well, maybe this holiday will give you an opportunity to get to know me better." He looked at my drink. "So is that the sweetest pineapple in the world?"

"It is sweet!" I said, taking another delicious sip.

"Don't drink too much. Not with our afternoon plans."

"What afternoon plans?"

"We're going snorkeling. A boat leaves for the reef in one hour."

"Are we all going?" I was still blown away by this making of plans that was happening.

"Your mom said you loved snorkeling."

"I do, but . . ." I didn't finish that part of the sentence, which would have been something to the effect of *I'd really rather go snorkeling without you and your dad.*

"I don't have a bathing suit," I said instead.

"They provide wet suits."

"Oh." Well, now I didn't have an excuse and, besides, I did love snorkeling. In fact, it was the one thing I'd been looking forward to the most. I suppose I shouldn't let the fact that Jagger and his dad seemed to be tagging along for everything ruin the holiday I'd wanted for so long. A little stab hit me in the ribs. I wished my dad was here with us. He'd have loved this place. A part of me felt like I needed to make the most of every moment to honor him. He would have wanted that.

"Sounds fun," I said.

Jagger got up off the rock and towered over me. "See you later, then."

I shot him a thumbs-up.

"Seriously, who's dick ring?"

I shook my head quickly and sucked on the drink again. "No one. *Shit!*" I grabbed my temples as the brain freeze hit me.

Jagger gave me a long, slow smile, and I quickly turned my back on him and looked out over the sea.

Chapter **Seventeen**

"*Pssst*, Mom," I hissed from the galley of the small boat that had taken us out to the reef. *"Mom!"* I whisper-screamed when she didn't hear me.

She finally turned and looked at me. "What's wrong?"

"Uh . . . please come here." I stuck my head through the small window and tried to sound casual, as if this wasn't an emergency.

"What's wrong?"

"Please come inside. I need help with something." I blinked at her, attempting to convey a sense of secrecy and urgency with my eyes.

"Do you have something in your eye?" As usual, my mom's ability to pick up on these kinds of things was slim to none. She seemed oblivious to normal nonverbal social cues.

I went along with it. "Yes, Mom, I have something in my eye. Can you please come inside and help me get it out?"

"Sure, darling." She merrily walked into the small galley where we'd all taken turns changing into our provided wet suits. As soon as she was inside, I closed the door behind her and turned around.

"I can't get it over my bum!" I pointed at the defiant wet suit that had refused to be pulled up.

"Aaah, I always said you inherited Great-Aunt Anneke's bum."

"Yes, yes, I know. You've told me since I was a child how uncanny the resemblance is."

"Even the little dimples on the sides. You've had those since the day you were born. Such a wonderful birth."

"Mom, please don't tell my birth story again. Just help me with this thing."

"You know, when I reached down and pulled you out of the water and put you to my breast, I finally understood what it meant to be a woman."

"So you've said, Mom. But please can we focus on pulling up my wet suit?" I didn't mean to sound dismissive, but when you hear the story of your spiritual water birth at least once a year, you tend to get a little blasé about it. My mom didn't stop, though, as she gripped the wet suit and yanked at it.

"Your dad cried like a baby when he saw you, first and last time I ever saw him cry . . . jump!"

"What?"

"Jump up as I pull," my mom said.

I jumped as she tugged the wet suit. "He was never a man of many tears."

"Huh?"

"Your father. Jump again," my mom commanded, and I jumped as she yanked once more. "Even though he felt things very deeply . . . JUMP!"

"Mom, as much as I love talking about Dad, right now, with my ass sticking out of a wet suit, it just doesn't seem to be appropriate."

"Oh, Margaret-Skye, always worried about what's appropriate." My mother stuck her head out the door and to my horror shouted, "EDDY, JAGGER, can you come here and help us with something?"

"*Mom!* What are you doing?" I turned around and pushed my bum into the wall.

"What's up?" Eddy's and Jagger's heads appeared at the door.

"Margaret-Skye is having some trouble with her wet suit."

"*No!* It's fine. I'm fine. I don't need your help." I glared at my mom and then hissed at her through my teeth. "Right, Mom? I don't need their help."

"She can't get the wet suit over her bum. She's always been very abundant in that area too."

"*Mom!*" I turned to Jagger and Eddy. "It's fine. I'll sit this one out. You guys go."

"Absolutely not—you love snorkeling," my mom said.

"I'm fine, Mom. I'll be fine here."

Eddy stepped into the galley. "We're not leaving you alone. This is a team activity, after all."

"A team?" Since when had we become a team?

"Margaret-Skye, I don't see the problem. It's not like your bum is naked or anything. Besides, we are all adults here."

"Oh god." I moaned into the hands cupping my face. My mother existed in a completely different reality to this one. She followed none of society's rules, ever. And she didn't see anything wrong with that. "I am not letting Eddy and Jagger help me get into my wet suit! And that is final!"

"I'm sure with them helping it will only take one tug! Just turn around and we'll do it quickly!"

"We'll close our eyes," Jagger said.

"Closed," Eddy echoed.

They both looked sincere, and strangely enough Jagger did not look like he was mocking or teasing me.

I sighed. I did want to snorkel, but the idea of Eddy and Jagger helping me into my wet suit was so utterly mortifying—there was literally nothing worse I could think of.

"If not, then you'll have to swim in your bra and panties!" my mom said, and now I could think of something worse.

I deadpanned her. "They are white and cotton."

"Turn around, then." My mom snapped her fingers at me.

I sighed again and looked from my mom to the Villains. *How had I gotten myself into such a humiliating situation?*

"Eyes closed!" I pointed at Jagger specifically. I didn't mind if Eddy saw my ass; if we weren't in wet suits, we'd be in bathing suits, and he would have seen it like this anyway. But the idea of Jagger seeing it and his hand being so close to it made me feel incredibly uneasy.

I turned reluctantly when Eddy and Jagger closed their eyes. "Don't open them. Mom, you'll have to guide their hands. No opening your eyes for anything. Got it?"

Eddy and Jagger both answered in the affirmative.

I shook my head in total resignation and dismay. This was not what I'd imagined for my life, ever. I felt hands around the wet suit and then my mom loudly ordered a tug, and everyone tugged so hard my feet lifted off the ground.

"Tug!" my mom said again and this time I bounced, almost launching into the ceiling.

"Okay, okay! It's fine, thanks." I cast my eyes back as the suit slipped on and that's when I bloody saw it!

Chapter **Eighteen**

"You looked at my ass!" I hissed as I walked past Jagger.

"It was an accident, I swear. I lost my grip on the wet suit and had to open my eyes to grip it again."

"Good excuse!" I sat down to put my flippers on.

"I promise, it was a mistake. I would never do that without your consent."

"And in what situation would I ever give you consent to look at it?"

He shrugged.

"There would be none." I glared at him. "And if you ever tell anyone about this . . ."

"I would never!"

"And if you ever mention it again . . ."

"Never."

"If you ever think about it, or . . ."

"Think about it?" A smile lit up Jagger's eyes. I didn't like it. "And how will you know if I think about it?"

"So you *are* going to think about it." I pointed an accusatory finger at him.

"I can't help it if I think about it. I won't try and think about it consciously, but it might pop into my mind from time to time."

"Why? Why would it pop into your mind?" I asked, flabbergasted at this admission.

"Well, it was . . ." He paused.

"What?"

"It's not like it would be a completely unpleasant thought if it did."

I rolled my eyes. "That is such a Jagger Villain thing to say!"

"I wouldn't be embarrassed if I were you, seriously," Jagger said. His voice was so soft that I almost didn't hear it.

"What's that supposed to mean?" I met his eyes. In this light, this bright sunlight, they were almost silver.

Jagger held my gaze, and I stiffened when the features of his face knitted into an expression that looked deadly *serious*. He opened his mouth, and I leaned in, waiting to hear what words were about to come out of it. Nothing came out. Instead, he shook his head, wiped the serious look off his face, and smiled at me again. "Nothing, Margaret-Skye. Come, the reef is calling us." And with that, with some unsaid thing hanging in the air between us, he dived off the edge of the boat and disappeared underwater. Jagger was a very confusing man.

I looked at the sea. Eddy and my mom were bobbing up and down together, still laughing, still chatting. They never stopped, even though every time they laughed one of them coughed and had to spit water out of their mouth. It occurred to me that their endless laughter might actually cause one of them to drown. What on earth were they still finding so funny? After all these hours, surely they'd laughed about everything there was to laugh about?

The reef exceeded all my expectations. I don't think I'd ever seen beauty like that before. The coral was startling. It came in an array of colors, shapes, and textures that all seemed so otherworldly. Orange clumps of tentacle-like things swayed rhythmically in the water. Coral that was soft, that you could run your hand through, and coral that was hard and prickly stood upright like miniature forests of trees. The sun broke through the surface of the water, leaving a glittering dappled light on the seabed below.

And then there were the little creatures teeming on the reef and in the water around it. I'd never seen such a concentration of fish before. Orange, black, and white ones seemed preoccupied with nibbling the pink coral. They would dart in and out of the soft tentacles, rubbing their bodies against them as if they were enjoying the feel of it. And then there were the curious ones: little yellow fish that seemed to watch us, completely aware of our presence. They hid behind the coral and peered around the corners as I floated past them.

After an hour spent snorkeling, submerged in the magical marine world that existed below the water, I was glad that I'd been helped into my wet suit, despite my initial embarrassment. The experience had been incredible, something that I would remember forever, especially that moment when a curious octopus had started following me. There was something amazing about the creature, and you got the feeling that there was so much going on inside its mind. As if it was weighing you up and then playing with you as it darted toward you and then receded quickly again, only to disappear into the coral once more.

The boat started back to shore as the sun began dipping down low, painting the sea and horizon in vibrant oranges and reds. I sat at the back of the boat, looking out over the scene.

"This is amazing," Jagger said, sitting next to me. "It's like a van Gogh painting."

"It is," I agreed, and then smiled. Jagger had hit the nail on the head with that one. The image in front of me was straight off one of the artist's impressionist canvasses.

"Did you know that when he was alive he only sold one painting?" I said without really thinking.

"Did you know that he painted his most famous painting, *The Starry Night*, in an asylum?" Jagger replied.

I turned and faced him. His cement-colored eyes were reflecting the vibrant hues bouncing off the water. "I did, actually. How come you're so good at general knowledge?"

"You're not the only one who goes down long Google rabbit holes."

"I don't go down Google rabbit holes!"

"Last week when you finished your article on xenophobia, you researched the mating habits of seahorses."

"Well, I was wondering what sea creatures I would see in Zanzibar. Did you know that they mate for life and that the males carry the eggs and give birth?"

Jagger grinned. "I do now, because when I got home, I also wanted to know why seahorses were so interesting."

"Hey, how did you know that's what I was doing?"

"The coffee station is right behind your desk."

"So you spy on me while you make coffee?"

"Only when you're doing something interesting."

I sat up straight. "That's just . . . that's . . . you should not be spying on me. I mean, what if I'm writing something confidential or . . . or . . . besides, spying is rude."

"I'm joking. I don't deliberately spy on you, but sometimes I can't help but notice what you're googling. Your computer screen is huge."

"I don't spend all day googling, you know. Only if I have a break, or if I've finished my articles."

"I know. You would never do something like that." He sounded amused and I ignored this.

"So what else have you seen me googling?" I asked.

"The history of anesthesia and how many people have woken up from it."

"I was having dental surgery."

"I know—you had a swollen cheek for a week."

"What else?" I asked.

"Well, there was one that had me somewhat confused . . ." He pitched his voice low.

"What?" My brain did a quick internal sprint, running backward and forward over all my Google searches. I cringed when I realized that a few of them might be seen as somewhat questionable, but I'd only researched stripping and porn for an article, and I'd only researched salacious sex scandals of the '80s because the press had gotten hold of an old photo of Leighton in his prime and printed it along with a sordid tale of a sex party in a hot tub. Of course he'd outwardly pretended to be deeply offended by the whole ordeal, but I knew he loved the attention. And then there had been the other time when I'd googled what "edging" was, because when I'd had my one single night of sex, the orthodontist had kept saying how hot I looked when he was edging me. Upon googling, though, I discovered that he'd misinterpreted my lack of orgasm for some kind of sexual practice, rather than what it really was: a lack of orgasm. Although I can see how he might have been confused, since shortly after that I'd faked so many so quickly. *Oh shit*, then there was that other time I'd googled how many women faked orgasms and—

"Looks like your brain is ticking away," Jagger noted with a chuckle.

"No."

"Trying to figure out what I may have caught you googling at work?"

"There is nothing to catch." But I wasn't feeling that confident anymore since remembering that there was also that time I'd googled Jagger himself quite extensively.

"Oh my god, you are!" Jagger pointed at me. "You actually look terrified right now, like I may have caught you in the act!"

"What act?"

"I don't know—you tell me. Because you're looking pretty red-faced and guilty."

"I am not! I'm just . . . just . . . sometimes I have to google things for work, okay?"

"Ooooh, Margaret-Skye. What has gotten you so worried?" Jagger teased me.

"Absolutely nothing."

"It's definitely something." Jagger leaned in and whispered, "Porn?"

"What? No! I do not do that at work!"

"Only at home, then." Jagger laughed.

"You're twisting my words! I do not google porn at work, or at home." Okay, so that was a lie. I had googled and watched porn at home, but only the stuff that Pornhub marks as female friendly.

"Well, you googled something you shouldn't have, or else your left eye wouldn't be twitching."

"What do you mean?"

"Every time you try to lie, your left eye twitches."

"How do you know?"

"I've shared a desk with you for half a year."

"My eye does not twitch when I lie." I folded my arms across my chest.

"It does. When you were telling me that voice note wasn't from Lesego, your eye twitched."

"No, it didn't . . . *shit*!" I slapped my hand over my eye as it betrayed me with a twitch, which caused Jagger to burst out laughing.

"Wait, was that what you were googling? Dick rings?"

"Oh my god! Stop!" I put my other hand over my face.

"Margaret-Skye," my mother called from the other side of the boat, "what are you two talking about? It seems very interesting."

"Body piercings!" Jagger called across to them. The boat slowed as it pulled up to the dock, and I immediately stood up.

"I have a few of those," Eddy said, and I flicked my head up and looked at him. He was smiling mischievously and my mother, my bloody mother, was now looking at him like *THAT*!

"Okay, that's it! I can't." I'd stood up before the boat had docked and almost fell over when it swayed. "I can't be here anymore as this conversation descends into the flaming pits of utter inappropriateness." Apparently, what I'd said was amusing, because everyone laughed.

"I'm not being funny," I added, trying to get my balance.

They laughed more as I grabbed my bag and, waving my arms in the air to keep my balance, jumped off the boat and onto the dock.

"Don't you find Eddy so intriguing?" my mom said when we'd made it back to our room.

"Mmmm," I mumbled. I knew if I told her I didn't she would probably argue with me, but I also knew if I agreed she would probably pull me into an hour-long discussion about his manifold intrigues.

"And I just love that he writes jingles. *So when it's hot, ask your mom to buy you a fruit pop.*" She sang the jingle that everyone knew growing up.

"It's very catchy." I had to agree.

"And he wrote the jingle for Top Insurance, and the theme tune to so many TV shows we've watched."

I nodded at her.

"So strange to think that in a way I've known him all my life through his music." She looked out the window and smiled. My insides knotted.

"I thought we could go to a restaurant tonight. There's this one built on a rock in the ocean, serves traditional foods, great reviews on Tripadvisor," I said quickly, hoping to steer the conversation away from Eddy.

"Oh, did I forget to tell you?"

"Tell me what?"

"We're meeting Jagger and Eddy at the hotel restaurant at seven." She got up and walked to the bathroom.

"Oh!"

"Maybe we can all go to that restaurant tomorrow night?"

"All?" The knot in my insides tightened. "I was thinking, Mom, maybe you and I could do something, just the two of us?"

"Definitely. I've already booked us a spa day at the hotel spa."

"You did?"

"Crystal massages followed by a hot tub and sauna."

"That sounds amazing," I said, perking up.

"I'll obviously ask for rose quartz," my mom said, and then took a long, contemplative pause. "Maybe you should ask for carnelian."

"Why? What does that do?"

"Nothing." But she said it in a tone that clearly didn't mean "nothing." In fact, it definitely meant "something."

I walked over to the bathroom. "Mom? What is so special about carnelian?"

"You don't want to know," she shouted from inside over the sound of the now-running shower.

"I *definitely* want to know," I shouted back.

"It awakens sexual energy and opens the root chakra."

I rolled my eyes. "There is nothing wrong with my root chakra."

The shower stopped and the door swung open. "You know I worry about you, Margaret-Skye."

"You worry because I'm not running around having sex! You do realize what an inappropriate conversation this is for a mother and daughter to be having."

"Not if we used to be best friends in a past life."

I shook my head. According to her, we'd been best friends back in feudal England some hundreds of years back and, before that, sisters in ancient Egypt.

"Just don't close yourself off to love because of your past. That's all I'm saying. Be a little more open with your heart."

"Maybe my heart doesn't want to be open," I said, sitting down on the bed. "Maybe I'm perfectly content the way I am."

She shot me a sideways glance. "Thirty-three, living at your parents' house, sleeping in a single bed with a Labrador to keep you warm at night?"

"That's unfair. I only moved in because you needed help, and maybe I like the single bed. Maybe I don't like the idea of having to choose a new side now that no one sleeps next to me, and maybe Lucy is a better cuddler than Matthew ever was."

"I don't doubt that last part, but seriously, Margaret-Skye, it's been over a year since your divorce, and by your own admission your marriage was over long before that anyway. You need to climb back on the horse. Put yourself out there. Open your heart to romantic possibilities."

I flopped onto my back and looked up at the ceiling. A bubble of anxiety rose in my throat. "I don't think I'm ready yet," I confessed.

My mom walked over to me, sat on the edge of the bed, and then she did something that she hadn't done in a while. She pushed my hair out of my face like she used to do when I was a child, sick at home from school with a temperature.

"Love doesn't work like that, sweetheart. It doesn't sit on the sidelines and wait to be called in to play. It comes when it wants to. That's how life and love and grief work. They wait for no man."

"Mmm, well, they should!" I muttered and looked up at my mom. She looked good, great even. The sun had kissed her cheeks a light-pink color and she had a cute pattern of freckles starting on her nose.

"I better get showered," she said, rising from the bed and going back into the bathroom. I watched her walk. She had a lightness in her step that I hadn't seen in a while.

Chapter **Nineteen**

The dinner was awkward. My "I Love Zanzibar" T-shirt was way too tight, squeezing my boobs together to form some kind of singular uber-boob. One mega boob that strained against the cheap made-in-China fabric that had zero stretch in it. Only larger women can know this—that a too-tight shirt can compress what should be two into something that looks very much like one. I felt like a strange alien creature with one boob as I sat at the table, feeling even more alien because Jagger and Eddy were there too. I stabbed my fork into my shrimp over and over again while I watched my mother and Eddy gasp collectively when they discovered that they'd had a mutual friend in common when they were teens.

What was this ritual that people did? This seeking out of commonalities —any commonalities? The fact that both might like the color purple could take on such a significance in this strange social ritual of seeking out tenuous links. Men did this a lot at social events, I'd noticed, gathering awkwardly in little groups of two or three away from their wives, discussing the rugby score or why they now preferred light beer.

I stabbed the lobster tail with my fork as I watched them pull more commonalities out, this time ones as thin and waiflike as strings of spider-spun silk: they both liked the Beatles. *Well, who didn't?*

"Margaret and I both used to wear black eyeliner when we were teens!" Jagger piped up, pulling my mom and Eddy out of their conversation. "I'm just trying to do that thing that you guys are doing," he said with a huge smile, as if he was highly amused by all of this. A flicker of recognition swept over my mom's face, and then she laughed.

"That's right! I remember that. Margaret-Skye's only ever attempt at rebellion."

"Mom." I rebuked her, knowing that she was probably now going to divulge something utterly mortifying, a party trick of hers. Like that time she announced to all her friends that I'd just started my period. They'd all hugged me and talked about harnessing the great shamanic power of the moon cycles and honoring my inner sacred female, then they'd all gone back to their drumming circle.

"You know, I had such high hopes for that rebellion, but it was very fleeting and rather disappointing."

"You are the only parent on the planet who's disappointed you were never called to school because I was caught skipping or smoking pot."

Jagger laughed. "I cannot imagine you skipping school and smoking pot." He said it in a way that seemed to challenge me. It stoked a kind of irrational competitiveness in me. I put my fork down.

"I'll have you know that when I was sixteen, I smoked cigarettes."

"But that was only for a week." My mom gave her head a disappointed shake.

"It was more like two weeks, but anyway."

"You could hear her coughing from all the way across the garden," my mom said fondly.

"I almost tried Ecstasy at a rave once!" I added quickly.

My mom rolled her eyes at me affectionately and then shook her head again.

"I'm sure I got high from secondhand smoke at a trance party!"

My mom put her elbows on the table and rested her head in her hands with a loud sigh.

"Fine! I almost shoplifted a lipstick tester from a store but then got too worried about the prospect of cold sores. But I did pick it up and almost put it in my bag."

My mom shook her head again.

"I protested topless at a feminist rights march!"

"You strategically wore a cardboard sign around your neck so that no one could see your boobs. I saw the photos."

"I know. I chafed against the cardboard." I slumped my shoulders, clearly unable to score any points for my rebellion.

"Margaret-Skye has always been our good girl, despite my best efforts to lead her astray. I thought it might happen when she became friends with Leighton George, but alas."

"Wait." Jagger's eyes widened. "Leighton George. *The* Leighton George?"

I nodded at him. "Yup."

"*The* Leighton George as in *Melt my skin, say it again, your love is like a sin, forever in my heart we will never be apart.*" Jagger sang the chorus to his most popular song of all time, "Love Is Like a Sin." And soon my mom and Eddy had joined in. Everyone who was alive knew this song. It had become one of those staples that was played at every party and wedding. This song had become a song that, despite having some of the world's worst lyrics, had taken on a cultish, legend-like status. A very famous hip-hop artist with solid gold teeth had even done a remix of it. Leighton had been in the video with him, which had only elevated his status to legendary.

When they stopped, I took a slow sip of my water and nodded for further confirmation.

"They've been best friends for about twelve years now," my mom added.

Jagger asked the question everyone asked: "Wait, how on earth did you become friends with Leighton George?"

"I met him in 2010 when I was researching and writing an article that included pop culture trends of the eighties."

"And Leighton George *was* the eighties," my mom said.

"God, he is more than just the eighties. He's a living legend," Jagger added. "Where does he live?"

"He's been living in Cape Town very quietly for years. I reached out to him for the piece. I didn't think he'd get back to me but he did, and we've been friends ever since."

"Wow!" Jagger leaned back in his chair and Eddy followed, looking equally wowed. "I didn't think you could get any cooler, but you just did."

I laughed. "Oh please. You don't think I'm cool."

"Yes, I do."

"Uh, no you don't," I argued with him. *Cool* was the last word I would ever use to describe myself. I'd always been very self-assured and known exactly who I was, and "cool" I was not.

"What's cool about you is that you don't know you're cool." Jagger eyed me over the rim of his drink.

"I don't believe you," I said.

"It's true."

I *tsk*ed, rolled my eyes, and then turned back to Eddy and my mom, who were still talking about Leighton.

"And he's the absolute sweetest, sends us bunches of flowers at least once a month, calls me once a week too, especially since"—my mom paused—"my late husband crossed over."

My mom always referred to death as a crossing-over. It was never a passing or a death—it was always a crossing. Eddy looked at her, sympathy etched into his face.

"I'm so sorry. When did he cross?"

I wanted to chime in with a "pass" or even a "kick the bucket" but left it.

"Just over a year ago."

I think he almost reached out and touched her hand but didn't. "Jagger's mom, my wife, crossed when Jagger was only four."

My mom moved closer to him, mirroring his sympathetic look. "Poor man, poor you." She looked at Jagger. "And you raised him all by yourself."

"Well, except for those brief times I had stepmothers, but they never seemed to stick around for very long." Jagger shot his dad an amused look.

"I've been very, very unlucky in love," Eddy confirmed.

"They say you only have three great loves in your life," my mom said.

"And did you have a great love before your late husband?"

My mom smiled broadly. "Oooh, I did. I was nineteen and I'd run off to join the circus."

"You ran off to join the circus?" Jagger laughed. "I thought that was an urban legend. No one runs away to the circus, do they?"

"I did!" This was another one of my mother's great tales that had been etched into her mythology. My shoulders relaxed and I put my elbows on the table. I quite liked this story—it epitomized my mother to a T. In fact, when I was asked to explain my mother to someone, I often leaned on this story as her summary. "My mom ran away with the circus when she was a teenager." I felt this summed her up perfectly.

"The circus came to town one year, and I fell madly in love at first sight with Lars, this gorgeous Swedish fire-breather. He was so magnificent, breathing fire like this perfect human dragon."

Jagger and Eddy laughed, and I joined in too. She had this way of telling stories that swept you up in them. "He did this act where he flew through the air on a trapeze while breathing fire out of his mouth. It was magical. He spotted me in the crowd, and an hour later we were kissing by the lion cages. It was very exhilarating. So that night I wrote my parents a letter and told them I was off to see the world with Lars. Of course, 'the world' meant traveling from one small South African town to another."

"She worked as a psychic crystal ball reader." I added to the story that I'd heard so many times before.

"I did! That was before I discovered my gifts, though. I made up this terribly strange quasi-Russian accent, which in my mind at seventeen was just the most enchanting-sounding accent I'd ever heard. I would swish my hands in the air and say things like 'I see a man with green eyes on the horizon.'" She put on her strange accent, and we laughed even more. "I was very, very mysterious." A massive smile lit up her face, and I must say, I hadn't seen her this happy since before my dad had died. She always used to have this wild, unbridled twinkle in her eyes, the kind of twinkle that told you she was only moments away from getting up to mischief or causing a ruckus, and I hadn't seen that in a while.

"I lived traveling and telling fake fortunes like that for three years, but when we arrived in Cradock, this tiny little town in the middle of nowhere, Lars dumped me for a real Russian. A sword-swallower called Svetlana." She looked over at me. "My daughter and I have that in common, both of us dumped for gorgeous Russian woman."

"Mmmm." I nodded in acknowledgment. "It's probably the only thing my mother and I have in common."

"Nonsense, darling, we have lots in common. You just hate to admit how similar we really are."

I sipped my drink and shook my head. "Nope. Just that."

"So how did you meet your late husband?" Jagger asked. I could see he was totally caught up in my mother's story.

"Well, there I was, standing on the side of the road with my bags in the middle of nowhere hitchhiking—of course you could hitch in those days without worrying that you were going to end up limbless—and this young man driving an old rust-colored Ford Cortina pulled up, and it was your dad, Margaret-Skye."

I smiled. I loved this story too.

"He was a real gentleman, you know. Wore this brown suit and a blue paisley tie, even though it was a Saturday. He was driving back to university to start the new year and he offered me a lift. He drove a full six-hour detour to take me back home. It was so far out of his way that he had to stay the night in our guest room."

"And let me guess, you were in love the next morning," Jagger offered.

"No! I thought he was the most boring man I'd ever met! Terribly lovely and sweet, but boring. The next morning he left, and I was sure I would never see him again."

"But fate!" Jagger snapped his fingers.

"Fate indeed. After the circus I tried my hand at university, but it wasn't for me, so I dropped out and decided to backpack through Europe for a while. In Romania I met up with some Romani travelers and lived and learned from them for a while."

"You did not!" Jagger shook his head. "That I don't believe."

"It's true. I've seen the photos," I said. Because if I hadn't, I wouldn't have believed this story either.

"Why has no one made a movie of your life yet?" Eddy asked.

I jumped into the storytelling that I knew so well by now. "Wait, there's more. And then she lived in a hippie commune for a while—"

"Don't forget the nudist colony too," she added.

"My god!" Eddy exclaimed, transfixed and hanging on her every word.

"And then after Europe she accidentally boarded a plane to South America," I said, relishing this slightly.

"Accidentally?" Jagger had almost leaned all the way across the table.

"I was trying to get back to South Africa but I misread the board and bought the wrong plane ticket. I realized one minute after they closed the door and almost said something, but then I figured I was meant to be on that flight."

"And then what?" Eddy was engrossed.

"Well, I landed in Peru, where I worked on a farm that grew aya-huasca for shamanic rituals."

"No. Stop!" Jagger held his hand up in the air. "You can't be serious. That actually happened to you? In real life?"

I nodded. "I know. I wouldn't believe it either if I hadn't seen the evidence of it."

Jagger smiled at me. "No wonder you're so cool," he half whispered, and then winked at me. I was just about to ask him what the hell he thought he was doing with his eye when my mom continued.

"And that's when I ended up having my true spiritual awakening."

"During a twelve-hour trip she had a vision that she needed to come back home." I said, adding to this story, which had been told so many times that it had become like a script.

"I was in the Amazon rainforest. It was drizzling this soft rain, almost like being inside mist. I was sitting on the bank of the river staring at the water and then . . ."

My mother paused. She always paused at this point in the story—it gave everyone a chance to lean in with anticipation.

"The water moved, a ripple, and then a wave, and then this fin broke the surface of the flat water and it was pink! It was a pink dolphin, and for a moment I thought I was hallucinating."

Jagger and Eddy burst out laughing. "You clearly were hallucinating if it was pink."

"No, that's the crazy thing! They actually have pink dolphins in the Amazon. And then, I swear, it stuck its head out of the water and looked at me. Looked me straight in the eye and it seemed to say, in its mind of course, *Go home!* So I boarded the first flight I could find back to South Africa, and guess who I bumped into at the airport when I arrived home?"

Everyone at the table gasped, including myself, who, even after hear-ing this story so many times before, could never really get over the kismet of this moment.

"And he was still wearing that exact same brown suit and tie!" She clapped her hands in delight. This was the detail she loved to tell the most. Not the pink dolphin and her strange encounters around Europe, but the fact that my dad was wearing the exact same clothing as he had been two years prior.

"He was on his way to a job interview, and it was his only good suit." She burst out laughing at the memory. And then her laugher slowed and finally stopped. "I gave all his clothes away to charity, except that suit."

We all sat in silence for a while. There was a beautiful poignancy to the moment that I could feel everyone was absorbing.

"I've never thrown out my wife's hairbrush. I know how strange that sounds, but I still have it," Eddy said, looking across at my mom. They stared at each other with a mutual understanding and sympathy, and I wondered if my mom had ever gotten to talk to someone like this before, someone who really understood what she'd gone through.

"We think we can hang on to them by holding on to their possessions, but really we don't need to, because they're still here with us, just in another form." She looked at me first, and then at Jagger.

"That was beautiful," Eddy said slowly, unable to hide the emotion in his voice. He raised his glass in the air. "Let's all drink to that."

Everyone clinked their glasses together and looked over at me—I hadn't raised my glass yet. I was too busy looking at my mom and Eddy. Something between them seemed to have changed; they were staring at each other as I could only imagine my mother stared at that pink dolphin on the banks of that river. I was suddenly overcome with the most awful feeling. It hit me out of the blue and it was very hard to understand.

"I . . . have to—" I stood up and pointed. "I'm getting tired, long day. I think I'll head to bed." I excused myself and left. I needed to be alone for a moment to compose myself. Rein in whatever these feelings were, even though I wasn't totally sure I understood them.

Chapter **Twenty**

The morning light streamed through the window, waking me up. I turned over and found my mom under the covers.

"Hey, Mom," I said, assuming she would be awake. She was always such an early riser. But she didn't move.

"Mom?" I tapped her on the shoulder, and she moaned.

"I'm so tired. I was up all night."

"Up?"

"Eddy and I got talking." Her words were sleep strangled.

"I see. And how long did you get talking for?"

She let out a long, exhausted moan. "Only got back at about five."

"Five?" What on earth did they have to talk to each other about until five?

She rolled over and pulled the covers close, cocooning herself. "I haven't watched the sun come up in years. Can I sleep some more?" she asked with a smile on her face, as if remembering something nice. "It was so beautiful. When did you last watch the sun come up?"

"A very long time ago," I confessed. "Sleep, Mom. I'll see you later."

I climbed out of bed and scratched around for one of the "outfits" that I had with me. I would phone the airline first thing and see if there was any progress on finding my luggage. I grabbed my underwear, which I'd washed last night and hung up in the bathroom to dry, and got changed into whatever strange combination of clothes I could concoct with what little I had, and that's when I caught sight of myself in the mirror. My usually pin-straight hair was curly from the humidity.

"No!" I tried to flatten it, but without my hair straighter—which was in my bag—it was pointless. I hated my hair like this, out of control, all over the place, bouncing about with a mind of its own. I liked it tame and under control. But there was no way I was going to be able to fix it; the only thing I could fix today was getting to some kind of a clothes store, even if it was just for underwear.

Once dressed, I headed for the breakfast buffet, picking up a brochure as I went. Walking through the undergrowth to the restaurant, I called the airline and got the same news I'd received yesterday: *no*, my bag was nowhere to be found, but *yes*, they would still keep looking.

At breakfast I ate a fruit salad followed by bacon and eggs, while paging though the brochure that advertised all manner of tours and Zanzibarian experiences, looking for something to do today with my mom. I also took note of where the nearest shops were and made a note to ask the reception how to organize a taxi to get there. When I'd eaten and found something that I knew my mom would love, I headed back to the room. I took a slow walk there to give her more sleeping time, but when I arrived, she still could not be roused.

"But, Mom, there are some ancient ruins that date back to the sixteenth century within walking distance from the resort. And a cave. Ancient ruins and mysterious caves with who knows what crystals in it, and you can swim in the cave!"

"Honey, I'm exhausted. Let me sleep a little longer."

I looked at my watch. It was already ten—the day was ticking away and I still wanted to get to a shop.

She said nothing and I gave her shoulder a little shake. "Mom!"

"Honey?"

"Should I go on without you and come back later?" I asked.

She nodded but didn't open her eyes or mouth.

"Okay, sleep well. See you later."

I walked out of the room and closed the door behind me, feeling a little disappointed that my mom wasn't joining me. I headed for the reception area where the path for the ruins began. I'd done a little googling before coming, so I knew what to expect: an old Portuguese coral house built about four hundred years ago for a family. The path to the site was well signed, even if the sign did read RUINED HOUSE, which I supposed, if you thought about it, was completely correct.

The path led me through more dense, tropical jungle. The jungle was wild and overgrown here; huge palm fronds stretched across the path, creating a natural canopy, while a tangle of moist ferns and vines nipped at my heels. This place had such a mysterious feeling to it, and I only had to walk a little way until the ruins came into view. I hadn't expected them to be so large and sprawling. Bright-green moss covered most of the aged walls, and ferns exploded from all the cracks. I walked through an archway, which had once presumably been the front door. It led into a long hallway with rooms that jutted off it. I stepped over small mounds of coral bricks, which had once been the walls of the rooms. A place like this tickled all my senses, firing up my imagination and bringing out the journalist in me who wanted to know who'd lived here. What their life might have been like here. What stories they could tell, what things they'd witnessed. I walked through the ruins, running my hands across their cool surfaces, imagining what it would have been like to walk these very passages. I rounded the corner and then—

"Oh my god! What are *you* doing here?" I asked as I picked myself up off the ground from a rather frightful, dramatic fall backward.

"You okay?" Jagger helped me up.

"Fine, I just . . . why are you here?"

"You mean, what brings me to this ruined house?" He smiled, clearly as amused as I had been with the sign.

"Exactly!"

"I'm not following you, if that's what you think."

"Why would I think that?" I asked.

He shrugged. "You always seem to think I'm up to no good . . . but I'm not. My dad is asleep. Apparently, he and your mother spent the night on the beach talking and watching the sun come up. I thought I would do something to kill time until he wakes up."

"Me too," I confessed. We were clearly in the same boat here. "Why did you bring your dad?" I suddenly asked.

Jagger's features twisted into confusion. "Who should I have brought?"

"I thought you would come with one of your many, you know, girlfriends."

He smiled. "I don't have a girlfriend, let alone many."

"You don't?" I shot him a very unconvinced look.

"No. Why didn't you bring your boyfriend?"

"I told you—"

Jagger cut me off. "You don't date. I remember."

"If you remembered, why ask?"

His smile grew and I knew the answer.

"Ahh, just to irritate me."

"You irritate too easily."

"And you are too irritating."

"You know, you're the only person who finds me irritating. Most people find me quite funny and charming. In fact, I've even heard myself described as delightfully gregarious."

"Who on earth said that?"

"My grade-four teacher."

I eyed Jagger for a moment, and then shook my head at him as he continued with that stupid, childish smile of his.

"My dad is my best friend," Jagger said, no longer smiling. There was such an intensity to what he was saying. No pretense, no joking, no bullshit. He was sharing something honest and personal with me, and I didn't quite know how I felt about that, or what to say to him, so I just nodded.

"After my mom died we became very close. Still are."

I felt uneasy suddenly. Jagger and I didn't share personal information with each other; that was not how the parameters of our relationship had been defined. And I for one did not want our relationship going there.

"My mom says we used to be best friends in ancient Egypt in a past life," I said, deflecting with humor.

He smiled and I was thankful that our "sharing moment" was over. "I was about to head to the cave. It's supposed to be amazing to swim in it. Have you been there yet?" he asked, holding up the towel he was carrying.

"I was also going to see it."

"Cool, let's go." Jagger turned and pointed at the wooden sign that read WATERY CAVE.

"Together? Just the two of us?"

Jagger looked around. "Unless there's someone else here that I'm not aware of?"

I stepped back. "It's all right. I'll go see if my mom's awake." I started walking away, pushing my towel back into my bag so it wasn't so obvious.

"I can see the towel. Are you really not going to come to the cave with me and swim?"

I swung around. "Maybe I've changed my mind."

"Upon seeing me here? That seems a little childish, don't you think?"

I was about to blast out an argument but . . . *He does sort of have a point.* Was I going to deprive myself of this cave adventure just because Jagger was here? Oh, who was I kidding. I didn't care if it was childish—I didn't want to go on a cave adventure with Jagger. What if the bloody cave collapsed and Jagger and I were trapped inside together, and never rescued, and thus he was the last person I got to see while I was alive? Jagger's laughter pulled me from my thoughts.

"What?" I asked.

"Looks like you have a movie playing in your head there, Maggie May. Let me guess, it's something catastrophic, on par with a midair engine shutdown or catching a deadly disease from your wastepaper bin?"

"No," I lied, trying very hard to control my twitch. A smile parted Jagger's lips, then moved into his eyes, causing little creases in the corners of them. "Come. Let's go to the cave." He beckoned me with his arm, and I stared at it.

I really wanted to see this cave. I'd seen pictures—it looked amazing—but I also didn't want to spend my holiday with Jagger bloody Villain. How had my peaceful holiday with my mom started to feel like a Contiki tour for four?

Jagger sighed. "It's okay. Why don't you go? I'll come back another time." He started walking off and I actually felt bad. Felt bad for Jagger.

"Shit," I mumbled under my breath. "Okay. Let's go. You and me . . . whatever. When in Zanzibar, or something like that," I added at the end to give it some kind of laissez-faire attitude. As if I wasn't actually as bothered by this as I really was. But these efforts were for naught, because it was clear that Jagger knew exactly how bothered I was with it, or he wouldn't have offered to leave.

I paused. Had Jagger just offered to leave so that I could go on my own?

"Huh!" I said out loud, surprised and totally thrown by what was, I must admit, a rather chivalrous sort of offer.

"What?" he asked.

"Nothing." Not that I would ever tell him that.

We arrived at the cave entrance and, just like the pictures, it was one of the most magnificent things I'd ever seen. The cave was open to the sky in parts, so light streamed onto waters so crystal clear that you could see all the details of the rock bottom. A man-made staircase descended into the cave; it wasn't very deep, but it was still impressive. Large stalactites hung from the roof, looking like massive drops of water that had been flash frozen and turned into stone. I hoped they didn't unfreeze themselves and drop on our . . .

"I'm sure they won't drop on our heads," Jagger said, and I looked at him in shock. "That is what you were thinking, right?"

"Uh . . . how did you know?"

A smooth chuckle slid out of Jagger's lips and then he shrugged. "Told you, we have basically been sharing a tiny desk for half a year and, like I said, I think I've gotten to know you pretty well in that time."

"Impossible. We don't even talk at work. We argue, at most."

"It's not only what people say that helps you get to know them." He smiled knowingly, as if he really did know something about me.

"Are you some kind of body-reading expert now too?" I asked, trying to arrange my face and limbs into a neutral pose that could not be read in case he really could read me.

"No, but I'm observant. And you are a creature of routine and habit. I've gotten to know those habits. I could even set my watch by them."

Surely I wasn't that predicable, was I? But as soon as I thought it, I knew it was true. I enjoyed doing the same thing over and over again. It gave me a kind of control over my environment, even if that control was imagined.

"Well, you have no habits," I said. "You're unpredictable and erratic. You come to work at whatever time you like, leave at whatever time you like. Sometimes you're gone from your desk all day doing god knows what."

"So you do take notice of me at work, then?" His face lit up, and I quickly realized my mistake.

I shook my head fast and vehemently, my hair flopping from side to side as I did.

"I love your hair like this, by the way."

Instinctively, I tried to smooth it down with my hands.

"Don't," Jagger said, his voice low and soft. "Don't flatten it."

"I hate it like this." I put both my hands on the sides of my head.

"Do you straighten it every single morning?" he asked.

I nodded.

"Well, you shouldn't." And with that, Jagger started pulling his shirt off. I turned around quickly and heard him laugh again.

"Swimming sort of involves talking off some clothes," he teased me. I heard him walk down the rickety wooden staircase, and then I heard a splash. I turned.

"Get in! It's freezing!" Jagger was out of breath, huffing and puffing as if hypothermia was setting in.

"You make it sound awful."

"It's not. It's amazing! Just get in quickly."

I hesitated for a moment and then peeled my clothes off. I left my T-shirt on. I wasn't in the mood for Jagger seeing me in a bikini top, especially since it was my mother's ill-fitting one. I raced down the stairs and shrieked when I hit the water.

"It's freezing."

"You have to dunk yourself."

"Shit!" I closed my eyes, took a deep breath, and plunged into the clear, cold water. My body reacted instantly to the shock. All my senses felt as if they'd exploded at once. I opened my eyes and looked around. I was officially on another planet. The green water was completely transparent. In fact, like a magnifying glass, or goggles, it seemed to clarify all the details below. The rocks of the cave were jagged and protruded into the pool. Strange stone structures stood like underwater pillars; oddly shaped pebbles and boulders littered the cave floor. Air bubbles rushed out of my nose as I slowly pushed myself back up to the surface, where I inhaled the cool, crisp air of the cave.

"And?" Jagger asked. I met his eyes. He was standing in a beam of light that shot out in a straight line, cutting his face in half, one side illuminated, the other side in shadow.

"It's amazing." I turned onto my back and floated, putting my arms out to the side for added balance. I lay there, suspended in the cool water, looking at the ceiling above me, the abstract world of rock art. Jagger also lay on his back, swaying gently next to me, and I cast my eye over at him. He, like me, was examining the ceiling. My ears were underwater, and that muffled the sounds of the world outside. The cool water lapped at me, and I could feel an easing of tension in my body, as if the water was pulling it out and then carrying it away.

"Who do you think lived in that house?" Jagger's words echoed in the cave.

"A Portuguese spice-trading family," I said quickly.

"I was going more with Portuguese pirates."

I stopped floating and stood up in the water. "You would think that, wouldn't you?"

Jagger also stopped floating. "Why do you say that?"

"You know, I'm more partial to actual facts, whereas you prefer sensationalism."

"But sensationalism is so much fun."

I rolled my eyes at him and shook my head.

"Come on. Pillaging. Pirating. Swashbuckling, plank walking, one-eyed, parrot on the shoulder, bottles of rum, and buried treasures?"

I shook my head again, opened my mouth to speak, but was interrupted.

"You must be talking about Kiki," Eddy said. Jagger and I turned to find my mom and Eddy at the top of the stairs.

"Who's Kiki?" I asked.

"Me! Kiki is me. Isn't it lovely? I've never had such a good nickname before." My mother looked as if she was about to turn effervescent and explode forth like Mentos in a bottle of Coke.

"I don't get it," I said.

"Oh, I get it. Cute. It suits you," Jagger said.

"I think so too." My mom beamed.

"I still don't get it," I said.

"Anke. Kiki," Jagger said to me.

"So, because she has a *K* in her name, she becomes Kiki?"

"Exactly." Eddy walked down the stairs to the water and then held his hand out for my mom.

"That still doesn't make sense. That's like calling me Mimi because my name has an *M* in it."

"I love that!" My mom gasped as she hit the cold water. "Mimi and Kiki—we sound like old country and western singers."

"Huh?" I gaped at my mother while everyone else laughed. Eddy and my mom swam into the water and suddenly this cave felt very full and loud. And just when I thought it couldn't get any louder, merry laughter bounced off the walls and ceilings in duplicate as my mom continued to joke about our potential careers as traveling singers.

But I felt unsettled by all this joviality and camaraderie, *and I felt something else*. My mom and I used to laugh with my dad like this, when we went to theme parks, and on Christmas holidays, and at family dinners. But my dad wasn't here, so why were we all laughing like this, like we were some kind of fam—

I shook my head. I didn't want to think that word right now because it felt so wrong.

"I think I'm going toooo . . ." I stopped everyone's laughter. I hadn't expected such a dramatic delivery, one that stopped everyone in their tracks and made them turn, but the cave had enhanced my voice somewhat and then tossed it around a few times.

"Uh . . . lunch. Hungry," I managed, and headed for the stairs.

"What a great idea! I'm starving," Eddy bellowed, and I froze. Hang on, what the hell was going on? How did "I'm hungry" get twisted into some kind of communal invite for lunch participation?

"Wasn't there a restaurant you were talking about, Mimi?"

I unfroze myself and gave my mom a very pointed look.

"Not working for you?" she asked, smiling ear to ear.

"What about Titi?" Eddy offered thoughtfully.

"Nah, that doesn't sound right either," Jagger said, shaking his head. "Gigi?"

"Where the hell do you get Gigi from? That sounds like an exotic dancer's name!"

"Maggie. Gigi." Jagger was smiling more than my mother; clearly he was loving this misnaming moment. Relishing it, no doubt, like he always did.

"Oooh, no, she hates being called Maggie. Her ex-husband called her Maggie."

"Is that what it is?" Jagger's gray eyes probed me uncomfortably and I'd had enough.

"Okay!" I walked up the stairs and loomed over everyone in the pool. "Can we all just please stop trying to rename me on my holiday. I already have way too much of that at work. My name is Margaret to you two"—I pointed at Jagger and Eddy—"and Margaret-Skye to you." I pointed at my mom, and everyone just looked amused.

"I know! Skylee." Eddy completely ignored me. "Kylie, but with a Sky."

"That's it!" I stomped up the stairs, aware that my bum was probably shaking like I was twerking for a TikTok and everyone was watching. I got to the top, grabbed my towel, and wrapped it around my cold shoulders.

"The rock!" my mom yelled from the cave. "The restaurant you were telling me about, it's on a rock in the middle of the sea. You can only get there by boat."

Jagger and Eddy both made appreciative *oooh* sounds. I waved my hands at them; I didn't want to hear it from them. I wanted to go to the restaurant without them. I didn't want every single thing I did to include the Villains.

I suppose I lost that one, though. Because an hour and a half later, we were all in a traditional little dhow boat being taken to the rock restaurant in the middle of the turquoise sea.

Chapter **Twenty-one**

When we got back to the resort later that day, a tight feeling had taken up residence in my stomach, a feeling of unease I couldn't shake despite my afternoon spent in one of the most unique and beautiful places I had ever seen. The rock restaurant was just that: a rock in the middle of the water, with nothing but a restaurant on it. And the seafood they served was caught straight from the sea below you. The food had been amazing, the scenery had been amazing, and the way the smell of salty sea air filled your lungs while you ate fresh lobster was amazing. The breeze flicked drops of water up into the air, turned them into fine vapor that bespeckled your shoulders and cooled you down. It was all just so perfect, except for one thing, or, should I say, two things.

Despite this place's many beauties, there had been something so strangely uncomfortable about the day, and it was not just the way my mom and Eddy were looking at each other. It was also the way they seemed to already be sharing in-jokes, the kinds of jokes that best friends or partners shared. They were laughing and clinking glasses and acting like they had known each other for years.

"I'm going clothes shopping," I announced to the party on our return.

"Brilliant!" Jagger spoke up instantly. "I also need a few things."

"Like what?" I asked.

"Sunscreen, and my toothpaste burst in my bag, so I need another tube, and a few T-shirts since I ruined two."

I blinked at Jagger. This announcement had not been an open invitation for him to tag along. "Why don't you wash your shirts? I can lend you sunscreen and you can use my toothpaste," I said quickly.

"Sounds like you don't want me to come with you?" He seemed amused.

"Well, I . . . it wasn't an invitation," I said.

"Oh, Margaret-Skye," my mother chided me. "You're being ridiculous now."

I swung around and looked at her. She probably wanted to get rid of us both so she could spend time alone with Eddy.

"I won't cramp your style, promise. We'll just share the taxi ride to the shops—that's all. And then I'll turn a blind eye to whatever you're *really* buying, because clearly it's a secret." Jagger winked.

I scowled. "I'm buying clothes," I reiterated.

"Sure you are." He winked again.

"Something in your eye?" I shot back sarcastically.

"Nope." He stretched his arms above his head, really showing off his impressive height. I wasn't sure the stretch was necessary. I think it was more to annoy me than anything else. "So what time should we go?"

I looked down at my watch. "The taxi will be here in five minutes."

"Great!" He sprang into action and trotted off to the reception area. I walked behind him wondering not only how it was that he was joining me, but how he now seemed to be the one leading me there too.

We sat in the back of the taxi. It was a lot smaller than the airport shuttle and, as such, each pothole that it went through felt like a shock wave that started in my coccyx and then traveled up my spine. At certain points my body levitated off the seat entirely, only to come crashing back down, my legs and arms flopping down in places I'd really rather they didn't.

"Sorry, I didn't mean to." I pulled my arm off Jagger's knee quickly and braced myself for the next bump. The roads here were worse than the potholed roads in South Africa, and that was saying something.

"Shit! Sorry!" I said again, as the next bump sent another wayward limb flying into his chest. The next bump was even more unfortunate as it required two things of me. One, to grab hold of my boobs as they bounced uncontrollably on the way up and down, and two, grab something to stop myself from falling sideways, and that something happened to be Jagger's upper thigh.

"Sorry!" I gushed again.

"I'm irresistible—I get it," he teased me.

"Oh please. I'm certainly not touching you on purpose. I'm touching you under duress," I said, turning my back to him and quickly stuffing my one boob back into my bra, hoping that Jagger hadn't noticed.

As we got closer to the small town, the potholes began to lessen on the tarred roads.

Town was perhaps the wrong word to describe the place we were standing in when we climbed out of the taxi. We were in a small fishing village and the shops in a row on the main street were small thatched huts with open sides. Many were filled with tourist trinkets—paintings, carvings, and shells—but I was looking for one that contained clothing. We walked along the road in silence, peering into the shops as we went. There was a small convenience store that looked as if it sold some basic foodstuffs and had a refrigerator of ice. Next to it was a shop that had the words INTERNET SERVICES AVAILABLE HERE painted on a sign. Next was a woman sitting on a big blue drum, a makeshift table in front of her laden with bananas, then a cell phone shop in a painted metal container that did repairs and sold airtime, and after that, what looked like a place that sold fishing supplies. But then another store caught my eye. Colorful sarongs were tied to the low-hanging roof, flapping in the warm breeze. I made a beeline for the shop and peered inside. It was a curious mix of brightly colored tourist clothing, traditional clothing, and piles of what looked to be cheap made-in-China fakes. Jagger walked straight up to a T-shirt that had "Guchi" embossed in the middle of it. He picked it up and laughed.

"Love it!" He looked at the sizes inside and once he'd found the right one, slung it over his shoulder. Next he found one that claimed to be an "Adidos," and the one after that was a "Hugo Hoss." Jagger continued to laugh as he moved from one pile to the next. I turned my attention to the other end of the shop, where I saw bathing suits, socks, and underwear. I peered over my shoulder to make sure Jagger wasn't looking in my direction. When I was sure he wasn't, I moved over to the folded packs of underpants. One, a selection of lacy pink and red things, was named "Victoria Whispers." I picked it up, searching for the right size.

"Found what you're looking for?" Jagger asked. I spun around, hiding the undies behind my back and leaning against the table, blocking its contents from view. Jagger shot me what Shawn would call a "sus" look, and then stepped around me.

"I see." He sounded amused again, and I flushed with mortification. It was one thing sharing a holiday with this man, but sharing the purchase of underwear was a line I did not want to cross.

Too late for that, a voice echoed in my head.

"You could always just go commando," Jagger said with a smile, and then did something strange. He raised his eyebrows up and down repeatedly, as if he was alluding to something . . . *what?*

"NO!" My eyes involuntarily drifted down to his crotch area and then shot back up again. "You do not . . . no! That's just . . . I don't want to know, Jagger. Stop!" I held my hand up in the air, the one holding the lacy whispers. Jagger eyed them and I quickly put them behind my back again.

"Jagger, I have no desire to discuss my underwear with you, and certainly no desire to discuss your lack of underwear. Gross."

He laughed at this.

"It's not funny! It's revolting, and . . . at work! No. This is too much, even for you."

"Hey, I wear underwear to work. But sometimes, on weekends or on holidays, I like to—"

"*Stop!* I said no more."

"I once wrote an article about why it's not actually good to wear underwear all the time. It gives your skin a break from chemicals such as fabric softener and laundry detergent. It can also reduce chafing and improves circulation—"

"Stop, stop, stop. I beg you."

My pleading fell on deaf ears. In fact, all it seemed to do was inspire him to continue.

"It also feels pretty liberating. You should try it sometime."

"Certainly not! You sound like my mother now."

"She's a wise woman."

I shook my head and pursed my lips. "No, thanks."

Jagger stepped closer, looming over me. "Why? You scared?" He raised a brow in challenge and I felt my competitive streak flare again. God, Jagger did know me! He knew where to get me. He knew that it was hard for me to back down from a challenge.

"I'm not scared," I insisted.

"Prove it!"

"Are you challenging me *not* to wear underwear?"

He shrugged, and I stared him down.

"For how long?" I asked. I could not believe I was even entertaining this.

"At least an hour. And you can't just do it sitting in your room or by the pool. You need to go out into the world like that. Feel the breeze."

"Maybe I don't like breezes . . . there."

"You'll enjoy it. There's a sense of freedom to it."

I shook my head at him and then moved off to the rack of women's clothes, grabbing T-shirts, shorts, and skirts. "Not happening, Jagger. And I would prefer it if we never spoke about underwear again."

"Suit yourself." He had a smile in his voice, and I fantasized about sticking one of those pairs of "Docha & Cabanna" socks in his mouth.

When we'd paid for our items and were back on the street again, my eyes drifted down to his crotch area. I had to tell Lesego. I knew how much she would bloody relish this tidbit of information. It would brighten her day. Brighten her life. So I pulled my phone out behind Jagger's back and shot her a quick message.

> **Margaret**: Do not send me a voice message back. JAGGER DOES NOT WEAR UNDERWEAR!

She replied immediately. I knew she would. She was clearly so desperate to learn more that she was even prepared to use her fingers and type.

> **Lesego**: Oooohhhh… how do you know? 😉
>
> **Margaret**: I know because he told me!
>
> **Lesego**: Ooooh… and why would he tell you something like that? 😉
>
> **Margaret**: Stop these winky faces and oooohhhs
>
> **Margaret**: Nothing is going on, or ever will go on between us. Ever!
>
> **Margaret**: As much as for some mad reason you think it might
>
> **Lesego**: What's that wise quote again…
>
> **Lesego**: Oh, I remember, something about fine lines between love and hate
>
> **Margaret**: If you don't stop, I might hate you soon
>
> **Lesego**: You could never hate me. I'm too damn loveable
>
> **Margaret**: That's unfortunately very true
>
> **Margaret**: Got to go. I'm about to get into a taxi with Jagger, and don't you dare say ooh
>
> **Lesego**: 😉
>
> **Margaret**: That either!

Chapter **Twenty-two**

When we got back to the resort, instead of heading to the room I decided to go for an evening walk on the beach. The warm sand felt good beneath my feet. It glistened like diamond shards in the moonlight. There's something about the beach that feeds the soul on a deep level. The point at which the earth beneath your feet ends and tapers off into the vast waters encompassing our planet. When I was younger, I remember asking my father after seeing the globe in his study why the waters didn't just fly off the earth and shoot up into space. That's when he'd explained gravity to me. My father was this treasure trove of knowledge, a well that I was always dipping my bucket into, trying to take up as much of it as he offered. The idea that there was a force so strong that it held things together and kept them from flying apart seemed so incredible to me. He used to say that the only other force that strong was love. It was the glue that held families together and stopped them from breaking apart and spinning away from each other. My father had very much been the gravity in our family, and without him my feet didn't quite feel as firmly planted on the ground as they used to be. In many ways I still couldn't quite believe he was gone. My father had always been such a strong presence in my life that the idea of having a life without him in it had never crossed my mind. And since he'd been gone, time seemed to have moved in a very different kind of way: slow, stagnant. Mind you, it seemed to have started moving differently when he'd gotten sick.

The year my dad was sick stopped being about the days, or weeks, or months. Instead, time was measured by a very different metric. Second chemo treatment, six-week checkup, day after radiation, three-month checkup and second MRI. Time moved from one appointment to the next, each one seeming to take a little more of my father away from us. The treatments stripped him of little parts of himself as he got weaker and smaller until he barely resembled the man I used to know.

That's the thing about cancer, one of the nurses had said to me as the vile red liquid snaked into his veins—the treatment makes you feel sicker than the disease itself. My dad deteriorated before our eyes that year as chemo made him bald and thin, as steroids made his cheeks puff up, and medication constantly dilated his pupils, so meeting his eyes was like looking into the center of two black holes.

It's amazing how many types of pleas one can make; I hadn't known quite how many until then. You can be so desperate that your day turns into a series of moments that happen in between those pleas. Pleading that the chemo and radiation worked, pleading with the doctors to get him onto the new drug trial, pleading with the universe and God that he would not be taken from us, pleading with myself to be stronger, to be less emotional, to not fall apart. My pleas had fallen on deaf ears, it would seem.

I continued to walk up the beach, taking slow, contemplative steps, enjoying the fact that all my senses were alive and engaged. There was smell: salty and floral. Tactile: the sand between my toes, the breeze on my skin, and every now and then, when the wind chose to, it flung a few cool droplets of water my way. I concentrated on all the feelings, and, for a few blissful moments, my thoughts ceased to exist. It was always hard to escape the confines of my chaotic, anxious brain, but when I did, I relished the quiet calm that came with it. And for a second, there was no anxiety gnawing away at me. There was only a sense of freedom . . .

Free.

An unwanted thought arrived in my consciousness. And the second it did, I blushed stupidly. I stopped walking, pulled my skirt open, and looked down at my underwear. I burst out laughing. *What was I thinking?* I carried on walking, shrugging off the ridiculous thought. But it only went away for a little while, because moments later I had stopped walking and was looking down my skirt again.

I shook my head and continued walking, but when I stopped for the third time, I looked around to see if the coast was clear. It was, and I tentatively slipped my hand up my skirt. I wasn't doing this because Jagger had dared me to—I was only doing it for research purposes. I was a journalist—by nature we are curious beings, and I was just being curious. Besides, he was right: going commando did have health benefits. I'd googled it. I was doing this for health and research and to have another unique human experience that I could . . .

Oh, who was I kidding! I was doing this because Jagger had irritated me when he'd assumed I wouldn't do it. And even though I would never tell him about it, I wanted to prove him wrong. *Even if it was only for my own private gratification.*

And I hated to admit this, even to myself, but there was something utterly freeing about it. The breeze whipped my skirt up and swished it from side to side. It was rather refreshing! I continued my commando walk off the beach and into the resort. I passed some people on the way and had to stifle a laugh as I greeted them, knowing something that they didn't. It was quite exhilarating having a little secret that no one else knew, and by the time I'd reached my room, I was in a great mood. That is until a noise stopped me from slipping the key into the door. I looked around at the other rooms, at the tropical undergrowth, behind me at the path, but couldn't make out the source of it. I turned the key with a loud *click* and was hit with a commotion.

"Margaret-Skye? Is that you?" my mom screeched. She sounded

hysterical and out of breath. Her voice had a frantic, high-pitched quality to it, but something stopped me from barging inside to see if she was okay. More commotion came from inside. This time I heard something bang, and then a giggle. Wait . . . two giggles. Was my mom . . .

"NO! Mom!"

"But you messaged me and said you were going for a walk?" my mom returned.

"I've been on a walk, Mom. A long, long walk." Why did everyone who was clearly up to no good ask this kind of question? As if it was *your* fault that you had turned up at some inopportune time, not *their* fault that they were doing something inappropriate.

"I'm sort of . . . in the middle of something," my mom said through what sounded like suppressed laughter.

"I kind of figured that," I replied sarcastically.

"You think you can give us another"—she paused—"thirty minutes, maybe an hour?"

"*Mom!*" Oh my god, I can't believe my mom was busy with *that* in our room, on our bed. Did no one have respect for the sanctity of a shared space?

"Sorry, honey, it's just that my . . ."

"Her hands are tied!" Eddy shouted, and I physically hit my forehead with my hand. Face-palm emoji. I'd never thought people actually did that in real life until now. I'd always viewed it as one of those hypothetical emojis, like that winky-eye, tongue-out-of-mouth emoji. No one does that in real life, but here I was having a real-life emoji moment. And now all I could hear were the almost hysterical shrieks of laugher coming from my mother and Eddy. And did they really think I was going to come back to that room and sleep in that bed after *that*?

Everywhere I turned, I seemed to have a Villain man invading my personal space. My desk, my bed, my mother. I shook my head, trying to fling that image out of it, but it clung on stubbornly. I stormed off, not even sure of where I was going. I pulled my phone out and did the only thing I could think of.

Margaret: MY MOM IS HAVING SEX WITH JAGGER'S DAD!!!!!!!!!!!!!!

Leighton sent me a series of laughing emojis. I did not find this funny, though. So I sent angry faces back, followed by a green nauseated face.

Leighton: Go, Anke!

Margaret: OMG, I knew I shouldn't have told you. You're probably all for this?

Leighton: And why not? At least she's getting laid

Margaret: You know I HATE that word, and I did get laid

Leighton: Bad sex is not sex, it's yoga

Margaret: Yoga?

Leighton: There is some uncomfortable stretching that no one really enjoys, noises that sound ridiculous, and afterward strange muscles feel sore and you are totally unsatisfied

Margaret: That was not a good analogy

Leighton: Fine, like brushing your teeth. Has to be done, too much friction, and leaves a bad taste in your mouth

Margaret: Still not. But I'm sorry, did you miss that part where I said my mom was having sex with JAGGER'S DAD???!!!

Leighton: I got it. That was the part I was laughing at

Margaret: You're useless. I can't have this conversation with you

Leighton: Is he at least hot?

Margaret: If you like ZZ Top?

Leighton: You know I did LSD with Frank Beard in the Nevada desert once

Margaret: Of course you did!

Leighton: Mind you, in those days taking LSD was like drinking coffee in the morning

Margaret: You are officially zero help. So I'm going to stop messaging you, forever

Leighton: You'll miss me

Margaret: Unfortunately

I slipped my phone back into my pocket and looked around. Where to now? My mother had "kicked" me out of my room with her shenanigans. If anyone should be having holiday sex, shouldn't it be me, the recently divorced daughter who wasn't even wearing underwear, *not* my recently widowed mom?

For a moment I thought of messaging Lesego but didn't. The need to reach out to someone with this information and have them respond to me in the same way I was feeling—with shock and horror—was totally overwhelming. I needed a sympathetic ear badly but didn't have one, so instead I focused my energy on working out where I was going to sleep that night. Because it certainly wasn't going to be in *that* bed.

I headed in the direction of the reception hoping—silently praying—that a room might have miraculously opened up. Surely there must be one, *one* spare room *somewhere* in this place? But I was given the same information twice by the receptionists: "No, there is no room." When I asked them whether it was an option to sleep in the broom closet or laundry room, they looked at me so strangely that I thought it was time to leave.

I found myself walking back to the beach without even thinking about it. When I got there, I was sad to see that the comfortable loungers had been moved and all that remained were those hammocks between the palm trees. Hammocks, wildly romantic in thought, but in practice, not so much. I walked up to one and gave it a push with my hand. It swung violently. It wasn't even vaguely sturdy looking and the ropes looked as if they'd been handwoven with grasses or dry seaweed. I began to lower myself into it to see how it responded to my weight. It swung wildly again and delivered an ominous-sounding squeak. I stood up again and looked at it, trying to decide the best way in which one might mount this beast. It reminded me of those mechanical bulls that were just waiting to throw you off. And throw me off it did. Because on my first attempt I was unable to stop the swing and it tossed me onto the beach. Spat me out like old, chewed gum. I stood up and dusted off the sand. Thank god I'd put my underwear back on, or else I would be trying to dust sand from a very unfortunate place. I looked back down at the hammock. My leg-first approach had not worked. Perhaps an all-in-one, less staggered approach might be the ticket. Jump on in a single move and let gravity settle you.

I said a quick, silent prayer and then, with zero confidence in my ability to make this move successfully, I jumped into the hammock all at once. It swung like crazy and I clutched the ropes, trying to steady myself. My stomach muscles felt as if they might rip apart, but finally after what felt like an exorbitant amount of time, the swinging slowly came to a stop and I was (somewhat) successfully lying in a hammock. I felt a little nauseated from the swinging. The ropes were not comfortable, cutting into my bum and back. I could imagine little bits of bum fat oozing between the openings, like when you squeeze those fluid-filled stress balls wrapped in netting that everyone watches videos of on YouTube. The word *satisfying* is usually attached to the video. It's amazing how many videos on YouTube claim to be "satisfying": a box of Crayola crayons getting squashed by a hydraulic press, or a car slowly driving over tubes of toothpaste. I always wonder who's going to clean that stuff up afterward. I don't feel soothed and satisfied by videos like that. On the contrary, it sends my anxiety soaring.

I wiggled around trying to make myself comfortable but realized quite quickly that if I was going to have to spend the night sleeping here, I would wake up with all sorts of pains in my neck and red marks on my bum, as if I'd been at some BDSM club. That's how you know you're over thirty, by the way: those twinges and aches in your neck and shoulders and knees. They seem to start as thirty hits and get progressively worse as the years roll on. Until one morning, after sleeping funny, you have to go to physio to get rid of the sharp, stabbing pain under your shoulder blade. Gravity is also less kind in your thirties; it starts to pull on things that were previously buoyant. Boobs, eyelids, and, one day after hours writing at my computer, I looked up to see two indelible lines between my eyebrows.

"What are you doing here?" Jagger's voice came out of nowhere and I jumped. The hammock swung again, and I gripped the sides.

"Lying down," I replied casually, when it had stopped swinging.

"I can see that. But why?" His tone had a slight looseness to it, a languid quality that led me to believe that he'd probably just come from having cocktails with someone.

"You know it's scheduled to storm soon," he said.

"According to whom?"

"The weather app."

I turned to face Jagger. He was silhouetted against the hotel lights, which made him look even taller.

"You know you can't trust weather apps, right?"

"Why not?" Even though he was silhouetted, I could see the smile twitch on the corners of his lips.

"When has a weather app ever been right?"

"Mmm, I don't know. I think meteorologists are pretty good at predicting these things."

"Meteorologists are incapable of making any prediction about the weather correctly!" I said quickly. On the day my dad died, it was scheduled to rain. I knew this because my insurance company had sent out one of those storm warnings. *Severe storm, chance of hail.* They claimed to do this because they cared, but really they just don't want you to go skidding about in the rain and have a bumper bashing, or leave your car uncovered only for it to get battered by hailstones.

But there was no storm that day. The weather had remained bright and sunny. I hated that weather. I felt that, on the day my dad died, it would have been far more appropriate for the sky to blacken, to rip open and spew ice and water at the world below destructively. And then on the day of the funeral, when I'd wanted sun, some light, some warmth, which the weather app had promised me, it rained. Poured on us all.

I looked up at the sky. There were clouds—I couldn't deny that. I also couldn't deny that the wind had picked up in the last few minutes and that the temperature had gone from a balmy warm, to a less-balmy cool. Jagger looked up at the sky for a moment, too, and then down at his phone, his features lit up by the bright screen.

"I don't even know why meteorologists still exist. Imagine working in a profession where you get most things incorrect! You would be fired immediately. But it seems like meteorologist are exempt from this."

"I don't know, I would go to your room if I were you." He scrutinized the sky again.

I could have told him that I couldn't go to my room, that very bad things were happening in my room, but didn't. One more person knowing what was going on in there would make it even more real. And I didn't want reality right now. I wanted a blissful state of ignorance.

"I'll take my chances out here." I turned back to what I thought was my former (almost) comfy position, only I couldn't find it.

"You look like you're settling in for the night?" Jagger sounded amused, as I wiggled back and forth.

"Maybe I am," I replied defiantly. "Maybe I like sleeping under the stars in this . . . hammock." The last word came out of my mouth with disdain. I'd decided, for good reason, that I didn't like hammocks. Hammocks were for stranded pirates, forest-dwelling hippies, and tight-rope walkers. They were not for people like me.

"But there're no stars," Jagger pointed out.

"There will be."

"Not if the weather app is anything to go on. It says that at eleven there is an eighty-nine percent chance of a storm. It's ten fifty." Jagger walked over to the hammock next to me and got into it. I rolled my eyes. Of course he got into it smoothly and effortlessly. He was probably an old hand with hammocks, probably did advanced *Kama Sutra* positions in them with those aforementioned tightrope walkers.

"What are you doing?"

"Waiting here until eleven," he said with a yawn.

A silence fell between us. It felt like the usual silences we experienced at work, where I fantasize about him getting fired, or him quitting, or a giant crack opening in the earth's crust and pushing him to the opposite side of the building.

"Ten fifty-six," Jagger stated matter-of-factly.

I *hmph*ed nonchalantly in response but was a little concerned by a flash of light in the distance.

"Ten fifty-seven."

"Are you going to do that every minute?" I asked.

"No, I'll do it every second when we get to the last minute."

"Well, that won't be irritating in the slightest."

Jagger snickered. "Oh, I'm sure it will be. Very irritating."

"Obviously, since it seems to be your life's mission to constantly irritate me."

"Untrue. You just irritate easily."

"I do n—"

"Ten fifty-eight." He cut me off, proving his deliberate irritating intentions. "What's that?" He pointed at the horizon.

"Don't know."

"Looks like lightning to me."

"Could be something else," I offered in a very unsure-sounding voice.

"Name one other thing it could be."

"Uh . . . it could be . . . one of those lights that people shine into the sky outside a nightclub!"

Jagger looked as if he was considering that for a while, only he didn't answer. Instead he started counting down.

"Sixty, fifty-nine, fifty-eight—"

"Please stop!"

"Fifty-six, fifty-five, fifty-four—"

"Oh my god! Do you have to do that?"

"Fifty, forty-nine, forty-eight—"

"Fine! Fine! Do it and we'll see who's right." But as I said that, a massive bolt of lightning split the black sky in two.

"Looks like that's going to be me."

"Just because there's lightning doesn't mean there's going to be rain," I said, not believing that anymore. The trees were starting to bend in the growing wind, and the birds were all flying away.

"Twenty-five, twenty-four, twenty-three—"

He hadn't gotten any more numbers out when another bolt of lightning turned the sky white. And then a single drop of rain fell and landed right on my face. I knew Jagger was looking at me. I knew he was smiling, and I knew he was basking in the glow of his victory.

"It's one drop!" I wiped the water off my face and another one hit my leg. "Two? Two drops do not make a downpour. It's a drizzle."

"It's rain, though."

"You said a storm. This is not a storm."

"I agree—it's not a storm."

We sat there for another five minutes or so as the odd stray drop fell from the sky, and then the drops stopped completely. I looked up as two of the clouds parted and revealed a star.

"Well, you were right!" Jagger said, getting up off the hammock with the kind of ease I knew I would never be able to achieve when I needed to do the same. "Okay, I guess, good night, then. Enjoy your night under the stars." He looked up. "Looks like they might be coming out for you after all."

"Looks like it," I said, counting another two stars peeping out from behind the clouds.

"Sleep well." Jagger walked away and I was alone again. Maybe this would be nice: sleeping in a hammock under the starry African sky, breeze in my hair, sounds of night birds, hammock swaying gently, enveloped in the intoxicating scent of jasmine. Yes, this would be good. This would be great! Who needed a bed and a room and a blanket when you had the magnificence of the African sky above you and . . .

"Oh my god!" I jumped and toppled out of the hammock as the remaining clouds ripped apart and water gushed down as if someone had tipped the contents of a giant cosmic jug over the edge of the clouds. It was like standing under a waterfall—one minute there had been no rain, the next I was drenched. I scrambled to my feet. In seconds my clothes were sticking to me like a second skin. The wind had picked up, and the gusts left me shivering. I hugged my body and ran for cover under the nearest thing I could find, which provided zero coverage. A palm tree. The wind was so gusty that the tree was dancing left to right like those inflatable people with the flapping arms that you see outside car dealerships. I needed to get out of this rain. With each passing moment, it was coming down harder and harder until it felt as if I was being whipped all over my body.

Perhaps this had something to do with cursing the meteorologists. Perhaps this was some kind of revenge weather. I was left with zero options here, bar one.

Chapter **Twenty-three**

"Here." Jagger passed me a dry towel when he opened the door, as if he'd been anticipating my arrival.

I attempted to dry my hair first and then wrapped it around my dripping body, still on the threshold.

"How did you know I would come here?" I asked.

"Well, I sort of guessed you wouldn't be going back to your room."

"Wait, you know what's going on in there?"

"I didn't know for sure, but when I found you settling in for the night in a hammock, I suspected there had to be a very good reason." Jagger held the door wide and gestured for me to come inside. I paused. This felt very . . . *weird*.

I'd often imagined what Jagger's life would be like outside of work, but not in *that* way. Not in the way Lesego seemed to think I thought about him. Not at all. But I had thought about it, and it wasn't a stretch to imagine what it would be like, given that he wrote about it constantly. His dating escapades, his sex toy tryouts, not to mention all the other things with which he experimented. I'd always had a pretty good idea of what Jagger's life was probably like, but this felt different somehow. This felt so personal, entering the place that he was sleeping in at night.

The room was identical to ours, just an inverted version of it.

"Maybe I should . . ." I looked at the bathroom. This all felt very wrong. I couldn't bring myself to say it. *Maybe I should go into your bathroom and dry myself.* I would need to take my clothes off and wring them out in the basin, maybe my bra and panties too. In fact, I might be completely naked in his bathroom for a little while.

"Sure," Jagger said, a slightly loaded tone in his voice, as if he knew what I was thinking.

I walked into the small bathroom; it was just like ours. I closed the door and then checked the frame carefully, making sure there weren't any gaps that Jagger could see through. I turned the key in the lock. I was hoping for a quiet turn, but it clicked loudly and, as soon as it did, I heard him laugh.

"Scared I'm going to forget you're in there and accidentally walk in on you?" His voice wasn't that far away, and it made me think he'd walked up to the door.

"Uh . . . habit," I said. Reluctantly, I started peeling off my shirt. *Peeling* was the correct word, because it stuck to my wet skin like a coating of wood glue that had dried. I pulled my shirt off and grimaced at the sucking sound it made as it detached itself from my breasts. I looked at myself in the mirror. My bra was soaked too—not the most comfortable of feelings. I squeezed my top into the basin and the water poured out.

"How's it going in there?" Jagger asked.

I stopped squeezing. Impertinent question. "Do you want a running commentary?"

Another soft laugh. This time definitely closer than before. "A running commentary would probably be overkill. I just meant are you okay in there? You need anything, another towel, some dry clothes?"

"Whose clothes?"

"I can lend you a T-shirt, if you want."

It was my turn to laugh. "No, thanks."

"What's wrong with my T-shirts?"

"You mean other than the fact most of them have holes in them?"

"They don't *all* have holes in them."

"Sometimes they look like they've been lying on the floor for a year."

"Hey, I follow Lesego's advice."

"And what's that?"

"Well, since reading her article about how unsustainable the fashion industry is, I've been buying more clothes at secondhand stores."

"Secondhand! Your clothes look like they come from fourthhand stores."

"At least I'm doing my bit for the environment. As you pointed out, climate change doesn't just affect the weather—it also shapes the future political landscape of the world."

I paused midwring. "You read my article?"

"You sound surprised."

"Well, I mean, I am . . ."

"You're surprised because I read your article or surprised because I'm interested in how 'water management and food insecurity will lead to a change in global political policies, and a shift in the socioeconomic landscape too'?"

"You're just reading it now, aren't you?"

"Nope. Read it a while ago."

"You expect me to believe that you read it a while ago but are able to quote it verbatim."

"I have a good memory."

"Mmmmm . . . like you're good at general knowledge?"

"You still think I cheated?"

"Did you?" I stopped what I was doing and walked up to the door, resting my forehead on it. I got the sense that Jagger was just outside.

"No, I didn't."

"Mmmm . . ." I mumbled through the door.

"Ask me anything," he challenged me.

I asked the first question that popped into my mind. "What the hell are our parents doing?"

"I believe they call it intercourse." Jagger laughed, and I launched myself off the door.

"Do you have to say it out loud?"

"You brought it up."

"Yes, but I didn't think you would actually say *that*."

"Sex?"

"Jesus, Jagger. Stop."

"Our parents are shagging."

"*Stop*. Oh my god! Please."

"I mean, good for them."

"What? How is this even vaguely good?"

"Well, just because you reach a certain age doesn't mean you shouldn't have a healthy sex life."

"You would think that, wouldn't you?"

"What's that supposed to mean?"

"Well, it's clear you're obsessed with sex and all the sex you have. All your threesomes and warming lube and panda suits and whatever else you seem to get up to."

"You think I'm a slut, don't you?"

God, that is a horrible word.

"You think I am a giant man slut?" He paused as if he was genuinely asking the question and wanting a reply. "Just because I write about wax play doesn't mean I'm doing it."

"What the hell is wax pla—? *No*, actually, I don't want to know. I can imagine it, so thanks very much for putting that image into my mind. Not to mention the imagine of my mom and your . . . oh *god*, now the images have combined . . . stop!" I slapped the side of my head as my mom picked up the imaginary candle and dripped wax on Eddy's mystery piercings.

Jagger let out a full-blown laugh, and if I hadn't been seminude I might have flung the door open to deliver a really top-notch death stare.

"Why do you do that?" I asked.

"Do what?"

"Revel in being utterly contrary. You are the most contrary person I've ever met."

"I could say the same for you, Contrary Mary."

"Margaret!"

"I know, just living up to my contrary reputation."

"You're infuriating. Deliberately infuriating and constantly contrary!"

"I'm totally offended," Jagger joked, because he wasn't offended. Nothing seemed to offend Jagger. He seemed to go through life in a manner where nothing serious ever stuck to him. He was the duck and everything else was the water pouring off him.

I finished in the bathroom after about thirty minutes of drying my hair and clothes with the small hairdryer attached to the bathroom wall. They were still slightly damp when I emerged, but overall much better than they had been. I found Jagger sitting in the chair reading through the resort brochure.

"Now what?" he asked.

I shrugged. "I, um . . . I don't know where to go."

He looked at me and then at the bed.

"Well, I'm not sleeping in that bed with you, if that's what you think!"

"Where are you sleeping, then?"

I peered out the window. The rain was still coming down in sheets.

"Perhaps our parents are fin—" Jagger started.

"Stop!" I held my hand up. "And even if they are fin—" I shuddered at the thought and could barely get the word out "—ished, I'm not sleeping in that bed until it has been thoroughly disinfected and the sheets have been changed . . . twice."

"Seems like you're in somewhat of a predicament then. Where to sleep tonight, where to sleep." He said it with a smile.

I sighed and looked around the room.

"Is there something you want to ask me?" he teased me.

I shook my head.

"I didn't think so. The Margaret I know would rather stubbornly sleep out in the rain than share a room with me."

He walked over the door and opened it. The rain was coming down so hard that I was sure I was standing behind a waterfall, peering out through a water curtain. "I guess good night then."

I puffed my chest out and walked to the door. "Cool. Okay. Bye," I said, but didn't move.

"Careful not to get blown away," he said as a particularly forceful gust of wind splashed drops of water in our faces.

I stared at the rain, and then looked back into the dry, comfortable-looking bedroom and sighed again.

"Something you want to ask me?"

"Can I—" I took a deep breath. "May I . . . would it be okay if I . . . can I sleep in your room tonight, please!" I spat the last part out and Jagger laughed immediately.

"You sure you want to sleep in the same room as the guy who inspires you to build a Great Wall of China to avoid looking at him?"

"God, you are such an exaggerator! They are hardly great walls!"

"Small walls?"

"They are not walls!"

He laughed again and I walked back into the room and grabbed a pillow off the bed. "I'll sleep on the floor!" I declared and puffed the pillow between my hands.

"The floor is tiny," Jagger said, looking around.

"I'm not sleeping in that bed, with you!"

"I could build a wall in the middle of the bed." He said this with the kind of smug relish unique to Jagger.

"Stop talking about walls!"

"Why?" He was acting all innocent now. "You like walls. They're your thing."

"I would hardly call walls *my thing*." I put the pillow down on the thin sliver of floor next to the bed and lay down. God this was truly uncomfortable. I'd hate to think how much worse it would be if not for my extra padding. Jagger walked around the bed and looked down at me.

"Comfortable?"

"Very," I said, breathing out deeply as if I was feeling all Zen.

"Looks comfy. I'm sure that gecko also agrees."

"What geck— Oh!" I jumped as a gecko skidded across the floor. I'd forgotten about those. They were everywhere here. I jumped off the floor and grabbed my pillow. I didn't hate the geckos per se. From a distance they were really cute, but up close like this, on my pillow, not so much.

"I'll sleep in the bath." I walked into the bathroom and closed the door behind me. The bath was like ours, a small shower-bath combination. I dried the wet patch in the middle of it and then climbed in with my pillow.

Just imagine it as a soft bed, I repeated over and over in my head as I tried to wiggle into a comfortable position. And as soon as I *almost* had, a droplet of water dripped from the shower and landed on my leg. I sat up and looked at the showerhead. Another drop was clinging to the side of it. I closed both taps, turning as hard as I could. They moved a millimeter. I lay back down, satisfied that I'd stopped the leak, but when three more drops landed on my foot, I realized that this was one of those perpetually leaky showerheads and no amount of tap tightening was going to fix that. I walked out of the bathroom, clutching the pillow to my chest, and stopped dead when I saw what Jagger had done.

"The showerhead leaks." Jagger was lying on the bed next to a wall of backpacks and cushions he'd put down the middle of it.

"I noticed that." I stood at the foot of the bed and stared down at it. I was tired, my body hurt, and the bed did look soft and comfortable. I put my pillow on the bed and climbed on. I shuddered. There's nothing more intimate than sleeping next to someone. *Nothing*.

I rolled over into my usual sleeping position. I always slept on my side, one leg curled up, the other straight behind me. Sometimes I liked to put a pillow under my knee, especially since sleeping alone. Sometimes having a pillow there makes the bed feel less empty. Jagger must have also rolled, because the bed shook and the wall swayed. And then we lay there in total, awkward, cringe-inducing silence. The silence stretched and the awkwardness grew until it was all I could feel.

"So, you're divorced," Jagger suddenly said.

"Is that a question, or a statement?"

"Both. I guess."

"You want me to lie here and tell you about my divorce as if we're in some kind of confessional?"

"No, I just thought I would break the awkward silence with something totally out of left field."

I smiled. "It was out of left field. And yes, the silence was awkward."

"God, wasn't it!" Jagger replied.

"I've been divorced for just over a year now. But the marriage was over long before that." I paused when I thought of something Jagger had said to me once. "You were wrong. Not marriage material, I guess."

There was more silence, and I felt the claws of awkwardness grab hold of us again. As if awkward was a giant bird sitting on this wall between us and every time it wanted to make its presence known, it dug its claws in.

Jagger broke the silence once more. "I hated your ex-husband's book."

"What! How do you know who my ex-husband is?"

"I overheard people talking about it in the office. I may have googled him and bought his book."

I sat up and peered at Jagger over the wall. Men like him usually praised my husband's books. What had that one reviewer said? *Captures the essence of the thirtysomething-year-old man's psyche.*

"But you're the exact target market for it."

"Doesn't mean I can't hate it." Jagger propped himself up, too, bringing us face-to-face. "It was so fucking pretentious."

"God, wasn't it!" I almost squealed in delight. It wasn't beneath me to take any opportunity to dump on my ex-husband's book—his book about a man who hits thirty-five and realizes that he doesn't want to be married with kids and begins a sordid affair with every woman he can.

When he'd written it, I'd seen absolutely zero comparison to his life. He wasn't thirty-five, he didn't have kids, he wasn't an attorney—it was a work of fiction. But what do they say about life imitating art?

"What part did you hate?" I wasn't even trying to hide the childish glee in my voice.

"All of it."

"Okay, I'm going to need specifics here."

"I haven't seen you this excited since the infamous Pandora Papers were leaked and two South African politicians were named in them."

"How did you know I was excited?" I asked, taken aback that he'd noticed my delight at finding out that one of our ministers had been illegally squirreling millions offshore and had bought a penthouse in Dubai for his mistress. Journalism gold right there.

"You always get this twinkle in your eye, like a naughty pixie."

"A naughty pixie?"

"Mischievous elf?"

"Pixie or elf would be the last thing I would describe myself as, but do tell me what parts of the book you hated."

"Well, the writing was so self-indulgent."

"I thought so too!"

"I mean those long-winded inner monologues the character has on every page, as if the entire universe revolves them. What an ass!"

"Yes! Finally someone agrees with me." I was so thrilled by this, even if it was Jagger who was agreeing.

Jagger smiled, and I didn't even try to hold mine at bay. Our eyes locked, our smiles grew, and for the first time ever, I felt like Jagger and I were finally on the same page about something. Oddly, it happened to be a page in my ex-husband's awful book. I'd never held Jagger's gaze for this long, and far from feeling awkward, there was something familiar about the moment, even though we'd never shared anything like this before.

"Seems like we've found something else in common, then." His voice was a whisper.

"You know, you are one of the only people in the country who thinks that his writing is rubbish. Me, Leighton, and you. But I can't trust my best friend to be honest about things like that. He would literally hate chocolate if I had a run-in with it."

"I can guarantee you that other people feel the same way. They've just been told to like the book because of the review that Susanna Marshal gave him when it first came out. And no one dares argue with Susanna Marshal's opinion."

There was an edge to his voice that made me sit up. "Do you know her?"

"She taught me creative writing at UCT for nine months, before I dropped out because I couldn't stand it and her."

"Really?"

"We had a difference of creative opinions."

"What, she didn't like your writing about sex parties and wax play?"

He shook his head. "She didn't like my writing, full stop."

"So, you didn't study at the school of hard knocks, after all."

"Have you been reading my LinkedIn profile?" Jagger sounded way too pleased with himself, and I knew I needed to cut him down to size.

"Lesego told me that," I said as dismissively as possible.

"You and Lesego talk about me, do you?"

"Please!" I scoffed. "Do not let that inflate your ego even more. I guarantee we do not sit around discussing you." That was a lie. All I seemed to do these days was discuss Jagger. "If not hard knocks, then where and what did you study?"

Jagger's head popped over the wall again and he looked down at me. "Wait, are you asking me a question about myself? A question that sounds like you might be genuinely interested in something to do with me?"

"Not at all. I'm just making casual conversation." I met his steel-colored eyes. I guess one could call them attractive. Not that I was attracted to his eyes, but logically, unemotionally, I could appreciate their aesthetic qualities. Their cool, mirrorlike appearance, the way their paleness accentuated the darkness of the pupil, the way the edge of the iris looked as if it had been ringed with black liner.

"Good, because I wouldn't want us to break with convention."

"What convention?"

"You know, you hating me, me getting on your nerves, you rolling your eyes."

"I don't roll my eyes," I cut in, rolling my eyes, and then stopped. "Okay, I roll my eyes. But you do a lot of things that call for very justifiable eye rolls."

"And sighs," he said.

"I do not sigh!" I protested, and then almost sighed. "You tap your feet a lot. It makes the desk wobble," I shot back.

"When you disinfect your work surface, it also makes the desk wobble."

"When you work, you listen to music that I can hear through your AirPods. It's very distracting."

Jagger's face lit up like a firecracker. "Are you going to tell the teacher on me?"

"When I was in fourth grade there was this boy called Peter Clifton."
I paused after I said his name. I hadn't thought about Peter Clifton in
years, and I had no idea why I was thinking about him now.

"What about him?"

"He sat behind me in class and used to drive me insane. He flicked
my ponytail with his ruler when the teacher wasn't looking. Once, he put
a whoopee cushion on my chair. Another time he blew chewed-up bits
of wet toilet paper at my back through a straw. He pretended to sneeze
behind me nonstop. He basically made my life a living hell."

Jagger laughed. "He liked you. When you're in fourth grade, if you
like the girl, you drive her mad."

"He drove me crazy."

"And that's because you secretly liked him too."

"I don't think so," I said quickly, but with an uncomfortable feeling
growing inside me.

"It's obvious. You guys liked each other. That's why he did it, and
that's why it drove you so mad when he did."

"That's not the point of this story, Jagger," I replied, trying to steer
the conversation away from who liked who. "The point I'm trying to
make is that not since fourth grade has anyone driven me as crazy as you."

"So, what happened between you and Peter? Did you hook up?"

"We were in fourth grade!" I tried to deflect, starting to get uncomfortable with this conversation and the way in which Jagger seemed to
have seen something deeper in it.

"Later?" he asked.

"Fine, whatever. It was seventh grade, our first boy-girl party and we
kissed behind the school hall. But that's not the point of the story. The
point is—"

Jagger burst out laughing, and I leaned over and slapped him on the
shoulder.

"Stop it! What I'm trying to say is that—"

"You want to kiss me behind the school hall?"

"No! Oh my god, how on earth did you get that out of the story?"

Jagger flopped down on the bed. "How was the kiss?"

I followed his lead and flopped down too. "Terrible."

"My first kiss was horrendous. I bit her tongue."

"Seriously?"

"It was a reflex. She put it in my mouth, and I just bit it."

I burst out laughing. "Did she ever kiss you again?"

"No! Did you ever kiss Peter Clifton again?" he asked.

"No," I said. We both kept silent for a while. I was thinking about Peter and how when we'd gotten older, despite how crazy he'd driven me, I'd started to think how hot he was and how he reminded me of Justin Timberlake.

"Cute story," Jagger said on a long yawn, which set me off to yawning too.

"Do you know why you yawn if someone else does?" Jagger asked.

"No. I actually don't."

"Social mirroring. It's more common in people who are friends or family."

I laughed. "Maybe I'm just also tired."

"Maybe," Jagger said, and then I felt the bed move, as if he'd turned around. I hoped he had his back to me. "Or maybe despite your best efforts, we're becoming friends."

"You wish!" I said.

"Maybe I do," he said in a strange soft tone that made me creep closer to the wall, and right there between the backpacks was a little gap. I stuck my eye to it and . . .

"Fuck!" I jumped back when I saw Jagger's face. "Sorry, I was . . ."

"Spying on me!"

"No! I was just . . . checking." I flushed with heat. I was spying, but not for any other reason than checking to see what direction he was facing.

"It's okay—you can admit it if you were spying."

"I wasn't."

"It's all right. I'm flattered."

"Seriously, don't be."

Jagger gave one of those signature chuckles of his. The kind that told me he was amused and that his ego had just been stroked. I sat up and looked down at him over the wall.

"Would it be okay if we turn off the lights, or does baby need a night-light?" I mocked his childhood fear of the dark.

"We can turn off the lights as long as you don't wet the bed."

"Oh my god!" I scowled and flopped down on my back.

"Don't dish it out if you can't take it, Margaret-Skye."

"I know I don't have to tell you *not* to call me Margaret-Skye."

He gave yet another throaty chuckle. "Good night, Margaret."

"You're chuckling too much," I said quickly.

"I can't help it—you're funny."

I *hmph*ed in response and the light flicked off. I turned over, mumbling a quiet good night, and looked at the window. There was a gap in the curtains and the rain was softer now, the droplets slipping down the window in a less frantic manner. I watched them. They were relaxing, hypnotic even, and soon—despite the fact Jagger was sleeping next to me—my eyes began to get heavy.

Chapter **Twenty-four**

When I woke up, for a terrifying moment I forgot where I was. That was until a shirtless Jagger walked out of the bathroom, brushing his teeth.

"Morning." The word came out through the foamy toothpaste.

"What are you doing?" I pulled the blankets over me, feeling very exposed.

"Brushing my teeth." I watched him dig in his bag and pull out a crumpled shirt.

"Don't people usually brush their teeth in the bathroom?"

"I'm a multitasker." Jagger turned and walked back into the bathroom.

For a second I allowed myself to look at his naked torso. I'd seen it yesterday, but I'd tried not to look at it then. I had to admit, it was not what I'd expected. There were no tattoos, no wayward piercings or other signs of body modification or wax scars. In fact, it was all very smooth and squeaky clean and contoured, apart from that one silly tattoo on his arm. I had an urge to report this back to Lesego immediately. If his top half wasn't pierced, the bottom half probably wasn't either. His father on the other hand . . .

"Noooo!" I cringed and put the pillow over my head. Why had that thought just popped into my head? My mom and Eddy were probably waking up together now. There was sure to be giggling and chatting and maybe even some morning sex. I buried my face farther into my pillow and let out a dramatic moan.

"What's wrong?"

"Our parents are having sex," I mumbled into my pillow.

"It would seem so."

"Doesn't it freak you out?"

"Not really."

"Is there something wrong with me that it's freaking me out? Am I supposed to be so evolved and mature that I'm totally okay with my mom having sex in our once shared bed?"

"It's okay to feel anything you want to feel."

"I usually see my therapist on a Tuesday, but thanks so much for that."

"You see a therapist?"

"There's nothing wrong with it." I sat up defensively.

"I didn't say there was. I saw one for many years, after my almost divorce."

"What . . . you're divorced?"

"Almost divorced."

"What does that mean?"

"I was engaged—she broke it off. They don't have a word for that, but I think they should."

"Why didn't you tell me?"

"You never asked."

"We spoke about my ex and my divorce—you didn't think you could have slipped in a 'well, I'm almost divorced too'?"

Jagger shrugged.

"When did you get almost divorced?"

"It's been five years now."

"What happened?"

"She wanted kids. I didn't," Jagger said, dropping a fairly large bomb. "She always thought I would change my mind. I didn't."

"I don't want kids either," I heard myself say, even though I really hadn't meant to share something so personal with him, something that had caused a lot of judgment as I'd gotten older and more resolute in my decision that I didn't want to breed. When I told people this, usually women, they would all get that same look in their eyes. It was this kind of knowing, patronizing look, which was often followed by something like an arm touch, or a sympathetic tone delivering a variation of the same line: "Don't worry, you'll change your mind one day." As if not wanting to have children was some kind of affliction that if I knew better, I would get over at some stage.

"Was that a problem in your marriage?" he asked.

I shook my head. "No. Matthew was the problem in our marriage. Although he would probably say the same about me."

"Dr. Phil always says, 'No matter how flat you make a pancake, there are always two sides,'" Jagger said, and I shot out of bed.

"Wait, you watch Dr. Phil?"

Jagger nodded.

"Oh my god, you watch Dr. Phil! I thought I was the only one I knew."

"I totally disagree with people who say he's just Jerry Springer in a better suit!" Jagger added.

"Me too . . . Phil's suits are horrible!" I flopped down on the bed feeling this strange sense of familiarity and comfort with Jagger yet again. It still caught me off guard.

"So, Dr. Phil, the Potterverse, good at general knowledge, and a short-lived penchant for punk rock and black eyeliner . . . I wonder what other similarities we'll find," Jagger mused.

"Well, there is the fact that our parents are having sex."

"There's that too. How about breakfast?" Jagger asked, and I didn't even need to think about it.

"Oh my god, I'm soooooo hungry," my mother said, plowing into a plate of pastries. We'd spotted them when we'd walked into the breakfast area.

"Must be from all that exercise you got last night," Eddy said, and they both burst out laughing in this way that made the food in my stomach churn uncomfortably.

"Can we please not discuss this over breakfast?" I asked.

"Sorry." My mother smiled at me and then looked back at Eddy. "Margaret-Skye has always been uncomfortable talking about sex."

"No, I just don't want to talk about it with you while I'm trying to digest my fruit platter."

"Definitely some blockages in her root chakra."

"Mom!" I raised my voice and someone at the table next to us turned. I lowered my voice. "Can we also stop talking about my root chakra, please? This is hardly appropriate breakfast conversation, and certainly not in front of strangers."

"Strangers?" Eddy piped up, looking genuinely confused.

"Well, I mean, people we don't know well, not that I would like her to discuss my sex life with someone I know well, but . . ."

"Kiki and I know each other better than most people know each other, and didn't you and Jagger share a bed last night?"

"Okay, that's it!" I stood up and grabbed my toast. "I'm going to eat this by the pool. I prefer my toast served without a side of sex talk." I started walking away but stopped when I heard my mom.

"She really needs to let loose, you know. She's a bit closed, needs to open up."

I swung around. "I am loose and open, Kiki! Trust me. So loose and so, so open." I definitely said that too loudly, because a few people put their cutlery down and stared. I eyed Jagger. He had a crooked little smirk etched across his lips.

"What?" I asked.

"Nothing. Just admiring how loose and open you are," he said.

I turned and walked belligerently out of the restaurant in search of peace and sex-free quiet. But that was hard to get, because a few hours later it was clear that my mother had turned into an infatuated teenager.

We were sitting poolside while Eddy swam and Jagger sat by the bar with his laptop.

"Isn't he marvelous?" She waved at Eddy, and he waved back. Her cheeks flushed pink. It was a very familiar color. I had seen it many times before on various women in the office. What was with these Villain men and their ability to make woman turn pink? Villain pink. Maybe that should be an actual color. Maybe Pantone could make it their color of the year. If they did, I would not buy it.

"Mom, seriously, what are you doing?"

"What do you mean?"

"Mom, you're having sex with him. You hardly know him. I mean, I know you're all free and lived in a bloody hippie colony or whatever, but that was in the sixties. It's 2023—you can't just have sex with strange men!"

"He's not strange to me."

"You have known him for forty-eight hours!"

"It feels like I've known him a lifetime."

I shook my head. "Sex releases all kinds of feel-good hormones. They facilitate the bonding experience. It's a very primal, chemical reaction. That's what it is: you're on a dopamine high right now, but when you come down from it, you'll see."

"Maybe I don't want to come down from it." She tilted her head and stared at me over her sunglasses. "Maybe I'm having fun and enjoying myself."

"What if the fun ends badly and you get hurt?"

"Then the fun ends and I get hurt. That's part of life, darling. You can't protect yourself from hurt all the time. Sometimes you have to go with the flow and see where the river takes you." She raised her glasses again and I knew there was no reasoning with her. When my mom got an idea into her head, that was it. My ribs constricted as I thought about my dad and what he'd be thinking.

"Well, I hope you're not planning on getting to know him better tonight as well, because I would like to sleep in my bed again, and not next to Jagger!"

"I believe you built a wall in the middle of the bed." She chuckled.

"Jagger did that, and how do you know about the wall?"

"Eddy went back to his room later but he said he found you two fast asleep, so he came back. I take it nothing happened with you and Jagger, then?"

"*What?* No, Mom. Absolutely nothing happened. *Nothing.* Unlike you, I don't come to tropical islands and roll into bed with strange men that I do not know."

My mom pulled her glasses down again and glared at me over them. "If I didn't know you better, I would say you were slut-shaming me."

I sighed. "It's not about the sex. Well, it is, to a degree, but it's also not."

"You just don't approve of who I'm having sex with."

"No, Mom, I don't. I mean of all the people in the world to have sex with, you chose Jagger Villain's dad! Jagger Villain! The man I reluctantly share a desk with at work and who drives me to drink, literally. I don't mean that in a figurative way—I mean it in an actual *Jagger made me so mad one night that I drank too many pink cocktails* kind of way."

"To be honest, darling, I don't think it's got anything to do with you who I decide to sleep with."

"It does when you choose to do it in our shared bed."

She pursed her lips together for a moment and then unpursed them. "Okay, I can't argue with that point, but where else should we have done it—in those hammocks?" She pointed at them, but I was already all too well acquainted with them to need to look. "You know I've always told you that women living in bigger bodies, like us, can do everything that people in smaller bodies can, but . . ." Her face flushed, and it wasn't from the sun. "I'm not sure that extends to having hammock sex."

"Wow, this conversation deteriorated rather quickly." I held my watch up to my face. "It's only ten o clock in the morning and we're already talking about having sex in a hammock."

"Who's having sex in a hammock?" Eddy came up behind us and my mom let out a loud belly laugh.

"Not me, that's for sure." I got up and walked off as Eddy ogled my mom in a way that I'd rather not witness. I walked over to Jagger and his laptop.

"What are you doing?" I asked.

"Some research for my Zanzibar piece."

"Oh right." Jennifer had agreed to let us go for an extended holiday on condition we both came back with a piece on Zanzibar. "What are you writing about?"

"I was thinking of going into Stone Town today and visiting the Freddie Mercury museum and then going to Mercury's Bar this evening. Queen songs in the background, live music, cocktails."

"He was born here. I forgot."

"Farrokh Bulsara. I thought it would make a cool piece. Review the restaurant, add some interesting facts in about his early life here. A feel-good piece about him in general, that kind of thing. What are you writing?"

"Well, it's *not* going to be a feel-good piece."

"I wouldn't expect anything less from you," Jagger said.

"What's that supposed to mean?"

"Margaret-Skye, hard-hitting, award-winning journalist. What's it about?"

"The forgotten and largely undocumented story of the intra-African slave trade. Did you know that before the transatlantic slave trade,

Zanzibarian people were being traded in South Africa as slaves? They have a tour here in Stone Town that you can do."

"Oh wow!" Jagger said.

"*Ja*, I know, not your thing."

"I wasn't going to say that. I was going to say that I had no idea there was an intra-African slave trade."

"Most people don't. When you think about slave trade, you think about shipping slaves off to America, Britain, and Arabia."

Jagger closed his laptop and looked at me earnestly. "When are you going into Stone Town to do the tour?"

"Tomorrow. I already organized it."

"I would love to come with you."

"You would?"

"Yes. I would."

"Oh. I didn't really think you'd be interested in something like that."

"Something like what?"

"I don't know. I suppose something other than sex toys, swingers' parties, and swiping right."

"Did you do that alliteration on purpose?" Jagger smiled.

"I think it has a certain ring to it."

"A snappy, snarky, sarcastic one. More alliteration." Jagger put his elbows on the table, leaned his chin into them, and looked up at me. "I actually *would* be interested in coming on that tour with you. I'll be your research partner. Question is, would you be interested in being my research partner?"

"I actually like Queen."

"Really?"

"My dad used to play them a lot."

A look flashed across Jagger's face suddenly and I got immediately suspicious. A sneakiness had crept into his gray eyes.

"What?"

"I just had a thought. Well, it's more of a challenge, really, and I know how much you like challenges, being as competitive as you are."

My ears pricked up. "And what is it?"

"How about this: you write my article and I'll write yours. Let me prove to you that I'm not just a shallow 'sex toy, swingers' parties, and swiping right' kind of guy."

"Let you write my article on the atrocities of slavery?"

"Don't you think I can do it?"

"Honestly? No, I don't."

Jagger stood up. He towered over me, looking down his nose with an undeniable determination. "I think you're just scared you can't write my article. You can't let go and have some fun and write a funny, feel-good piece. Despite your claims to be loose and . . . *what was it again?*"

"Open. Loose and open." I folded my arms defiantly and stepped closer to Jagger. Our bodies touched, although I hadn't meant that to be the case.

"What do you say?" he asked.

"You are more insane than I thought if you think I'm going to let you write my article and then submit it."

"Tell you what—we'll both write our own articles and each other's, then we'll send them off to Jennifer and see which ones she thinks are best."

"Really?"

"And we won't put our names on them. A neutral judge."

I thought about this. I was still stinging from the quiz night *almost* defeat and, honestly, I'd love a chance to get even with him. "Fine. Challenge on! I'll show you how bloody funny and feel-good I can be. I can be sooo funny and feel-good—you have no idea."

"Believe it or not, I actually do find you very funny."

"Sure, in a mocking way."

"Not at all. I think you're genuinely one of the funniest people I've ever met."

I inspected Jagger's face. No smirks curled the corners of his lips; no amusement twinkled in his gray eyes. He seemed serious. "Oh." I didn't know whether I should take that as a compliment or as something else entirely.

"So . . . leave at four?" Jagger asked, still gazing down at me from his lofty position. Our bodies were still touching, although I'm sure we should have moved away from each other by now.

"You're too tall," I said, and Jagger burst out laughing.

"I've never had a woman tell me I was too tall before."

"Well, I'm not like other women."

Jagger moved back, opening the space between us while he locked eyes with me. "Oh, I'm well aware of that."

"What's that supposed to mean?"

"Just what I said. You're not like any woman I have ever met before, Miss May."

I *tsk*ed at his ongoing deliberate misuse of my name, which had apparently turned into some kind of sport for him. But at least it wasn't Maggie May.

"Shall we leave at four, then?" he inquired again.

I glanced down at my watch. "Sure."

"What are you going to do now?" he asked, probably also calculating that there were six hours until four o'clock.

"Go to the beach."

"Cool." Jagger sat back down at his laptop again.

"Why? What are you going to do?"

"A little more research, and then I'll also head to the beach. See ya later, then."

I didn't like the way he'd said *See ya later*. It implied an easy familiarity between us that was almost friend-like. *See ya later* was what you said to your friend when you hung up after making dinner arrangements. I didn't want a *See ya later*.

"Well, I might not be on the beach the whole day. I might change my mind and go somewhere else. It's not like I can spend six hours on the beach anyway, what with my pale skin. Too much sun . . ."

Jagger looked up from his computer and smiled again. "Seriously, one of the funniest people I've ever met!"

I scrunched my face and walked away.

"By the way . . ." he called from behind me, and I turned. "How did my other challenge go?" His eyes twinkled like the devil's might do upon concocting some evil plan.

"None of your business, actually!" I pulled my bag in front of me to obscure that general area.

"Ahhh, so you tried it."

I blushed. "I did not, and even if I did, I would not tell you."

I turned and started walking away again.

"You totally did!" Jagger called after me again. "And you loved it! Admit it. I was right."

I flicked a hand at him and continued to scurry away with Jagger laughing behind me.

Turns out I did spend all day swimming in the divinely warm water, then lying in the dappled sun under a palm tree and reading a book. I then repeated this perfect activity over and over. At one stage I simply floated on my back in the sea, my body swaying gently in the tide. I watched a flock of birds fly above me. Every now and then one would swoop down to skim the water.

I took another slow stroll up and down the beach, collecting small purple shells on the way and wrapping them up in a sarong. I made it back to Jagger's room at two thirty—plenty of time to shower and head to Stone Town. And when I got there, he was sitting cross-legged on the bed with his laptop still open in front him.

"What kink is it this time?" I asked as I walked into the bathroom.

"Why assume that I'm researching kinks?"

I looked at myself in the bathroom mirror. My blond hair was even more curly. I ran a hand through it to shake out the flecks of sand. Freckles had sprung up across my cheeks and nose, and my face was flushed a vibrant pink color from the exercise and sun.

"Aren't you?" I asked.

"You look like you had a good day."

"Shit!" I turned in fright, surprised that Jagger's voice was so close and found him leaning on the door frame.

"How do you know I wasn't getting undressed?"

"If you were getting undressed you would have locked the door and checked underneath it!"

"Still, you can't sneak up on people like that!"

"I didn't sneak. You were just too busy looking at yourself in the mirror to notice me."

I shot Jagger a quick disapproving eye roll.

"Katoptronophilia," he said. "The kink."

"What's that?"

"The fetish of watching yourself in the mirror."

"Ha, ha!"

"I don't blame you—you look good. Relaxed."

"I feel relaxed," I said, brushing some sand off the tip of my nose.

"It suits you."

"Honestly, I haven't felt this relaxed in . . ." I paused. Truthfully, I couldn't remember the last time I'd felt like this. Certainly not in the last few years. "I can't even remember," I said.

"Hopefully, we'll continue that when we end the day with icy cocktails at Mercury's."

I had to admit, that sounded nice. I stepped on something. I looked down to see Jagger's twisted T-shirt on the floor. What thirty-plus-year-old man drops his T-shirt on the floor? That was just the height of sloppy laziness. Thank god I wasn't sharing the room with him again and, before leaving for Stone Town, I gathered all my things together and walked them over to *my* room. I looked at the bed; the sheets had been changed—this was evident by the presence of one of those handmade swan towels that graced the foot of the bed, although it looked more like a baby dragon than a graceful swan. I grabbed a pen and paper from the desk and left my mom a little reminder note.

Sex in our bed . . . cul-de-sac of NO!

Mercury's Bar was situated right on the beach and, upon entering, you were whisked away by a lively patchwork of color, patterns, and textures, which seemed to sum up perfectly the life that was being celebrated here. A life that I'd gotten better insight into during our walk around the museum, situated in Farrokh Bulsara's first home.

Each chair and tablecloth were made of different color materials, each wall a different texture, and the ceiling was a checkerboard of patterned tiles.

"Wow!" I said as I walked through the rainbow-colored restaurant and onto the veranda. It overlooked the beach, which was scattered with traditional wooden dhow fishing boats. The sea, too, was full of them, anchored in the shallow waters and swaying from side to side. Farther out, beyond the boats, cargo ships piled high with crates also bobbed in the water. The sea here was busy, not empty and quiet like at our resort.

"Let's sit here." Jagger surprised me by pulling out a chair.

"I can't remember the last time a man pulled a chair out for me."

"I don't do it very often." Jagger lowered himself into the one opposite me.

"Not even for all those many Tinder dates?"

"Nope. Not even for them."

"Mmmm . . ." I hummed thoughtfully. "I could argue, though, that chair pulling is an outdated, fundamentally sexist act that holds no place in our modern society, especially since women have spent decades fighting for gender equality and, as such, can pull out our own chairs, thank you very much!"

A slow smile snuck across Jagger's lips and his eyes sought mine out in a long languid movement. "I agree wholeheartedly," he said.

"You do?"

"You are *more* than capable of pulling out your own chair."

"If you agree, then why did you do it?"

Jagger leaned back and put his hands behind his head. Typical Jagger. "Maybe I just wanted to hear you say something like that."

"Ahh. Back to purposefully goading me, are you?"

"It's just too much fun."

"You know who you are? You're that kid who keeps asking 'Are we there yet?' on a twelve-hour flight, which drives his parents to literal insanity and excessive alcohol consumption."

Jagger laughed and, before I could stop it, I heard a soft laugh escape my lips. The atmosphere between Jagger and me had been different all afternoon; there was a certain ease to our interactions that had started at the museum. A server came over with menus and we ordered drinks immediately. It was swelteringly hot, even though the sun was about to go down, and the resort had warned all the holidaymakers about an upcoming heatwave. My Coke arrived moments later in a tall glass bottle, and Jagger's unfamiliar-looking beer was also served.

"'Leopard Safari Premium Lager,'" he read from the label. He held it out and we clinked bottles, before he raised it to his lips and took a long, contemplative sip.

"And?" I asked.

"Well, if you're going to be writing the article, don't you think you should also be sampling the local beers?"

Jagger held the bottle out for me, and I raised my brows.

"Sorry." He pulled it away and then, with great precision and effort, wiped the rim of the bottle with a serviette. "Better?" He passed it back to me.

"Vaguely." I raised the bottle to my lips. "I'm not a big beer drinker. Never really liked the flavor."

"Then you might not like this one—very malty."

I took a sip and swirled it around in my mouth.

"And?" he asked.

"Mmmm, very, uh, earthy," I offered, and passed it back, grimacing as I did. "Some soil on the palate there."

Jagger took another sip. "A very robust, yeasty body."

"A brawny bitter bouquet," I added.

"With a heady herbaceous mouthfeel."

We laughed and, when we finished, I found myself smiling at him, looking into those cement-colored eyes of his and then before I could stop myself . . .

"You know your eyes are *actually* gray. I've never seen anyone with gray eyes before."

"And your eyes are actually a mixture of blue and green. At first I thought they were blue, but when you look closely, you have a line of green around the pupil. They're very . . . well"—he paused and took another quick sip—"you have very nice eyes."

"Wow, two compliments in one day! First, I look good and relaxed and now I have nice eyes," I joked, and took another sip of my refreshing Coke.

"I compliment you all the time but you never seem to take them as such."

"Not true! When did you compliment me?"

"Last week I told you I liked your new haircut."

"No, you didn't. You said, 'Hey, Maggie May, nice hairdo.' It was sarcastic. Not complimentary."

"I actually meant it. And a month ago I told you I liked your new lipstick. The one Lesego gave you to try as a tester. The one you hated because you thought it made you look like your oxygen saturation was low."

"Uh, you didn't say you liked it—you said it made me look like I'd been eating blueberries."

"I love blueberries. I bring them to work every day to snack on."

I watched Jagger over the rim of my Coke. "You have a seriously strange way of doling out compliments."

"Maybe you have a strange way of taking them," he countered, and then gestured to the sea. "Sun's going down."

We turned our attention to the water. The sun was beginning to dip and the orange light show was not disappointing. The sunsets here were dramatic; the sun could never just go down—it had to depart in flames, painting everything in reds and golds. We sat in silence and watched. As the light drained from the sky, the ones on the ships in the distance began flickering on, casting splashes of light on the water like fallen stars.

"I never want to leave here," Jagger said softly, gazing across the water, his eyes reflecting the dusky colors.

"Me too. Hey, I love this song." I perked up as "We Are the Champions" started playing in the background. "My dad and I used to listen to this all the time. He . . . he . . ." I swallowed hard at the thought and put my Coke back down because my hand had started to shake.

"He what?"

"Used to call me his little champion." I clasped the bottle between my hands and squeezed it, trying to force away the feeling that accompanied this thought.

"What was he like? Your dad?"

"He was . . . amazing." I turned back to the orange sea. "He was the kindest person you ever met. That's what everyone said at his funeral, how kind he was. How he never had a bad word to say to, or about, anyone.

And so patient." I smiled. "You need to be if you live with my mom, I guess. He used to come to every single one of my school events, even that ill-fated time I played in my one and only netball match because most of the team came down with a stomach bug and the coach needed someone to stand in. She told everyone *not* to pass the ball to me and told me to stand still. And I did. I didn't touch the ball once, but my dad was still there, cheering me on."

"That's sweet," Jagger said.

"It was. He was. He wasn't the fanciest, or the funniest, or the best looking, or the most successful—he was just himself, you know? Nothing more, nothing less. And he gave me the best life he could. He really loved me. And I felt loved every single day." I sighed and reached across the table for Jagger's beer. I raised it to my lips and took another sip.

"Nah, still not sold on this." I shook my head and passed it back to Jagger.

"If you don't mind me asking, how did he pass?" Jagger's voice had become soft and low, warm even.

"Cancer. Brain," I said, and looked back out at the sunset. The warm, vibrant colors stood in stark contrast to the colors that had been present at his death. Bright-white fluorescent lights that drained their surroundings of any saturation. Washed everything out. Cold, white walls, sickly-green bedsheets. A hospital has got to be one of the worst places in the world to die, surrounded by machines and beeping sounds and the smell of disinfectant permeating your lungs.

"He died in the hospital," I heard myself saying, even though it hadn't been my intention to open up to Jagger. But there was something about us being here, being so far away from our everyday lives that made me feel like I could share. "If I'd known he was going to die that day in the hospital, I would never have called the ambulance." My eyes and throat burned at the thought. "I would have picked him up off the floor, put him in his favorite sunny chair facing the garden and the birds he loved to feed. I would have thrown seed onto the lawn, like he always did, and let him die there in the chair watching that cheeky pin-tailed whydah chase off all the other birds like it always did." I smiled at a memory. "He used to scold it affectionately, as if it understood English. 'Bugger off, you bloody nuisance!' He didn't mean that, of course. Actually, I think he liked that bird best of all. I think he admired its pluck and audacity." I reached up and wiped a tear from my cheek and then pulled my eyes away from the colors and looked at Jagger. He was watching me as if his life depended on it. His gray eyes, far from being the usual striking cool color, were warm, and they urged me to continue.

"The day he died, the doctor came out of ICU and told me that it was time to say good-bye to him." My jaw clenched. "How the hell do you say good-bye to someone after an entire lifetime together? How do you sum up the entirety of an existence together, in just a few words, delivered bedside in the cold, sterile environment of a hospital?"

"What did you say to him?"

"Not enough. Not nearly enough. I regret not saying more. I regret not telling him how wonderful and special he was. What an amazing human and father he'd been. How he'd filled my life and my mother's life with so much joy and laugher. I could have said so much more, but seeing him like that, this shadow of a man . . . sickly gray skin, dents in his cheeks and under his eyes, barely conscious . . . all I said was, 'I love you.' I should have said more."

Jagger reached for my hand. I looked down as his covered mine. This was the first time that Jagger had done this, the first time I'd ever felt his skin on mine in an intentional way. I didn't pull away. Instead I laced my fingers through his and gripped them.

"What you said was perfect." Jagger ran a thumb over the top of my hand. "What you said is the most important thing anyone can say to someone else."

I nodded but bit my lip. "You know what he said to me? 'I wish I'd had more time.' *Time.* That was it. The last thing he said. And then he just closed his eyes and drifted away."

"Did your mom get to say good-bye to him?"

I shook my head. "She was at a friend's house when I rushed him to the hospital. Her friend raced her there, but she arrived ten minutes too late. She said she could feel him go, though, as she was driving there. She already knew when she arrived at the hospital."

We sat in silence for a while. I stared down at Jagger's hand, his thumb still rubbing back and forth over the top of mine. I couldn't remember the last time someone had held my hand like that. It felt good. "I have so many regrets that I didn't say more."

"You can still say more," Jagger said.

"That's what my mom says. But it would feel weird just saying stuff now, hoping that somehow he hears me."

Jagger's face was filled with sympathy, and I'd never felt closer to him than in that moment.

"And you? Do you remember your mom?"

Jagger shook his head and then also looked over to the sea, as if it could offer some solace to the feelings that were welling up in both of us. "I wish I did, but I don't. Sometimes, if I close my eyes and concentrate really hard . . ." He closed his eyes as if he was doing it right there and then. I leaned closer. This was such an intimate moment, and I felt drawn in by it. "I think I can hear her singing. She was a singer, that's how she and my dad met. But I'm not sure if it's real or if it's just something I've made up over the years."

My heart broke for Jagger. A small, four-year-old boy without a mom and, unlike me, without even a single memory of her. I had memories of my dad that would last a lifetime, that I could pull out and sift through when I needed to, but Jagger had nothing.

"I have a framed photo of us in my room. We're in the pool and she's throwing me up in the air and catching me. I don't know how old I was, but I was laughing and so was she. It looked like we were having a lot of fun."

"Sounds like it," I said, and then I was the one running my thumb over the top of his hand. His hand was big in mine. His fingers were long and felt smooth and soft.

"If you don't mind me asking, what happened to her?"

"Car accident. Very sudden and unexpected."

"Fuck, Jagger. That's . . . I'm so sorry. My mom believes that those who cross over are always with us," I said.

"Do you believe that?"

"I mean"—I shrugged—"I don't know. I'd like to think they are, but . . ."

Jagger finished my thoughts: "You're a woman of science and facts," and I looked at him again. Every now and then he came out with some insight into me that was so accurate. These astute observations also caught me off guard.

"But I guess talking about my dad and my favorite song playing at the exact right time at a restaurant halfway around the world, so . . . who knows? My mom would definitely take that as some cosmic sign."

"Apparently, my mom's favorite color was orange." We both cast our eyes over the sea again, watching as the last of the golden orb finally disappeared. Jagger finally pulled his hand from mine and held his bottle up again. "To potential cosmic signs and Freddie Mercury." He smiled at me. It was one of those forced smiles, the kind you make when you're trying to put on a brave face but underneath you're crumbling. I could relate to that smile. I had used it often. Another thing Jagger and I had in common, it would seem.

I clinked my bottle with his, and then we both raised them to our lips and sipped at the same time, holding eye contact with each other. I pulled my eyes away from Jagger's and ran them over the features of his face. He looked different. I don't know whether I was seeing him differently or if it was the play of the orange light on his face, but his features seemed softer somehow. Diffused. There wasn't that sharp edge to him anymore, and I had a desire to reach out and put my hand on his cheek to see what it would feel like. But I didn't.

Chapter **Twenty-five**

Jagger and I got back in a rather jovial mood that night, despite our conversation. This was possibly helped by the local drink we'd been talked into sampling—for research purposes, of course—a mysterious spirit called Konyagi. A quick Google search yielded very little information, and certainly no indication of what it was made from, and of course when I'd asked, I was told it contained "the tears of a lion," but was assured it was perfectly safe—even though upon further Google searching, I discovered it was barely legal outside of East Africa. A thought that was not comforting since I'd already drunk it. One of the waiters had shown us the ritual involved in opening the bottle. Legend has it that before you open the bottle, you're meant to smack the bottom a few times to release the spirit inside.

We'd only had one each, but the warm, buzzy effect lasted for a while afterward and all the way back to our resort. We gave each other a friendly wave at the fork in the path and walked off in opposite directions. But when I got to my room, I paused. I hadn't heard anything, and nothing seemed out of the ordinary, except for that nervous, sick feeling that niggled in my belly.

"Nooo, she wouldn't," I whispered, while bringing my knuckles down to the door.

"Come in," my mom called, sounding as innocent as anything. I walked in and was greeted by a sight that took me a few silent moments to digest.

"Uh . . . Eddy, Mom." They were sitting on the bed, sipping champagne, and watching a movie together.

"Hello, darling, how was your evening?" she asked casually, as if it was nothing that she and Eddy were sharing alcoholic beverages on our bed.

"Fine. How was your evening?" I looked at the bed for telltale signs of sex: clothes on the floor, the tangled disarray of unbridled lust. There weren't any.

"We didn't have sex on the bed, if that's what you're thinking." My mom took a long slow sip of her champagne, mischievousness flashing in her eyes. I looked around the room and noticed the desk and chair had been moved.

"No! God, no, Mom!" I flung my hands over my face and slumped against the door frame.

"You said the bed was in the cul-de-sac of no," she protested. "Not the entire room and bathroom."

"Not the bathroom too!"

"The bathroom wasn't in the cul-de-sac either."

I shook my head in utter disbelief.

"Eddy was about to leave anyway, we were just watching a movie until you got back."

I looked around the room again, the door to the bathroom was ajar and so were the bathroom cupboards.

"Nope! I can't. You guys stay here, and I'll go find another room. I'm sure there's something available. I saw people checking out this morning, so . . ."

I paused, waiting for my mom to jump in and protest. *No, darling, we can't kick you out of your room*, etc., etc. She did not. Instead, she jumped up and hugged me and thanked me for being so "understanding."

"But I saw people checking out this morning," I said in a pleading voice to the receptionist who'd told me there were still no empty rooms.

"The one room has been occupied by new guests and the other rooms are having maintenance done on them."

"What maintenance? I can live in a room having maintenance," I gushed enthusiastically.

"I'm sorry, that's against hotel policy." I could hear she was getting weary of this conversation.

"And you're sure you have nothing else? Absolutely sure?"

She shook her head. "I'm afraid not." She gave me an apologetic smile, and I headed out again. I was officially homeless, and my horny mother had been the one to render me this way. I walked past the hammocks on the beach, past the loungers by the pool, and then did another walk past them all. And by the end of it, I was dripping with sweat. The hotel had put up a sign warning all guests of the impending heatwave, and I could feel it tonight. There was no way I was going to be able to sleep outside. I needed the AC. And I needed the weather gods to stop punishing me with their weird weather revenge. I sighed, slow, depressed, and resigned, when I realized that I was left with only one option.

"Miss Margaret May." The door opened slowly, and Jagger leaned against the frame. "And what brings you to my room in the middle of the night?"

I rolled my eyes. "Don't get too excited. I need a place to sleep—again."

"Our parents . . . ?"

"Do you have to ask?" I walked past Jagger and into the room, where

I plonked myself on the bed. "They're having champagne and a movie night."

"That sounds like a great idea. What are they watching?" Jagger reached for the TV remote. I shrugged. I had no idea what they were watching and, frankly, I didn't really care. I wanted sleep. I'd spent the day in the sun, and the evening had been spent sipping beers and drinking strange alcoholic beverages that, for all I knew, were snake wines.

"Look, *Pretty Woman*." Jagger pointed as an image of a young Richard Gere filled the screen.

Pretty Woman and champagne in bed. What a romantic cliché.

"When did you watch this last?" Jagger asked.

"Can't remember," I admitted, and pulled myself to the top of the bed, resting my back against the headboard and stretching my legs out in front of me. "This is Leighton's favorite movie of all time." I reached for my phone, took a photo of the screen, and sent it to him. A message came back instantly, and I burst out laughing when I saw it.

"What?" Jagger asked.

I held my phone up for him to see: Leighton was also watching *Pretty Woman*, and Jagger laughed as Leighton sent another message through.

Leighton: Big mistake. BIG. Huge. I have to go shopping now!

Leighton: You know I partied with Richard Gere and Cindy Crawford at Prince's house in L.A.

Margaret: Of course you did

Leighton: Richard Gere is even better looking in real life if you can imagine that. Speaking of good looking, how's our favorite Villain?

Margaret: I don't know a good-looking Villain

Leighton: He's hot. You just won't admit it

Margaret: He's okay. He's also right next to me, so I would rather stop talking about how hot he is

Leighton: Ahhh, so you do think he's hot

Margaret: 😳

Leighton: Are you guys watching *Pretty Woman* together? 😂 😂

Margaret: Absolutely not!

Leighton: Wait … this is interesting

Margaret: What is?

Leighton: You and Jagger are kind of like Edward and Vivian

I scoffed out loud and quickly typed a response as Jagger looked over at me. I tilted my phone away from him.

Margaret: NO WE ARE NOT

Leighton: Sure you are. Polar opposites

Margaret: Am I the sex worker in this scenario?

Leighton: No. Jagger is

Margaret: I'm an uptight, no-fun, coldhearted billionaire businessman with prematurely graying hair who perpetuates toxic masculinity?

Leighton: Exactly!

Leighton: I gotta go. They're about to have fade-to-black sex on the piano!

I tossed my phone onto the bed and looked up at the TV as Julia Roberts engaged in a classic '90s musical montage of trying on clothes.

"Please turn that off," I said.

"Why? She's about to walk into that shop and tell those rude shop attendants off."

"Just how many times have you watched this?" I walked over to the small bar fridge in the corner of the room. There was nothing in there except a hotel bottle of water. I took it out and sipped.

"Shall I order us some champagne?" Jagger asked facetiously.

"Absolutely not. And you should turn this off. It's actually a very degrading film about power and patriarchy. A rich man and his money and its ability to turn a prostitute into a lady with a fancy dress and a hat. Assuming that there's something wrong with being a sex worker, of course."

A smile twisted across Jagger's face again and he looked at me. "You just don't want to watch a romantic movie with me, do you? No one hates *Pretty Woman*! Even if, true, it has dated somewhat, and if it were remade today, it would definitely be changed a little."

"How would you change it?"

"Well, for one, I would make Julia Roberts the businesswoman. Richard Gere would be the male escort hired for the week while she's on an important business trip."

"And what business trip would she be on?" I asked, playing along.

"Well, she would probably be in a powerful IT job, perhaps even the creator of a very successful app, like the woman who created Bumble, a female-centric dating site, which would make it even more interesting that she's hiring a male escort for the week, as she runs a dating app."

"Okay." I relaxed into this story a little and, to be honest, was enjoying playing this make-believe game. "So, she's off on a business trip, she's contacted a male escort agency, and hired . . . who? Richard Gere wouldn't play the role anymore?"

"Jamie Dornan. Mr. Grey himself in a role reversal."

I laughed. I kind of liked this idea. "Who's Julia Roberts?"

Jagger scooted up the bed and rested his back against the headboard and then looked straight at me. My breath caught in my throat for some inexplicable reason. "Well . . ." His voice was softer, a little breathy. "She would have blue-green eyes, for sure."

The breath didn't quite catch in my throat this time. It sort of didn't make it up to my throat. My lungs forgot how to exhale for a second as I looked back at Jagger.

"Shit, can you turn up the AC? It's so hot." I broke eye contact and took another sip of my water.

Jagger was still watching me as he reached for the remote and blasted the AC. "Better?"

But it wasn't better. The heat I was feeling seemed to be coming from the inside, not from the outside. "Much. I think I'm going to sleep now. Big day tomorrow. In Stone Town. The article." My sentence came out in word bursts, with none of my usual smooth articulation. I walked into the bathroom to brush my teeth and stepped on the same shirt I'd stood on earlier. "If we are going to be sharing a room—which is obviously highly regrettable and not ideal—we are going to need to have some rules in place. Like using a laundry basket."

Jagger agreed and, when I came back out, he'd rebuilt the wall in the middle of the bed. I nodded in approval and then climbed into bed and turned away from him.

"Do you mind if I watch this, or is it too distracting to go to sleep to?" Jagger asked.

"No, it's fine," I lied. Watching a rom-com with Jagger in the room felt highly awkward and somewhat inappropriate. We stopped talking as I made myself comfortable, the only sound in the room was of Julia Roberts trying to learn which fork went with which course of the meal.

The sentence repeated in my head: *She would have blue-green eyes . . .* coincidence. Definitely not loaded with some strange meaning and subtext. *Surely not?*

"Uh . . . in this remake of *Pretty Woman*, what color hair would our actress have?" I asked.

"Oh, that's easy." Jagger paused, and I raised myself off the bed in anticipation. "Red. It has to be red. That's a given."

I dropped back down and breathed a sigh of relief.

Definitely coincidence.

"And curly, has to have curls."

The relief disappeared; Why did it feel as if Jagger was talking about me?

Chapter **Twenty-six**

The next day we were back in Stone Town, the ancient-looking town with its thin, winding streets and intricately carved wooden doors in every wall. We went into a totally different part of it today. Up every street, vendors lined the small alleys, selling fruits and touristy paintings. People riding bikes navigated through the chaos of the narrow passages without bumping into anyone or anything. But today's trip would not be as pleasant as yesterday's. It would be a trip through history, a look into the past, but not a very nice one. *It was an essential look, though.*

We arrived at a beautiful Anglican cathedral. It was an unusual mix of Gothic architecture with detailing that was typically Islamic in aesthetic. It was hard to imagine that beauty could exist in a place where the worst human atrocities had been committed. Jagger and I were led into the old slave chambers below the church. We had to duck our heads in order to enter the dank, dark room. Two tiny windows were the only openings that provided light and ventilation in this cave-like space, the most depressing room that I'd ever been in. It had a feeling to it: dark and foreboding and evil—pure evil. You could almost taste it, like something bitter on the back of your tongue. It crawled up my spine and made all the hairs on my body stand up.

"They used to keep up to fifty slaves in here," Jagger whispered somberly.

"Impossible." I looked around the tiny room, trying to measure it in my mind. There was no way that fifty people would have squeezed in here—ten at most.

"They used to die from lack of ventilation." Jagger looked out the tiny slit windows and then sat down on the stone slab. He ran his hands over it. "Can you imagine spending your last days in this room, no food or water, having to go to the toilet right here, and then twice a week being led out into a market and sold as if you weren't even human? A mere commodity to be traded."

My stomach lurched and nausea rose up inside me. I sat down, too, trying to imagine what it would have been like to be here. To be ripped away from family and friends and brought to a place where you were alone, hungry, thirsty, and afraid.

I ran my fingertips over the old stone walls. They were cold, icy even, despite the heat outside. You could feel the human suffering that had been embedded in them. If these walls could talk and tell you of the horrors they had witnessed, you would never be able to sleep again. I closed my eyes and inhaled. The most oppressive feeling curled around me and pushed my body into the ground, weighing so heavily on me that it was almost hard to breathe.

Jagger's voice echoed in the empty room as if an invisible ghost was copying him. "Zanzibar was the center of the East African slave trade and at one stage human trafficking was the most lucrative business here."

"How do you know that?"

"When you thought I was researching kinks, I was actually researching this. Do you know they estimate that fifty thousand slaves were sold here annually in the market? They were taken to the market, chained up, and whipped. Those who didn't cry or faint fetched the highest prices."

I swallowed down the bitter taste of bile in my throat. I gazed around the room again, making sure I took in all its details, committing each and every one to memory. Nothing about this place and what had happened in it should ever be forgotten. Something caught my attention and I moved toward it. Old, rusty shackles built into the stone pillars lay dark and ominous. I touched one, aware that it would have been around someone's wrist. Many wrists.

"This place is so beautiful—the beaches, the sun, sea, sand—but behind that is such a dark, ugly past." I looked out the small window and tried to imagine what it would be like if this was my only access to the outside world.

"Imagine if this was your only window onto the world outside." Jagger moved closer to me.

"I was thinking the exact same thing."

We sat in silence for a while, taking it all in and, in the silence, I suddenly heard a small, choked noise coming from me. I put my hands on my face and realized that it was wet.

I felt an arm slip around my shoulders. It was warm and comforting, like a beacon of light in this dark, awful place, and I let myself lean into the comfort. I shifted closer to Jagger and melted into the side of his body, putting my head on his shoulder, and allowing myself to be held by him.

"You okay to go look at the museum now?" Jagger asked.

I nodded and wiped my eyes. "Let's go."

We stood up and, before walking out of the room, Jagger reached for my face and touched it.

"What?" I asked, as he trailed a finger down my cheek. My initial response was to pull away from him, but I didn't. Instead, I closed my eyes and allowed his finger to trace the contours of my face.

"Nonwaterproof mascara." Jagger ran two thumbs over my cheeks gently and then shook his head. "Nope, it's not coming off."

I shrugged. "If I'm leaving with only smudged mascara, then I'm doing better than the thousands who left this room before me."

A comforting smile spread across Jagger's lips, and I matched it warmly.

We went out into fresh air and freedom, and I did not take that moment for granted at all. I was able to walk away when so many others hadn't. For many, these four walls had been their last place on earth. It represented the very worst of humanity, and I was eager to put words to this story that so many didn't know. This was a story that should never be forgotten—the undocumented trafficking of Zanzibarian people into South Africa—and if I could in some tiny way breathe life into it, then I would be incredibly proud of that fact.

We got back to the resort again in less-than-jovial moods, very different to how we'd arrived last night. Two journeys to the same place, with very different outcomes. Jagger and I grabbed our laptops. We had two articles to write, and I headed for the bar area by the beach. I picked a table under the shade of a palm tree and sat down. The resort had put fans outside, and the breeze coming from them was the only way you were able to sit in the open air. I started writing but stopped when I heard footsteps.

"Well, hello there," Jagger said, standing in front of my table.

I looked up. This was all too familiar: Jagger looming over my desk, my neck crooked up to look at him.

"Is this seat taken?"

"Uh . . ." I hesitated.

"I could build a wall, if you want?"

I looked around the restaurant. "There are other tables, you know."

"I know. But this feels familiar and right, doesn't it? You and me, sharing a workspace?"

"You know I never wanted to share a workspace with you in the first place."

"I know, but you secretly love it."

"I do not secretly love working with you in my space. I much prefer my own space. Hence the wall."

"It's cute how we do this."

"Do what?"

"This little back-and-forth banter we have where you pretend to hate me and everything I do but secretly enjoy it."

I burst out laughing. "I do not enjoy it. I find it energy-draining and time-consuming. It cuts into my work time and concentration."

The amusement on his lips grew into a full-blown smile. "Shall I still go sit at another table?"

I shrugged. "Sit where you want."

"I will, then." Jagger lowered himself into the chair opposite me and I watched him take out his Moleskine notebook and flip it open.

"Are those notes?" I asked, leaning over to peer into it.

"Yup."

"You actually write stuff in there?"

"What else would I do with it?"

I shook my head, bit back a smile, and looked back down at my screen. "Nothing."

Jagger slammed the notebook shut with a soft bang. "Do you think I carry it around for show?"

"Maybe."

"Would you like to look at it?" Jagger passed it over and the journalist in me was desperate to peep inside. And so I thumbed through it. Each page was full of words and notes, some underlined and highlighted in color.

"Believe it or not—because I know you don't—I actually take what I do very seriously," he said as I read through a page on the history of the polygraph machine and the technical notes on how it worked.

"Truth serum?" I touched the words on the page with my fingertip.

"Sodium thiopental. Yeah, I had this idea to get someone to inject me with it to see it if worked for a *Tries*. . . video."

I slapped his book down. "See. This is what I don't get. Why, *why* would you do that to yourself?"

"Well, firstly, I didn't. But if I did, it would be for the same reason that your curious and analytical brain chases truth so relentlessly in your work."

I shook my head. "It's hardly the same."

"Why, because you think your truths are more valuable than mine?"

"Frankly, they are. Digging up the truth behind government corruption is more valuable than digging up your truths about truth serum." I passed Jagger's book back and his face fell. He took it with far less enthusiasm than when he'd handed it to me, opened his laptop, and then, without another word, looked back down at his computer screen. A feeling hit me in the ribs, I felt . . .

Shit.

"I'm sorry," I said quickly. "I didn't mean to imply that—"

"You didn't imply." Jagger looked up at me again. "You stated. You stated that your truths are more valuable than mine."

"You're right, and I'm very sorry. That was wrong of me." I said it and absolutely meant it. "I'm being a total snob."

Jagger looked up at me again, his face still devoid of that smile he'd had plastered across it moments ago. "You are!"

"Am I snobby?"

"Most of the time it's rather endearing, sometimes not so much."

"Endearing?"

"Very." Jagger held my eyes and didn't let them go.

"That sounds somewhat patronizing," I said.

"It's not meant to be."

"What's it meant to be, then?" I challenged him.

"I just mean that I find all your quirks quite—" He stopped talking. Something inside me stopped too. Everything became very still as he looked at me in a way that did something strange to me. Strange, yet familiar. I'd felt this feeling before. I'd just never thought I would ever feel it with Jagger. I cleared my throat and quickly looked away, perturbed that he'd made a little something inside my stomach flip.

"Entertaining." He said the word after such a long pause that for a moment I didn't know what he was talking about. I looked back up at him and was caught in his stare once more.

"I entertain you?"

"Put it this way, I've never looked forward to coming into work every day as much as I do now."

Whoosh! The feeling that knocked me in the chest had a sound to it that I could hear clapping in my ears like thunder. It came out of nowhere. Hit me hard, pushed my breath out in a short, sharp exhale. *Fuck, what was happening to me?*

"I need to . . . work." I looked down at my screen.

I didn't look up at Jagger again.

Chapter **Twenty-seven**

We spent the afternoon writing at the table together, and I was surprised by how easily the words flew out of me for the piece on Mercury's. The piece on slavery I was finding much harder to write. It was difficult to document something so terrible, to assign words to it that that did the story justice. Jagger was typing away too; in fact, he'd barely looked up the entire day. It caused something competitive in me to stir.

"What have you written?" I asked, after I'd counted the keystrokes he was typing per minute, which was faster than me.

"I'm about to finish the article on slavery."

"Oh." I sat up and tried to look over the top of his laptop

He closed it. "No cheating."

"I'm not cheating—I'm just curious."

"What are you writing?" he asked.

"Freddie Mercury."

"Oh, I finished that one last night," he said casually.

"When?"

"I stayed up for a few hours after you went to sleep."

"And you've also almost finished the slavery piece too?"

"A few last paragraphs to write then I'll give it a quick edit." He opened his laptop and continued typing, leaving me to stare at him slightly slack-jawed. I thought I would be the one winning this—not that it was a race to the finish, but it might as well have been. I hated the idea that Jagger would finish his work before me. I stared back down at my computer, willing the words to come, but they were much slower than usual.

"You want your iced coffee?" Jagger asked after another hour had passed. "You usually get one at this time of the day."

I looked at the time. Three o'clock. That's when I hit my afternoon slump.

"That's probably why you're not typing as fast as you were, your afternoon slump."

I closed my computer and stared at Jagger. This was yet another one of those comments he made that completely caught me off guard.

"How do you know about that?"

"Like I've said, several times, I've shared a desk with you for six months. You start typing slower and yawning at about two thirty and that's when you get your coffee. Always iced in the afternoon, cappuccino in the morning."

Without answering, Jagger waved down one of the waitstaff and ordered an iced coffee and a glass of water for himself.

"I never drink coffee," Jagger said when I looked at his glass of water. "But you probably hadn't noticed, right?" he asked.

I felt that knot in my stomach again because he was right: I hadn't noticed.

After writing our articles for most of the day, we wandered back to the room and collapsed into our respective books. I sat on the bed listening to my audiobook while Jagger lazed in the rattan chair. I was amused to see him read. I hadn't imagined him as a reader, and certainly not such a serious reader. I was almost embarrassed by my thriller, considering he was consuming Kazuo Ishiguro. The hours passed in silence, and I realized that I hadn't felt anxious all afternoon. Since coming here my anxiety had all but disappeared. This holiday really was what I'd needed. Over the years, my therapist had taught me coping techniques—breathing, pressing pressure points, placing cool towels on my forehead. None of them had really worked, but something was working now. Whether it was just this place, or something more . . .

I looked at Jagger. I narrowed my eyes and squinted at him, studying him. His relaxed way of being, one leg up on the chair, hair flopping to one side, his old, stretched shirt, which looked comfortable and worn.

Surely, he had nothing to do with my current relaxed feelings? But the more I stared at him, the more I wasn't so sure. I looked away quickly when Jagger looked up, as if he'd sensed I was staring.

"Let's go out." He rose from his chair. "I've had enough reading for the day, and we are far too young not to be out at eight o'clock on a tropical island bursting with possibilities.

"Where do you suggest we go?" I asked, pressing Pause on my book.

"The hotel bar and disco." Jagger rushed to the bathroom only to emerge about thirty seconds later, declaring he was ready to go. I eyed him up and down. All he'd done was change his shirt. "Let's go." He stood there beaming in his Guchi.

"Give me a moment. I need to try to create something that resembles an outfit." I walked into the bathroom, closed the door behind me, and looked at myself in the mirror. I'd been walking around in clothes I would never wear under normal circumstances. Clothes I would only wear if my bag went missing and all I could buy were some rather ridiculous-looking clothes from the only clothing shop near me. I pulled on one of my fake designer shirts, stretching it to fit across my bust until I heard the *pop, pop, pop* of threads breaking. I was still wearing my mother's bikini tops as bras and she was right, of course—my boobs were bigger than hers, and as such, the bikini did not do its required, and rather simple, job of covering them all. Instead, some jiggly, now slightly pink, mounds of flesh ballooned out of the cups, and if I bent down to pick anything up off the floor, they squished together and pushed against my chin. I wrapped a colorful sarong around my bottom half and tied it in front with a knot. It flapped open and my also slightly pink thigh peered out.

"Right!" I said to myself in the mirror as I let my hair out of its ponytail. The curls bounced around my shoulders as if they were made of trampoline springs.

I was just about to leave the bathroom when an urge hit me. I reached for my makeup bag and unzipped it slowly. The sample lipstick that Lesego had given me, the one that I thought I'd hated, fell out.

"Whatever," I said with a shrug and then dragged the color across my lips. I ran some mascara over my lashes and spritzed my neck with perfume before walking back into the room. The second Jagger saw me, his face almost split open with a smile.

"Blueberries," he said.

"Indeed."

"And you don't look like a corpse."

"That's always a bonus, I guess."

"Shall we?" Jagger held his arm out for me, and I stared at it.

"What is this? Prom? Are you going to give me a corsage next?"

"Do you want a corsage?"

I thought about it for a while. "You know what, I didn't get a corsage. Perhaps I should have taken that as the first sign that the night was going to go downhill."

"If it makes you feel any better, my prom was a total disaster too."

"What happened?"

"Well, the girl I really wanted to go with—I had such a crush on her—went with someone else. I had to watch her with him all night having the best time. And I had a massive pimple on my chin that night, too, which obviously I squeezed before going, but then it just got inflamed and infected, so I had a red mountain on my chin all night."

"Ahhh, poor you. Didn't get the girl?"

"Nope. Destroyed my fragile teen heart."

I chuckled. "God, mine too."

"And everything is so intense when you're that age. Everything feels like the absolute end of the world. I wrote seriously angsty poetry in my journal when Emily Stone went to the dance with James Crawford."

"I cried for days after my dance. I'd just gotten my braces off and was so ready for a serious make-out session, maybe even more. But instead he made out with my best friend. We weren't friends after that."

Jagger laughed loudly. "Wouldn't it be great if we could all relive that night over again, older, wiser, less awkward, pimple- and braces-free?"

"I guess it kind of would."

"Although we'd still keep Nickelback," Jagger teased me. *"Luuuk, uuhh, thuuuss, phuuutogruuph,"* Jagger sang at the top of his very put-on nasal voice, and I burst out laughing.

"You do that so well."

"I missed my calling it seems."

"You know, Nickelback are actually a completely misunderstood and underrated band if you think about it."

"Defending them. You must be a really big fan."

"I'm not a fan. I'm just saying that perhaps it's unfair that everyone hates them so much."

Jagger stopped, looked at me, and attempted an eye roll. I had never seen him roll his eyes before and he did it very awkwardly.

"Are you trying to copy me?" I asked.

"Ow, that actually hurts." Jagger closed his eyes and massaged them through his lids.

"It's a muscle you have to exercise, and I've a lot of occasion to exercise it." I swished out of the room and into the balmy night. Jagger followed me.

"What music do you listen to if you're not really a Nickelback fan?" Jagger asked.

"Nothing in particular. I usually have music on as an afterthought, you know? Something on in the background. It doesn't really matter, to be honest. And you?" I asked.

"Music was a big part of my life growing up, my dad being a musician and my mom a singer. I'm sure you know who I'm named after?"

"Well, I guessed."

"What's it like being friends with the great Leighton George?" Jagger asked.

I stopped walking and turned to face him. "Leighton is amazing. He's exactly what you would expect him to be in real life too. Loud and funny and over-the-top and completely weird. But he also has this other side, a soft, gentle one. He doesn't show that to many people, and that's the thing I like most about him."

Jagger smiled at me. "It's nice to have someone like that in your life."

"It is," I acknowledged, resuming our walk. The farther we went, the balmier the air seemed to become. The weather people had definitely been right this time: this *was* a heatwave—the temperature had soared. Jagger and I walked in silence but the sounds of our feet on the wooden boards were perfectly in tune. We finally arrived at the beach disco.

It was about as cheesy as they came: a mirror ball, a smoke machine that gave a lame intermittent puff like a smoker coughing up cigarette smoke, and one purple flashing light. It was set on the beach under a thatched roof and was filled with barefoot, lobster-pink Europeans who'd clearly had way too much sun and were now on their second round of drinks. But despite all its imperfections, it was perfect. It had a retro charm about it and oozed holiday atmosphere, that atmosphere where anything and everything seems possible because you're not your usual self. You're a holiday version of yourself. You laugh more easily, dance more easily, and converse with strangers because you're on bloody holiday, Margaret. You don't care that what you're wearing is ridiculous because you're a little loose-limbed and loose-tongued thanks to those coconut cocktails with twirly straws and bits of pineapple floating on top.

"Want another one?" Jagger slid up to me holding a large neon-yellow drink that had not one but two straws sticking out of it. He seemed to be relishing the fact that I was drinking with him, taking great delight in the fact my cheeks were getting redder by the minute, which he was pointing out rather frequently.

"I don't usually do this," I said, pulling the drink away from him and immediately angling my mouth over the straw.

"So you've said." He smirked.

"Ahhh! I see what you're doing there." I pointed at him. "You're trying to imply that I drink more than I let on. Sneaky."

Jagger smiled. "You're fun when you're drunk."

"Firstly, I am not drunk. *Drunk* is an ugly word. I am simply basking in the warm glow of tropical alcohol!" I sucked on the straw again. "Mmm, this is delish! What is it?"

"I think it has coconut and pineapple in it."

"They all have coconut and pineapple. In fact, it seems to be a basic tropical prerequisite to add coconut and pineapple to everything here. Even the fish we ate today had coconut and pineapple in them!" The cocktail went down quicker this time, and the next one slipped down even faster. Jagger drank whiskey on the rocks and fancy gin and tonics, which I've always thought have a certain pretentiousness to them. Whiskey and gin tastings had become such a thing in recent years, and you could barely go to a bar these days without finding someone who was making gin out of cow dung, or whatever other fauna or flora was fashionable, and dropping little sachets of freeze-dried botanicals and pink peppercorns into the liquid. But I should not judge a man on the drink he chooses, lest he judge me on my choices, which at this current moment were beyond fruity! We were both leaning against the bar and, although we'd not consciously agreed to it, were watching the socially lubricated crowd in front of us. Every now and then one of us would give some sort of commentary, as if we were watching a sports game.

"Move on, buddy, move on. She doesn't look interested," Jagger said after we'd watched a man try and fail to buy a particularly pink-skinned girl a drink for the last five minutes.

"Ooops!" I winced as someone tripped and fell while trying to dance.

"Lucky it's a sand floor," Jagger commented.

And we went on like this together, doing a running commentary of the events happening around us. It was a little like watching my favorite reality TV show playing out in front of me. It was odd. Jagger's presence was also starting to feel less strange and jarring. And then . . .

I should have guessed it. Because I knew it was coming. It always came in places like these. Suddenly "Love Is Like a Sin" was blasting through the bar.

"It's your friend!" Jagger pointed at the air. And then the next thing happened, the thing that always happened when this song came on. A sudden atmospheric shift in the room. It seemed to hold a place in everyone's heart and, god, it was catchy. Maybe the catchiest song ever recorded, and everyone knew the lyrics. And like clockwork, people descended onto the dance floor and sang along.

"Your eyes like diamonds in the night, these feelings we cannot fight."

"A real musical Shakespeare," Jagger teased me.

"He is!" I pulled out my phone; I had a habit of messaging Leighton every time I heard one of his songs, which was often. He loved it. I stood back and took a photo of the club and then send him a message.

Margaret: When love is a sin fever sets in

I sent the picture and waited for the blue ticks. They came immediately and then his response.

Leighton: Is that Jagger?

Margaret: Hey, they are playing your song. Be interested in that, not Jagger

Leighton: Mmmm, but look how interesting he is …

Margaret: Dot, dot dot? Please don't give me dots. I don't want dots. I know what dots mean

Leighton: Oh, come on. Admit it. Just a tiny bit … he's hot

Margaret: He's not my type

Leighton: Darling, that man is everyone's type

Margaret: Excuse me. I didn't message you to talk about Jagger. I messaged you to tell you that a whole nightclub of drunken people are embarrassing themselves on the dance floor to your song

Leighton: That's the way I like it. Have you and Jagger taken to the dance floor yet to throw some shapes?

I burst out laughing. He had such a funny turn of phrase.

Margaret: No, I was messaging you first

Leighton: Get off this phone immediately and go to the dance floor and shake that sexy juicy ass your mama gave you

Margaret: No reminders of mama please

Leighton: Oh, I forgot

Margaret: No, you didn't. You totally remembered and you're just trying to make me picture my mom's ass now

Leighton: Ha-hah! You know me too well

Margaret: You're incorrigible

Leighton: I know!

Leighton: Now go dance! Have some drinks. Let your hair down. Enjoy yourself

Margaret: I'll have you know I have had THREE tropical cocktails already! Maybe more, I might have lost count actually

Leighton: That's my girl. Make it four for me and have some fun

Margaret: Love you!

I slipped my phone into my bag, and when I looked up, Jagger had his hand held out to me.

"It's practically the law," he shouted over the music.

"What is?"

"To dance like an idiot when this song comes on."

I shook my head. "I'm afraid I'm one cocktail too short of idiotic dancing."

Jagger winked and then pointed to the bar. "I thought you might say that."

Two bright-pink shot glasses looked back at me. They had sugar crystals around the rim of the glass and something pink and fluffy floating on top. I moved closer.

"Wait, is that . . ."

"Cotton candy shots."

"Seriously! Oh my god, I love cotton candy."

"I know."

"How do you know?"

"I heard you telling Lesego how you feel more desserts should come topped with pink cotton candy, so . . ."

"Were you listening to my conversation?" I asked, raising the glass to my lips.

"You two are always talking at your desk and forgetting I sit behind the partition."

Actually, he was right. I think I try to block him out at work and carry on as if he wasn't there. I looked at Jagger as he raised the shot to his lips. I wondered what things would be like when we got back to work; I didn't think I would be able to ignore him anymore after we'd gotten to know each other these last few days.

"Bottoms up? And then dance?"

"Why not?" I threw the pink thing back and sucked the melted candy cotton off my lips. The last of my inhibitions were washed away by the sweet pink drink, and when Jagger extended his hand again, I took it. He led me onto the dance floor, and I burst out laughing when he attempted to twirl me, which the sand didn't allow for.

"Wasn't there a dance for this?" Jagger asked.

I nodded and mouthed that there was.

"Didn't it go something like this?" He put his hands on his hips and then swung them left to right.

"You're a terrible dancer," I shouted over the music.

"I never claimed to be any good. But what I lack in skill, I make up for with enthusiasm." He put more energy into the dance, and I laughed. He looked ridiculous and I don't know why—maybe it was the drinks, the holiday spirit, the way Jagger was smiling—but I joined in. I swept my hands around my face mysteriously as Leighton had done in the music video and we both laughed when at least ten other people around us did the same. I felt rather caught up in it all. The music, the lights, the sand beneath my feet, the warm feeling in my heart that my best friend had created something that caused so much joy for so many people and had done so for over forty years now. We danced and laughed and, by the end of the song, were drenched in sweat and out of breath. I hadn't done that much exercise since the time Lesego had thought we should start spinning; we lasted one session and then had to buy talcum powder for the week-long chafe we'd endured between our thighs. We'd walked around at work smelling like babies and leaving little white powdery patches on things when we sat down. That was my last foray into any kind of organized exercise.

We walked over to the bar again and collapsed into the stools. I grabbed a cocktail menu and fanned myself frantically. The cool air that hit my skin was a welcome relief. It was so hot and humid here, and dancing like an '80s synth pop star just made that all worse. Jagger waved the barman down and I was relieved to see two bottles of water arrive. We tore the tops off our bottles and gulped, but when I looked back at Jagger, he'd put his down, leaned back in his chair, and was staring at me. *Really staring.* As if he was examining me.

"Why are you looking at me like that? And why are you leaning? When you lean, I know you're up to no good."

"Why do you think I'm leaning and looking at you like that?"

"You sound like my therapist. *Why do you think that? And how does that make you feel?*" I tried to imitate my therapist's voice but it just came out sounding French and I gave up. "My ex and I did a lot of therapy. And you know, they never, and I mean *never*, tell you anything! You're paying them for advice but they refuse to give it to you. So basically, you're paying someone to listen to you while you give yourself your own advice."

Jagger shook his head and tutted. "They should be out of a job. Them and meteorologists."

"Exactly!" I smiled and took another sip of my water and then eyeballed him again. "But seriously, why are you looking at me like that? Like you're really thinking about something."

"Maybe I am *really* thinking about something."

"What?"

A peculiar looked washed across his face, his lips parted, and I scooted closer to him to hear what he was about to say, only he closed his mouth and shook his head.

"No, you can't do that. Tell me what you're thinking about."

"I can tell you, but it might make you feel rather . . ." He paused.

"Rather what?"

"I don't know, actually. You could react badly . . . you could react well. Hard to predict."

I stood up and pulled my chair closer to him, imbued with a kind of confidence I don't usually have. "You are not leaving until you tell me what you're thinking, Jagger Villain."

Jagger stood, too, and stepped toward me. I gasped at his sudden proximity and the smell of gin on his breath as he tilted his head down to meet mine.

"Okay, but don't say I didn't warn you," he said.

"Consider me warned."

"You sure?" he asked again, and I gave him a very intentionally over-dramatic eye roll.

"Fine, I just hope you can handle it."

"Oh, I can handle it," I assured him.

"I was thinking how hot you are."

I was sure all the lights and the smoke and the music stopped.

"Sorry, what?"

"Hot." He smiled. It was slow and seductive and . . .

"NO! No, no, no, no, no! You are not pulling that with me, Jagger bloody Villain. I'm not falling for it. For those smooth smiles and steely gray eyes and *ooh, baby, you're hot* nonsense!" I tsked and reached for my water again. "Nope! Not. Falling. For. It!"

"Falling for it implies some kind of lie or trickery on my part. And I can assure you, I'm not lying at all."

I put my water bottle down with a thud; a few drops splashed onto the bar. "You think I'm hot?"

"Unbelievably so."

"You think I'm unbelievably hot?" I repeated, almost on the verge of uncontrollable laugher.

"Yes. I do."

"Interesting," I mused.

Jagger laughed. "I tell you you're gorgeous and you say 'interesting.'"

"What should I say? There doesn't seem to be a right way of replying to that sort of thing. If I say thanks, I'll just come across as vain, and if I say no, I'm not, I'll just come across as one of those people who can't take a compliment."

"You should take the compliment, Blueberries."

"Did you just call me Blueberries?"

"Maybe, Maggie May."

"Okay. Fine. I graciously take the compliment, Jagger. Even though I'm feeling very suspicious and unsettled by this sudden and extremely unexpected declaration that I may or may not actually believe."

"What is it so unexpected and unbelievable about this declaration?" Jagger inched closer to me. Or did he? I wasn't sure if he'd moved or if the floor had shifted and I'd tilted or if I'd moved. "It really shouldn't be so unexpected."

"What do you mean?"

"You haven't noticed that I've been staring at you and flirting with you for the last six months?"

"What?" I gasped, and then choked on a fleck of saliva. I beat my chest with my fist.

"I didn't know this news would affect you so badly." Jagger pulled a bar stool out and I sat back down. "You can't be *that* surprised. I've overheard Lesego make comments about it."

"She was joking!" I stated quickly.

"Many a true word."

"Wait, so what are you saying? That you've been flirting with me?"

"I thought it was pretty obvious."

"NO! No, it's not obvious. Unless you consider driving me to literal drink and office partition DIY flirting? And what do you mean you've been staring at me? You know that makes you sound like a total creep, and I am sure HR would have something to say about staring."

"Glancing, then. I've glanced at you from time to time, and some of the glances may have lingered. Sound better?" He was smiling at me as if this was all a Jagger joke. *Was it?*

"Let me get this straight. You've been flirting—badly, I might add—with me?"

"Yup!" Jagger looked so amused that I just couldn't figure out if this whole thing was a joke.

"Okay, so let's assume that's true, for the purpose of this discussion. Tell me: Where exactly did you expect that flirting to go?"

"Where flirting usually goes."

"And where might that be?"

"It usually leads to a date, maybe a kiss, if I'm lucky. Potentially more if we find we're compatible."

"I can tell you right now, for free, we are *not* compatible! We don't need to go on a date, or kiss or 'more' to know we are not compatible."

"And yet here we are, on holiday together, drinking and dancing in a bar, sleeping in the same bed, and sharing a bathroom."

"There is no merit to that argument. We've been forced to cohabit because of our parents."

"I didn't force you to come to this bar and dance with me, did I?"

"Not technically. But I did succumb to holiday peer pressure."

"Pressure? Please! No one could pressure you into doing anything you didn't want to do. I think I know you well enough by now to know that for a fact."

"Well, that's true." I eyed Jagger for a while, trying to decide whether or not he was being serious. I hadn't, not for a single second, suspected that Jagger might be into me in any way, despite Lesego's jokes. Besides, I wasn't his type. I was too serious for him, too not into wax play and having threesomes and whatever else was to be served on Jagger's sexual smorgasbord.

"You don't believe me?" He looked at me and I stared back at him—stared straight into his eyes and probed them for the answer. And then I got it and burst out laughing.

"Good one!" I laughed, and slapped Jagger on the arm. "For a second there, you almost had me considering it, even though it's the most ridiculous thing I've ever heard! Come on, let's dance again." I ran back off to the dance floor feeling that my holiday spirit cup definitely runneth over.

But when I looked back at Jagger, he hadn't followed me.

Chapter **Twenty-eight**

"How's your head?" Jagger asked, dropping two aspirin into my hand and passing me a glass of water the next morning.

"Not too bad actually." I swallowed the aspirin and thanked him. God, what time did we get home?" I asked.

"Around two."

"How did we get here? I don't really remember."

"Yes, I didn't realize how strong those cotton candy shots were. We probably shouldn't have had the third one."

I held my forehead. "I hate cotton candy."

"That's not what you were saying last night when you were walking up to strangers telling them how cotton candy was the floss of the gods and how more desserts, and perhaps even savory dishes should be made with it."

"I didn't!"

"You told the chef that instead of duck à l'orange he should make duck à la cotton."

"I did not," I protested.

"You did, trust me. I decided to take you home when you stuck your hand into the cotton candy machine and made a candy hand."

I stood up. "Now I really don't believe you . . ." I blinked a few times as it came back to me. "Oh god! I remember that." I sat down on the bed and clutched my head, not because it was sore, but because the shame of my cotton candy escapade was now coming back to me in vivid detail. "I'm so embarrassed."

Jagger laughed. "No need to be—it was pretty adorable, actually."

"A grown woman with a candy-coated hand is not adorable. A grown woman running around a bar and talking to total strangers about cotton candy is not adorable. It's unstable and unhinged, and I wouldn't be surprised if the hotel had called for someone in a white coat to take me away."

"Honestly, it wasn't that bad."

"What else happened last night that I've forgotten?"

A strange look came over Jagger's face.

"Oh god, what else did I do?"

"Nothing. Don't you remember the conversation we had?"

"I remember Leighton's song coming on, you and me talking about work a bit, and then it all descended into cotton candy chaos."

"Is that all you remember?" he asked, seeming a little disappointed now.

"Is there more?"

Jagger opened his mouth, and before he could speak—

"That's right, you tried to make me think you liked me and were flirting with me!" I laughed and pointed at him. The thought was even more ridiculous than the cotton candy hand. "Good one."

"Yup, you said that last night." Jagger turned and walked off; he didn't seem to be as amused as I was. "I'm going to shower."

I climbed out of bed and stretched my sore muscles. God, I really must have danced for hours last night. I walked around the room, shaking my stiff legs, and that's when I saw it. Jagger's laptop. I glanced at the bathroom door. The shower had started. I looked back at the computer. It was open. Virtually an open invitation to look. If it had been closed, well, that would have been another story. But it was open—it was practically screaming to be looked at. By me.

I raced over as quickly as I could and went straight to the article he'd written on slavery and then started reading it.

"Margaret-Skye," I heard as I walked past the pool.

"Mom! I've been looking for you. You weren't at breakfast."

"I'm saving my appetite." She walked toward me, her robes and sarongs swishing even more today. She was extraswishy.

"For what?"

She paused. Something flashed across her face that looked like . . . guilt? My mom never looked guilty. She didn't believe in guilt. Guilt was a self-inflicted negative emotion.

"Mom? What's going on?"

She ran a guilty-looking hand through her extraguilty-looking hair. "So I know I said I'd booked us a spa day, but Eddy booked this picnic for us on this little island just off the coast and—"

"Mom, are you serious?"

"It's supposed to be beautiful there."

"I've hardly seen you and this was the one thing that you said we were going to do together."

"I know, I'm sorry, but . . ." Her face blushed, her cheeks went pink, and she smiled. She looked like a giddy schoolgirl with a crush, and she was certainly behaving like one too.

"I'll make it up to you, Margaret-Skye! I promise." She looked at me with puppy dog eyes that, if I was honest, were hard to resist.

"Fine, okay, go have your gorgeous romantic picnic. I'm sure we can cancel the spa day."

"Well, that's the thing: we can't. I already paid, so I thought you and Jagger could go."

"Jagger and me? A spa day! Hot tub and massages." I burst out laughing. "I don't think so."

"But you two are getting on well."

"We're not."

"It certainly looks like it."

"Jagger and I don't even like each other. We're just tolerating each other because we've been thrown together."

My mom smiled—all the guilt on her face was gone now. "Margaret-Skye, I don't need to be psychic to tell you what's going on here."

"What's going on, Mom?"

"You like him!"

"Jagger?" I spat the word out with explosive consonants. "I don't like him: I despise him, I hate him, I—" I stopped.

That's no longer true now, is it? a voice in my head pointed out. I sighed. "Okay, fine, I don't hate him anymore, but I don't like him either. I'm neutral to him."

"Neutral, but having so much fun together?"

"I'm forced to have fun with him. It's not out of choice—trust me."

"Just because you didn't choose it, or it wouldn't have been your first choice, doesn't mean it's not true."

"I'll rephrase, then. We are tolerating each other and, yes, sometimes it is vaguely pleasant, okay?"

"Vaguely?"

"More or less. Somewhat. Sometimes."

"I'd say it's definitely more, rather than less." My mom eyed me very suspiciously, as if she was concocting something in her head.

"Mom! I don't like the way you're looking at me."

"I'm not looking at you like anything. I just think that maybe you're not seeing this clearly."

"My eyesight is perfect, thank you very much. You're the one with eye problems, not me. Now go and enjoy your picnic and stop staring at me with your one good eye!"

"I'll have you know this one good eye can see more than what lies in front of us in the here and now."

"Mmmm, the all-seeing eye."

"Oh yes, this eye sees it all. And right now, it is seeing a lot."

"Mom, you're making zero sense, as per usual," I said affectionately.

"No, it makes sense. You're just not ready to seek out the sense."

I held my hands up. "That made even less sense."

"Sense is what you make of it."

"Untrue. Something either makes sense or it . . . god, why am I arguing about the nature of sense with you? Go on your picnic and I'll go to the spa, but I'm not inviting Jagger. I'll ask them if I can use the other booking later."

"Oops," my mom said.

"Oops what?"

"I already told Jagger. He's meeting you there at eleven."

"Seriously, Mom. You expect me to get half naked with Jagger in a hot tub and then have a hot-stone massage with him?"

"I told them to make sure they used the carnelian." She started walking off.

"My root chakra is fine. I told you that." But my mom didn't listen. Instead she sashayed off into the undergrowth.

"It's open, Mom. It is wide, wide open. Trust me. I am so bloody open, I'm gaping." I stopped talking when a family with kids stopped dead in the path.

"Sorry, I didn't . . . it's not . . . never mind." I turned and quickly ran away.

Chapter **Twenty-nine**

The doors to the spa oozed Zen relaxation before you even set foot inside. Two lush green palms—fluttering and swaying gently through the air, although I wasn't quite sure there was a breeze—stood either side of a large carved wooden door. Two big bowls of water flanked the door beneath the palms, pink petals floating rhythmically in the water, almost in time to the sway of the palms.

Why is the international symbol for trying to make someone feel relaxed and find inner peaceful equilibrium always floating foliage? I stared at the petals, trying to figure out what was making them move, and how I was supposed to derive my inner peace and relaxation from them. Because I would need more than a floating petal to make me relax today if Jagger was going to be joining me. I could think of nothing less relaxing than sharing a hot tub and having a massage with—

"Hey, M." Jagger was swaggering toward the door.

"M?"

"Not working?" he asked.

"Why don't you stop trying to come up with a nickname for me and call me Margaret? Why are you so obsessed with coming up with a new name?"

"I call all my friends by a nickname."

"Are we friends?"

"Well, we're not enemies anymore, are we?"

I folded my arms across my chest and my T-shirt bunched. I tried to fix it.

"Still no word on your suitcase?" Jagger eyed my ill-fitting tourist tee.

"I called again this morning and they found a black suitcase fitting the description. The name tag has been damaged, but there's enough to make out my name on it. They're sending it over later."

"Great!"

"I can't wait to wear actual clothes again. Things that look good on me, not"—I opened my arms and gestured—"this!"

"What's wrong with 'this'?"

"Have you seen me?" I said sarcastically.

"Yes, I see you," he said in a slightly lower tone. *Why was he using that tone?* But before I could ask, the doors opened and we were greeted by a serene-looking woman in flowing white robes. We were handed cool, lemongrass-infused cloths to wipe our brows, which were already sweaty due to the relentless heat and suffocating humidity. Then we were led inside—more bowls of floating petals appeared, candles flickered, and there was a sound of trickling water as it ran down one of the walls. This place was relaxation personified. If relaxation was a person, they would be named Reef Spa in Zanzibar.

"What is it about floating petals that is so relaxing?" Jagger whispered as we were led down a dimly lit passage. This was the kind of place in which you dared not raise your voice above a whisper. It's as if you signed some kind of psychic contract upon entry, agreeing to a certain vocal volume at all times. We arrived at the end of the passage and another intricate Zanzibarian door was opened for us. The first thing that hit me was the smell: sweet and powdery.

"There is baobab oil in the water, very moisturizing for the skin and hair," one of the therapists said as she glanced at my hair. I tried not to take offence at that, though I was sure she was implying that it looked as if something might be able to nest in it. I forced a smile at her and peered into the room covered in brilliant, intricate mosaics, seeing, in the middle of it, a sunken hot tub. The next thing I noticed was the light: warm, soft candlelight. Candelabras with flickering candles, floating candles. So many candles. And then there was the sound of it all, the soft, soothing pitter-patter of raindrops hitting palm leaves and the faint singing of tropical birds. I laughed nervously.

"I'm not . . ." I pointed into the room. "With him . . ." I pointed at Jagger. "In there." I pointed back at the room, but before I could continue protesting, Jagger pushed past me and walked inside.

"Amazing," he said.

"Not amazing," I replied, eying him.

"Is it not to your liking?" one of the therapists asked, looking genuinely surprised and maybe even a little hurt.

"No, it's not that. It's beautiful, it's just that it's very romantic, isn't it?"

The therapist smiled. "Thank you." She started pushing me in and closing the door. I shot my hand out and stopped it.

"I don't mean that as a compliment. It is a compliment, or course. Well done, very romantic, but him and me, we're not, so I don't think—" She cut me off, pushed me inside, and closed the door.

"I think she cut you off," Jagger said.

"Hey! Hey, what do you think you're doing?" I asked as I turned to find him shirtless and walking toward the tub.

"Getting in."

"You can't," I said.

"I can and I will."

"Well, I'm not getting in." I walked over to the bench on the side of the room and sat down.

"Suit yourself." Jagger pulled his shorts down, revealing his swimming trunks, and I immediately averted my gaze as he climbed into the hot tub.

"This is amazing," he said, making a huge show of how amazing it all was. I wasn't going to pay him any heed. Sharing a bed with him was one thing—at least there was a wall—but climbing into a candlelit hot tub filled with floating petals, half naked, I drew the line at that.

"So warm," he continued. "And the smell!"

"I can smell it from here," I countered.

"And I can already feel the oil seeping into my dry skin," he said, a huge smile across his face, and I knew what he was doing.

"My skin is fine, thanks."

"It might soothe that sunburn on your shoulders."

As he said it, I reached up and touched my shoulders. They were a little sore from my day spent in the sea. The skin felt tight. It also stung, and the promise of the moistening baobab water did sound appealing. Only problem, Jagger was now immersed in that moisturizing water.

"Get in. This is just like the cave."

"Only a lot smaller."

"It's also warmer. Tell you what." The water splashed out as Jagger moved to the other side of the tub, making space for me. The hot tub was small, and Jagger's knees were poking out of the water as he pulled his long legs toward himself.

"What are you doing?" I asked as Jagger started doing something with his hands in the air.

"Building an invisible wall!"

I watched him, my smile growing as he mimed laying bricks and smearing cement.

"You look ridiculous doing that!" I laughed at him.

"Done!" He wiped from his brow the imaginary sweat of hard labor and I rolled my eyes at him playfully.

"I prefer visible walls," I said.

"Your need for walls is strong."

"Only when you're around," I teased him.

"I think you need to get over that now. We're sharing a bed, for god's sake. We shared personal details of our lives with each other last night, and I practically tucked you in after your cotton candy exploits."

"You didn't tuck me in!" I protested.

"How do you think you got into bed without your sandals?"

"You took my sandals off?"

"You were trying to climb into bed with them on," he said. The warm light of the candles bathed him in an orange glow, taking away all his sharp edges once again. "We went underwear shopping together."

"No, we didn't. I did and you just tagged along."

"Just get in."

I looked at him, then looked at the water. Looked around the room, and then back at the water.

"Fine! But I'm not taking my clothes off." I stood up and walked over to the hot tub, still wearing my shirt and shorts, and stuck my toe into the water. Steam rose from it, bringing with it another scent that I hadn't noticed before. Was it lemongrass? Something citrusy, something divine, something that made you want to slip into the water.

I lowered myself into it, gasping this time at the warmth, and sat down on the seat. Jagger's legs and body took up most of the space, and no matter how I adjusted myself, our legs remained pressed up against each other's.

"You have very long legs," I pointed out.

"I'm tall," he said flatly.

"Just how tall are you?"

"Six foot three. I was six foot in grade seven. I looked like a spider." He stretched his legs out and stuck them over the edge of the tub. "Believe it or not, I only grew into my looks in my late teens."

I burst out laughing and the water around us shook. "You're so arrogant. Breaking news: not every woman finds you attractive."

"And I suppose you are that 'not every woman'?" He stretched his arms behind his head now, elongating himself until it looked as if he barely fit in the hot tub at all.

I nodded and folded my arms across my chest; the water was making the shirt stick to me and I didn't want him to see any nipple protrusions.

"You don't even find me a little bit attractive?"

I shook my head and tried to bite back a smile.

"And if I was the last man on the planet?"

I laughed again and made a real show of shaking my head even more. "You could be the last man in the universe and I still wouldn't be attracted to you."

Jagger suddenly pulled his legs back into the tub; the water around us splashed and his legs pressed into mine even harder. The move caught me off guard and I let out a little gasp, especially when he leaned in closer to me, his face lining up with mine, his eyes on the same level as mine, looking straight into me. I felt that falling feeling again, that feeling that I'd had before, where either I was leaning, or he was leaning, or the world was tilting. I tried to arrange my features in a way that didn't betray what I was feeling, although I wasn't entirely quite sure what that was. All I knew was that I didn't want Jagger to know. But he *did* know. His eyes seemed to be reaching into mine, pulling out all the answers. My skin prickled under his gaze, and I pulled back.

"We should . . . massage," I said, shooting out of the water.

Chapter **Thirty**

"We'll give you five minutes to change. Take off whatever you feel comfortable with," one of the therapists whispered, so softly that we had to lean in to hear her.

I stuck my head into the massage room. It was a couple's room—I was expecting that, but there was something I wasn't expecting.

"There's nowhere private to undress."

"I'll turn my back," Jagger said, walking into the room.

"Uh . . ." I hesitated.

"I won't look, promise."

I hesitated again and Jagger swung around to face me.

"You don't trust me not to look?" He caught my eyes and smiled.

"No. I don't," I replied, holding his gaze. His eyes left mine and swept up and down my body.

"You're hot, Maggie May, but I can resist gawking at you. I swear."

"God, you're so full of crap, it's unbelievable. Fine. Turn." I gestured a circular motion with my hand, and he followed that prompt. When I was satisfied he was facing the other way, I quickly whipped off my shirt and wrapped myself in the lavender-colored towel. I did some major one-handed ninja maneuvering to remove my bra while still holding the towel but managed. I climbed onto the table and pulled the other towel over my back.

"So, do those lines usually work for you?" I asked.

"What makes you think that was a line?"

"Most of the things that come out of your mouth are lines."

"Not true. Sometimes they are circles too."

I laughed. "That was really corny!"

"But it made you laugh."

"Only from the sheer secondhand embarrassment I'm feeling on your behalf."

"But it did make you laugh." His voice was softer now, not as playful. "I love your laugh." He delivered that "line" in a way that stopped my smile. In a way that made me raise my head and stare at his back. In a way that made something inside me pull and tighten, like it had done before. In a way that thrilled me but that downright terrified me too.

"Can I turn around yet?" he asked.

I looked away and buried my face in the hole in the table. "Sure." I was lying as flat on the bed as possible, so Jagger couldn't see anything. I could hear a towel being pulled off the hook, clothes being removed. He was stripping and a thought, a terrible one, came to mind. I froze. Against all rational and decent thinking, I wanted to turn around and sneak a peek so I could report back to Lesego. That's if one could decern the shape of piercings through clothes. A tiny look. A very quick one. So brief it would almost not even be a proper look. A glimpse. And I was only looking for research purposes. To report back to someone. This look was not for me at all—it was for . . . *science*? Journalistic investigation. I tilted my face ever so slightly and . . .

"Oh my god, Jagger! What are you doing?" I caught a flash of him out of the corner of my eye and almost fell off the table.

"What?" he asked innocently.

"You're not supposed to take off *all* your clothes." I covered my eyes but it was too late. I had seen his naked side which, trust me, was more than enough, but still not enough to be able to report back to Lesego. "This is not *that* kind of massage. It doesn't end happily! Put your clothes on."

"The masseuse said to take off as many clothes as I was comfortable with."

"So you took them *all* off! That's how you feel comfortable?"

"You have your top off."

"I have to, or else they can't get to my back. Mine are not out and about swinging about merrily like yours."

"I'm not swinging it—you turned around and looked."

"I did no—" I stopped. He was totally right, of course. "It was an accident! My face was uncomfortable—I had to turn, and I . . . I didn't see it. Just your side!"

Jagger laughed, and my face went red.

"But seriously, you have to put your underpants back on. I don't think it's massage etiquette to have them off."

"I wouldn't know. I've never had a massage."

"What? How is that possible?"

"I struggle to sit still. Always have."

"I've noticed."

"It used to drive my teachers mad. I was always in trouble at school for fidgeting, even though I couldn't help it."

"That's horrible." I turned toward Jagger. I'd heard him climb onto the massage bed. I propped myself up on my elbow and looked across at him. He was wearing underwear now and lying on the massage bed, looking out the window in front of us at the sea and palm trees. He looked as if he was recalling an unpleasant memory, and suddenly, I didn't feel that good.

"I'm sorry I kick you under the table when you tap your foot," I said.

Jagger turned and looked at me too. "I'm sorry it irritates you."

I sighed. "It doesn't irritate me as much as I say it does."

"You just like kicking me under the desk?" He sounded amused again and I looked away and nodded.

"You're lucky it's only been a kick. I once fantasized about plunging a pencil into you kneecap."

Jagger roared with laughter but it was interrupted by the therapists knocking on the door. "I believe you requested carnelian stones for the massage," one of them said.

"Well, my mother suggested them."

"Great, we'll do carnelian on both of you," the other therapist said.

"On him too?" I lifted my head and looked at them.

She nodded.

My mom's words echoed in my head. *Opens the root chakra.*

"Uh, wait. Not him. Maybe we shouldn't, I mean . . ." Everyone in the room looked at me expectantly as I paused. If there was even the slightest chances of chakras opening during this massage, then this was clearly something to park in the cul-de-sac of *no and absolutely never.*

"Variety. Isn't it better we have variety?" was all I could manage as an explanation for my outburst, which had been above the vocal volume threshold.

But clearly variety was not good, because soon Jagger and I were both being rubbed down with carnelian stones. I clenched my root chakra just in case it would explode open, or in case something else might happen to it. But I stopped clenching when my body began to relax and melt into the bed when the warm stones moved up and down my back in long, slow motions that turned my muscles into soft butter. I closed my eyes and took a deep breath as my mind and body started to float away, but I didn't float away for too long.

"Can we talk about something?" Jagger asked in a whisper.

"Not relaxing?"

"Nope. My brain is racing."

"What do you want to talk about?"

"Well, is there anything you want to tell me?"

"Why would I have something to tell you?"

"I thought I would give you a chance to get something off your chest while you're in a relaxed state?"

I pulled my head out of the hole and tilted it toward Jagger. He was looking in my direction. "What might I want to get off my chest while in a state of relaxation?"

He smiled. Slow and sneaky as if he knew something. *What did he know?*

"What did you think of my article?" he asked.

"How did you know?"

"You minimized the window after reading it."

"Shit," I mumbled, and put my head back in the hole so he couldn't see the guilt on my face. I looked down, another obligatory petal-festooned bowl of water below me. Scents of lemongrass and lavender filled my lungs and my muscles felt warm and relaxed. I took a long, slow in-breath.

"It was . . . amazing. It was amazing."

"What?" An above-volume commotion broke out next to me as Jagger sat bolt upright on the bed, much to the chagrin of the therapists, who both stepped back in shock. "Would you mind repeating that? I'm not sure if I'm high on lavender oil and having an auditory hallucination or—"

"It was an incredible piece, Jagger. Beautiful, actually. Your idea of writing a first-person narrative account that actually took the reader on the journey with the slave was brilliant and moving and also heartbreaking. I couldn't have written a better article if I tried. In fact, I'm not going to submit mine to Jennifer—it's pointless. Yours is better."

Jagger swung his legs over the side of the table and leaned across the space between us. By this stage, both therapists had stepped aside. I felt physically compelled to sit up so, clutching my towel as close to my body as possible, I did. I watched Jagger as his eyes left mine, as he dropped his head and shook it slowly from side to side.

"Will you give us a moment?" I asked the therapists, sensing a huge shift in Jagger's demeanor. "We'll call you back in when we're ready." I smiled at them reassuringly as they exited. "Are you okay?" I turned my attention back to Jagger.

He finally raised his head, and when he did, a look I'd never seen before lit his gray eyes silver. "You have no idea how much that means to me."

I baulked. "Why . . . why would it mean that much to you?"

"Because—call it ridiculous, it probably is—but I want your approval."

I burst out laughing and then stopped when Jagger didn't. "Why the hell would you want my approval?"

"Because I've always admired your work and I was really excited when I got the job and was going to be working with you."

"*You* admire *my* work?"

"Massively."

I frowned at him. "Well, you have a really strange way of trying to gain someone's approval."

"Not true, you were just determined to dislike me and everything I did from day one. Not even from day one, but rather the second you laid eyes on me. And since then, you've never even given me half a chance."

I looked away and sighed. I couldn't hold his gaze. I felt . . . it was hard to put it into words. But it felt cold and heavy in my throat. "Your piece on dating as a nonbinary individual was also good. It was very . . . sensitively written." I took another deep breath. "Your video, the barbershop and that stupid checkerboard, what you said about him and his family, was lovely, although I still hated the checkerboard." I sighed again and continued before I lost my nerve. "And your article on dick pics was really good and I'm sure women all over the world are very glad you wrote it . . . I was glad you wrote it."

Jagger jumped up off the bed suddenly and without any kind of warning, threw his arms around me and pulled me into a hug. Hot and cold panic gripped me instantly as I felt my towel loosen and then slip. It pooled on the floor by my feet, and when I felt Jagger's muscles relax, as if he was about to let me go, I wrapped my arms around him and clung on as if my life depended on it.

"Don't move. Do. Not. Move."

"I didn't know you liked hugs so much. If I'd known, I would have given you one sooner."

"It's not that—it's . . . *my towel*!"

Jagger looked down.

"Don't look down! Oh my god, Jagger," I shouted at him. "Please, do not look down."

"Wait, are those your . . . ?"

"YES!"

"And they're against my . . . ?"

"YES!"

Jagger started laughing but bit his lip when I glared at him.

"It's not funny." I wrapped my arms tighter around him, making sure there was no space between us, not enough for him to tilt his head down and look at my boobs, which by the way, were bulging up as if they had been squeezed into a corset and my nipples—*oh god, my nipples*—they were pressed into his chest. My naked nipples were rubbing up against Jagger's chest and I . . . I . . .

Something warm that tingled and twitched moved through me. It started in my feet. My toes were touching Jagger's—unintentionally, of course—and the feeling surged up my legs, into my stomach, and next thing I knew my nipples hardened against him.

Fuuuuck! I screamed in my head as I tried to mentally retract them and also to mentally ban the feeling in my stomach that was swirling like a pair of socks in a spin cycle, getting lower and lower until the feeling settled in my—*I was going to kill my mother when I saw her again*—bloody root fucking chakra. I inhaled a sharp, panicky breath, which did not go unnoticed by Jagger. I blame the carnelian rocks for this mess! This mess where the heat of Jagger's body against mine was physically doing things to me while I mentally panicked about the things that were happening. I had to get away. I had to extricate myself from this strange surreal moment where my naked breasts were pressed against his chest and . . . *oh god, help me, I've gone insane, but I think I was enjoying the feeling.*

"Your article on Freddie Mercury was also amazing." Jagger's voice was so low it was almost just a rumble.

"When did you read it?"

"I might have . . . seen it."

I couldn't scold him for this because that's exactly what I'd done.

"I loved how you made it so much more. How it was about the power of music to evoke memories and connect people. It was lovely. I also won't be submitting mine."

"You won't?" I looked up at Jagger; for some reason his approving compliment meant something to me.

He leaned down. His face coming closer to mine. I blinked, and my eyes didn't open right away. I could smell him. Feel him. I could almost taste him.

"Margaret." His voice was so soft it was almost inaudible, and it did something to me. It did something to me and my nipples that terrified me.

"I have to . . . t-t-t-towel," I stuttered. "Bend." Still with my hands around Jagger, I forced him into an awkward bend and as soon as it was within reach I grabbed my towel and, with sound barrier–breaking speed and the agility of a contortionist who can put their toes on their clavicles, I was once again covered in a towel. And, as soon as I was, like a swimmer pushing off the wall, I pushed myself off Jagger, all the way to the other side of the room, grabbed my clothes, and then disappeared out the door and into the nearest bathroom I could find.

Chapter **Thirty-one**

What the hell had just happened?

I panic-paced the bathroom a few times, trying to work out why on earth my body had betrayed me in such a humiliating way and made me want Jagger. *Want him?* Of all things! I crossed my legs and cursed my mother and the carnelian and anything and everything I could. I had to get away from here, away from the floating petals and intoxicating smells and soft whispers and Jagger's naked chest that I'd been pressed up against. My nipples twitched at the memory, and I cursed them too. I slipped my clothes on and the moment I was decent, I ran.

Out the door, down the paths, and all the way back to our room. *Our room!* I couldn't carry on sharing a room with Jagger after this. I would need to inform my mother of that as soon as she bothered to reappear. I don't care how in lust she and Eddy were with each other—they could hook up in the hammocks and in alleys for all I cared—I was just no longer prepared to share my room with Jagger. My mind raced, thoughts doing hopscotch, but when I came to my room a tiny wave of relief washed over me. My suitcase was waiting outside the door.

I rushed over to the small black case and hoisted it into the room and onto the bed. It felt the same weight as it had been when I'd packed it. I checked the name tag, and it had obviously been damaged during travel—but there it was, "Miss Mar . . ." The first three letters of my name were still visible. I unzipped the suitcase as fast as I could and reached in immediately. I couldn't wait to change my clothes and wear something that actually made sense—since everything right now was no longer making any sense to me. But as I did, my hand encountered something that felt strange; I didn't remember packing something that felt like this. I pulled it out of the bag and stared at it. Despite the previous hopscotching of my thoughts, they were very slow to catch up this time. Too damn slow, because by the time I knew what I was looking at—not to mention holding in my hand—I heard a loud burst of laughter coming straight from behind me.

"Well, well, Margaret-Skye, what do we have there?"

I jumped in horror and without thinking tossed the purple thing over my shoulder as hard and fast as I could.

I ran into the bathroom and washed my hands frantically, lather sloshing all over the mirror and the floor. But when I'd finished, loud moans of pain made me rush back into the room.

"Jagger!" I raced over to him; he was lying on the floor clutching his eye, blood dripping through his fingers. "Are you okay?"

"I don't know!"

"Shit. Put pressure on it." I pushed my hand over his and then grabbed the phone with my other hand and pressed 1 for reception. "Hello, I need a nurse or a doctor or . . . someone. My friend's eye is bleeding. We're in room one fifty-four!"

The woman on the other end said that she would send the lifesaver over immediately; I was hoping for someone with the letters D and R attached to their name, but this would have to do for now. Jagger put his hand over mine and I turned back to him.

"You just called me your friend."

"What?"

"On the phone, you just called me your friend." Jagger sat up and, despite the obvious pain and the blood dripping down his face, he smiled.

"You called me your friend but you tried to kill me with your purple vibrator."

"It is not my vibrator. That is not my bag!"

His smile grew. "Suuurrre."

"I swear, it's not my vibrator. I swear."

"Whatever you say, Maggie May."

"It's *not* my vibrator!"

Jagger burst out laughing again but stopped when he winced. "You tried to kill me with a dildo."

"It was an accident! I didn't try to kill you. And stop calling it *that*!"

Jagger's laugher escalated to near hysterics, and I wanted to die of embarrassment. "You tried to kill me with a purple rabbit vibrator."

"Stop laughing!" I purposefully pressed my hand to his eye even harder and he cried out in pain. "Oh my god, I'm never going to hear the end of this, am I?"

"Never. It's too damn good! You've blinded me with a purple vibrator! If I land in the emergency room for stitches and eye surgery and the doctor asks me what happened, I'll have to tell him that you attacked me with your sex toy!" His laugher was reaching a fever pitch.

"I didn't attack you! And it's not my sex toy and you won't go blind or need stitches . . . at least, *I think you won't*." I wasn't that convinced; the blood coming from his face did seem like rather a lot.

I didn't think Jagger was able to laugh any more, but soon tears were trickling down his face, mixing with the blood and making it even more of a mess. "This is, quite literally, the funniest moment of my entire life!"

"I'm glad you find this so funny, because I find it utterly mortifying."

Jagger sighed and his laughter finally tapered off. "Margaret-Skye . . ." He squeezed my hands and looked me straight in the eyes, with his one eye.

"Jagger?" I replied.

"I think you have just become my best friend!"

I smiled at him for the first time since the purple phallus went flying through the air and shook my head. "Clearly you have a very strange definition of what best friends are, then."

"No, I'm never wrong with these things. I've had the same friends since I was three years old. Trust me, I know what makes a friendship. And hitting someone in the eye with a sex toy is just about the best way to start one!"

I hung my head and felt a smile creep across my lips, but that was quickly wiped off by a shudder. "God, I was holding someone's vibrator. In my hand!"

"You know the rabbit vibrator is the bestselling sex toy of all time?"

"I don't want to know."

"Did you know that before the rabbit vibrator, there was a beaver, a kangaroo, and a turtle version?"

"Stop saying vibrator!" I pleaded with him.

"Did you know that the first modern vibrator was invented by a doctor to use on women to cure them of hysteria?"

At that, I became hysterical. The laughter burst out of me like a fountain; it was so sudden that I had to sit with my back to the wall to brace myself and, once I started laughing, I simply couldn't stop, until tears also ran down my face.

"Shall I carry on?" Jagger asked, also still laughing.

"No. It hurts." I clutched my ribs as the laughter rattled them about and then cupped the sides of my face as the muscles there ached.

"Because there's plenty more. I've written an article on the history of sex toys," he said, moving to sit next to me, his hand still over his eye.

"I'm sure you have." I shook my head at him in playful disapproval.

When our laughter finally fizzled out, a strange, silent lull pushed into the space between us. But the silence wasn't empty. It felt as if there was something in it, hanging between us, that neither of us wanted to acknowledge or name.

"I came looking for you." His voice was a mere whisper. "You left very quickly."

"I . . . I . . . suddenly felt a little strange." I looked away from him.

That was the truth. But I wasn't going to say why I'd felt strange. That my body had felt as if it was on fire next to him. That an ache of wanting had started deep in my belly, that for a moment there it had taken all my strength not to stand on my tiptoes and press my lips on his. "I think the lavender and lemongrass were a bit overwhelming." That was a lie. He, *he* was overwhelming me.

Jagger turned. In the periphery of my vision, I could see him looking at me. Feel him looking. I also turned, meeting his eyes with the faux confidence someone who wasn't lying might have. But as soon as I did, I felt all that put-on bravado melt away as Jagger's gray eyes probed me deeply.

"You sure that was it?" he asked in a way that told me that . . .

He knew! He knew! Shit.

"I'm sure!" My face flamed red. A thumping sound started in my ears as my heart moved into my head and beat rapidly. I turned away only to come face-to-face, so to speak, with the rabbit to our left. I looked away in the opposite direction, not daring to make eye contact with him or the sex toy. The presence of the toy was making the whole situation so much worse, making the tingle return, this time in my shoulder, pressing up against his.

"Are you sure that was it?" His voice was even softer now, and I nodded in response and then almost died of relief when a lifesaver, still wearing a dripping wet swimsuit, ran into the room and put an end to our awkward conversation.

As it turned out, Jagger did need exactly four tiny stitches, which a small local clinic down the road provided—albeit in a very long and protracted manner. And by the time we got back to the resort, it was already dark. I called for some room service. Our parents were still nowhere to be found and, as the evening progressed, so did the bruise around Jagger's eye—and my accompanying embarrassment and guilt and multitude of apologies delivered in several ways. I'd made him an ice pack for his eye, but with the rising heat, the incessant and indescribable heatwave in which we were gripped, it melted faster than it had time to dull the bruise.

"I want this heat to be over," Jagger moaned.

"Me too."

"It's your fault that Zanzibar is in the grip of a heatwave. You shouldn't have pissed off the weather gods!"

"It's like a sauna in here." I walked over to the AC and checked that it was working. It was, but it wasn't making even the smallest dent in the stifling room. I went into the bathroom and wet two towels under the shower. With a dripping wet towel on my head, I walked back into the room to find Jagger lying on the floor.

"They downplayed it. This is not a heatwave. This is hell opening up and swallowing us in flames." Jagger wiggled his shirt off and tossed it onto the bed. "Are you sure the AC is on full blast?" He looked up at it as it blew out some pathetic wisps of cold air that melted immediately in the heat.

"Yup!" I flopped down in the rattan chair, which actually felt as if it had been left out in the sun all day.

"Try the floor." Jagger patted the floor next to him.

"Okay, shuffle over." I lowered myself to the floor. "Oooh, that feels good," I said as my body came into contact with the cool tiles.

"Enjoy it while it lasts. It will warm up soon."

"We could move around the floor, rotate places like they rotate crops!" I suggested, and we both laughed through the heat and sweat dripping off our bodies. I looked at the open windows and doors. "Breeze! Breeze!" I moaned at the open cavities. "Not even a tiny breeze!" I watched the trees outside willing one to come, but the leaves were as still as statues.

Suddenly, I felt a breeze, but it wasn't coming from the door—it was coming from next to me. Jagger was flapping a brochure at me and the cool wind on my face felt like heaven.

"Oh my god." I rolled over to give him more access to me. "More! More!"

Jagger continued to flap the magazine and I closed my eyes in bliss.

"Faster!" I moaned, and Jagger laughed. "And don't you dare make a joke about how that sounds. I know how that sounds and I don't care. I want it hard and fast, Jagger!"

I opened my eyes and smiled at him through the blur of the impromptu fan.

"If I do you, will you do me?" he asked cheekily.

"Perhaps," I teased him.

"Look at us—who would have thought."

"What?"

"Well, if you'd told me last week that you and I would be lying on our backs together, scantily clad and sweating, I wouldn't have believed it."

"Very funny." I leaned into the fan wind even more until I was almost on top of him. But the second he stopped fanning, and I stopped fanning him when it was his turn, the heat rushed back as if it had never been gone at all.

"We can't keep this up all night," I said, crawling to another, cooler part of the floor.

"I know." Jagger crawled after me and we both flopped down on the cool tiles.

"What is the temperature?" I groaned.

"Now you're willing to trust the weather app?" Jagger quipped, holding his phone in the air above us. I scooched closer as he thumbed the screen.

"Now that, *that* I believe. Finally they get it right!" I pointed at the number on the screen. "It's ten at night and it's ninety-eight degrees. And with the humidity, it says a real feel of one hundred and four!"

"That's it. I can't take this anymore. I need to cool down." Jagger stood up and looked down at me.

"How?"

"Well, this is an island you know."

"A night swim!" I jumped up at the idea. "Yes."

Jagger grabbed the towels, and we dragged our hot, heavy limbs into the oppressive, humid night. We walked through the dense vegetation, each move making us hotter and hotter. We passed the pool and found a few people there—we were not the only ones who'd had this idea. And when we got to the shore we saw a few bodies lying on the sand, feet in the shallow waters. We walked up the beach until we arrived at a secluded spot. The sea was so still it looked solid, as if you could walk across its surface. But the still surface was quickly broken as Jagger ran into the ocean. He dived and disappeared, and when he emerged, he looked like a different man.

"This is amazing. Hurry!"

"I am!" I pulled my dress off and tossed it onto the ground. I was wearing one of my mother's bikinis, and I hoped the top would do a good enough job of holding me in. I was about to walk into the sea but stopped when I saw how Jagger was looking at me.

"What?" I put my hands on my hips defiantly and felt things jiggle. "I'm sure you're not used to seeing women's bodies like this but get used to it." I threw my head back and marched into the sea.

"Why do you do that?" Jagger asked. "Always make these assumptions about me."

"Like what?"

"What kind of person I am. What I might like or dislike. What I may or may not be used to. It actually kind of pisses me off."

I stopped walking again. He sounded genuinely angry.

Something hit me in the stomach. He was right, and I knew I needed to say it. I steeled myself. "You're right. I'm sorry. I haven't tried to get to know you, and I do make assumptions. When half the staff was laid off and the paper went online, and then you came along and you were doing and writing things that we never used to do . . . I guess it unsettled me. I get anxious and . . ." I took the biggest in-breath I think I'd ever taken. "I've treated you unfairly. And I'm sorry."

Jagger was silent for a moment, and then he smiled again. "Apology accepted."

"Is that it? Just 'apology accepted'?"

"Yes. Why?"

"You're not angry anymore?"

"I don't hold grudges, and when people apologize, I'm quick to forgive."

"Huh!" I eyed him, not sure I believed him. "So you're over it? That quickly?"

"Shouldn't I be?"

"I mean, I don't know. I don't think I get over things that quickly, but I suppose there's no timeline to these things . . ."

Water whipped across my face, and I jumped.

"What the hell?"

"Stop overthinking my accepting your apology and just get in. Seriously, you have no idea what you're missing."

I didn't need any more convincing. The cool water that Jagger had splashed across my body felt amazing, as if it was putting out a fire. I rushed into the sea and as soon as I was deep enough, I dived. The water engulfed me and cooled me and soothed me as I cut through it, feeling very elegant and mermaid-like.

"This was a good idea," I said when I popped back up.

"I'm full of good ideas," Jagger said, and then moved closer to me. "If you'd ever listen."

"Ah, so you're *not* totally over it?"

"I am, but I thought I would rub it in one last time, just for added effect. Did it work?"

"Yes," I admitted.

"So, when we get back to the office, you think we could try and be friends? Call a truce?" Jagger moved closer to me and, even though I was submerged in cool water, something felt as if it was warming me up.

"A truce? That would be nice," I said.

Jagger stopped his approach and sat down in the shallows. I did the same, and we sat shoulder to shoulder in the water. We gazed at the horizon, which seemed so far away. The moon was making everything around us a silvery color and the sky above us looked like a sea of glitter on a black canvas.

"It's beautiful," I whispered in absolute awe. "And cool. So, so cool." I swished my hands through the water and then said the first thing that popped into my head. "I love this moment." I blushed as the words flew out into the night air around us. They seemed to have a sense of weight to them, and they didn't quite dissolve immediately. Instead, they lingered, swirling around us.

Jagger shifted. He was facing me now. "I love this moment too." And then he did something that made everything inside me boil all over again. He reached out and brushed the sand off my cheek. I flinched but didn't pull away. Instead, my eyes found his and that feeling began to build inside me again.

I couldn't shift my gaze away from his. His eyes were by far his most startling feature, gray and highlighted by long dark lashes. And with the addition of this ghostly silver light, they were almost ethereal. After cutting the checkerboard out, his dark hair was much shorter on the sides, but the top still had that ruffled, messy quality to it. His hair always looked as if he'd climbed straight out of bed and hadn't run a brush through it and, being in such humidity, I'd noticed a definite curl to it. Unruly curls that made it stand up in all directions. His hair was messy and somewhat rebellious, which suited his personality. He had a little white scar on the bridge of his nose, which I now knew how he'd gotten, and this gave his face a feeling of comfortable familiarity. He had the start of a holiday beard; he was always stubbly and never cleanly shaved, but I'd never seen his facial hair this long. It framed his face, which was angular.

His features were not soft and subtle, they were not rounded and cute; they were the antithesis, and for the first time ever, I think I got it. I got what everyone said and thought about him. He *was* hot. And for some bizarre reason, the small, fresh cut above his eyebrow and the bruise round his eye added to this hotness. Clearly this was some biological throwback to the times when men dueled over women, the stronger winner emerging bruised and battered to claim his prize.

"What's going on in that brain of yours?" he asked breathily.

"Nothing." *Another lie.* I looked away, hoping he wasn't asking that because he already knew the answer and just wanted to hear me say it out loud. But of course he knew the answer; the little twinkle in his eyes and skewed, self-satisfied smile confirmed it. Two options here: I could either continue with my bad lie or . . .

"I find you attractive, even if you're not the last man in the universe," I said brazenly, turning back to him. "There, I said it. I'm a cliché, another woman who thinks you're good looking. Happy?"

"I am, actually."

"Mmmm, of course you are. You like having a fan club."

"That's not why I'm happy," he said, and then the water around us rippled as Jagger moved even closer. "I'm happy because *you* said it."

I tried to swallow but couldn't. "Happy you've finally won me over?"

"Why is everything a competition with you? Can't I just be happy? Full stop. No hidden agenda. No ulterior motives—just happy that the woman I've had a crush on for the last six months has finally noticed me."

I was about to scoff, roll my eyes and laugh again when . . . "Wait, you *are* being serious this time!"

"I was being serious last time too."

"You're serious?"

"Deadly."

"Okay . . . wait . . . I need a moment to absorb this."

Jagger chuckled. "Take as many moments as you like."

I looked out over the ocean again, trying to find the horizon line in the silver glow. My mind raced. Thoughts like those small fishes swimming around the reef flitted through my brain, weaving in and out of my gray matter.

"So, you've liked me for six months now—the entire time we've been working together—yet you've purposefully driven me up the wall on several occasions and take great delight in deliberately doing it?"

"I know, it's all very Peter Clifton," Jagger said.

"Ah . . . very. Why didn't you just act normal and ask me out like an adult might have done?"

"I did."

"No, you didn't!"

"Yes, I did. Multiple times. I asked you if you wanted to come to that new gin bar I had to write a review about, and a week after that I invited you to that theater show and that restaurant I needed to review."

"Those weren't dates, were they?"

"They were dates. I was asking you out on dates. Multiple times."

"And end up in one of your columns? I don't think so."

"Is that what you think I do? Ask women out just to write about them all?"

"Well, you are writing a weekly, single-guy dating column, dating how many people I would hate to hazard a guess."

"I'm not dating anyone. I'm going on dates for work and writing about it. I'm not getting intimate with any of them, not going on second dates. Besides, I would hardly call a speed-dating evening *dating*."

"You wrote an article about how to set up a good, more right-swipeable Tinder profile."

"I didn't go on any dates with anyone who swiped on me."

"You wrote an article on threesomes and sex parties and—"

"I didn't participate. I went as a journalist."

"Sex toys?"

Jagger cleared his throat and went a little pink in the cheeks. "Those I did personally try, but—"

"Okay. Stop. I don't want to hear about your experiences with those, uh, things."

"Fleshlights."

"God, it feels like every conversation today leads us back to sex toys," I said, and shook my head. "It's ridiculous."

"I'm not this big, single player like you think I am, by the way. I'm dating because I want to find someone to settle down with. I'm not looking to play the field—I told you this. To be a total cliché here, I'm looking for love."

"On Tinder?"

"On Tinder, at speed dating, at a bar, at a club"—he paused—"on a tropical island in the sea."

His words stole the breath from my lungs, but I managed a strangled whisper. "I told you: I don't date."

Jagger sighed. "I know. It's a pity."

"I'm sure you'll get over it." I turned away from him and looked back out over the sea.

"I guess I'll have to, won't I?"

We settled into silence again, but this time the silence was loaded with awkwardness. A thought was beginning to take shape; it sat in the front of my brain but I didn't quite know what it was yet. I felt this energy building up, this coiling, roiling, boiling energy that turned the mystery thought into actual words and I finally knew what I was thinking and feeling.

I was flattered.

A little bit thrilled.

I was bloody turned on . . . again!

I caught the faint whisper of a song. A familiar song. There was a light on the sea in the distance, a yacht maybe, and it was playing one of Leighton's songs.

"Listen." Jagger pointed in the direction of the yacht.

"I know! He's everywhere. I can't escape him."

"Spin me on your love access, baby. Spin me, kiss me. Kiss me in the dark," Jagger whisper-sang next to me, and I joined in softly.

"Spin me, kiss me. Kiss me in the dark."

We turned and looked at each other, smiling, waiting for the falsetto to kick in, which we both knew was impossible to sing. We bobbed our heads in unison, waiting for the vocals. Our smiles grew and we both took deep breaths and . . .

"Kiss meeeeee! Kiss meeeee!"

It was impossibly high, and I grabbed my throat trying to make it. Jagger's face went red and a vein in his neck bulged as he tried to reach the note but failed dismally and started coughing. And then, as suddenly as it started, the music went off.

"Kiss me," I said.

"In the dark," Jagger sang back badly.

"No, kiss me," I repeated.

"The song's stopped." Jagger pointed in the direction of the yacht. The lights had gone off.

"I wasn't singing. I was saying, kiss me."

"Now?"

"Right now." I leaned closer, making my intentions crystal clear. He leaned, too, and then stopped abruptly.

"Do you know what you're saying? I told you that I liked you."

I nodded, even though I had no idea what the hell I was doing. I had no logical explanation for this other than I was caught up in a perfect moment. Sea and cool and stars and Jagger and songs from my best friend that I was taking as some kind of cosmic sign.

"You sure?" Jagger's lips were centimeters from mine.

"I've never wanted anything more." *Wait, had I just said that? And was that actually the truth? Because if it was, I had certainly not been aware of that. Or had I . . .*

I stared into his eyes, trying to communicate with him as the warm, tropical waters lapped against our sticky skin. This moment felt so perfect. The silver moon bathed us in an iridescent glow as our faces moved closer to each other and the gap between our mouths disappeared and our lips touched. We stayed like that, lips brushing each other's ever so softly and then . . .

We kissed.

The kiss was slow and sexy—and familiar. I hadn't expected that. His hands on my face, in my hair, stroking the back of my neck, his cool fingertips across my jaw. This kiss didn't feel like the kind of kiss strangers gave each other. This kiss felt like it was the culmination of something that had been building between us for a while now. Maybe it had?

But soon the kiss was no longer comfortable—it was desperate and wanting. Hard and fast and messy. We pressed our bodies into each other's until there was no room left between us. The air was hot and humid but not nearly as hot as the blood coursing through me. My insides felt as if they were on fire, and the man I was kissing was gasoline. He'd ignited something inside me, something so inexplicably big that it couldn't be contained. A sense of urgent need—the greatest need I have ever known—pulling, clawing, screaming need, and suddenly, without any real conscious memory of how I'd gotten there, I was straddling his lap. Somehow, in the hungry kissing, I'd climbed onto him. My breasts pushed into his chest once more. He pulled me closer, dragging me across his lap. He was hard—I could feel it—and all that separated us now were mere pieces of fabric. I ground into him—I wanted to push that fabric aside and feel him. All of him. I threw my head back and moaned loudly as Jagger's hands slipped over my breasts, grazing my nipples, stopping to tease them between his fingers. I looked down at his hands. *His* hands. On *my* body. *His* hands were on *my* body, and it was as if it was only dawning on me now. And when it did, I burst out laughing. I laughed so hard that I fell off his lap.

"Are you okay?"

"We're kissing," I managed between snorts of laughter.

"I think we're doing more than that," Jagger said.

"I *know!*" I half shouted into the night.

"Do you want to stop?" he asked, which brought my laugher to an abrupt stop. I stared at him. He stared back.

"So, do you?" he asked again.

Did I want to stop kissing him? It should have been such a simple question: Yes or no? But it wasn't. It was the most complicated question I'd ever been asked. Because I wasn't just kissing anyone—I was kissing *him*. The man I'd thought I absolutely despised. The man I'd been forced to share a desk with at work for the last six months, whom I'd fantasized about getting fired more times than I could count. Who drove me to literal drink, drove me crazy, drove me up the bend and sometimes even drove me to have thoughts of physical violence. But despite all this, the answer flew out of my mouth.

"Absolutely not!" As fast as I could, I climbed back onto his lap and wrapped my arms around him, our lips finding each other's immediately.

"God, I've wanted to do this for so long," he whispered against my mouth, his warm breath making my skin prickle. I arched my back, creating a space between us, a space in which he could explore me with more ease. He lowered his mouth and ran his tongue across my chest. It was warm against my cool skin, sending shivers down my back. I ground into him and he moaned in response, which was the hottest thing that I'd ever heard in my life. "You're so fucking hot!"

Correction, *that* was the hottest thing I'd ever heard in my life, and it was enough to throw me over the edge, even though I was already teetering on its precipice. I pulled my bikini aside, allowing my naked breasts to tumble into his hands as I ground into him, again and again and again. Jagger took my nipple in his mouth. He sucked and licked and moaned against me as we swayed back and forth like this, the water rippling and splashing around us.

"We . . . we . . ." I panted, "can't. Not here . . . we—"

"Can't go back to that room," Jagger said as he squeezed my nipples between his fingers, and I almost flew off his lap and into the sky.

"We'll die of heatstroke," I managed.

"Here?" Jagger pulled away and looked at the water around us.

"And risk getting a sea urchin somewhere you wouldn't want to? I don't think so."

"Hammock?"

"Too much swing!"

Jagger stood up in the water and pulled me with him. "Well, room it is, then."

We both ran back to the room. I don't think I'd ever run so fast in my life, and running was not an activity that women my size are usually good at. Things tend to bounce and jiggle and hurt, but this time I ran like a bloody gazelle and, before I knew it, we were inside. We both stood there, out of breath, and looked around.

"Too hot!" I moaned.

"Way too hot," Jagger agreed, and then stepped into the bathroom and turned the shower on.

"You want to . . . in the shower?" I stared at the water in shock.

"Is that a bit too . . ."

"Too?" Heat pulsed between my legs.

"Yeah, maybe the shower isn't the best idea. And this obviously doesn't need to go any further," Jagger said, and then turned the shower off.

"What?" The heat between my legs was now screaming at me and I crossed them to squeeze it away. That didn't work—it only made it more intense. "You want to . . . *stop?*"

Jagger walked out of the bathroom, smiling, and stopped in front of me. "No, but we can. It's your choice."

I grabbed his hips and pulled him closer to me. Our bodies slammed together with a sweaty thud. And that thud was enough to set it all off again . . .

"Turn that shower ON!" I pushed Jagger away from me and gave him a pat on the ass as he ran back into the bathroom.

"Yes, ma'am," he teased me as I rushed inside and then slammed the door behind us. I immediately reached for his pants and then a thought hit me. I pulled his pants away and looked down. A wave of relief washed over me.

"Oh, thank god!" I said out loud, and Jagger laughed.

"Are you checking I don't have a dick ring?"

"Shit, how did you know?"

Jagger pulled me into his arms and kissed me on the forehead. "Do you want to message Lesego quickly and tell her?"

"No."

"You sure? We can stop for a while, and you can let her know."

"NO!" I said a little louder this time. "I do not want to stop!"

And then Jagger's face dropped. "I don't have protection."

My brain raced and suddenly I knew exactly what to do. Thank god for lost luggage . . .

"The suitcase! I saw some in the suitcase."

I jumped out of the bath, raced over to the case as fast as I could, feet skidding across the floor, and was back with Jagger before he'd almost had time to blink.

"You really want to have sex with me?" he teased me, and all I could do was nod.

And we certainly did have sex. Crazy, hot sex. We slipped around the bathtub, trying to get at each other in as many ways as possible as the cool water cascaded down on us. And then, when we seemed to have found the thing that worked best—me bent over, clutching the towel rail, Jagger behind me, driving into me, while our bodies bashed together, sending the water flying all over the bathroom floor and nearby mirror—just as I was about to come, Jagger stopped.

"Not like this," he panted, pulling out of me so suddenly that I gasped.

"Wh-wh . . . huh?"

Jagger pulled me from the shower and then, with surprising strength, picked me up and put me on the bathroom vanity. The vanity was small and the tap pushed into my back, but it was also the perfect height. I opened my legs and Jagger slid between them. He took my face between his hands and kissed me.

"I want to look at you."

I think I melted into the faux marble counter as everything changed again. The sex was no longer hungry and desperate. Instead it became slow and deep; the kind of sex strangers do *not* have. The kind of sex where your eyes are involved; the kind of sex where you can't stop kissing each other, even when you're coming. And then when he comes, he grips your face and looks into your eyes as you watch that blank look of unfocused pleasure wash across his.

The kind of sex where you hold each other afterward, as if you're actual lovers instead of sworn work enemies.

Chapter **Thirty-two**

"Morning," I said, not daring to look at Jagger. I'd avoided looking at him since he'd released me and I'd slid off the bathroom vanity, casting my eye back at the mirror to see the red mark the tap had left across my back. And I'd definitely avoided eye contact when he'd pulled me close and given me a slow, tender kiss on the forehead that seemed to say more than we'd ever said to each other before. The only time I'd actually looked at him was when he'd fallen asleep, and I'd stared at him for what felt like hours, trying to figure out how the man I'd thought I didn't like had just given me multiple orgasms.

I reached for one of the breakfast croissants, not because I was particularly hungry, but because I was scared that if anyone had to ask me any question today, I might blurt it all out.

Coffee, Margaret-Skye?

I SLEPT WITH JAGGER LAST NIGHT!

Can I pass you the sugar, darling?

AND IT WAS GOOD!

No, I was lying to myself. It hadn't just been "good"—it had been amazing. Mind-blowing. I pushed the entire croissant into my mouth and coughed a few times, sending little flakes of puff pastry flying across the table. I picked up a serviette and held it in front of my mouth as I tried to chew what was clearly too big for one bite. I could see Jagger looking at me from the corner of my eye.

"Hungry?" my mom asked. She and Eddy had finally emerged from obscurity and were seated at the breakfast table with us.

I nodded because I couldn't open my mouth to speak.

"Well, I'm glad you're both here, because Eddy and I have something to announce." My mom laced her fingers through Eddy's in a way that made me stop chewing.

"Eddy and I . . ." She blushed and pushed a long strand of gray hair behind her ear. "Have decided to . . ."

"Get married!" Eddy jumped in excitedly.

"Wfffat?" I sprayed little machine-gun bullets of pastry across the table. They landed in cups of coffee and glasses of orange juice.

"I know!" my mom gushed. "It's amazing. And perfect and we can't wait!"

I downed a glass of water, trying to wash down the croissant while chewing as fast as I could. I felt like one of those competitive eaters, but I needed to respond to this madness as quickly as possible.

"And won't it be so funny," Eddy said, "when you and Jagger are related?"

At that . . . *it happened.*

I beat my chest as the first flake of pastry was inhaled. I could feel it in my lungs. Large, wet chunks of the croissant exploded out of my mouth in a melodramatic coughing fit. One piece flew across the table and landed on Eddy with a thud. I grabbed for the nearest liquid, a cup of coffee, and threw it into my mouth. It scalded my tongue and I spat it out in a shower.

"You okay?" Jagger reached for me, but I grabbed a serviette and beat him with it. I did not want him touching me.

"Margaret!" My mom jumped up.

"No one panic." Eddy stood up dramatically, tossing his serviette onto the table. "I used to work as a lifesaver at the local pool in 1955."

He rushed over and wrapped his arms around me. "I know the Heimlich maneuver."

"I don't need the Heim—" I coughed and spluttered, trying to stop him as he started bouncing me up and down, my feet lifting off the ground as he did it. I felt like a weightless rag doll in his overly exuberant hands. "Stop!" I yelled, my rib cage feeling as if it was going to cave in.

"Dad, I think that's too hard!"

"You have to do it vigorously," Eddy countered. "In order to Get. It. All. Out!" He heaved me hard with each word.

"Harder!" my mother shouted in panic.

"Stop! Stop!" I tried to pull away from what was becoming an over-zealous rescue. Jagger grabbed Eddy's hands and pulled them off my body and next thing I felt gravity disappear. I was falling. I waved my arms in the air, imitating a bird, which I knew was a totally futile attempt to stay afloat. Needless to say, I didn't, and I crashed straight into Jagger's outstretched arms. We swayed for a second as Jagger tried to hold us up, but alas, all dignity was lost when we toppled to the floor and a small crowd gathered around us.

I'd closed my eyes somewhere in the tumble, and when I finally opened them, I was face-to-face with Jagger. Those same gray eyes I'd looked into when I'd come last night—*a few times, more than a few . . . SHIT, stop thinking about that*—were boring holes into mine.

"You okay?" he whispered.

I didn't respond. I thought it was obvious that I was far, *very far*, from being okay.

"You okay?" he asked again, and I felt like crying. Because I was the opposite of okay. Was there even a word for this, a word that could point me so far away from "okay" that it was not even in the same dictionary?

"We . . . we . . ." I stutter-whispered, as one last pastry crumb shot out of my mouth and landed on Jagger's shirt. I tried to wipe it away, but Jagger placed his hand over mine.

"We what?" He squeezed my hand gently.

"Sssss . . ." I sustained the *s* for far too long, but the other letters did not want to come out. Letting them all out would be like releasing horror into the world. But they came out anyway. "Sssstepsiblings! Ssstep!" I cringed in revulsion and felt the nausea rise up in me. "I think I'm going to be . . ." I jumped off Jagger and ran across the restaurant into the bathroom as quickly as I could.

I didn't physically get sick, but I did have to splash my face with water to douse the clammy, nauseating feeling that crawled across my skin like a nest of baby spiders had hatched on me. I grabbed the basin and held myself up with shaky arms as the bathroom door opened.

"Mom"—I spun around—"you can't be serious."

"Are you okay?" She moved toward me but I blocked her approach.

"Mom, you can't be serious about marrying Eddy!"

"Why not?"

"You don't even know him!"

"I do. We haven't stopped talking for the past six days!"

"Exactly, six days! Mom, this is a holiday fling. This is like an episode of *The Bachelor*: crystal bloody lapping waters and snorkeling and sunsets and fucking tropical bloody fish. This place is designed for romance. That's what this is. A holiday romance. God, if everyone went off to marry the person they had a holiday fling with, the divorce rates would be twice as high!"

She folded her arms. "Well, I think that's very rude and patronizing, darling."

"Mom, you can't fall in love with someone in six days—that's impossible."

"Who says?" She was starting to sound combative, which was a very unfamiliar side to my mother. My mom usually "went with the flow" but now she was standing in front of the flow, stopping it like a dam.

"Besides, you're a widow!" I added.

"So you want me to close my heart forever after your dad?"

"Uh . . . no. I mean . . . but why so soon? It's only just been a year."

"Well, at my age one year is like seven dog years. I'm sixty-five—there aren't as many good years left when you get to my age."

"God, Mom, you're hardly a geriatric case."

"Margaret-Skye!" my mom shouted, and I froze. I'd never heard her shout before. "In five years' time I might not have the hips for sex anymore!"

"God!" I covered my face and felt the first wave of cringe rock me.

"I've fallen in love! I didn't mean to. I wasn't expecting it, but it happened. And I'm going to marry Eddy, and I would like it very much if you would be my maid of honor!"

"Maid of—" I shook my head, took a deep breath, and tried to control the tone of what I was going to say next. "You miss Dad. I get it. You guys were together forever, and I know your heart is broken, and I've seen you struggle this year, but you can't replace him to make yourself feel better with the first infatuation that comes along. It will never work, Mom."

My mom's hand flew up to her chest. "Replace him? You think I could ever replace your father?"

I shrugged. "I don't know, Mom. You tell me."

"Marrying Eddy does not mean I don't still love and miss your dad. It doesn't mean that I'm replacing him and the memories I shared with him. I could never replace him."

A tear slipped down my cheek. So many emotions had welled up inside that they were physically leaking out. Jagger and I'd had sex last night, and now my mom thought she was in love with his dad. It felt as if the entire world had gone mad and reality had been flipped on its head.

"How can you still love Dad but want to marry someone else?"

My mom straightened up and ran a hand over her kaftan. "You are my daughter, and I love you very much. But I'm also my own person, and as such, I think I know my own heart. I'm going to be marrying Eddy on this island before we leave, and it would be wonderful to have you standing next to me, but if you won't, then I'm still doing it." And with that, she turned and walked out of the bathroom, and I was left staring after her.

Chapter **Thirty-three**

Margaret: MY MOTHER HAS LOST HER MIND!

Leighton: Let me guess, you've just heard?

Margaret: Wait, you know??

Leighton: Anke called me this morning and asked me to come for the wedding

Margaret: You're coming???

Leighton: I've booked my jet and everything

Margaret: Thank god! Maybe you can talk some sense into her

Leighton: Doubt it. The heart wants healing love

Margaret: Stop quoting your song lyrics at me. This is not the time for jokes

Leighton: But how funny is it that you and Jagger are going to be related?!

Margaret: I HAD SEX WITH HIM LAST NIGHT

Leighton: OMG! What?

Leighton: 😂😂😂😂😂😂😂😂😂😂😂😂

Leighton: Babe, seriously, there are not enough emojis for that

Margaret: So stop trying and take this seriously

Leighton: Okay, was it good?

I paused, an involuntary smile crawling across over my lips, and I immediately berated my mouth for betraying me.

Leighton: Hello, was it good?

Margaret: Amazing. Okay. Happy now?

Leighton: You're like the title of one of those Pornhub videos. "Stepbrother gives stepsister ten orgasms!"

Margaret: STOP!

Leighton: Stepsister seduces her stepbrother

Margaret: Stop!!!

Leighton: Family sinners; my stepsister seduces me

Margaret: STOPPPPP!

Leighton: Okay, okay. But seriously, stepsiblings aren't real relations when you didn't grow up together. And you're both adults! And there was something between you long before your parents even hooked up

Margaret: There was nothing between us before our parents hooked up!

Leighton: 😳

Margaret: Seriously, why does everyone keep saying that? I didn't even like Jagger

Until now, I thought.

Margaret: OMG I feel sick to my stomach

Margaret: I had sex with my soon-to-be stepbrother!

Leighton: I hope you used protection, otherwise your baby will be your cousin, or something

Margaret: Yes, we used protection

Margaret: I feel so dirty!!!!!

Leighton: But sometimes being dirty feels so goooood!

Margaret: Song lyrics again. Stop!

Margaret: My mom can't really love him, can she?

Margaret: She's in lust. This is a lusty holiday fling, right?

Leighton: I don't know, she sounded totally smitten when she called. I haven't heard her sound that happy in ages

Margaret: That's all the sex hormones. They're gushing in her brain, overwhelming her reason and logic. She is high on oxytocin and dopamine right now, so she only thinks she's in love. But she's not. She needs a twelve-step program, not to step down the aisle

Leighton: What's the worst that can happen? They go back home and in a month realize it was all the dopamine, get divorced, and go their separate ways. At least she was whisked off her feet and had some great sex

Margaret: What if he breaks her heart?

Leighton: And what if he doesn't?

Leighton: What if she's happy and loved and high on dopamine for the rest of her days?

Leighton: It's better than being high on ayahuasca

Margaret: Only barely…

Leighton: Listen, I should be there in a few hours we can talk about it then!

Margaret: Hey, where are you staying? This place is fully booked

Leighton: Not the presidential suite

Margaret: I should have known they wouldn't let us common folk stay in there for the night. This is their fault then. If they hadn't said they were fully booked we wouldn't have had to share rooms and then this would not have happened. Can you sue a hotel for this?

Leighton: Sue them for the best sex of your life. I'm sure everyone will take great pity on you. Poor little Margaret who came like a steam train last night… just how many times by the way?

Margaret: Cul-de-sac of NO!

Leighton: Cul-de-sac of tell me later when I'm there

Margaret: Cul-de-sac of not in your wildest dreams

Margaret: When will you be here. How many hours?

Leighton: About five

Margaret: Okay, I need to spend the next five hours hiding from Jagger. I can't look him in the eye again. How am I going to work with him? I'll have to quit. I'll have to quit and flee Joburg

Leighton: You're being such a drama queen now

Margaret: I learned from the best, didn't I?

Leighton: Well, go and hide and I'll see you later

Leighton: You know you're living in a soap opera right now

Margaret: It certainly feels like one

Despite the size of the lodge, the jungle-like surroundings, and the beach that stretched on for ages, hiding was hard. Especially because I was lugging a suitcase that wasn't mine around with me now! I'd snuck into our room when Jagger wasn't there, threw everything I had into that suitcase—at least it was good for something—and then made a stealthy retreat. I'd walked around for a while, trying to decide what to do with the hours that stretched out ahead of me. The resort was filling up with people heading to the beach and populating the pool and, if I didn't get away from these common areas, I knew I would be spotted soon. I walked down one of the wooden paths that cut through the undergrowth. I'd noticed a sign that read NO GUESTS BEYOND THIS POINT and I headed for it. Usually, I was not one for breaking rules, unless in a work capacity while chasing a story, but today called for rule breaking. I'd already broken the worst rule I could last night: sleeping with the enemy.

Enemy . . . that word no longer seemed right. I was starting to forget why I hadn't liked Jagger in the first place. My feelings of dislike for him had started to be replaced by feelings of . . .

"No!" I said out loud. "I don't like Jagger, do I?" That was impossible. Liking Jagger Villain was utterly impossible.

And yet you did have sex with him, mocked a voice in my head. I walked past the NO GUESTS sign, which seemed to lead to a series of small rooms. I looked in the first one: pool pump; the second one seemed to be a workshop of some kind, and the last one was a large laundry room. There was a small chair outside the laundry room, and I plonked myself down and took out my phone. Four hours and forty minutes. What on earth was I going to do, sitting here in the middle of the undergrowth by a laundry room in this heat? This seemed like a low point in my life, very, very low. My phone pinged suddenly.

> **Leighton**: Go hang out in my room. I called the resort and told them you would be coming. I hate the idea of you running around incognito for five hours. It seems so undignified

Margaret: OMG, thank you. You're a lifesaver. I was squatting in the bush by the laundry room

I slipped my phone into my pocket, grabbed the suitcase, and dashed for the reception desk. I couldn't wait to get into Leighton's room. Maybe I'd order a cocktail. I needed one. Maybe I needed two. But on my way to reception, much to my horror, I saw *him*.

"Shit!" I turned, looking for a place to hide. A large potted plant caught my attention, and I slithered behind it as quickly as I could.

"Hey!" Jagger called, and I froze. *If I freeze, will he see me?* But this rather obviously moronic question of mine was quickly answered.

"Where have you been all day?"

"Jagger, oh, hi. I didn't see you there."

"I've been looking for you."

"You have?" I adopted the sort of nonchalance that only someone like Jagger might have. I made my limbs all floppy in an *I don't care* way, and barely opened my mouth when I spoke. I didn't care! I was chill! Cool . . . that's what my attitude was meant to convey, anyway, but judging by the smile creeping across Jagger's lips, I doubt it was coming close to achieving any of that.

"You've been hiding from me all day, haven't you?"

"No, I haven't."

"Then why are you standing behind a potted plant?"

I opened my mouth to speak but nothing came out. Jagger's smile wavered and he stepped closer to me. A serious, purposeful step. The kind of step that told me something big was about to go down.

"Are you okay? After last night. You seem . . ." He let the unfinished sentence hang in the air and it was clear he wanted me to fill in the blanks with words that might explain my current behavior.

Confused?

Embarrassed?

Uncomfortable?

Horny?

"I'm fine!" I chirped, forcing bright, sparkly positivity into my voice.

"Then why haven't you been able to look me in the eye since we had sex?"

"Shhhh!" I shushed him, looking around.

"There's no one around to hear us."

"I can hear us."

Jagger's brow knitted in confusion first, and then something else when his eyes drifted down and settled on the suitcase. "Jesus, was it that bad?"

"No, no, it's not that . . . Leighton is coming here for the wedding, and I haven't seen him in a while and I thought it would be more comfortable, for both of us, if I stayed with him."

"Okaaay." Jagger looked hurt. "Did I . . . uh, did things maybe go too fast and far last night?" He looked at me with these vulnerable puppy eyes that caused my insides to melt.

"No, things didn't go too far. What happened . . . I wanted it to happen, and it was . . ."

Fucking amazing?

Multi-orgasmic?

Hot as hell?

I bit my lip. *Shit.* I hadn't meant to. But the image of me with my back pressed into the wall, my one leg up resting on the edge of the bathtub, Jagger on his knees, his face buried between my legs while I grabbed the showerhead to stop myself from falling over from the pleasure, flashed in my head.

"Look, can't we just pretend that never happened?" I said quickly before I lost the nerve.

"What?"

"Or it did happen, but it was a mistake. We'll put it down to heatstroke. We were suffering some kind of fever and, you know, fevers can affect your thinking."

"You're saying we were out of our minds when we slept together?"

"Exactly!" I snapped my fingers, so glad he was getting this.

"I wasn't out of my mind," Jagger said firmly. "And, quite honestly, it didn't look like you were out of your mind either. I mean, you were very clear and specific about the things you wanted me to do to you."

"I was not."

"Um . . . I wasn't the one who told me to me go 'faster' and 'harder' on multiple occasions!"

"Oh god!" I dropped my face into my hands and groaned. "Stop! Please. We're going to be stepsiblings. Does that not make you feel repulsed?"

"It's not like we grew up together!"

"You sound like Leighton now."

"Leighton sounds wise." Jagger slithered even closer. His approach was slow and sexy, and he was staring at my lips and all I could think about now was how my lips had been around a very intimate part of his last night and how he'd wiggled and grabbed the back of my head and thrust into my . . .

"*Whoa!*" I held both my hands up this time. "Back off. Do not take another step. Stay away from me, Jagger."

"How the fuck am I meant to stay away from you after last night?"

"Like I said, forget last night happened."

"Forget it? Forget you on top of me like that? Naked. Forget your head between my legs, me between yours. The way you looked and tasted. The sound you made when you came, the way your legs shook and clenched around me." His voice was soft and low and now I was staring at his lips too. Staring and stepping forward.

"Stop it. You're deliberately trying to turn me on, and that's not fair."

"All's fair in love and war, don't they say?"

"This is not love, Jagger." I started walking up the path again.

"Call it whatever makes you happy, but that doesn't change the fact it happened."

"Many things happen, Jagger. Many, many things happen every single day to many, many people. That doesn't mean we should talk about those things."

I heard another one of those Jagger chuckles behind me. Those chuckles that told me he found me amusing. That he found my quirks, what had he called them, charming? I stopped walking and swung around indignantly.

"Is this some kind of a joke to you?" I looked at him and his smile faded.

"What's the punchline, then?" he replied.

"The what?"

"If this is a joke, what's the punchline? A guy walks into a bar, leaves with the woman he's liked for half a year, they spend one night together, an amazing, amazing night, and next morning she's packed a bag and gone? That's not a very funny punchline, don't you think?"

I stared at him. I didn't know what to say. He kept telling me how much he liked me, for how long, and I'd started to believe him. The only problem was I just didn't know how I was supposed to feel about this.

"Where are you really going, anyway? This place is fully booked."

"Not the presidential suite."

"Seriously? I would pay to see that. Can I come with you?"

"I don't think so."

"Just to stick my head through the door, that's all. And then I'll leave you to carry on hiding from me."

"I wasn't hiding from you!" I said, even though we both knew that wasn't true. "Okay, I was hiding."

"But you weren't hiding very well, so clearly you wanted to be found."

"I did not want to be found!" I protested, and then my eyes scanned the features of his face and came to rest on those eyes. Gray and cool and shiny. They were magnetic. The kind of eyes that drew you in, making it impossible to look away. The kind that made you take steps forward even before you knew it, as if in some kind of gray, foggy trance. That made reality slip away until you were reaching out, wrapping your arms around waists that belonged to people you should not be wrapping arms around. They made your lips find their way to his lips and your hands roam his taut back and pull at clothes and hair and . . .

Chapter **Thirty-four**

We barreled into the room, a tangle of lips and arms and legs and hands. An explosion of body parts grabbing and pulling at each other. We hit the wooden post of the four-poster bed first; my back collided with it so hard that the breath was pushed out of my lungs—it was so bloody hot.

"You okay?" Jagger pulled away and rubbed my back. "Sorry, my eyes were closed and I—"

"Stop talking." I pushed him. He fell into a chair, and I climbed on top of him. I had never, *ever*, been like this before. But for some reason Jagger ignited something inside me, or maybe it was those bloody carnelian stones. I straddled Jagger and moved my hips against him as we both moaned into each other's mouths. He reached out and grabbed my ass, and then started to lift me.

"Oh my god! You can't lift me!" I wiggled as he picked me up. "You're going to drop me," I squealed as I clung to him.

"Yes, I *am* going to drop you."

And then in one hasty movement, I felt myself fall back onto the bed and bounce. I laughed loudly as I hit the bed and even louder when Jagger threw himself through the air and landed next to me. I climbed onto Jagger, both of us still laughing.

"And now I have you exactly where I want you!" Jagger wrapped his arms around me.

"Or maybe I have you where I want you!" I squeezed my thighs together, trapping him.

"Maybe, this is exactly where we're supposed to be," Jagger said, and then released his arms. His smile faded and he pulled my chin toward his lips. He kissed me softly on the edges of my mouth. It was this gentle side of Jagger that was so unexpected. I'd seen it last night, and now I was seeing it again.

"If someone had told me last week that this is where I would be today, I would never have believed it." I touched his face, ran my fingers over the bridge of his nose, and down over his lips. He kissed the tips as they traced him.

"Life is full of surprises." Jagger slipped his hand up my skirt, slid it under my bikini, and squeezed my ass. "You have no idea how long I've wanted to do this."

"Are you an ass man?" I asked.

"Guilty as charged." He rolled me off him and climbed on top of me. I opened my legs and let him fall between them, like I had last night. He helped me wiggle out of my dress, and then without removing anything else, he pulled my bikini top down, exposing my breasts.

He sat up on his haunches and pulled something out of his pocket. I knew what it was the second I caught the flash of shiny plastic.

"You bought condoms?"

"I did." He ripped the packet with his teeth.

"Somewhat presumptuous, don't you think?" I watched, transfixed by his teeth as he tore the foil open.

"Hopeful. Not presumptuous." He pulled the condom out, holding it up in the air. "But aren't you happy I bought some?"

"So happy!" I pulled him back down on me. He pushed my bikini bottom aside and slowly, much slower and softer than last night, slid inside me in one drawn-out move. He remained still when he was inside me, and looked down, running his thumb over my lips, down my neck, and then making circles around my breasts. I let out a whimper when he moved, just ever so slightly. It drove me wild. I clenched around him and tried to pull him in deeper, tried to make him move again, but he returned to stillness. I moved my hips against him, dragging myself across him. He still didn't move, only smiled down at me. I grabbed his ass and lifted my legs as far back as they could go, trying to force him deeper, trying to get him to move inside me like he'd done last night.

"Oh my god, Jagger, what are you doing to me?" I said, rocking my hips back and forth under him, creating that movement that I was so desperate for and that he was completely denying me.

"Savoring the moment," he whispered against my neck.

"Well, can you stop savoring it and just fuck me!" The words flew out of my lips. Words I'd never heard myself speak before, and they were the words that ignited everything.

The desperate thrusting, the tight gripping of my legs around him, holding him in place in case he did that to me again. Fast and hard and loud.

"God," I panted as Jagger flopped down onto me, his weight crushing me into the bed, the sweat on his forehead making my neck wet as he buried his face into me. We lay there like that until Jagger softened and slipped out of me. I gasped at the loss of him and was shocked by how much I still wanted him inside me.

He rolled onto his back and we lay there panting. My heart beat like a drum. Jagger put his hand on my chest, and I took a long, slow breath in and placed my hand over his.

"My heart is racing," I said.

"So is mine." Jagger took my other hand and placed it on his chest. We lay there like that, feeling each other's hearts as they slowed down and returned to normal. My eyelids felt heavy and when I looked over at Jagger his were closed and his breathing had become long and slow. I got up and went to the bathroom and when I came back, Jagger was fast asleep. I climbed back onto the bad and wiggled up to him, putting my head on his chest, and I too closed my eyes.

Chapter **Thirty-five**

A voice drifted through my sleepy haze: "Well, well, well, well, well . . ."
It took me a few moments to recognize it and, when I did, I sat up in bed.

"Leighton!"

"Margaret-Skye." He looked at me with a smile.

Jagger opened his eyes and gasped. "What?"

"Jagger Villain, I believe," Leighton said, and then dropped into the
chair. "I see you two put the room to good use."

Jagger grabbed the nearest pillow and covered himself as quickly as
he could.

"Oh, it's too late for that. I've already seen it all." Leighton raised his
brows up and down a few times. "Lucky girl."

"Leighton!" I shot him a warning look.

"What? It's not like I saw it on purpose. It was out there on full
display when I walked in."

Jagger laughed. "This is so not how I wanted to meet you. I've been
such a big fan, for so long and this wasn't really . . . I mean . . . it's you
and me . . ." Jagger stumbled over his words.

"Are you feeling a little starstruck over there?" Leighton asked.

"Um . . . yeah," Jagger admitted.

"You'll get over that. It usually wears off pretty quickly when you get to know me." Leighton waved a hand in the air. "However, I'm not sure I'm going to get over this anytime soon."

I buried my face in my hands.

"I'll give you guys a moment to pull yourselves together, shall I?" Leighton got up and walked out of the room.

"Oh my god, that was so embarrassing," Jagger said, removing the pillow and climbing off the bed to find his pants.

"Oh wow! You're actually embarrassed! I didn't think you got embarrassed. You're the guy who shaves checkerboards into his head."

"Well, I am. Not every day you meet someone like that with your dick out. Literally."

I burst out laughing. "I'm sure that's not so unusual for him."

"Are you guys decent yet?" Leighton shouted through the door.

"Decent!" I shouted back, and then looked over at Jagger. "Uh . . . maybe you should . . ."

"Go! Right." Jagger started moving off, but then stopped. He turned and walked back up to me.

"See you soon?" He leaned down and placed a small kiss on my forehead. I melted. That's how it felt as everything inside me went soft and warm and fuzzy. And then he walked out of the room. I knew I was smiling after him like an idiot. I could feel it as the muscles in my face strained against the fullness of the smile.

"Mmmm . . ." I heard a murmur and looked toward Leighton, trying to pull my lips out of the massive smile. I knew what was coming, and I also knew there was zero way I was ever going to wiggle myself out of it.

"How? Where? What? Who and everything? Go!"

Leighton pointed at me and then flopped down dramatically in the chair again. "And don't you dare try and leave out any of the important bits—especially since I've just come face-to-face with the most important bit."

"We had sex again. What else would you like to know?"

"Everything!"

I flushed. "It was good. Really good."

Leighton's face lit up and he leaned forward. "Okay, so are we talking like rock my world sex or I think I saw God sex or fainting goat sex?"

"I think we created a whole new category."

"Like?"

"Transported to another dimension sex."

"Oh my god."

"But it can never, ever happen again."

Leighton shook his head at me. "Are you still hung up on that whole stepsibling thing?"

"We are going to be related!"

"I know, it's so *Game of Thrones*! Or is it more *Blue Lagoon*?"

"You're taking far too much delight in this!"

"I can't help it—this is the greatest storyline ever created. Office enemies to extradimensional sibling lovers."

"Stop saying *sibling*!" I got up off the bed and paced the palatial suite a little. It took a long time to walk the entire thing. Leighton watched me curiously as I marched.

"Training for a half marathon?"

"I just thought I would pace a bit."

"Shall I join you?" he asked.

"Sure, why not?"

Leighton jumped up and walked next to me as I paced the suite once more. "How many more times are we going to do this?"

"I don't know, until my mind stops racing."

Leighton grabbed my arm and stopped me. "This is not how to stop the mind from racing."

"Champagne?" I asked.

"Exactly!"

Leighton walked over to the bar fridge. In places like this, the fridge was always stocked with overpriced finery, from real champagnes to truffle-covered chocolates. I'd stayed with him a few times on some travel we'd done, so I knew what kinds of things came in fridges like this. He emerged moments later with a bottle of Dom Pérignon, one glass, and a sparkling water. Even though he no longer drank, he was always quite determined to get everyone else around him to. He sat next to me and poured me a glass. I took a gulp as he sipped his sparkling water.

"Jokes aside now, tell me everything," he said in a completely serious tone, and this was the Leighton I liked the most. The serious one that not many people got to see. Most people only saw the jokes and flair—not many people got this side of him—and I knew how lucky I was to get it. And so I told him everything.

Chapter **Thirty-six**

That evening, Leighton insisted on throwing a dinner party to end all dinner parties in his suite. He had jumped into almost immediate action, calling reception and ordering flowers and a private chef and someone to stand there and mix cocktails for us. And by the time eight came around, the place looked gorgeous. The dinner table had been set on the large balcony overlooking the sea. The view from up here was spectacular. The presidential suite was on a hill, elevated above the mere mortals down below. It's amazing what money and fame can do: snap your fingers and within a few hours you can have a full seven-course meal at your doorstep with a butler who hands out warm, lemongrass-scented hand towels as the guests arrive.

"Welcome to Chez Leighton." Leighton welcomed my mom, Eddy, and Jagger, ushering them inside. I quickly looked away so as not to make eye contact with Jagger, and took a very long sip of my champagne.

"I'm so glad you're here!" My mom embraced Leighton, and they rocked from side to side in a big hug. They both gave such great hugs, so hugging each other must have been extragreat. Nothing could beat a hug from either one of them. Mind you, Jagger's hugs were also . . .

I took another long sip. *Stop thinking about Jagger!* I scolded myself like a naughty child as my mind wandered to places it shouldn't go.

"Thank you so much for organizing this," my mom said. They were still hugging.

"Are you kidding? It's my pleasure. I wouldn't miss this for the world," Leighton said, and looked at me very pointedly. I rolled my eyes at him and took another long, slow sip of my drink. The bubbles made my nose itch and I sneezed.

"Bless you," Jagger said loudly. "You know in some cultures people believe that when you sneeze it means that someone is thinking about you." He said that last part with too much relish.

"Did you hear that, Margaret-Skye?" Leighton teased me. "Someone is thinking about you."

For some reason, I sneezed again.

"You know that in some cultures they believe that if you sneeze three times in a row that means that someone is in love with you," Eddy added.

"Really?" Leighton put his hands on his hips and swiveled to look at me. "That is fascinating, don't you think?"

I opened my mouth to talk and suddenly felt the sharp and uncontrollable inhalation of a breath. I slapped my hands over my mouth as the sneeze built and everyone looked at me in anticipation. Leighton was grinning like the Cheshire cat, and I shook my head at him vigorously as the sneeze built.

"Don't fight it," my mom said.

"If you try to stop a sneeze, your eyeballs will pop out," Eddy added.

I pointed at him. "That is an urban le . . . le . . . le . . ."

Leighton clapped. "Here it comes."

"I am not going to sneee . . . snee . . . eee."

"You're going to sneeze." Leighton looked delighted.

"I AM NOT GOING TO . . ."

I sneezed. So hard. So loudly that my toes lifted off the ground as if I'd been propelled up by exploding jet fuel.

"Well, how 'bout that. Someone loves ya." Leighton eyed me.

"You know in some cultures the sneeze is viewed as a bad omen," I countered, and flashed Leighton a very hairy eyeball.

My mom swished her hands around in the air again. "I'm starting to get the feeling that we're not talking about sneezing here?"

"You know, if you think about it, sneezing is very similar to having an orgasm." Leighton pursed his lips together as he said this, as if holding a laugh at bay. I was going to kill him.

"Okay, can we stop talking about sneezing?" I demanded, perhaps a little too forcefully, because my mom was now looking at me very curiously.

"Okay, now I know we're definitely not talking about sneezing." She turned to Leighton and raised her eyebrows.

"Oh, it's a long story. Very long." He shot me another look and I squirmed in my skin. Yup, definitely going to kill him before the night was over, especially because I was now thinking about orgasms and Jagger's long, very long . . .

"A toast!" Jagger said loudly, looking about as uncomfortable as I felt. Oh god, was he also thinking about orgasms? "To the future Mr. and Mrs. Villain."

"Wait!" I widened my eyes in shock and stared at my mom. "You would be Mrs. Villain? As in Villain. Anke Villain?"

"No, I don't think I'll take on another surname. Too much admin at my age." My mom put her hand on Eddy's shoulder.

"Thank god!" I said on a relieved out-breath. The mere thought that my mom might actually be Mrs. Villain made it even more real that she would be related to Jagger and, therefore, by proxy, so would I.

Eddy placed his hand over my mother's and smiled at her. "It's your choice," he said, and then looked at her with awe and utter adoration.

I turned and walked onto the balcony. This was too strange. I stood there staring out over the dark sea when I felt him come up behind me. I could feel the warmth first, and then the scent hit me next—that sandalwood fragrance that mingled with the salty smell of sea air and coconut sunscreen. They'd combined into something that was uniquely Holiday Jagger.

"You okay?" he asked softly.

"Honestly." I turned around. "I have no idea! Do you know?" I asked, and then put a hand over my face in frustration.

"Hey, what's wrong?" Jagger peeled one of the fingers away from my face and made eye contact with me.

"What have you done to me?" I whispered accusatorily at him.

"What have I done to you?"

I pulled my hand away, looked around, and lowered my breath. "Yes, Jagger. You. What have you done to me? I'm not myself. I'm impulsive and crazy and I can't stop having sex with you—why can't I stop having sex with you?—and—"

"Because it's amazing?"

"Well, make it bad, then," I insisted.

"We'd have to have sex again for me to deliberately make it bad."

"Well, that's not happening." I took another large sip of my champagne, and Jagger's eyes lit up as they fixed on my lips.

"Honestly, I don't think you and I could ever have bad sex." His eyes moved off my lips and blazed a trail up to my eyes.

I pointed my finger at his face and swirled it around in the air. "Stop doing that!"

"Stop what?"

"That sexy, steamy thing you do with your eyes."

Jagger's laugh came out breathy. It rumbled low in his throat and made my skin prickle. I took a step away from him, which only seemed to add to his amusement.

"Fine, I'll stop," he said, pulling his eyes from mine and flattening out the corners of his lips. "Shall we?" He held his hand out for me.

"We what?"

"Looks like everyone is sitting down. We'd better join them." He tilted his head toward the table where my mom, Eddy, and Leighton were all sitting down, chatting and laughing as if they'd known each other all their lives.

Jagger started to move off, but I grabbed him by the shirt and pulled him back. "Seriously, though, we have to stop having"—I looked up as my mom got up from the table and walked across the room, and then leaned into Jagger—"*s-e-x*"

"Are we back to spelling it out again?"

"Our parents are getting married. We have to stop." When I realized how close I was to him, I quickly pulled away as his scent filled my nostrils: warm and spicy and intoxicating. I could feel his breath on my cheek; I could see the rise and fall of his chest as he breathed in and out, in and out. His breathing got faster; so did mine, and I felt myself being dragged toward him, as if he was a magnet and I was a flimsy little paper clip, unable to fight his pull.

"Hey! What are you two up to in the corner there?" Leighton shouted from the table. "The first course is about to arrive!" He pulled the chair out next to him and patted it. I was glad of the distraction and without looking at Jagger again, I marched to the table and sat. Jagger joined me.

"I want to make a toast." Leighton stood up and held his glass of water in the air. Of course he wanted to make a toast—he was always making toasts. It was his favorite thing to do.

"But for this toast, I'm going to rely on words that I wrote many years ago, because I have a feeling they are still very applicable now." He grinned at me, and I stiffened. What the hell was he up to?

"Forty years ago, I wrote a ballad called 'Blue Love.'" I swallowed hard and then tried to inconspicuously shake my head at him. He ignored me and then, much to my horror, started singing softly. I wanted to melt into the chair.

"I couldn't have dreamed you up before I met you. No magic potion to

manifest you. You were perfect before I knew you. I just didn't know I needed you, until your love hit me out of the blue."

He stopped singing, cleared his throat, and then raised his glass into the air. "Sometimes love just comes out of the blue and finds us when we least expect it. And sometimes it comes from those we least expect it to. And that's the inexplicable magic of love, to take you by surprise!" Jagger, Eddy, and my mom held their glasses in the air, and everyone looked at me to do the same. I scowled at Leighton as I raised it slowly.

"To love coming out of the blue when we least expect it to." Leighton took a sip of his water, and everyone followed suit. But as I did, I caught Jagger looking at me. I felt it again. Magnetic pulls and flutters deep in my belly, and suddenly it was taking all my energy *not* to look at him, which was proving excruciatingly hard to do, because I was now hyperaware of him.

In fact, Jagger was almost all I saw and felt and smelled. God, he smelled good. God, he felt good, the way heat radiated off his body. The way the heat seemed to move over you like your favorite blanket in winter. He'd gotten under my skin and into my mind. I reached for the champagne and took another sip, not in toast, but to douse the hot feeling that was rising inside me. Someone grabbed my hand under the table, and I flinched in fright, until I felt the warm, smooth movement of his fingers sinking through mine. His thumb made circles on the top of my hand, and it was both soothing but also . . . *shit!* I crossed my legs.

I crushed his thumb with mine to stop the circles, but this was only met with a smile. Jagger stuck his other hand under the table and placed it over mine, trapping my hand between his. I didn't pull away this time, because despite myself, it felt good to have my hand in his. Jagger rested my hand on his knee, and that's how we stayed until we ate. But as soon as our knives and forks were down again, our hands found each other under the table. This thing that was going on with Jagger had taken me by surprise.

It really had come out of the blue.

Chapter **Thirty-seven**

I lay in bed, staring up at the ceiling. The only thing I could think about was Jagger.

Jagger Villain.

How he'd slipped his hands over mine under the dinner table. How he'd looked at me with those steel-gray eyes over the rim of his glass. How he'd glanced back and then almost walked into the door frame when saying good-bye to me. Once again, Jagger was occupying my thoughts, but not in the way he'd been occupying them for the last six months. *But he has been occupying them* . . . I could almost hear Lesego and Leighton sing in unison.

I nearly fell out of bed when my phone beeped. The synthetic sound was so out of place among the soft stirring of waves and the breeze through the palm trees.

> **Jagger**: I can't stop thinking about you

My heart raced and I sat up in bed with a smile.

> **Margaret**: You should try harder
> **Jagger**: Are you thinking about me?
> **Margaret**: No
> **Jagger**: I don't believe you

Margaret: You are so full of yourself

Jagger: You love it

Margaret: Do not

Jagger: Well, now you're just lying. Want to know exactly what about you I'm thinking of?

Margaret: Sure

There was a long pause, and the dancing dots were killing me with anticipation.

Jagger: I was thinking about how hot you look naked. How amazing you taste; how good you feel when I'm inside you

Margaret: Is this you trying to sext me?

Jagger: Is it working?

God, yes, it was working! My internal temperature had risen by about a degree and a thumping feeling had started deep in my belly.

Margaret: I'm not sure, carry on and I'll let you know

Jagger: 😄

Jagger: I want you so bad

Margaret: And what are you planning on doing to me?

Jagger: How detailed do you want this to be?

Margaret: You're a writer. Use many adjectives

Jagger: That's the first time you've ever called me a writer . . . I'm even more turned on now

Margaret: So?

Jagger: First I'm going to undress you slowly. Then I'm going to run my tongue over every inch of your naked body. And when I get to your nipples, I'm going to suck on them and make you wiggle like you do when I suck your amazing tits

Margaret: And then what?

Jagger: Then I'm going to spread your legs open and slip my fingers inside you while I lick you until you come

My brain short-circuited. Every rational thought I'd ever had about *not* having hot sex with Jagger seemed to be such a distant memory. Logic turned off. Rationality left me. All I was left with was the hot feeling in my blood and the throbbing, which had moved from my belly to between my legs. It felt as though if I didn't let Jagger do those things to me, I would die some kind of strange death.

Margaret: OKAY, I'LL BE THERE NOW!

I tiptoed through the suite and then, as quickly and inconspicuously as possible, ran through the resort like a beast possessed. I was totally out of breath when I finally made it to Jagger's room. I pushed the door open and there he was—lying naked on the bed waiting for me, hard and ready.

"What if that hadn't been me?" I asked, racing over to the bed and jumping on.

"Well, then it would have been fucking awkward."

Jagger grabbed me the moment I was on the bed and rolled us both until he was lying on top of me.

"So, what're you waiting for?" I asked, rather desperate to play the sexting out in real life.

"What's the rush?" He smiled down at me and then moved the hair out of my face.

"Don't ever straighten your hair again." He twisted a curl between his fingers playfully.

"Don't ever wear anything else but these stupid clothes you've been wearing." He pulled at the neck of my new nightie, a Vyctoria Peckam design.

"Don't ever cover these freckles on your nose with makeup." He ran the tip of his finger over my nose. He started moving his hand down my body and I gasped each time he touched me.

He reached my knees and I felt him wipe something off them. "Don't ever wash the bits of sand off your legs."

I let out a soft, whispery laugh. "Why?" I asked.

"Because you're perfect like this." All the energy of moments ago was gone, and when he kissed me next, this feeling of melting completely into another human being was the most overwhelming of my entire life. This feeling of totally collapsing into Jagger as if I'd known him all my life. As if he was a safe place, warm and familiar and all mine. Something between us was completely different and it felt, it felt . . .

. . . *right.*

"And just where do you think you've been, young lady?" Leighton asked the second I opened the door.

"Shit! You're supposed to be asleep. You never wake up before nine."

"Well, someone woke me up in the wee hours of the morning when they snuck out of bed for what I'm guessing was a late-night booty call."

I slapped my hands over my face and wailed. "I had sex with my soon-to-be stepbrother again on the day of our parents' wedding, okay! Are you happy now?"

"No, but clearly you are." He pointed at my neck.

"What?"

"The last time I had a hickey was in 1989!"

I rushed to the mirror. "I have a . . . *god*! I have a hickey! It's huge."

"It looks like you had a wrestling match with a vacuum cleaner and lost."

"Help me get rid of it!"

Leighton picked up some concealer and very gently dabbed it on my neck. It only did so much to hide the bright-purple mark, though. I slumped across the dresser and put my head in my hands.

"Whyyyy, why, why can't I stop having sex with him? It's all I think about now. I want to hate him again. I want to find him unattractive again. But now when I look at him all I can think about is sex! Sex with Jagger. How has this happened?"

"Well, I think it's pretty obvious." Leighton slapped a cloudburst of powder onto my neck, and I coughed as some landed in my mouth.

"What's obvious?"

"From day one of Jagger arriving at the office, that's almost all you've talked about. He's driving you mad, you hate him, he's always wiggling his foot, tapping his pencil, walking with his hips, leaning, laughing, blah, blah, blah. And you know what they say: there's a very fine line between love and hate."

"I don't love him!"

"You just love having sex with him."

"I do! I do love having sex with him. I don't know what he's done to me. I mean, he's turned me into some sort of sex demon. I'm saying and doing things I've never done before. I asked him to fuck me. ME! I said those words to him!"

"Maybe the sex demon was always there—Jagger just helped it come out."

"No, that's not it! Maybe it's because I haven't had sex in a while. Maybe it's not even that good. I've just been without it for so long that I've forgotten what it's like. That's it. I probably need to go out there and have sex with a few more people and then I won't be so obsessed with having sex with him because I'll realize that he's actually not that good . . ." I buried my face in my hands again. "No. He's good. So, *so* good!"

Leighton laughed.

"It's not funny! Why can't he be crap in bed?" I walked away from Leighton, shoulders stooped, and then threw myself onto the bed dramatically.

"God, this is so *Dynasty*. I should just hand you a Daytime Emmy, flopping on the bed like you're some hard done by Krystle Carrington."

"New *Dynasty* or old *Dynasty*?" I asked.

"Old one, obviously."

"Are you Alexis Carrington in this storyline?"

"I'm always Alexis Carrington. Would you like me to push you in the pool, snap you out of this mopey sex spell?"

"Please!" I rolled over onto my back and felt the bed bounce next to me as Leighton climbed on.

"The world has gone mad," I said, reaching for Leighton's hand. "My mother is getting married, *married*, of all the crazy things she could be doing, and I'm having sex with my sworn enemy." I paused; the word *sex* seemed somehow wrong after last night. "Can I tell you something?" I rolled over and faced him.

"Anything."

I paused again. I wasn't sure I could say it out loud, even though it had been racing through my mind all night. "Last night . . . with Jagger, it didn't feel like . . . *just sex.*"

Leighton couldn't hide his smile. "What did it feel like?"

"I don't know . . . just something *more.*"

"Mmmm, I think someone is falling for their co-worker."

"I'm not falling for him." I *tsk*ed and then rolled over onto my back again, a strange feeling clawing up inside me. "Am I? I'm not, right? This is nothing more than sex. A holiday fling, right? Tell me this is just a holiday fling and it will be over as soon as we touch down back home."

"Why does it have to end?"

"Um . . . because our parents are getting married in a few hours' time. God, Leighton, my mom is getting married to a total stranger in a few hours' time, and she wants me to be in her wedding. What should I do?"

"Why do you have to do anything?" Leighton propped himself up on his elbows and looked down at me. His eyes peered out of wrinkled lids. He had a face like Mick Jagger's. The years of sex, drugs, and rock 'n' roll had been etched into him, despite the regular Botoxing.

"Your mom seems genuinely happy. She's glowing. I haven't seen her like this in a year. Don't extinguish it. Maybe it works out for them, and maybe it doesn't. So what? That's life. You can't predict anything. All you can work with is the here and now, what's right in front of you. What you can see, and touch, and hear. And what I see is a woman who's been given a second chance at love and happiness, when only a year ago love and happiness were ripped away from her. You can't begrudge her that."

I pushed Leighton's hair back with my fingers and watched it jump straight back up again. "This is a terrible haircut."

"I know. The stylist was gorgeous, though."

I chuckled.

"Go and talk to your mom. I don't want you to regret not being in her wedding someday."

I raised myself off the bed. "You think so?"

"I do, and I'm usually right about these kinds of things."

"If I'm her maid of honor, I'll feel like I'm betraying my dad."

Leighton sighed. "You've got complicated feelings about this—I get it. But that's why you need to talk to her."

He was right, of course. My feelings were so complicated it was hard to distinguish one from the other. I wanted my mom to be happy, but *what did that mean for the memory of my dad?*

"Okay, I'll go." I got up and walked out of the room.

Chapter **Thirty-eight**

I stood in the doorway. For some reason my feet had decided they didn't want to carry me inside. They'd stopped dead at the threshold, as if there was a line they were unprepared to cross.

Will you be my maid of honor? How could she even ask that of me?

But when I watched her from the doorway, her oblivious reflection playing on the reflective glass of the window, an unexpected feeling came over me. She looked happy. And she looked so beautiful too.

She stood in front of the full-length mirror, the pretty, casual white dress accentuating her tanned holiday skin. She radiated an aura of relaxed happiness and this made me feel . . . made me feel . . . ? *What?*

Heartbroken.

A thumping pain in my chest made me take a step back. This picture of my mom in the mirror was all wrong. It was incomplete. *Where was Dad?* Wasn't he supposed to be standing next to her? Basking in the glow of her happy relaxedness. He, too, would have sun-kissed holiday skin and a slightly sunburned bald patch on the top of his head that no matter how much sunscreen he put on, always went a little red. He would probably be wearing those ridiculous Hawaiian Bermuda swimming trunks that he always wore when he watered the garden or washed his car in the yard with that high-pressure hose he loved so much. He was always finding excuses to use that thing, like the time he dropped by my house to clean the "muck off my driveway." He'd spent hours spraying it, only for it to be dirty a few days later.

But he wasn't here. And he would never be here again. He would never stand next to Mom in the mirror, and I would never have him clean the muck off my driveway again.

I was forced to take another step back as the unwanted thought seemed to reach arms out and shove me in the chest. A hot, searing sensation wove around my heart, up my throat, and into my mouth. I took another step back, bigger this time. And it all became crystal clear to me in one moment.

I can't do this! I cannot be her maid of honor. I cannot be in this ceremony.

I turned and was about to call on my feet to carry me away as quickly as they could, when I stood on a stick and heard it snap. I looked over my shoulder to see if my mother had heard it. She had.

"It's bad luck to see the bride in her wedding dress before the wedding," she called, a girlish giggle in her voice as she grabbed for the hotel gown and wrapped it around her. "Unless you want me to take my wedding dress off?"

"Stop! Gross! It's me, Mom."

"Margaret-Skye? Oh dear!" She laughed, even though I didn't think there was anything funny about this, and then appeared at the open doorway. "Oh, sorry, I thought you were—"

"Yes, yes! I know who you thought I was." I folded my arms across my chest as that searing sensation snaked back down my throat and then decided to wrap itself around my ribs like a too-tight corset.

She smiled at me. It was so big and wide and happy, and it felt so out of place in this moment. As if it had no right to be here at all. "You're just in time. I have your dress." She ran up to me and slung it over my shoulder. "And you won't believe it, but the hotel made these divine tropical bouquets for us to hold. Come in, come in—you have to see them."

She waved me in and then rushed back into the room, picking up one of the bright pink-and-yellow bouquets. "Aren't they fabulous? And you have to smell these frangipanis." She stuck her face to the bouquets and inhaled deeply. "You just want to bottle the scent and wear it forever. It's glorious!"

"Mom—" I tried to interrupt her but she continued.

"They've even made these beautiful bougainvillea arches on the beach, all the way down to the water's edge. Eddy says he wants to get married with the water lapping around his ankles. How lovely is that?" She looked as if she was about to continue, and I stopped her.

"I can't," I said quickly.

"You can't what, honey?"

"I can't be your maid of honor, Mom."

She smiled at me. "Of course you can. Everything is already arranged. The dress, the flowers, and you don't even have to make a speech. It's going to be so informal that you can just—"

"No. I won't," I said, cutting her off again, taken aback by the abrasive tone in my voice. I hadn't meant for it to come out so harshly, but her girlish excitement was rubbing me the wrong way. The more "excited and happy bride" she sounded, the more it tore strips off my already damaged heart.

"You . . . won't?" Her face dropped like hot wax melting down the side of a candle.

I shook my head. "No."

She looked at me expectantly, as if waiting for me to continue. But I didn't.

"Will you at least tell me why?"

I took a deep breath, trying to fight back the tears that I could feel were coming. It didn't feel good having to say this to my mom. Having to ruin it all by sticking a sharp pin into her happy little bubble. But I had to. It was now or never unless I waited for that moment when they ask *if anyone has any objection to the marriage*, but that would be way too dramatic!

"I just can't," I managed quietly.

"*Just can't* is not a reason, Margaret-Skye. You're going to have to do better than that on my wedding day."

"Well, sorry I'm not giving you the right answer, Mom," I said sarcastically, and regretted it instantly when I saw the hurt that swept across her face. But I continued. "I can't dress up and carry flowers, no matter what they smell like, and walk down the beach and have bloody water lapping at my ankles and pretend I'm happy for you when I'm *not*!" The force of that last word punched a hole in the air between us and the room suddenly went very still.

"Wh-what?" My mom looked so taken aback, and this pissed me off. *How was any of this news to her?*

"Mom! Honestly, I don't know what you're thinking. I mean this 'wedding' is the most ridiculous thing I've ever heard of! You have known this guy for seven days. *Seven*, and you are marrying him! Have you even stopped, for a second, to consider what that actually means? 'Till death do us part, better or worse' and you don't even know what this guy's 'worse' is! You don't know him at all. He could be a bloody serial killer and you wouldn't even know it—that's how little time you've actually spent with him. He could be a weirdo who collects mannequins and keeps them in his attic or he could be a total asshole who hogs the TV remote and doesn't let you watch your favorite program because it's at the same time as the cricket. He could never cook or clean, or what if he's a disgusting pig who leaves skid marks in the toilet, or what if he's allergic to dogs? What if he swells up at the sight of Lucy and then he makes a 'me or the dog' ultimatum, or what if he hates the way you decorate the house and let the creepers grow through the window and onto the ceiling and what if he wants you to get rid of your favorite chair or . . . if he . . . if he . . . ?" I couldn't talk I was crying so much now. I hadn't intended to cry, but I was, and it was shaking my shoulders and voice and making me suck in short sharp breaths that hurt my solar plexus.

"Honey." My mom stepped closer to me, concern now etched into her face. "No one knows all those things about anyone when they get married—you of all people should know that." She gave me a small, sympathetic smile. "Besides, I'm pretty sure he's not a serial killer and, if you want, you can come and snoop in his attic with me, and so what if we disagree on the finer points of decorating or—"

"*What if he makes you take the photos of Dad down?*" I heard the words fly out of my mouth, hoarse and raw-sounding and full of this unbridled emotion that I just couldn't hold back anymore.

"What?" My mom looked shocked, her face frozen for a second. "No one is going to make me take the pictures of Dad off the wall. And I'm sure he has photos of his late wife up on the walls too. Just because we have pasts with other people doesn't mean we shouldn't have futures with each other."

I started manically wiping the tears away from my face, but my fingers were wet and all I was doing was moving the wetness around in circles. I hated coming undone like this. Unraveling in this messy manner, emotions on full display for the entire world to see. I grabbed the hem of my shirt and raised it to my face, wiping it. The shirt came away wet.

"Let me get you some tissues." My mom's voice softened. It was the same voice she'd used whenever I was home from school sick, running a fever and stuck in bed. *Can I get you anything else, honey?* she would always ask, stroking her hand over my cheek, and I would feel instantly better for it. But today it didn't make me feel better at all.

"You're just forgetting about him, Mom," I said as I reached for the offered tissue.

"No, I'm not. I've already told you that."

I blew my nose loudly. "You're marrying someone else. You're moving on, you're getting over him, you're letting him go . . . *you're forgetting him.*"

"I can't believe you still think that's what I'm doing!" She turned away from me and moved for the box of tissues herself. My guts twisted in the guilty knowledge that I'd made my mom cry. I watched as her posture changed. It seemed to fold in on itself, like a paper doll being folded in half. Her shoulders slumped. Her aura of happiness was gone . . . I was the pin. I had popped her bubble.

"Margaret-Skye." She turned around and looked at me. "I still love your father. I will never stop loving him, but he's gone. He's gone and he's not coming back and I, I, am still here! You are still here, and we have to keep on living. Just because he died doesn't mean that we have to die too. What do you want me to do, rip my heart out and pack it away in a box, put it on a shelf and let it gather dust until the day I die?" Her voice broke.

"Mom, no . . . I don't want you to . . . I mean . . ." I shook my head. "I don't know what to say to you. This is just so sudden, and I haven't had time to process it and I wasn't expecting it and . . ."

"And I wasn't expecting your dad to die! But he did. You weren't expecting your husband to cheat on you and to get divorced. But it happened. Life is full of things we don't expect—that's how it works. It's messy, it's unpredictable, it twists and turns in directions that we can't control and that, *that*, is something you need to learn. And it's exactly what Leighton was saying last night. You should listen to him more."

I inhaled sharply, anxiety tugging at me from all sides. "I don't like that." I swallowed; the ball of saliva stuck in my now-dry throat.

"You can't control everything, Margaret-Skye." My mother took a step closer to me. "Surely your father's death must have taught you that?"

"No, his death taught me that life sucks!"

My mom stopped walking toward me and looked at me. Her eyes bored into me as if she was trying to bring something up to the surface. "If that's what you got out of his death, then I feel very sad for you, my love."

"What do you mean?"

She walked up to me and then reached out and ran her hand over my cheek. I exhaled in relief; I didn't know I'd been holding my breath.

"Honey, your father's death taught me the complete opposite. Life doesn't suck. Life is precious, and magical, and wonderful. It is a gift, the best gift that we will ever be given, and we have to enjoy it, because it can be taken away from us like this." She clicked her fingers together and I flinched. "That's what your father's death taught me. That is the final gift your dad gave me, to appreciate every single moment that I have left. To live it, to enjoy it, and yes, to fall in love again."

"Well, I don't think I'm ready to take lessons like that out of Dad's death, okay?" I said, and then stormed from her room. I felt like a child all over again, nothing about the way I was acting was even vaguely adult in any way, and I was ashamed of that. Shouldn't I be able to be more grown-up about all this? But the answer was that I just couldn't.

I headed straight for the beach, the place that had given me solace before, but today all the soft sand and lapping waves were just not able to calm me. This feeling rattled around inside me like a single coin at the bottom of a can. It was loud and tinny and, when it beat against the sides, painful. I paced the beach, and when I saw a familiar figure come into view, stopped and waited for the figure to walk toward me.

"So it didn't go well with your mom," Leighton stated. It wasn't a question. He knew me so well that just by looking at my figure in the distance, he could tell.

"No."

He eyed the dress that I'd slung over my shoulder. "Would be such a pity not to wear that. You'll look great in it."

I cast my eyes over the dress my mother had so thoughtfully chosen for me when she'd gone into town yesterday to look for wedding apparel.

"This is just happening so fast. I haven't had time to prepare for it, to wrap my head around it."

"And we know what a problem that is for you. It's all got to be carefully planned and thought out and analyzed. Like one of your brilliant articles. But seriously, when are you going to realize that life does not work like that?"

"You sound like my mom."

"Your mother is a very wise woman. And so am I."

"A wise woman?" I asked.

"Well, I'm wise. Let's go with that. And as your best friend in the whole wide world, I am going to dispense some wisdom."

"And what wisdom might that be?"

"Whether you're ready for it or not, your mom is getting married today. And you will absolutely regret it if you're not in her wedding. The marriage may last, it may not last—no one knows. But I do know one thing, you will regret it if you're not there with her in that dress looking amazing and supporting her."

I sighed. "Why do you always have to be right?"

"Because I'm old."

"And knocking on death's door?" I teased him.

"Exactly. Think of this as my parting wisdom to you."

I pushed Leighton on the shoulder. "You're not dying. Get over yourself and stop being so dramatic."

"I could say the same about you."

"Mmmm." I ruminated on his words as I looked out over the beautiful ocean.

"Come. Let's get ready for this wedding shindig. I'll even do your hair and makeup."

"Last time you did my hair you made me look like Bananarama."

"I'll go easy on the teasing this time."

"You better." Leighton threw an arm around me, and we started walking back to the villa.

"I have one more thing to say to you," he said, hitting me with his hip as he swayed.

"What's that?"

"Becoming a stepsibling with someone in your thirties doesn't make you related. So you can park that car in the cul-de-sac and have sex in the backseat."

I laughed. "I think we'll have to agree to disagree on that one. In a few hours' time Jagger and I will be related, which means . . ." My stomach dropped. No more sex with Jagger. The thought was awful. Sex with Jagger had been amazing, and now I couldn't imagine not having sex with him.

"Shit. This is a bit of a predicament I'm in, isn't it?"

"Not to me. You're clearly really into Jagger and—"

I stopped walking. "I'm clearly not *into* Jagger . . . am I?" And then it hit me. All at once. The thing that seemed to have been in front of me for a while that I just hadn't seen. Or maybe I'd refused to see. I face-palmed again. "Shit. I'm really into him. A lot."

"You like him," Leighton confirmed.

"I really like him." The thought terrified me, but it had a kind of clarity to it that was also a relief.

"Can I make an observation as your all-seeing BFF?"

"I'm not going to be able to stop you, am I?"

"Nope! I think you're using this stepbrother thing as an excuse not to get involved with Jagger because you've lost faith in romance and love since ex-hub decided to do the kalinka with Nadezhda."

"What's the kalinka?"

"It's a Russian folk dance. You know the one where they kick their legs in the air?"

"And she definitely had her legs in the air." I ran my hands through my hair in an agitated state. "But things with Jagger . . . they just . . . I didn't expect them!"

"I couldn't have dreamed you up before I met you. No magic potion to manifest you. You were perfect before I knew you. I just didn't know I needed you, until your love hit me out of the blue," he sang next to me.

"Whoa." I stopped him again. "It's definitely not love, though. *Like*, not *love*. Right?"

"You need to stop asking me the questions that only you know the answers to."

"Nah, it's not love." But as I said that I didn't quite believe it. Somewhere along the way, somehow, for some reason that I couldn't quite figure out, I had started to *more than* like Jagger. But how was it possible to feel so much for someone so quickly? How was it possible to have such utterly different feelings about someone in just a week?

"Well, you know what they say," Leighton said.

"What do they say?"

"What happens on vacation, doesn't always stay on vacation."

I stopped walking again. "Who says that? No one says that. That is not what anyone says. It's supposed to stay on vacation, not come with you after vacation."

"Well, that's what I say." Leighton pulled me again. "This is a vacation situation . . . wait, that's a really good line. That's a really catchy name for a song."

"*Sun-kissed cheeks, wind-tossed hair, dancing in the sand 'cos you just don't care.*" Leighton sang some off-the-cuff lyrics. "Hey, that's kind of catchy."

"It is. Totally cheesy, but catchy as hell," I admitted. This was the thing with Leighton: music was always on the tip of his tongue. The catchiest tune just waiting to be sent out into the world.

"Shit! I need to record that. Quick, I left my phone in my room. Run!" And with that, Leighton took off across the sand, humming, and I struggled to keep up.

Chapter **Thirty-nine**

"You look . . . *so beautiful,*" Jagger said, dragging his eyes up and down my body, which made everything inside me spark to life. The knee-length dress that my mom had picked out for me was perfect, and as for the color—it would have made Lesego proud. It was aquamarine like the sea.

"It matches your eyes," Jagger whispered. "Although nothing can really come close to them."

I gave him a playful eye roll. "Really dishing out the compliments today."

"Every single one of them true, and plenty more where they came from."

My body screamed for him. I ran my eyes over him. He was wearing, for perhaps the first time in his life, because he was pulling at the neckline as if it was scratching him to death, a collared shirt.

"Have you ever worn a shirt like that?"

"Never."

"Come here." I beckoned with my finger and his face immediately lit up. "Don't get any ideas," I chided him. I reached for his collar and then undid the top three buttons. The relief on his face was instant. I pulled the shirt open, and his chest came into view. Smooth and perfect, except for that red mark that my fingernails had left down it. My entire body hardened . . . *on top of him, nails digging into his skin as I came.* "Better!" I moved off quickly. Jagger ran his fingertips over the red marks, as if reliving the same moment that I was.

"Better . . ." I pointed at the beach. ". . . go."

"Better go," Jagger echoed in a voice thick with lust. Despite swearing off sex with him, all I wanted to do right now was rip his clothes off, push him up against the nearest palm tree, ravage him, and forget that we were about to be related.

You're using it as an excuse, echoed a voice in my head. Was I?

Jagger extended his hand toward me. I eyeballed it and shook my head.

"Are you scared if you touch me you won't be able to stop?"

"You are not that irresistible, I assure you."

Well, that's just a blatant lie! that irritating voice in my head, which seemed to have made itself judge and jury, screamed at me.

"Wait, before we go, I need to ask you something," Jagger said.

"What?"

"You and me . . . what's *really* happening between us here? You keep saying that you don't want to have sex, and then we keep having sex . . . but the thing is, the thing . . ." He stopped talking. Looking down at his feet, he ran what looked like a nervous hand through his hair. In that moment, he looked so vulnerable, as if he was about to say something that would have the power to change everything. I held my breath, waiting. He looked up at me again.

"Thing is, it's become much more than *just* sex to me. Much, much more. It was more than that before we even started having sex. You are more to me, and I want more with you."

"Want more what?"

"More everything. More of you. Relationship more."

"You want a relationship with me? Your soon-to-be stepsister?"

"God, you're so hung up on that. We are *not* going to be related."

326

I threw my hands in the air out of sheer frustration, exasperation, and I don't know what else.

"Even if stepsiblings is not a real thing—"

He cut me off. "It's not."

"Okay, even if it's not, I just don't know . . ." I stopped talking, mirroring Jagger's obvious anxiety with my own foot shuffle and hand in my hair. I didn't actually know what I was about to say to him. Because I still didn't have the words for what I was thinking and feeling. This week had been a whirlwind of so many emotions and I had been swept away in it all, and my feet were not on the ground. I was still spinning. I was dizzy and confused.

"Talk to me. Please," Jagger urged.

"It's the *more* I'm not sure about, Jagger. It's the more that frightens me."

"It's the having less that frightens me," he said.

I looked away, a salty sting in my eyes, a tightening in my throat. "I can't do this right now, Jagger. It's too much. My mom is getting married and I'm still not sure how I feel about it, and I can't do this now."

"Of course. We'll pick it up later." He smiled at me and, *fuck it*, I melted. I melted right back into that smile of his once more. *More*. He wanted more with me, not less. I just wasn't sure I was in any position in my life to give him, or anyone, more.

More meant trust. *More* meant letting go of control. *More* meant all the things that terrified me. He leaned over and kissed me on the forehead.

"Let's get to this wedding, then," he said. We started walking again and when we got to the beach, the scene in front of me stole my breath.

"Wow! Almost as beautiful as you," Jagger said softly coming up behind me.

"This is *way* more beautiful than me." I looked at it all in awe.

The beach sand was glittering orange with the light of hundreds of candles. A tiny breeze made them sway, just enough so that they cast patterns on the uneven sand. I could see that Leighton had definitely had a part to play in this, because the aisle was completely covered in rose petals. It looked like a thousand roses had been used to create the soft, velvety carpet across the beach. And then there was my mom. She looked so beautiful in the flickering light of the candles. The warm glow danced across the features of her face, accentuating the smile she had when she saw me. She rushed over and pulled me into one of her big bear hugs.

"I am so over the moon you're here." She looked at me, tears in her eyes, and I was so happy that Leighton had knocked some sense into me.

"Me, too, Mom. And I'm sorry for—"

"Shhh." She put her finger over her lips. "Never apologize for your feelings. I know this is hard for you and you're probably not sure how to feel about this."

I nodded and bit my lip to stop the tears.

"But I'm so grateful that you chose to be here with me today."

I put my head on my mom's shoulder and she stroked my hair. "I feel so . . . so . . . everything is just happening so . . ." I pulled away from her.

"I know. You've always hated surprises, even when you were little. I used to have to tell you what all your birthday and Christmas presents were before you opened them or you wouldn't open them. Mind you, your dad was exactly the same. I used to tease him about being allergic to surprises. You're so much like him, you know that?"

I pulled my head off her shoulder and straightened the hair that I'd flattened against her neck. "And you're not. You go with the flow. You never plan ahead, you live for surprises, and practically run toward obstacles." We looked at each other for a while. Physically we were so similar, but fundamentally, my mom and I were different people. She'd raised me but none of her personality traits had rubbed off on me. I was my father's daughter, through and through, and maybe that's why this day felt so hard for me.

"You look beautiful," I said to her.

"So do you."

"Are we ready for this?" Leighton's big arms came around us and squeezed us together tightly.

"We are!" I said, putting on the bravest voice I could.

The service was completely nontraditional—no one walked down the aisle, no one threw petals and confetti—but it was beautiful. And standing next to my mom as she exchanged vows with Eddy, I was swept up in the romance of it. I watched Eddy closely, and there was absolutely no denying that look in his eyes: it was the look that someone gives another person when they are the only thing in the world they can see. When nothing else around them exists, except that person in front of them and the moment they're sharing. I felt tears in my eyes when I realized that my mom was looking at Eddy in the exact same way. But this time, the tears were happy tears.

My father would have wanted my mom to be happy. He was the kind of person who only ever wanted the best for someone, and suddenly I imagined him sitting astride that glittery cloud again, but this time smiling over what was going on below. I suspect he'd also be smiling and shaking his head somewhat at my mother's choice in partner. The complete opposite to him in every single way, but that was my mom. She was always surprising everyone with her choices and decisions, and I knew that that was one of the things my dad had loved most about her. Her free spirit was what attracted him to her in the first place, and this right here, this wedding on the beach that had happened in seven days, well, if that wasn't the ultimate in free-spiritedness, then I don't know what was.

I looked past Eddy and my heart lost control of itself because Jagger was looking at me like that too. My knees felt weak and my feet felt unsteady and . . .

"Shit!"

Everyone looked at me.

"Sorry . . . the sand, uneven . . . lost my footing." I dusted myself off and I was sure my entire face was flashing Jagger pink. I avoided looking in Jagger's direction again, but it was no use, because I could feel his eyes boring into me for the remainder of the ceremony.

Chapter **Forty**

Jagger caught up with me on the beach later that night as I walked and tried to take it all in. He looked good coming toward me—*god, he looked more than good.* Over the last week, I'd come to believe that Jagger was perhaps the most gorgeous man I'd ever met. And certainly slept with.

"Hey." He stopped in front of me. There was a breeze, finally a breeze that had pushed some of the heat away, and it was tugging on his shirt and hair.

"Hey."

"Having a last walk on the beach?"

"It's hard to believe this is our last night here. So much has happened in seven days."

"So much," he echoed, his voice heavy with meaning. There was so much meaning between us now, and I wasn't sure we could ever go back to the way things had been between us. Everything had changed. I had changed.

"We have a conversation to finish," Jagger said.

"We do," I agreed.

"So?" he asked. "You know what I want—what do you want?"

I couldn't bring myself to say it because of the way he was looking at me, so I just shook my head. Jagger sighed.

"So, that's it. You're not going to change your mind about us." Jagger's eyes were pleading with mine and I shook my head.

"I can't say I'm not very, very"—it looked as if he was searching for the word—"disappointed," he finally said, and then shook his head quickly. "No, that's not the right word at all. Disappointed doesn't even come close to describing how I feel right now."

"How do you feel?"

"Honestly?" he asked. "No bullshit. No hiding. Just honestly?"

I nodded.

"Heartbroken."

Silence swirled around us like the wind did as it suddenly came out of nowhere.

"I think I might have underplayed it a little when I said I had a crush on you." Jagger held his shirt closed as the wind picked up even more. The weather had changed so suddenly, and so had the mood between us.

"Underplayed it?"

"Yes."

"If you don't have a crush on me, then . . . ?"

Jagger turned his body away from me and looked out over the sea as the waves slapped the shore. Dry sand was thrown up into the air. Water droplets flew off the surface of the water and sand crabs scuttled for the holes. He turned back to me, a look of determination on his face.

"I'm . . . I've . . ." Jagger seemed to have no words, or the words weren't coming. I leaned in as the wind got louder.

"What?" I urged.

"Fallen." The word rushed out of his mouth and the wind dragged it away.

"What?" I shouted over the howling wind and dug my feet into the sand for extra support as the rushing air rocked me back and forth.

"FALLEN," he shouted, and this time I heard him. "FOR YOU. I've fallen for you."

Jagger stepped closer as the wind got louder. He tried to say something but a crack of thunder drowned it out. He put his lips to my ear, touching it briefly. A shiver ran through me, and it wasn't from the sudden drop in temperature.

"I fell for you months ago. For months I've been coming to the office every day hoping that today would be the day you might actually have a proper conversation with me. You might actually take the time to get to know me." ·

"I don't know what to say," I mumbled into his neck, closing my eyes and taking another deep breath of him.

"I know you don't." Jagger ran his lips over my ear as he spoke. "I didn't tell you this because I need you to say something back—I told you this because it's the truth."

The wind was screeching now, the sand nipping at our ankles, and I could hear the hammocks whipping in the gale, snapping against their ropes. Another crack of thunder sounded as the sky went white. This storm had come out of nowhere. And Jagger and I were standing right in the middle of it. He wrapped his arms around me and pulled me into a hug.

"If you ever decide you might feel the same way as me, you know where I am." He pulled his head out of my neck and looked at me. He forced a small smile that broke my heart. "You could just pass a note over the partition, if you want."

I smiled at him. "Or knock three times on the wall?"

"I thought you said it wasn't a wall?"

"It's a wall," I teased him.

Jagger forced another smile, and my heart broke again. "We'd better get out of the storm before we're blown away."

My dress blew up and I pushed it down. Strands of my hair flew into my face like attacking tentacles. Jagger took my hand and we ran across the beach, through what was now a sandstorm. My body stung as particles of sand battered it. We ran until we reached that fork in the path and we stopped. The rain started. Leighton had given up his suite to the honeymoon couple, so Leighton and I were in my mom's room and Jagger was back in his. I couldn't help but remember how my mom and Eddy had looked at each other the first time we'd come to this fork, and now, my heart thudding, I realized I was looking at Jagger like that.

It felt as if once we took these separate paths, it would all be over. This fork in the road was a fork in our relationship. And if we went down different paths, a full stop too. The rain picked up. Water trickled down Jagger's face. It pooled in the corners of his slightly open lips. Tentacles of hair stuck to my wet cheeks, and I tried to push them back. Neither of us said anything; there was nothing to say. It was all about which fork in the road we were prepared to take, which one *I* was prepared to take.

Jagger stared at me expectantly, as if waiting for me to do something. I guess the ball was in my court. He'd made his intentions very clear. I was the one who needed to decide. Left fork, right fork?

Shit. This was too hard. I needed time to think, to weigh things, to make a pros-and-cons list. But instead of doing any of that, I pulled Jagger toward me and kissed him in the rain. Our warm lips tangled as the cool rainwater rushed down our faces, and then warm tears as they leaked from my eyes when I realized that this was a good-bye kiss. I pulled away and then without looking back I raced down the path. Jagger caught up to me and pulled my arm. I turned to face him.

"No! You don't get to do that to me. You don't get to kiss me like that and then just leave me in the rain. You owe me some words at least."

I tried to stop the tears. I hoped he didn't see them. I hoped the rain disguised them.

"You're a writer—please give me some words to explain this. To explain why you're ending something that feels so right and real and amazing."

But I didn't have words. It was all so fucking wordless.

"I don't know," I said and then carried on running. *Because, honestly, I didn't really know.*

Chapter **Forty-one**

Leighton had offered to take Jagger and me back in the private jet. It was awkward. I sat in silence at the back, Jagger sat in silence at the front, and Leighton sat in the middle trying to make conversation with both of us and failing dismally. Jagger and I said very stilted good-byes at the airport, and as soon as I was home alone the tears came again. It felt like a pent-up dam had been waiting to break open and break open it did.

And then I played out the ultimate cliché, for which I admit I was embarrassed, but I climbed into the most comfortable clothes I could find and ate ice cream on the couch watching a reality show about people trying to lose exorbitant amounts of weight. The cliché continued when I added a glass of rosé to the mix and then fell asleep on the couch clutching a pillow to my chest.

I dreamed about Jagger that night. We were playing a game of tennis and each time he hit the ball into my side of the court, I would stand there and watch it pass me by: I didn't swing. I didn't make a move for it. I was frozen like a statue. I woke up with a racing heart and drenched in cold sweat. My heart only raced more when I thought about having to go into work and sit across from Jagger as if nothing had happened. I spent Sunday in the same way as I'd spent Saturday. The only difference was that I'd finished the ice cream and had moved on to potato chips.

When Monday came along, I decided to go into the office early before anyone else did, to acclimatize and adjust to my surroundings without the pressure of seeing Jagger. But when I got there, I found Lesego looking busier than I'd seen her in a while. I walked over to my desk, put my stuff down, and greeted her. She barely looked up. She just moaned at me and clutched her head as if she'd been up all night.

"You okay?" I called over. She finally looked up.

"No, I'm trying to finalize that office shoot for tomorrow."

"What office shoot?"

"The prom retrospective."

"Is that seriously still happening? That wasn't a joke?"

She looked up at me properly for the first time since I'd come in. "You look so tanned! And I love the freckles—you know women are tattooing them on these days. You look amazing!"

"Thanks." I touched my face self-consciously. "This kid in kindergarten once called me freckle face."

She rolled her eyes. "Haters gonna hate!" She turned back to her desk. "The photographer canceled on us last minute, and I'm struggling to get a new one. Then the hairstylist's agent called and wanted more money because she needs to bring two assistants, not one. And obviously budgets being so tight, we can't afford it so I'm contemplating doing some of the hair myself or getting cheap wigs. I also had to go and source everyone's clothes and accessories, which was a lot, since we have ten people in the shoot."

"You sourced me clothes and accessories?"

"Yup, you can bring some of your own, though, if you want. But based on the prom photos everyone gave me, I've pretty much sourced very similar, if not the same, accessories and clothes."

"Wait, you got me . . ."

She laughed. "Yes, I found those strange fishnet arm sleeves you wore."

"Nooo! You can't seriously expect me to wear those?"

"Not to mention those hanging safety-pin earrings." She laughed again. "Don't feel too bad—Amy's dance was in the eighties, so she's wearing a metallic purple lamé ruffled and tiered dress with a permed wig and white stilettos. *White!*"

"We're all going to look ridiculous."

"Speaking of ridiculous, can you paint your nails like you had them at the dance too? That would really save time."

"I think I'm going to call in sick tomorrow." I opened my laptop, went to my emails, and started sifting through the hundreds that I'd received while I'd been away.

"You can't. While you've been lying in the sand, I've been sweating over this for an entire week. So was Zanzibar gorgeous and amazing and just the holiday you and your mom hoped for?" Lesego asked.

I swallowed. Her question was a particularly hard one to answer. "It was amazing."

"When this shoot is over, I want all the details and I want to see all the photos. But let me get through the next forty-eight hours."

I had read through the first ten emails in my inbox when I heard the door open. I looked up to see who'd arrived and my heart fell to my toes.

"Good morning, Margaret," Jagger said awkwardly, and lowered himself into his seat.

"Good morning, Jagger," I said as politely as possible, not daring to look at him.

"Margaret?" Lesego looked up and laughed. "What's gotten into you today?"

"Well, Margaret is her name," he replied.

"I know—you've just never called her that, and actually . . ." She walked over to my desk and lowered her bum onto it. "I literally don't think I have ever heard you call him Jagger. Ahhh, that's so sweet. Did you guys get close on the holiday?"

"No! We did not get close." I laughed; it sounded utterly ridiculous and forced and it needed to stop, so I reached for my bottle of water and took several gulps. Close didn't quite describe what had happened to Jagger and me over the last week.

"Jagger, I managed to source most of your prom outfit. Those leather gloves with cut-off fingers and that lime-green studded belt are winners. I didn't know what shoe size you were, though, and I'm not sure how I'm going to make them look so old and worn before tomorrow either."

"I still have those," he said.

"You do?" Lesego looked thrilled. "Cool. Don't forget to bring them, then! And can you also paint your nails? I've sourced some clip-in lip rings, so you'll be looking superauthentic, and I reminded the makeup artist to bring extra black eyeliner for our resident emos over here."

Jagger laughed, seeming to lose all the awkwardness he'd had a moment ago. "This is going to be so much fun."

I scoffed. "Fun? Hardly."

"I know what would make it fun for you," he said, turning to Lesego. "Make sure you have some Nickelback playing for Margaret. We know how much she loves it," he said cheekily, his voice dripping with something deep and suggestive.

"Shit!" My knees hit the desk, it wobbled, and my pen slipped off. I stuck my head under the table to see where it had gone. Too far to reach. "Jagger, would you mind passing me my pen, please? I seem to have dropped it on the floor and it's rolled over to your side of the desk. Thank you," I said, not looking up at him as I emerged from under the desk, careful not to hit my head on the way up.

"Of course, Margaret. I would be delighted to pick up your pen and pass it to you," Jagger said, and then got up and bent down. My eyes drifted across to his ass for a split second but I pulled them back as soon as possible.

"What's with you guys? You're both acting strange!" Lesego noted.

"*Nothing!*" I said too loudly, and then coughed. I reached for my water and sucked it down as fast as I could.

"Shit!" It gushed out of my mouth, dribbled down my chin, and onto my shirt.

"Shit!" I grabbed some tissues, knocking the box off the table, and tried to dab the water off my face and neck. The wet tissues stuck to my shirt and fingers. I tried to shake the tissue off my fingers into my bin but knocked it over with my hand and flung a wet tissue across the room.

"Shit!" I tried to pick up my trash can but my wet fingers slipped on it, and everything fell onto the floor.

"Shit!" I got down on my hands and knees and started picking up pieces of crumpled paper and pencil shavings.

"I have never heard you say shit so much. Seriously, what's going on?" Lesego probed.

"Nothing!" I said again, too chirpily. That sounded way too happy, and I chastised myself for not being better at the game of subterfuge. But then again, I had never slept with my co-worker—a co-worker whom everyone, including myself, actually thought I hated—and now here I was trying to hide that fact from my other co-worker.

"Let me help." Jagger got up and rushed over. He lowered himself to the ground and his knee touched mine, and I flew backward onto the carpet as if I'd been shocked. I got to my knees, pulling my skirt down, but it was too late. I could see that Jagger had looked up it. The color in his cheeks and the look in his eye told me so.

"I don't need your help!" I pointed at him.

"Let me help you," he insisted.

"No. I'm fine. It's good. Go back to your desk." I shuffled away from him on my knees.

"Jesus, what's up with you guys today?" Lesego looked down at me curiously.

"Nothing is wrong," I said, shoving stuff into my bin furiously and then putting it back.

Lesego pointed at my trash can. "You put it on the wrong side of the desk."

"Shit." I picked the bin up, slammed it down again, and got back into my chair, feeling flustered. I picked up a piece of paper and fanned myself but fanned too hard and threw the paper over my shoulder instead.

"Nooo, something is going on. You guys are acting really, *really* strange, almost like you . . ." Lesego lowered her face to mine and looked me straight into my eyes. "Oh my god, you guys hooked up."

"*What?* No. Shit. Shhhhhh! Keep your voice down," I hissed at her.

She jumped off my desk and rushed over to Jagger's side and then eyed him up and down as if she was able to read something off him. And clearly she was. "You guys had sex!"

"SHHHHH!" I whispered-screamed, and Jagger burst out laughing.

"And stop laughing." I swung my eyes over to him, and as soon as they came into contact with his, I felt that fuzzy, warm, melting feeling deep inside me. I looked away, grabbed my water and gulped again.

"It's about bloody time!" Lesego said. "I mean you could have cut the sexual tension between you two with a fucking sword."

"That's not the correct idiom," I pointed out, trying to deflect.

"I did it on purpose. The sexual tension has been so strong you needed a sword, not a knife."

"There has been none, and there is no sexual tension between Jagger and me," I insisted in a very stern tone.

Lesego clapped her hands in glee. It was obvious all her previous stresses were gone as she honed in on this. "You guys had sex! This is the most exciting thing I've heard all year."

"And no, I don't have a dick ring, by the way," Jagger teased her. Lesego gasped and then burst out laughing. I spat my water out of my mouth onto my laptop.

"Shit." I manically pulled tissues from the box again and shoved them onto my computer, hoping they would suck up the water that was no doubt seeping between the keys and sure to short-circuit the whole thing.

"Let me help you." Jagger raced over to my computer and in a few seconds had managed to dry it.

"Ahhhh." Lesego put her hand to her heart. "So sweet. Like a modern-day fairy-tale hero. Chivalrously jumping in to save the fair maiden's Word documents from vanishing forever into the dark delete bin."

"Stop it, Lesego!" I hung my head and then kicked my legs and did a full circle swing in my office chair. I felt so out of control that the constant, predictable swinging motion felt soothing. I did it again. And again.

"You've broken her, Jagger," Lesego said with mock concern in her voice. "What did you do to her?"

I swung again. And then again. And then once more before I came to a stop because I was starting to feel nauseated and dizzy. I stood up and looked around the room. It was starting to fill up with co-workers and I was sure that if Lesego had figured this out so quickly, soon every person in this office would know that I'd had sex with Jagger. As another person came through the door, I imagined a new, even worse moment of discovery, while I rolled around on the floor picking up tissues and papers.

"Margaret, you okay?" I heard Jagger ask as the anxiety built inside me with each new imagined scenario playing out in my mind. I would walk past Shawn and there would be something in my walk and they would know! Jennifer probably knew just from the way I'd written that article. Mary from HR would probably know and have something to say about it, and Tebogo from the security room—well, who knows how he would know, but one thing was sure, it was only a matter of time before everyone here knew what I'd been up to.

"Seriously, Jagger, bro . . . ken!" Lesego laughed loudly just as Shawn walked past.

"Hey. You guys are back," they said, looking up with one eye from their phone. "How was Zanzibar? I see you're both alive so clearly managed not to kill each other."

"They did more than manage that," Lesego chuckled under her breath, and I wanted to die.

"Hey, welcome back," Jennifer said, walking up to us.

Oh my god! My nerves bubbled and boiled, and my heart began to race.

"Great articles, both of you. Really enjoyed them. Glad to see you guys were able to work together."

"They did more than manage to work together," Lesego whispered at me and then giggled stupidly.

YEEES! I had sex with him! Okay, are you all happy now? I had sex with Jagger Villain and it was fucking amazing, I heard myself scream in my head, and that's when I knew I needed to get out of there before the words flew out of my mouth for real. I started grabbing my stuff frantically.

"I need a personal day," I shouted over my shoulder at Jennifer as I dashed out of the office.

"What's wrong?" she shouted after me.

"It's personal." I ran as fast as I could, and, not wanting to wait for the elevator, raced down the stairs. As soon as I arrived in the underground parking lot a sense of relief washed over me, but the relief soon vanished when a voice echoed around me.

"Wait. Stop. Please."

"No!" I replied, and continued my speedy approach to my car, but Jagger was clearly faster and soon I felt a familiar tug on my arm. I swung around to face him.

"Is this what it's going to be like?" he asked, out of breath.

WHAT HAPPENS ON VACATION

"What's going to be like what?" I asked, even though I knew exactly what he was referring to.

"Us? You? In the office like we just were. Tissues flying across the room and you barely able to stand up."

I threw my arms in the air and everything I'd been holding crashed onto the ground.

"Shiiiit!" I clenched my fists and moaned at the universe.

Jagger dropped to his knees in front of me and started picking things up, but as I looked down at him all I could think about was what he'd been doing to me last time he was on his knees in front of me. I felt a throb between my legs and wanted to part them, wanted to put one up on the bonnet of a car and let him make me come a million times over.

"I can't do this, Jagger. I'm not going to be able to come to work every single day and pretend what happened between us didn't happen and not look at you and want you to . . ." I bit my lip as Jagger stood up and stepped closer to me.

"Want me to what?" he whispered against my neck, leaning in.

"You know what I want you to do, but we can't, and I don't know if I can carry on like this. In the office, every single day, with everyone watching, seconds away from them all finding out."

"So, don't, then." He took my hand and placed it on his chest. "Give this a go. *Us.* Then you wouldn't have to hide it every day and toss tissues on the floor and drop your stationery every time you see me."

I shook my head. "We can't—our parents are married."

Jagger dropped my hand suddenly and stepped back. "You know, I'm actually getting a little sick and tired of hearing that excuse." He took another step back.

"It's not an excuse."

"Bullshit. It's an excuse."

I shook my head violently.

"You're scared—I get it. You had a marriage fall apart. You lost your dad, the man you loved most in the world. This thing between us came out of the blue and you don't like it when things come out of the blue and catch you off guard. You get anxious, and that terrifies you. And you certainly don't understand how you can go from thinking you hate me one day to thinking you might be falling in love with me the next day."

"I'm not falling in love with you, Jagger," I objected quickly.

"Your eyes say something else entirely, Margaret."

I pinched my eyes closed. "That's just your arrogance talking. Thinking every woman in the world falls in love with you, Jagger."

"And that is just your fear talking, Margaret. Thinking you can brush me off with constant sarcasm and snarkiness."

I opened my eyes and looked at him again. I felt as if I was falling again. Falling into those gray pools of water that seemed to mirror everything that I was feeling. Feelings that maybe I wasn't even aware that I was feeling yet. But there they were, in his eyes, showing me what it was that perhaps I'd been missing all along.

"We can't keep this up." Jagger broke eye contact. "This little game we play with each other where you say something crappy about me and I say something shitty back. Where you pretend to hate me and I pretend that I don't care. It's going to end in heartbreak, probably for me. Besides, you're a terrible, terrible liar. Apart from the constant eye twitch, you practically destroyed the office in there."

"I am a terrible lair," I admitted, and put my back against my car.

My phone beeped and I looked down at it to see a voice message from Lesego. I didn't need to listen to it to know what she was going to say—well, *ask*. Because she was going to ask a lot, that was for sure. "It's from Lesego. God, it's only a matter of time before she tells everyone in the office, and then everyone will know." I threw my head back and looked up at the lights above me. Bright, cold, sterile lights of the parking lot. I sighed loudly. It was sad and long, and it hurt.

"You know what," Jagger said, clearly taking a step back because the sound of his shoe hitting the ground echoed around the parking lot.

"What?" I tore my eyes from the lights and looked at him, white spots in my field of vision from their brightness.

"I also can't do this every day. I refuse. Coming to work and sitting opposite you and pretending that I'm not looking at you and thinking about you and desperately wanting you while you pretend that I don't exist or, worse, talk to me like a total stranger. It's going to kill me."

"I don't want to kill you."

"Well, you are. This hurts like a fucking breakup. We were together in Zanzibar and it was amazing. I loved every moment of it. And now we're not, and I hate it." Jagger looked at me expectantly, as if he wanted me to say something. I didn't know what to say.

"And, honestly, I don't see why it needs to end. I know how you feel about me, and I feel the same way about you."

"How do you know how I feel about you, Jagger?" I crossed my arms, suddenly angered that he was making these assumptions about me and then dishing them out as if they were facts.

Jagger rushed toward me and without a moment's hesitation took my face in his hands and pulled it close to his. I didn't pull away. Instead, I moved my lips toward his, until they were touching. I swept them across his. His breath came out in little bursts. It smelled so good: toothpaste and coffee and some kind of spearmint gum all mingled together to create this incredible aroma that I just wanted to drink in. And so I kissed him. It was slow and long and tender like our last night together. When it was over Jagger pulled away, took my chin in his hand, and tilted my face up to meet his.

"You wouldn't kiss me like that if you didn't feel exactly the same way as I do." He bent his head and planted a soft kiss on my lips. "The ball's in your court. You know what I want—now you just need to decide what you want."

"Balls?" My mouth fell open as the dream rushed back to me.

"Not my balls, obviously."

"I know, like tennis balls," I mumbled, and Jagger frowned. "And if I hit it back to you? Then what?"

He smiled. *God, I'd missed that smile.* "Then I'll hit it back to you, and hopefully we can start a rally. Rally being a metaphor for relationship, in case you didn't get that."

"I got it." We stared at each other for a while under the fast-flickering fluorescent lights of the underground parking lot.

"I better get back to work," Jagger said. It sounded like a question, as if he was waiting for me to say something back. Something like: *Don't go back to work, Jagger. Come home with me and let's fall into bed and have sex all day.*

But I didn't. I nodded, and Jagger turned and walked back into the building.

Chapter **Forty-two**

"Something is off with you, Margaret-Skye," my mom said, leaning into the computer screen that evening.

"It's nothing." I shrugged and tried to arrange my features and body parts into something normal and natural. If my mother smelled anything vaguely off with me she would come after it like a bloodhound until she found it and dragged it out.

"Noooo, something is not right here. I'm picking up some . . ." My mom stared at me. Her eyes felt as if they were boring holes into my soul, and I was starting to regret this little Zoom call with her.

"Mom, you're in Zanzibar—I'm at home. We are separated by a screen and hundreds of kilometers and a bloody ocean. You can't pick anything up through a screen."

"*Au contraire*, darling daughter, I do some of my best work through a screen."

"Mom, you're on your honeymoon. Go and enjoy yourself. Remember, you only have a few good hip years left." I tried to make a joke and I knew I'd made a mistake because my mom was now glaring at me.

"Waiiiit, what the hell is up with you. Something is up . . . *something* . . . I just can't figure it . . ." She leaned even closer to the screen, her nose almost touching it, and stared at me so intently that my cheeks went red.

"JAGGER! You and Jagger!" She pointed a pewter-bejeweled finger at me. "You and Jagger." She waved her hands around in the air. "I should have seen it. It's so obvious! I mean the sexual aura radiating off you is wild."

"Stop trying to read my aura."

"I can't help it—it's oozing off you. You had sex with Jagger, didn't you?"

"Did you and Jagger have sex?" Eddy's face appeared in the screen, and I face-palmed. I was acting out so many emojis lately that I might as well *be* an emoji at this stage. Download the all-new "Margaret emoji" for all those cringe moments in life that you need to express to a friend without typing any words. I held my face and shook my head. "Why can't I hide anything from you?"

"Because we've been together in at least four other lives now. And you're also a terrible liar."

"Apparently, even Lesego worked it out in two minutes. Okay, I had sex with Jagger! Is that what you want to hear? Are you happy?" I wailed.

"Are *you* happy?"

"Do I look happy?"

"Well, your aura is vibrating at a really high frequency, darling."

"I can't even read auras and I'm sure I can see it," my new stepfather—*oh god, stepfather, stepfather*—said.

"Both of you, please stop this!"

"You know, I don't need to be psychic to have seen this coming. Jagger has been crazy about you for months. You're all he talks about when he gets back from work. And he's always making me read your articles because they're so brilliant," Eddy said.

"He is?"

Eddy nodded.

I put an elbow down on the table and sank my chin into it, feeling defeated.

"Honey, what's wrong?"

My mom's tone had changed, and a tear rolled down my cheek.

"Margaret-Skye, talk to me."

I glanced at Eddy and then looked back down.

"I'll leave you ladies alone," he said, and walked away. I waited to hear the door shut before I started.

"You like Jagger?" my mom asked. I nodded. "Maybe even more than like him?" she continued, and I carried on nodding. "So what's the problem, then? Why does it look like you're fighting this so hard?"

"We are stepbrother and sister! It can never happen!"

"Are you being serious?" she asked.

"Yes!"

"Is that really what this is about?" she pressed.

"What else would it be about?"

"I don't know—you tell me." My mom carried on, "Because I'm sure I don't need to tell you that becoming stepsiblings with someone in your thirties you weren't even raised with does not mean you're related. And besides, Eddy and I aren't even married legally. Weddings in Zanzibar are not legally recognized in South Africa. So what's this really about?"

"I don't understand how this could have happened," I whispered.

"What?"

"This. Jagger and me. He's driven me mad for the last six months at work, and now suddenly we're having sex and I'm feeling all these feelings. It doesn't make sense."

"And you hate things that don't make sense."

"I do! Why can't things be simple? Cut-and-dried. Black-and-white. Why does life have to be this nebulous shade of ever-changing gray?"

My mom looked at me with something that resembled sympathy. "Sometimes we have to embrace the gray because that's often where we find the greatest joy. That's where the life-changing miracles reside."

An image of those gray eyes flashed in my mind, and I let out a long sigh.

"I'm a divorcé. I failed at the last relationship I was in."

"You didn't fail—you just weren't with the right person."

"And you think Jagger is the right person?"

She shrugged. "I do, actually."

"What?" I spluttered. I couldn't hide my shock. I was expecting her to say something less like that and more airy-fairy: *Maybe, maybe not, but you'll never know if you don't try.* That kind of thing. Not this!

"You wouldn't be like this if it was just meaningless holiday sex."

"I . . . have to go, Mom." I did need to go. I needed this conversation to end. My heart was pounding in my ears, making me feel dizzy.

"Wait, don't go like this," she called as I started to close the computer. "Are you going to be okay?"

I nodded at her feebly, but truthfully, I didn't know if I was going to be okay. The most disconcerting feeling took hold of me. How had I gone, in one week, from absolutely hating Jagger to this? Or . . .

. . . had I ever really hated him at all?

Were all those sayings about love and hate being inextricably linked true? That love and hate are the opposite sides of the same coin. They certainly felt the same: the roiling sensation in your stomach; the sensation of your heart knocking around inside you as if it wasn't tethered to the place it should be; circular, repetitive thoughts of that person going around and around until you're dizzy; riding a roller coaster of dopamine and adrenaline with every single encounter with them until you don't know whether you're up or down, left or right, backward or forward, in hate or in lo—

No! I couldn't be in love with Jagger. Jagger and I were complete opposites. We lived and breathed and existed in totally separate universes and yet, *yet*, the last six days with him had been some of the happiest and relaxed of my life. With Jagger everything had felt so easy. All my worries and anxieties had melted away as I'd melted into him.

I got up and paced the room. Lucy looked up at me with concern. She was right to be concerned. I was concerned. When I'd nearly worn a path in the carpet, I finally collapsed onto the couch, consumed by my own self-inflicted terror. Love and relationships always end in pain. Whether they're good or bad, they all eventually end in pain. Look at my disintegrated marriage. Look at my mother. Married to the same man for most of her life and then one morning she wakes up and he's no longer there. The unimaginable horror of having your heart broken like that makes it almost impossible to put your heart back out there again. And yet, that's what my mother had just done.

Despite it all, she'd placed it in someone else's hands, knowing full well that it could all end in heart-shattering pain. I wasn't as brave as my mother, though. I didn't step in front of spitting snakes and board the wrong planes to the wrong countries.

I fell asleep on the couch that night and dreamed about Jagger again: we were playing tennis like the night before, but this time my dad was the umpire and he kept telling me to hit the ball back.

Hit the bloody ball back, Margaret!

Hit it!

He got more frustrated and worked up as the balls passed me by and flew into the back fence, until he finally climbed down off the chair and walked right up to me.

Take your racquet and hit back. Don't just stand there—finish what you started.

And so I did. I held my racquet tightly and the next ball that came my way, I hit as hard as I could. It flew over the net, over the back fence, and then hurtled into the sky. It was sunset: the sky was orange and pink and looked as if it was made up of a million impressionist brushstrokes, or pixels, or small colored diamonds. The ball whizzed through the air, getting higher and higher, heading straight for the only cloud in the sky. And when it reached the cloud, I saw that my dad was standing on it. He held his hand out and caught the ball and that's when I woke up in a cold sweat, breathing heavily.

I jumped off the couch and raced for the kitchen. I needed a glass of water. My throat felt swollen and dry. I poured a glass with shaking hands and drank it in three gulps. And that's when I saw it, the pink and orange diamonds glittering from under the pile of magazines and papers and letters that had gathered on top of it for over a year.

I sat down at the counter and pushed the dusty debris aside, exposing the angel on the cloud and the colored diamonds. I'm not sure why I knew I needed to do this, why I needed to finish it, but I just did. Tears poured out of my eyes as I spent the next six hours meticulously placing the diamond dots onto the paper, until I finally finished what my dad had set out to do but hadn't had the time to complete. And when it was finished and I'd wiped the tears from my eyes, a sense of clarity settled in, and I knew what I needed to do.

Chapter **Forty-three**

I raced into work the next day and ran straight up to Lesego lest I completely chicken out. Which I was on the verge of doing. But the lack of sleep I'd had the night before seemed to be working in my favor. It, coupled with the several cups of coffee I'd needed this morning to get going, had put me in a somewhat delirious mood. The kind of mood where even though I was second-guessing my decision and vacillating between thinking it was the worst, cringiest, cheesiest idea I'd ever had, to thinking it was *still* the worst, cringiest, cheesiest idea I'd ever had—I was still going to do it.

Obviously, when Lesego heard the idea, she confirmed that it was indeed the worst, cringiest, cheesiest idea I had ever had, and therefore it was utterly perfect! And she was more than happy to help execute it. So, with Lesego waiting in the wings, there was only one thing left to do—go to hair and makeup.

All my co-workers were sitting in a line waiting to have their hair and makeup done. Everyone was in a good mood except Lesego, who was running around like a chicken without a head, checking in with the last-minute photographer she'd found, and dressing and styling people. I looked around and realized that Jagger wasn't there. A pit opened up in my mind as my imagination galloped: maybe he wasn't coming today because he wasn't coming back to work. He'd made it very clear yesterday that he was not going to be able to come into the office every day and work with me like this. But half an hour later, when I'd gotten into full hair, makeup, and clothing, the door opened and Jagger swaggered in.

He was already fully dressed and styled. His fake lip rings glinted in the overhead lights of the room and his loosely tied black-and-white checkerboard tie swayed around his neck as he moved. His eyes were lined in black kohl; it was so damn sexy. My mouth fell open. Sixteen years ago, Jagger would have been my dream date. I would have had his poster up on my wall and fallen asleep looking at it. He would have stopped my heart with those black painted nails and ripped black jeans. He would have been my ultimate teenage crush . . . *mind you* . . .

I inhaled as he came closer. The world stopped. Everyone in the room evaporated into thin air. All I saw now was Jagger as he walked across the room. This idea I'd had, this cringy, cheesy idea, which was completely out of character for me, suddenly seemed so right when I looked at him. He suddenly changed direction, and then he was coming toward me.

He locked eyes with me, and I stood up straight as a bolt of energy moved up my spine. He picked up speed and I think I held my breath the entire time, and only exhaled when he was standing in front of me.

"This is for you." He held his hand out. A bright pink-and-red corsage sat in his open palm, and I smiled down at it.

"You remembered?" I held out my hand for him.

"I know it doesn't make up for the crappy night you had all those years ago, but—" He stopped talking as he attached the arrangement to my wrist, his fingers grazing my skin as he went. The heat from his fingers entered my body, and once again, I found myself holding my breath.

"It's perfect. Thank you," I said when he'd finished putting it on. I inspected him. He looked absolutely ridiculous, but still so damn sexy.

"You don't have a pimple," I said.

"You don't have braces."

"I just got them off. I was kind of hoping I'd be able to have a big make-out session tonight with this guy who has a crush on me."

"Oh?" He raised his brows.

"It took me a while, but I figured out that I've also got a crush on him. Big-time." I clicked my fingers, and Lesego put the music on.

"Oh my god." Jagger burst out laughing. "It's your song!"

I put my hands over my hot cheeks and nodded at him. They were hot with the mixture of sheer embarrassment and giddiness rushing through me, made even more intense by the fact that I knew everyone was now watching us. I could feel their eyes on me.

"Does this mean what I think it means?" Jagger asked, taking my hand.

I nodded. "I didn't really get my kiss all those years ago, so I was sort of wondering if . . ." I wasn't able to hide anything. It was written in my smile, my eyes, my stance.

"You know everyone is watching us, right?" Jagger asked.

I closed my eyes tightly and nodded. "I know. And it's utterly embarrassing, but also the best way to announce it to everyone in the office so we don't have all that whispered gossip and all those awkward conversations with our co-workers as we explain to them all that we're together now!" I opened my eyes once I'd gotten it all out.

"Together?"

"If you still want to be?"

"Isn't this against some office HR policy?"

I shrugged. "No idea."

Jagger looked over my shoulder and called out, "Mary, would HR have a problem if I kissed Margaret?"

A few people laughed, including me. I couldn't believe I was doing this—this moment was so out of character for me—but it seemed that Jagger had made me do some pretty out-of-character things of late. What had my mom said? *Find someone who pushes you out of your comfort zone.* Well, I was being pushed.

JO WATSON

Before Mary could say anything, Lesego shouted, "Kiss him!" which was quickly echoed by Shawn.

"Mary?" Jagger asked again. I turned and looked at Mary. She looked confused and taken aback. This seemed to be heightened somehow by the metallic purple lamé she was wearing and the huge puffy sleeves that sat under her ears.

"Um . . ." She looked at Jennifer as if genuinely seeking guidance. "As long as it's . . . um . . . consensual . . . I mean, I think, I'm not sure. I'd have to go and check the company policy."

"That will take too long! Just let them bloody kiss each other," Lesego said.

I leaned forward and planted a soft, short, meaningful kiss on Jagger's lips. I pulled away and looked up at him. We held each other's eyes for a while, and then he leaned in and kissed me again. It was short and polite and appropriate for public consumption. We drew away from each other, and Jagger smiled at me.

"Let's go do this photo shoot." He pulled me by the hand and when I turned, all my co-workers were smiling at us. I smiled back, until I saw what Shawn was doing.

"What are you doing?"

They stopped filming us and started typing on their phone screen.

"What are you doing?" I asked again.

"The country's most eligible bachelor is officially off the market," Shawn narrated as they typed. "Hashtag office romance, hashtag couple, hashtag love, romantic couples, prom night, senior prom . . ."

"NO! You're not posting that, are you?" I rushed over to Shawn and tried to grab their phone.

"Too late!" they said and held their phone up in the air. "That's going viral—mark my words—and when it does, I will be asking for a pay raise." They looked at Jennifer and raised their perfect brows.

356

Turns out it did kind of go viral. A lot of sad-face emojis were posted, mainly from Jagger's adoring female fans, and he even wrote about it in his latest, and last, Swipe Write column. Jagger's column moving forward was going to be much broader, not just focusing on dating, now that he was no longer single.

Turns out something else went viral pretty soon after that. Leighton released his track "Vacation Situation" with an over-the-top music video to match. Slammed by music critics, it was absolutely loved by the public and sure to become another hit that would outlast him and still be played in nightclubs in 2053.

My mom and Eddy returned just as happy and in love, and I quickly realized that I needed to move out of my mom's house after one night of having them home—the walls might as well have been made of air. So much had changed in such a short amount of time.

But perhaps the most surprising change of all was that it seemed I had a new defining characteristic—that I was totally and utterly in love with Jagger Villain.

One Year Later

My mom and I stood at the edge of the water once more. Eddy, Jagger, and Leighton stood behind us on the beach. They were giving us the space we needed to do the thing we were finally both ready to do. The sun had set, and just like before, it had gone down with blazing drama. The sky had turned a blood-orange color, the clouds pink, and the golden ball of the sun disappeared over the horizon, casting an iridescent glow across the turquoise waters. My mom held the box in her hands and looked at me. I nodded at her as she pulled the lid aside and passed it to me.

"You first," she said.

My throat tightened and my chest pulled as I looked down into the box. I gazed at the tiny flecks of ash that had once been my father. I walked farther into the warm water until it reached my knees and then slowly, carefully, tipped some of the ashes into the sea. The blue water turned momentarily white, and then the current came, moving the ashes around in swirls, as if they were alive, like a school of tiny fish moving together as one. And then the white cloud disappeared under the water; they were gone. My dad had wanted an underwater scene—now he was getting one.

My mom come up next to me. She sank her hand into the remaining ashes and then she threw them forward. A cloud of whiteness moved through the air, dancing on the breeze. Then, as the breeze stopped, they fell. We watched as the last of the ashes hit the water and sank below its surface. We stood there for a while in total silence, waiting and watching.

"Come, let's go," my mom finally said, and turned back to the shore.

I shook my head. "There are some things I want to say to him. That I didn't get to say when he died."

She touched the side of my face and nodded. I watched her walk back to the beach, back into Eddy's arms. He wrapped her in his embrace, and she buried her face in his chest.

I turned back around and watched the sun sink lower and lower. I wrung my hands together awkwardly.

"Hey, Dad," I said in a soft voice. "Okay, this is strange. I'm talking to the sea, and I don't know if you're there, or if you can hear me, or if this is just crazy. I know it's crazy, but I'm going to do it anyway. I wanted to say some things to you. Things I should have said to you the night you left us but didn't. *Couldn't.*" I wrung my hands again. "You see, saying I love you wasn't nearly enough. Because I love you doesn't even vaguely sum up how I feel about you. Those words are too small for you because you were so, so big. The biggest thing in my life. You were the most incredible father anyone could have ever wished for, and you filled my life with so much joy and love. There wasn't a moment that went by when I didn't feel loved by you, and I just wanted you to know that. I wanted you to know how proud I always was to be your daughter. And how much getting to call you *my* dad meant to me."

I paused and wiped away the tears running down my cheeks. "I don't know if you can hear me, but if you can, you should know Mom still feeds the birds every day. Your favorite pin-tailed whydah has bred and now there are four more there to harass the other birds. I finished your diamond-art thing—it gave me a cramp in my hand. Seriously, be thankful you were spared that. I got a promotion too. I'm the editor of the paper now. We're mostly online, though, but we're doing really well.

I would never have been able to do that if you hadn't always believed in me so much. And I guess the big news, the really big news, is . . . I'm in love! I know! I know! I wasn't expecting it at all, and we're such opposites, Dad, you would laugh.

"Mind you, you and Mom were like that too, but you worked. I think it will work with Jagger too—that's his name—and yes, named after Mick Jagger. He drives me totally crazy sometimes but I'm so in love with him. I wish you could have met him. I'm not sure you would have approved of him right away—he doesn't make a great first impression— but when you get to know him he's the best person I think I've ever met, other than Leighton, of course.

"Mom's also happy; she's met someone too. I didn't like it at first, but he's good for her. He treats her so well and I know you would want that for her. She's still just as nutty as ever, though. In fact, I think she's getting more eccentric as she gets older. But we're all great down here, Dad. We miss you so much, and life is not the same without you, but we're happy and doing well and I know that would make you happy too." I stopped talking and took a deep breath. "I hope you can hear me, Dad. Wherever you are."

"Look!" my mom shouted, and I turned. She was pointing out at the sea. Leighton, Jagger, and Eddy were also all looking. I spun around, following the angle of her finger, and when I saw it, my breath caught in my chest. A dolphin. Gliding through the water. We all watched it as it jumped and surfed on the small distant waves as if it was having the time of its life. We watched it until it finally vanished from sight and the moon crept over the horizon. I felt an arm slip around me. It was Jagger.

"Hey, you all right? Did you get to say all the things you wanted?" he asked.

I nodded as I leaned my head against his shoulder. He reached for my hand and raised it to his lips, giving it a small kiss. The silver moonlight caught the stone on my finger, and it flickered like the first star coming out at night.

He kissed my hand again, and I turned to face him.

"So." He raised his eyebrows at me playfully, seductively.

"So what?" I asked.

"Well, the honeymoon suite is waiting for us, and I have it on good authority that it's very romantic in there."

"Really? And just what exactly do you want to do in the honeymoon suite?" I leaned in and ran my lips over his. Touching him still gave me the exact same feeling it had given me a year ago in this exact same place. The same waters, and sand, and sky, and the same us, only very, very different. He wrapped his arms around me and attempted to pull me up.

I shrieked. "What the hell are you doing?"

"Trying to carry you over the threshold. It's supposed to be a romantic gesture."

"Rushing you to the hospital because you've put your back out is not my idea of romance," I said, pushing him in the chest playfully.

"What's your idea of romance then, Mrs. Villain?" He gave me a provocative grin, slipping his hands around my waist and digging his fingers into the abundant flesh there.

"I don't think so." I stepped back. "I'm not changing my name."

"But Margaret-Skye Villain has such a great ring to it, don't you think?"

"No. I don't."

"We could send out those cute Christmas cards with a photo of you and me and Lucy all dressed up in matching Christmas sweaters and sign it off, *the Villains*."

"I'm going to pretend you never said that because I'd really like to go back to our room and have wild sex, but that image is a bit of a turnoff."

"How wild?" He raised his brows.

I grabbed him by the hand and started walking him back toward the shore with me. "You'll have to wait and see," I teased him seductively. Everyone else had gone. Sometimes when I was with Jagger, it was as if we were the only two people in the world, and that no other people had ever felt the same way about each other as we did. I knew I'd never love anyone as much as I loved my office nemesis. And there was no one I'd rather take a vacation with or go up against in our quiz night . . . even though this time I was going to kick his ass.

Acknowledgments

There are always so many people to acknowledge and I always write such short acknowledgments and probably leave everyone out. So this time I will do a very thorough acknowledgments section.

My agent, Louise, who is as brilliant as she is funny! She's the only person I know who can pull off fluffy animal slippers during the day at a lunch meeting (or can she?). Kate, a brilliant publisher and possibly one of the nicest people I've ever met; she does not wear slippers during the day, though. All the folk at Wattpad HQ, especially Deanna and Fiona and Caitlin and of course all my amazing readers there that made publishing books a reality.

I should literally credit my husband, Gareth, as a co-author on my books; he brainstorms each one with me and whenever I am stuck (it happens often) he will sit with me and figure out how to unstick myself. He also fixes my computers, helps when the Wi-Fi is not working or the plugs have tripped, helps when I lose my phone (at least twice a day), and makes my life so much easier because I don't have to think about any of the electronics around me, and electronics really stress me out. He's also just an amazing person! (I feel like I have said all this before in another acknowledgments section, but I've written so many books now that I don't know where or in which one), which leads me into probably the biggest acknowledgment: to all my readers who buy all my books and make it possible for me to write more books and write more acknowledgments.

I also want to acknowledge my dad, whose death from COVID inspired many parts of this book. *Inspired* sounds like the wrong word, but in this case it's the perfect word, and I think he would have liked that. We had a very complicated relationship—not an uncommon thing, but it makes mourning him very complicated, too, and I got to explore some of that in my book, which felt rather cathartic. My father gave me four great gifts, and I'm so grateful for them: he introduced me to Depeche Mode (yes, still obsessed); he instilled in me a work ethic that underpins everything I do (he was the hardest-working person I knew); he taught me to always give to others who were less fortunate (he was a great philanthropist); and finally he taught me to always stand up and speak my mind. His death also gave me another gift: some of his last words to me were telling me that he wished he'd had more time, which made me evaluate my life and realize that time is not guaranteed, and therefore I have to try and get the most out of the time I do have left. (I sound like an influencer now, #blessed.) But it is a fundamental truth: time is our most precious commodity; we shouldn't waste it!

I've also always wanted to write a book set in Zanzibar because it is one of the most amazing places I've ever been to, and if you ever have the chance to go, I really suggest you do. It's as fascinating as it is beautiful. I think that is the end of my acknowledgments—they weren't as long as I thought they would be, which probably means I should acknowledge more people.

I have one more thing to say, which isn't an acknowledgment; rather it's a weird and interesting story that I've always wanted to tell people but never really have because it is pretty unbelievable. When I was twenty-three, I was working in theater, but mainly working as a stylist. I was miserable doing that—the styling, not the theater. I was not writing regularly at all, apart from the plays I had written and was directing. I went to a psychic called Frank—I don't believe in psychics, but there is a long story as to how I ended up there (for another time maybe)—anyway, this man Frank told me that I needed to be a writer. I had never really considered writing as a full-time career, and when he told me that I was going to go on and write many books and become an author, I laughed. It was a ridiculous suggestion. But I swear this is what Frank told me. I'm not making it up! (He also had messages from beyond—again, another story.) Some months later I had a full-on dramatic meltdown at a shoot and ended up screaming at someone very publicly (it was very justified though) and then ended up on another shoot where I got physically assaulted (again, story for another time). With Frank's words ringing in my ears, I walked away from that career. Besides, I had zero passion for dressing models and actors (literally one of the most stressful jobs on the planet), and had decided to become a writer, but not of books yet.

I started writing articles for magazines, earning next to nothing, and then worked my way from that into TV/movie scriptwriting, copywriting, writing online comedy content and adverts to eventually opening my own writing and production business. I did that for many years until finally I (accidentally) wrote my first book at the age of thirty-four. I had not intended to write a book; it was an incredibly spontaneous and unplanned decision, but all the while I could hear Frank's little weird words in my head. I still didn't believe him, though. But then I entered my book into a writing competition, won the competition, and got a publishing contract, and here we are!

I still don't believe in psychics, despite the insane encounter I had (or maybe I do just a tiny, tiny bit, I'm not sure though, I'm still on the fence). But every single time I finish a book I think of Frank, so this time I wrote about him. I'm not sure whether he deserves an acknowledgment or not, but life seems full of these really weird things that you can't explain. I'll leave that story there. I have so many other weird stories; maybe I'll start writing one weird story at the end of all my acknowledgments.

About the Author

Jo Watson is the bestselling author of adult romantic women's fiction, rom-coms, and contemporary YA. Jo has sold over 600,000 copies of her books worldwide and travels internationally to promote them. She is also a story writer on Wattpad, where she has over 80 million reads and 120,000 followers and has been awarded the Watty Award for outstanding stories twice. She lives with her son and husband in South Africa.

Look out for Jo Watson's next book, *Love at First Flight*.

Coming soon from W by Wattpad Books!

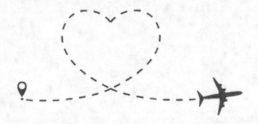

Heads turn when previously "unpopular" Pippa arrives at her school reunion weekend with a drop-dead gorgeous airline pilot on her arm. What her former classmates don't know is that she hadn't met Andrew until today, when they struck a deal to be each other's fake dates when the need arises. But unexpected turbulence could make for a bumpy landing.